MOLTEN DUSK

KARISSA LAUREL

Molten Dusk
The Norse Chronicles™
Copyright © 2017 by Karissa Laurel. All rights reserved.
First Print Edition: August 2017

ISBN-13: 978-0-615-81432-2
ISBN-10: 0-615-81432-8

Red Adept Publishing, LLC
104 Bugenfield Court
Garner, NC 27529
http://RedAdeptPublishing.com/

Cover and Formatting: Streetlight Graphics

To my wonderful guys,
for putting up with my flights of fancy

And all our yesterdays have lighted fools
The way to dusty death. Out, out, brief candle!
Life's but a walking shadow, a poor player
That struts and frets his hour upon the stage
And then is heard no more.

—Macbeth, Act 5, Scene 5, 22–26

CHAPTER 1

I HAD TOURED MORE OF NORTH America in the last few months than I'd expected to see in my entire life, and Lake Tahoe was another destination struck from my list—not that it was on my list of places to visit in the first place. But it should have been. From my vantage point on the patio of Baldur's home, set high on a ridge in the Sierra Nevada Mountains, the distant lake resembled a gemstone, a topaz sparkling in a god's diadem. In a way, that's what New Breidablick was: Baldur's crown, and he wore it proudly.

Somewhere inside the house behind me, Baldur and Thorin went about their business—namely, avoiding *me*. I hadn't expressly asked them to leave me alone, but they must have sensed the chip of ice that formed on my shoulder shortly after Thorin and I touched down in Baldur's living room over a week before. Processing everything that had happened—Val's revelations about his motives for revenge and Thorin's questionable culpability—required time and solitude. Thorin seemed to understand my need to resolve my feelings in private, and I hadn't failed to notice his empathy.

A breeze blew up from the valley below Baldur's home, stirring frigid currents that rushed past my ears and cheeks, stealing the warmth I'd hoarded under my parka's hood. High in these mountains, in the first week of December, winter had settled in and taken root. Back home, in North Carolina, humidity often lent weight and substance to winter's coldness, but here, in the west, dry air leached moisture and heat until my bones rattled like wind chimes.

Smoke spewed from Baldur's chimney, and the familiar musk of burning wood scented the air. Baldur kept a fire burning in the living room around the clock. Maybe I should have staked out a spot in front

1

of that blaze, those kindred flames and friendly heat, but I hadn't felt much like a reincarnated fire goddess for the past several days. Mostly, I felt sad, tired, and confused.

Behind me, the patio door *shushed* on its tracks as it slid open.

"You're going to stay out here all day?" Baldur pushed the door closed. "One would think you'd had enough of the cold for a while."

"It doesn't bother me." I snatched at the tiny dots bobbing on the breeze. Frozen flecks melted in my palm—minuscule snowflakes. The specks of precipitation came and went, itinerant visitors lacking the conviction to gather into something permanent. "I was thinking about Mani." My brother had loved the cold and adored snow. He was my complete opposite. "I wonder if he would have been able to generate ice the same way I make fire."

Baldur stepped to the railing at the patio's edge, and his big shadow fell over me. The patio was more like a huge balcony, supporting a fire pit, seating area, hot tub, and outdoor kitchen all done up in natural stone. The patio's edge dropped off like a cliff, and anyone unfortunate enough to stumble over the railing would fall several hundred feet before splattering on the rocky ground.

"I didn't know your brother in this most recent incarnation, and I regret it. But from what I've heard, he and the original Mani had a lot in common."

"He suspected something," I said. "It was why he went to Alaska in the first place—because of my dreams and premonitions and his own hunches. He was more open minded than me. I was in denial about the whole thing from the beginning."

He nodded. "I remember."

"I have *a lot* of strange dreams, you know? And they aren't always about me."

He leaned over, braced his arms on the railing, and knitted his fingers together. He stared out over the landscape. The Lake Tahoe sky, peering through patchy clouds, matched the blue in his eyes. "I am aware. Yes."

"I recently had one about Skyla. It involved you."

His posture remained relaxed and impassive, but he studied me— hard—from the corner of his eye. "I know what you're going to say."

I clutched the patio railing tighter, and my white knuckles stood out against skin that had gone pink with cold. "And?"

Baldur stood straighter, squaring his shoulders. He folded his arms across his chest, braced a hip against the railing, and exhaled. "And it's true. She's my granddaughter."

My heart rolled a somersault. I trusted my visions and dreams, but Baldur's confirmation solidified everything and made it real. Essentially speaking, Skyla was Aesir. The truth would blow her mind. *Hope it doesn't end up breaking her heart.* "Have you always known?"

"I sensed she was something *other* when I healed her, after she was shot in Helen's warehouse. Her blood, her healing, her body's response to my magic... It was all uncanny. But there, in the cabin at Rainier, after I'd brought Nina out of that hospital, after we had recovered you from Grim, after I saw Nina and Skyla together for the first time..." Baldur swallowed and shook his head as if shooing a pestering fly.

"You've been withholding the truth from her since then?"

His face contorted into a pained smile. He raised his eyes to mine, and as always, his otherworldliness pressed upon me like a physical weight. I hadn't bowed to him before, however. Why start now? "You don't want to hear my excuses, do you?"

I huffed a small chuckle. "No, but I can guess them. We've kept you busy, and you've been very single-minded about Nina. But you have her back now, so no more excuses. Skyla needs to know."

"Why haven't you told her yourself?"

"Not my story to tell. Besides, it would only piss her off more, coming from me. If you tell her the truth yourself, I think she'll be more inclined to understand and give you a break. She has one of the biggest hearts I've ever known. She just wants a family and someone to love. If you let her, I bet she'd love you."

Baldur pushed off the railing and strolled toward the end of his patio facing the valley that housed his horse herd. No surprise, the Aesir's attachment to four-footed steeds, especially considering their history with horses in the legends—Odin's *eight*-legged horse being an exceptional example, of course. "I know it's no excuse, Solina. I failed my daughters after Nina's last death. The Valkyries came right away and offered to raise them, teach them, train them, and it was easy to believe the girls were better off without me. You'd think after losing Nina so many times, over and over, I'd be numb to it."

He spun and faced me. His eyes burned as if he had a fever. "But it doesn't work that way. Each time, it gets worse. It hurts more and more. When Nina died after Skyla's mother was born, I was worthless—a zombie, as modern people like to say. I was in no state to raise three little girls, but I *know* it's no excuse. I neglected them, and Embla has made it clear she hates me for deserting her. I don't blame her. She asked me to leave her alone, and I've respected her wishes."

Baldur stepped closer to me. He rubbed a hand over his face and through his hair until strands poked up around his head like a prickly seedpod from a sweetgum tree. "Maybe that's why I've hesitated to say anything to Skyla. I'm afraid of her rejection. I'm afraid of hurting her more with the truth: that she has a family, and we abandoned her."

I squeezed Baldur's shoulder. "Skyla forgave Embla for keeping her distance for so long. She'll forgive you. Just don't wait until it's too late. Don't regret the time you could have been together with no secrets between you."

Baldur swallowed. His Adam's apple bobbed. "You're right. But I should tell her face to face."

"Sounds reasonable." I offered a conciliatory smile. "And maybe you'll get your chance, sooner than later."

Baldur arched an eyebrow. "Oh? Is Skyla coming here?"

"No." I shook my head. "We're going to her."

He blinked at me. "We are?"

"I spoke with her a little while ago. The Valkyries are already in Vegas, looking for leads. It's time I stopped hiding out here. I've got a wolf to kill, and it's not going to happen as long as I stay holed up in this fortress."

Baldur frowned. "Are you sure? If it's too soon—"

"It's been a week." I'd overdosed on self-pity during my stay at New Breidablick, and I didn't need more sympathy from Baldur or anyone else. "If I learned anything from Mani's death, it's that there is a time to mourn and a time to dance. I'm done mourning. Val doesn't deserve any more of my grief. Now it's time to dance, and preferably on some graves. Skoll's will be my first."

4

Baldur's lips curled into a cagey smile. "Thorin will be glad to hear it."

"I don't care what Thorin's glad to hear." I was still trying to figure out how I felt about the God of Thunder after learning of his participation in Loki's torture, Narfi's murder, and Val's abuse. Did something that happened eons ago matter anymore? Did I have the right to judge any of them after I'd murdered Mani's killer myself and would have done worse, given the opportunity? Did I have the right, when I was still seeking to kill Skoll and possibly Helen Locke and anyone else who threatened to harm me or those I cared about?

Baldur snorted and rolled his eyes. "Keep telling yourself that, Solina. You're the only one who believes it."

<hr/>

That night, as I had for many nights since arriving at New Breidablick, I dreamed of blackbirds, thunder, and rain. Dark places, roaring rivers, and darting fish. Fire and pain. The images swirled together, never coalescing into anything sensible.

A thunderclap woke me. Because thunder rarely occurred in winter, I attributed the phenomenon to Thorin expressing some unspoken sentiment. Frustration? Anger? He'd given me lots of space for most of the week, and I had a feeling he was losing his patience with me.

I stared at the bedroom ceiling and traded my questions about Thorin's emotional status for questions about the visions in my dreams. I'd lived much of my life with this ability to foresee and yet see nothing at all. What value was foresight without comprehension? Maybe I understood why the oracles in the legends always spoke in vague and quizzical terms. Without context, my visions had little worth.

From past experience, I'd learned the visions might become more specific over time, as I drew nearer to the event inspiring the premonitions. But that left me playing catch-up too often. Every task I had undertaken since Mani's death had come from a *reactive* position rather than a *proactive* one. Perhaps that would be my downfall, the undoing of us all.

I needed something more from my premonitions. I had to *do* something more to get those answers. My visions, no matter how stilted and unreliable, were a gift—one I had squandered for far too long. Perhaps, like a muscle, my psychic skills required training and exercise. As the development of my fighting and self-defense abilities had depended on the help of experts like the Valkyries, so too would my clairvoyant tendencies. But whom did I approach for that sort of training—Zelda, the palm-reading astrologist who worked from the little purple trailer on the outskirts of my hometown? *Hmm, I think not.*

If my abilities were real, maybe others like me existed—others with the same source of power: runes or ancient magic or Aesir blood. I simply had to find them, somehow. *But not tonight.*

I rolled over and punched my pillow, searching for a comfortable position. Nearly half an hour later, though, when I still hadn't managed to fall asleep, I slid from the bed and went in search of distraction.

Somehow, I found myself in Baldur's kitchen, studying the contents of a refrigerator stocked with enough provisions to supply a small army. After taking a water bottle, I backed away from the fridge and ran smack into Thorin. I squealed, flinched, and dropped the bottle. Thorin snatched it before it hit the ground and presented it to me.

"Sunshine." He bit back a grin.

My hands trembled as I took the bottle. "Thorin."

His closeness unsettled me—his dynamic presence, his body heat, and his fragrance of storms and summer winds. His casual elegance undid me. Long hair softened his warrior frame. His T-shirt stretched across imposing shoulders. His jeans sat low on narrow hips. My attention settled on his bare toes, peeking from ragged jeans cuffs, but even that set my heart racing—God of Thunder, barefoot and relaxed, unguarded. The familiarity of his presence was too much.

I stuttered something nonsensical, an excuse, an apology, and tried to push past, but Thorin held his place. When the son of Thor refused to move, he usually got his way.

"Don't you think you've avoided me long enough?"

I swallowed. "I wasn't—"

"Don't lie."

"It's easier," I blurted. Then I clamped my mouth shut before I said anything else I didn't mean to say.

6

One blond eyebrow arched. "You don't do anything the easy way, Sunshine."

I licked my lips. Mistake. Thorin's gaze darted to my mouth. My pulse quickened, and I imagined he could hear that, too. "What do you want?" I asked. "Are you here to give me a hard time?"

"No. I came to tell you Baldur's guys reported in. Your parents are home, and they're fine. There's been no sign of trouble."

My shoulders slumped. I sighed and blinked back a sudden welling of tears. Baldur's men had provided regular updates, and their news had given me no reason to worry, but with Helen and Skoll still on the loose, I took nothing for granted. "That... that's good."

"There's more news, though. Baldur's network got a hit."

I nearly dropped my water bottle again, but I snagged it and clutched my fists around it, squeezing. After he had recovered Nina, Baldur had dedicated his information network to finding Helen and the wolf, but those communication lines had been frustratingly silent. "Who did they find?"

"Your favorite incestuous nephew."

My upper lip curled, and a silent growl rumbled in my chest. "Nate. Where is he?"

"Baldur's people are holding him in an office in a new project that one of Helen's companies is building. I've already spoken to the Valkyries. Naomi and Amala are heading over there for backup until we get there."

I snapped into alert mode. "What are we waiting for?"

Thorin's head tilted, and his eyes narrowed as though studying a curious specimen. "Are you sure you're ready?"

"Ready for what?" I turned on my heel and hurried from the kitchen, heading to my bedroom to pack my few belongings and get dressed. If I had to face Nate again, I meant to do it in something other than pajama pants and a T-shirt.

He trailed me to my room but grabbed my shoulder and stopped me before I crossed the threshold. He spun me around to face him. "You may be one of the strongest and bravest people I've ever met, Solina. You're also stubborn and reckless."

I gritted my teeth and composed a rebuttal in my head, but Thorin continued before I could say anything. "Wait. I'm not trying to start a fight."

I sniffed. "Coulda fooled me."

His jaw worked, and I imagined his brain spinning like an old reel-to-reel computer calculating the right thing to say. "I know you, and I know what you're going through. You *know* I do. I've felt everything you're feeling right now, and that's how I know you won't hide from your demons. You'll face them and fight them no matter the danger or cost. You're in pain, and you'll do anything to make it stop—anything to pay back those who made you feel this way."

Thorin's grip on my arm softened. The severe angles in his expression and posture eased. "You'll take risks you don't need to take. You'll fight battles that don't belong to you. You do that enough times, and eventually, you'll lose. But your losses aren't just your own anymore. The things you do... they affect everyone. They affect me, Skyla, your parents, and millions of people who don't even know you."

He leaned in. His dark eyes bored into mine, emphasizing the imperative in his words. "I'll follow you out there, back into the world, back to the wolves and Helen and all the horrors she's surely waiting to unleash on us. Be sure about where you're going and what you're doing. Don't go jumping off any cliffs, because if you do, know that you'll be taking me over the edge with you."

Nobody asked you, I wanted to say as my heart thudded a slow, heavy beat. But, yes, I *had* asked him. I had asked him to be the wall everyone had to go through to get to me. I swallowed and bobbed my head. "No jumping off cliffs. Got it."

Thorin nodded and backed away. "I'll be in the living room. Come find me when you're ready to go."

CHAPTER 2

ALDUR HAD REFUSED THORIN'S INVITATION to come with us to Vegas, using Nina's fragility as an excuse to stay at New Breidablick. His newfound issues with Skyla might have also explained his reluctance to leave home. I'd let him drag his feet for a little while, work up the courage to confess, but I wouldn't let him put it off forever. I owed Skyla that much, and she deserved to know the truth of her history.

After collecting Skyla and Embla from the Bellestrella, Thorin drove us to the office complex where Baldur's men held Nate McNarry, Helen Locke's nephew and right-hand man. Thorin had arranged for another rental, a new 4Runner painted in flat black, insinuating aggression and fierceness. The SUV clearly stated: *Don't mess with me.* Skyla sat in the back with Embla, but we left the remaining Valkyries at the hotel on high alert, ready to come in an instant if we needed a show of brute force.

Half of me hoped Nate was on his own, and this wasn't another trick. The other half hoped Helen showed up with Skoll. Monsters were much scarier when they hid in the shadows. For the past few weeks, I'd held my breath, and I was suffocating. Confronting Skoll might mean my death, but it also might mean a chance to breathe again.

The tension of the pending confrontation kept us all quiet. Outside the 4Runner's tinted windows, the first hesitant rays of sunlight breached the horizon. A drowsy quiet had fallen over Vegas. Dawn was probably the only time in the day when noise and traffic gave the city a reprieve, and we travelled across town in half the time it would have taken at midday.

Thorin wheeled into the office complex's drive, pulled around to the front of a big building, and parked beneath its portico. The four

9

of us exited and stalked toward the entrance, everyone grim and silent. Naomi stood on guard at the front door, posture rigid. The Valkyrie was petite, dark skinned, and solidly built. Curls haloed her head in a dark poof, pulled back from her face by an elastic band. She wore combat boots and black cargo pants. Her whole attitude said: *I might be little and cute, but I* will *grind you in the dirt if I have to.*

Naomi waved, a salute, acknowledging our arrival. "Nate's inside. Amala and a couple of Baldur's men have him under watch."

Naomi led us up a flight of stairs to the third floor, down an empty hallway, and into a corner office framed by two massive windows facing downtown Las Vegas. Plastic sheeting covered the view and protected the room from the elements. The space smelled of sawdust and the earthy, mineral scent of fresh drywall mud.

Nate sat bound to a metal folding chair. Behind him stood a tall woman with glossy black hair and warm brown skin. Amala. I recognized her from visits to the Aerie. Despite Amala holding a knife to his neck, Nate smiled at me. He was as charming as usual, even in a rumpled suit and disheveled hair. I sneered at him as heat coursed through my veins, bringing my blood to a low simmer.

"Ladies and gents," said a man who I assumed was Baldur's contact. He stood by the door, his frame locked in a rigid stance. "If you have it under control, we'd like to move along." He nodded to another man in the corner, also militarily severe and blank faced.

Embla waved them out. "We can take it from here."

"Tell Baldur to keep an eye out for our bill." The spokesman for the two flashed a gesture, something like a salute. Then he and his partner withdrew from the room as quietly as a pair of ghosts.

Thorin stepped forward and addressed Nate. "I'll be up front with you. You're not leaving this place alive. But you can have a choice in how much pain you suffer before you die." He pulled something from his pocket and twisted his wrist. Mjölnir appeared in his fist. "We can make it quick and easy... or not."

Nate chuckled and shook his head. "Kill me if you will, but I have nothing to say. Make it as painful as you like. I won't give anything away. I'm not the betrayer. I'll die with honor on my side."

"You killed my brother." I spat. "He was an innocent. How was that honorable?"

"His death was a necessary sacrifice, the first step on the path of reparation."

"You're talking about some ancient vendetta," Naomi said. "We're here for justice *today*. You killed an innocent man and two Valkyries."

"They were not so innocent." Nate turned glittering green eyes on me. "The girl sold you out, Solina."

"She was naïve." I didn't hate Inyoni for her role in my betrayal at Oneida Lake. She was young, and the Valkyries lacked strong leadership. Anyone wanting to take advantage of them couldn't have picked a better time.

"And you aren't?" Nate asked.

"I know what I'm mixed up in. I know whose side I'm on and why."

"The Aesir will betray you, too."

I folded my arms over my chest and jutted a hip. "Then it's a good thing I'm not on their side." Thorin arched a questioning eyebrow at me. I ignored him. "I'm on *my* side. I'm on the side of humanity and life and survival. Ancient wars and prehistoric grudges mean nothing to me. I want my brother back, you bastard. I can't have him, so I want vengeance."

Nate sneered. "At least one of us is honest."

"No more games." Embla stepped in. "Amala, open his shirt."

Amala nodded and turned Nate's tie around, nearly strangling him in the process. She grasped his shirt plackets and ripped them apart, popping buttons and revealing his white undershirt. Her blade slit the thin cotton, exposing Nate's pale chest. She positioned the knife tip at Nate's breast, over his heart.

I lurched forward—to do what? Stop Amala? Help her? Before I could voice a question or protest, Embla issued another order, a single, harsh word. "*Ansuz*."

Amala's blade flashed. A symbol, akin to a tilting capital F, appeared in the flesh of Nate's chest. Blood oozed from the wound and dribbled over his pale stomach.

Thorin stepped closer and crouched before Nate, meeting him eye to eye. He seemed to understand what Embla and Amala had done. "Tell me where to find the wolf."

Nate shook his head and looked down. "I don't know. I haven't seen him since that night at the warehouses."

"I don't believe you."

"It's the truth." Nate nodded to his chest and the seeping blood. "Your Valkyries have ensured it, haven't they? I have no knowledge that can help you."

"Tell me where we can find Helen," I said.

Nate's eyes flickered to me. He shook his head. "You want some useful information, Solina? Nobody is who they seem. Trust no one."

Like I don't already know that. "Did you issue the order that killed my brother?" My flames crackled and popped beneath my skin's surface, begging me to let them out. "Were you there when Hati murdered him?"

Nate threw his head back and laughed. "Yes! Of course. You didn't have to carve a truth sigil in me to get that answer. I would have told you for the fun of it. I was there. My order set the wolf to action. I watched Hati's teeth tear through your brother's flesh. I listened to Mani beg for you, Solina. Did you know your name was the last word on his lips?"

His head jerked forward, his neck fully extended, and he bared his teeth at me in a maniacal grin. "I saw the blood drain from his body and the light die in his eyes. My only regret is that I won't be around to watch Skoll devour *you*."

My fire roared and shoved against my mental restraints like a rain-swollen river thrusting against a dam. This was not the time for self-immolation, though. An angry conflagration would burn down the building and destroy the possibility of answers, a transmutation that would steal my sanity. No, this was not the time, *not the time.*

I hunched over and struggled to contain the flames, but rage and frustration fueled my heat and sapped my self-control. I gritted my teeth. *Control, Solina. Control.* Firelight oozed from every pore. I fell to my knees and hugged my arms tighter around my waist, as if I could physically restrain my fire.

"No, no, no..." I muttered. But then an explosion of thunder rattled... and another.

A raging wind ripped aside the plastic sheeting over the windows.

Rain from nowhere and everywhere poured in and flooded the room. I stumbled to my feet and staggered to the window. The storm raged, my fire diminished, and a steamy fog enveloped me. When the last of my light died away, I eased to the floor in a puddle of embarrassment, anger, and rain.

"Holy shit," someone whispered. Naomi maybe.

Thorin took me by my shoulders and raised me to my feet. He tried lifting me into his arms, but I pushed against him. "No, I can stand. Just let me stand."

Concern swirled in his eyes. He frowned but nodded and held me until I regained my balance. Rain had plastered my hair to my face. I raked it back and plucked my sodden and scorched T-shirt away from my chest. At least I hadn't completely burned through my clothes.

He shifted, using his massive frame to shield me from the others. "Let me take you back to the hotel."

I almost accepted his offer, but no. Once I started giving in to weaknesses, when would I stop? "No. I'm okay. I'll be okay."

"Sunshine..."

I put my hand over his mouth to stop him. "No."

Thorin's eyes twinkled, and the blackness in them faded to brown. He pulled away and nodded. I stepped around him and faced the others. Skyla, Embla, Naomi, Amala, and Nate all stared, eyes wide. Yet, throughout the confrontation, Amala had not moved her knife from Nate's throat. *Now, that's a soldier.* They waited for me to say something, *do* something.

I held my splayed hands out at my sides. *Nothing to see here, folks.* "Can we pretend like nothing happened?"

The women glanced at each other. Naomi shrugged. "I didn't see anything."

My embarrassment drained away, and my shoulders slumped. I turned my attention to Nate. "So, you want to be a god again? That's your reason for doing all this?"

He shook damp hair from his eyes and leered at me. "*I* was never a god, Solina. Merely a legend."

"You love Helen and want to see her throne restored?"

He jutted his jaw. "She never lost her throne. She still commands the dead in her realm." His focus shifted to Embla. "Nothing can take that from her."

"Then what *does* she want?" I asked.

"What we all want. Justice."

"I don't understand."

Nate turned his attention to Thorin, and hatred burned in his green eyes. His cool composure receded, and he clenched his teeth while he spoke in a low and menacing tone. "The Aesir, their kind must be eradicated. Once and for all. They are a poison, tainting everything they touch."

Before I could ask for further explanation, Thorin stepped in. "*We're* a poison? Your grandfather killed Baldur, the most innocent and pure of us all. Loki murdered Baldur for his own amusement, for another of his self-indulgent, meaningless pranks. He killed him to prove he could."

"But my father was innocent," Nate said. "So was his brother. So was *I*."

Nate's father had been Narfi, who was also Val's brother. Therefore, Val was Nate's uncle. Throw Grandpa Loki into the mix and what do you get? One big tragic family.

"You just said yourself that no one was innocent," Embla said. "And you brought judgment upon yourself when you killed Mani and Khalani and Inyoni. Whatever mercy or justice you might have deserved, you have squandered. If you don't have anything useful to tell us, we won't waste any more time on you." Embla motioned to Amala. She raised her knife.

"Wait!" I shouted. "It can't be for nothing. Nate, don't die for nothing. Helen used you. Don't you know that?"

Anger drained from his eyes. His face softened. "This is not for nothing, Solina. I remained true to myself. I chose this. And when Skoll finally destroys you, we will all have our justice." His gaze flashed to Thorin. "Enjoy her while you can, God of Thunder. The wolf will kill her. She will die, in the end."

"No more," Embla said. "Finish him, Amala, before he can cause any more damage."

"No!" I screeched and lunged forward. "There has to be another way to make him talk."

"I'll talk." Nate grinned. "I'll leave you with one single truth. Helen is not your worst enemy—" Amala bent and dragged her blade across his throat. Blood welled up from the wound and cascaded down his throat.

"What?" Still on my knees, I lurched forward and clasped Nate's hand to my chest, over my heart so he could feel my desperation. "What do you mean? Nate?"

"It's too late," Embla said.

Amala stepped back and wiped her blade on her pant leg. Nate's stare fell on me. He smiled, a horrible rictus, as blood drained from his neck and cascaded into his lap. My stomach churned, and bile rose in the throat, acidic and bitter.

I fell to my knees at Nate's feet and peered up into the dying light in his eyes. "P-Please, Nate," I choked. "What did you mean?"

He gargled a terrible wet laugh. He stopped and wheezed, and pink air bubbles burst from his neck wound. I gagged and turned away but remained kneeling until he bled out. My mortal enemy—and I kept him company until the end. *What's* wrong *with me?*

While Amala and Naomi gathered plastic sheeting from the windows, Thorin eased me away from Nate's corpse. Then he collected the limp, bloodstained body and laid it prostrate on the plastic. A numbing coldness washed over me. Stomach acid burned in my throat, and yet my gaze remained glued on Nate, so pale, so... *dead.*

"Wha—" I coughed and cleared my throat. "Was that thing you carved in his chest?"

"*Ansuz?*" Amala said. "It is a master rune, the main symbol denoting the Aesir. It stands for wisdom, truth, and knowledge. It forced Nate to speak truth. Didn't mean he couldn't evade and avoid, though. Everything he said was true, but he never gave us the answers we really wanted. What a waste."

"What are you going to do with him?"

"Dispose of him," Embla said. "The same way we always have."

I stared up at Thorin, who stood back from the group, his expression dark, his gaze distant. "What was Nate talking about? Another enemy. Did he mean Val?"

He looked at me, but his expression did not change. His eyes remained unfocused.

I snapped my fingers at him. "Thorin?"

He blinked and shook himself. "I don't know. I don't know anything for certain anymore."

Skyla stepped to my side and crouched beside Nate's body. She patted his jacket and searched his pockets.

"What are you doing?" I asked.

She drew a keychain from one of Nate's pockets and found his wallet in another. "Searching for information. Maybe he has something useful in his pockets." She rifled through his wallet, ignoring the cash, but she pulled out a card, similar in shape and size to a credit card. Stamped on its front was the logo for Nastrond Industries.

"They sometimes used magnetized key cards like this to get around in Helen's warehouses," Skyla said. "The ones out in Laughlin."

I had hoped when we left those warehouses, we would never have to return to them. I should have known better. "You think there's something there?"

"What about the golems she keeps there?" she asked. "Or did Val use them all up in his fight with Thorin?"

I shook my head. "No. If all the shipping containers in that warehouse were full, the golems Thorin destroyed during the fight were a small percentage, assuming those came from the warehouse in the first place. Maybe Helen made up a batch especially for Val." I wrinkled my nose and resisted the urge to spit.

"Maybe it's time we find out," Skyla said. "And while we're there, maybe we can find something to lead us to Helen or Skoll. We've exhausted all our leads in Vegas."

Thorin stepped closer to us. The vacuous look had disappeared from his face. "Agreed. Embla, Skyla, let's regroup at the Bellestrella and gather the rest of the Valkyries."

I glanced at Skyla and back at Thorin. I shook my head. "This is never going to end, is it?"

Skyla patted my arm. "Don't say that, girlfriend. All bad things must come to an end."

"I thought it was all *good* things."

Thorin grimaced and looked away. "Those, too."

CHAPTER 3

UPON OUR RETURN TO THE Bellestrella, a dozen or so Valkyries piled into our hotel suite, bringing a low thrum of electric energy with them. Thorin, Embla, Naomi, Amala, Skyla, and I took seats at the dining room table, an impromptu convocation—Knights of the Oblong Table. Embla sat at one end, and I sat at the other. Thorin took the seat at my right hand, Skyla my left. Naomi took Embla's right hand, Amala her left. We formed a contiguous ring, yet the divide was obvious.

The Valkyries had come to Vegas to help us, but the ties binding the Valkyries to the Aesir were gossamer threads. Skyla's relationship to Embla might have been the only thing holding us all together. Whatever the reason, I was grateful for the Valkyries' presence, despite the uneasiness between us.

"You think these things at Helen's warehouses are golems of some sort?" Embla asked. "Containers bearing souls of the dead?"

Thorin leaned forward, braced his forearms on the table, and looked at me. "Do you remember the night you met Helen and the vision you saw outside the Westmark Hotel in Juneau, when I took your hand to help you from the car?"

"Yes," I said, "mostly." I rehashed it for the Valkyries' benefit. "Thorin stood in front of me in a misty field on the edge of some dark forest. Others stood around him, but a haze covered their faces, and I couldn't make out details. Somehow, I knew they were angry and ready to fight. They were scared. Their attention was focused on some invisible enemy on the other side of the mist. I remember a dog baying and wolves howling." I shivered. "There were voices, all hollow and empty sounding. Groaning and shrieking. It was such a horrible noise—it made me want to gag."

"Among many other horrible things that have no name," Thorin said, "that groaning and shrieking was Hela's army of undead. In the final battle, before Surtalogi's all-consuming flames were released, both sides fought—the army of Odin versus the army of Chaos. Hela raised the souls from her realm to fight on her side. She made constructs for them, bodies of a sort, from earth and rock and mud. The term 'golem' is a Hebrew one, but it is apropos for Hela's creatures."

"And everything that was done in Ragnarok," Skyla said, "she's doing again. We've already established that precedent. Helen is expecting another battle. But who is Odin's army this time? There's hardly anyone left."

"Baldur, me, the Valkyries, I suppose." Thorin leaned forward and braced his chin on his tented fingertips. "Point is, we're not going to let it get that far. We're going to kill that wolf, and we're going to destroy that golem army."

"Boss Man," Skyla said. "You've been to her warehouses. You can blip over, take a look, and tell us if there are guards or not. Tell us if the lights are on or if no one is home."

"I think it would be best to wait until after sundown," Thorin said. "I can move quickly through space, but I can't make myself invisible. Not without a lot of help."

"Fine." Skyla nodded. "That's step one. Step two is getting inside." She waved Nate's key card. "This should help."

If I insisted on coming along, I could count on an argument with Thorin about my safety. Normally, I didn't worry too much about our arguments, but the encounter with Nate had shaken me. A renewed fear chilled my blood, but I steeled myself against it. The only way to overcome fear was to face it, choke it down, stomp it out. "What's our goal?" I shifted my gaze to Embla. "Ultimately, we want to destroy these golems, right?"

Embla nodded. "Yes, but doing this takes our focus off the wolf."

I raised a finger. "Not necessarily. We've been waiting a long time for Helen to make a move. Killing Nate might antagonize her, but destroying her army certainly will, don't you think?"

She pressed her lips together. Then she nodded. "I see. Swat the hive enough times, and the queen will come out?"

"Exactly. We piss her off and force her into the open."

"Are we prepared to take down this army?" Naomi asked. "Our numbers are reduced. Many of us have never seen live combat before."

Embla's brows furrowed. "It is in our nature, Naomi. Why would you question our willingness to fight?"

Naomi shook her head. "Not questioning. Trying to be prepared." Her attention shifted to me. "Solina, you've fought these things before, yes?"

I glanced at Thorin and Skyla. "We all have."

"Then tell us about these creatures and what we should expect."

I glanced at Thorin again and inhaled deeply. "They move like skin and bone, more graceful than you'd expect. More flexible. But they are as tough as rocks, and my fire has little effect on them." I explained how I'd beaten them before. "Their weakness is their inability to think for themselves. They're single minded and don't seem overly concerned with self-protection. Imagine zombies made of flexible stone, and that's what you've got."

"But have you destroyed one?" Embla asked.

I shook my head. "No. Just outsmarted them. But Skyla shot one, blew apart his head, and Thorin took down a small army of them with his hammer."

The Valkyries swung their attention to Skyla.

"You shot one?" Embla asked.

Skyla nodded. "It was a big-caliber bullet. The bigger the better, I expect. Sort of like Thorin's hammer."

"They aren't invincible," I said. "Only a little more durable than the average monster."

Embla turned and addressed the assembly behind her. "Any more questions, ladies?"

A petite redhead named Siobhan piped up from the back. "Yeah... When can we start?"

After our meeting, the Valkyries dispersed, retreating to their rooms to assess their weapon situation and sharpen their knives and clean their guns, or so I imagined. I sat at the kitchen counter and studied the room service menu. My earlier flare-up had raided my energy reserves and stoked my appetite. Thorin eyed me from across the living room, wearing a thin-lipped frown. I turned my back to him and tried not to care what had made him look dour.

Skyla clapped her hands and bounced on her toes when the food service cart arrived. I lifted the covers, revealing stacks of French toast, pancakes, bacon, and sausage. She beamed at me as though I had revealed the last golden ticket to Willy Wonka's chocolate factory. Thorin wandered over to where and Skyla and I sat, stuffing our faces. Hands in his pockets, posture relaxed, he feigned nonchalance. It was as convincing as a hungry tiger wandering through a butcher shop hoping nobody noticed him.

I jabbed my fork at him. "I know what you're going to say."

His eyebrows arched. "Oh? Do tell."

I held up a finger and sipped my coffee. Then I swallowed and lowered my voice to mock his deep timbre. "Miss Mundy." Skyla choked and covered her mouth to keep from spraying masticated French toast across the table. "No one endangers my perpetuity. If you're thinking of putting yourself in the middle of this business with the Valkyries and Helen's golems, then you've got another think coming."

Thorin folded his arms over his chest. "I would never say, 'you've got another think coming.'"

I shrugged. "However you put it, the meaning would be the same." I looked at Skyla. "Am I wrong?" She snickered and shook her head. "And then you would say..." I lowered my voice again. "'Are you going to be stubborn about this, Sunshine? I will chain you if necessary.'"

Skyla's snickers gave way to a boisterous coughing fit.

"You're no help," Thorin said to Skyla. He shoved out a hip and readjusted his posture to something... feminine? He batted his lashes. "I'll tell you where you can stuff your perpetuity," he said in a high, wispy voice tainted by a bad Southern accent.

I glanced at Skyla. "Is that supposed to be me?"

Skyla jammed more French toast in her mouth and looked away.

"Well?" Thorin asked in his regular voice.

"You've got a point," I said. "I'm not a Valkyrie. I don't have warrior

20

blood flowing through my veins. But I'll tell you why I'm not too excited about staying here and sitting on my hands."

He huffed and rolled his eyes. "You mean, other than the fact that you insist on inserting yourself into the middle of every dangerous situation."

I slapped my fork down, pushed away from the table, and stood. "I won't sit back and let others fight my battles for me, Thorin. You know that."

"Why do the golems have to be *your* battle?" Lightning flashed in his eyes. "The Valkyries can do this on their own."

I stalked toward him, heat rippling across my skin. "What if Skoll's there, and this is our chance to end him?" I raised my hand, and flames engulfed my fingers. "I can defend myself."

"You can." He nodded. "But it doesn't mean you have to take unnecessary risks. Did you not make me swear I would be the wall that everyone has to get through on their way to you? Let me do my job."

"How about you give me some credit? I've done pretty well at keeping myself alive when there was no one else to depend on. I've saved your butt a few times, too."

Thorin smirked and shook his head. He probably had a smarmy retort all packaged up and ready to go, but he was smart enough, for once, to keep it to himself.

"This *is* my fight as much as it's yours, Baldur's, and the Valkyries'. The whole world's... You can't ask me to sit by and watch. You know me better than that. If you try to leave me behind, you know what'll happen. Didn't you learn that lesson when you went to fight Rolf?"

He growled and spun on his heel. He threw a fist into the wall, and it caved. Drywall dust scattered, and plaster crumbs dropped at his feet.

I raised my chin, put my hands on my hips, and arched an eyebrow. "Feel better now?"

He said nothing. My ears popped, and he disappeared.

I turned to Skyla, still sitting at the table before a half-eaten plate of French toast. She stared at me, blinking, her mouth half open. She closed it and swallowed. "You shouldn't do that to him."

"Do what?"

"Antagonize him like that. He's trying to protect you."

"He can do that and let me fight at the same time. He can't put me in a padded box, Skyla. I won't live like that."

"Even if it means saving the world?"

Well, damn. When she put it that way... At the moment, I was too angry and proud to admit it, especially to Thorin.

"You already said your fire doesn't have much effect on the golems," she said. "How do you expect to fight them? How much difference will your being there make?"

I had no answer, nor the patience to find one. Instead, I spun on my heel and stomped toward my room.

"Where are you going?"

"I think I have a swimsuit in my bags somewhere. It's either do laps or burn down this hotel."

She gaped at me and glanced at the patio door. "But it's freezing outside."

I snorted. "That's sort of the point."

Up and down and back again, I swam laps for what felt like hours. The Bellestrella heated its pools year around, but the chilly December temperatures had chased the other guests away. Mist rose from the warm waters, drawn by the cool air, and I probably looked half crazed out there, considering the inhospitable weather, but the cold and the exercise kept my flames under control. Never mind what anyone else thought.

Swimming pools made good therapy, in more ways than one. My frustrations and feelings of helplessness fueled each kick and stroke as I burned through them until serenity and reason returned. The water muffled exterior noises and distractions, and the exercise was mindless routine, allowing me to sink into my thoughts. Only then did I concede the logic of Skyla's and Thorin's arguments, although it took several hundred more yards of swimming before I could burn off enough pride to admit it out loud.

No living in cages or padded boxes, no letting others fight my fights, but no unnecessary putting myself in harm's way, either—especially if it put others at risk. What was so wrong with letting the Valkyries have the golems? Having reassurance of their support was why I'd asked them to come. Skoll was my fight, the one from which I consistently let myself get distracted. Helen's golems were ultimately another diversion. I needed to let them go and trust others to do their part.

You don't have to fight every battle, I told myself. *Sometimes, it's okay to delegate.*

After I dried off and changed into my street clothes, I went looking for Thorin and found him in the place that made the most sense. He and Amala and several other Valkyries had rearranged the workout equipment in the villa's private fitness room and made their own training center. Thorin stood in the middle, surrounded by three women. He had tied his hair back, and sweat had left dark rings on his T-shirt. The women prowled around him like hunters considering the best way to take down an angry bear. Golem fighting practice, I presumed, and Thorin was the golem.

I stepped back, watching from the threshold as Amala skipped forward and swung a right cross to Thorin's chin. At the same time, Siobhan struck for a kidney blow. He dodged both, moving as if water flowed beneath his skin instead of muscle. He was grace and strength—both the hurricane and the calm eye at the center. A thin layer of poise and civility masked his innate savagery, but that wildness burned in his eyes' dark depths.

He had revealed some of his true nature, his thunder god heritage, in that Portland field when he fought Rolf, but even then, it seemed as though he'd held back. I wondered what it would take for him to utterly drop his cool composure. What devastation could the God of Thunder inflict if his fetters were completely discarded? What could he do if there was no one and nothing, including his own remarkable self-restraint, to hold him back? A tongue of coldness licked down my spine, and I shivered.

Thorin followed through the path of his momentum and jabbed his knuckles at Amala's ribs. She jumped back, and his strike grazed her. She chuckled and bared her teeth in a wicked grin. Siobhan was not so lucky. He pivoted, kicked out, and swiped Siobhan's feet from underneath her. She had barely hit the floor when she bounced up, recovered her fighting stance, and grimaced. That fall must have hurt, but she shook it off.

Naomi moved in for an attack, but I interrupted before she struck. "Not to rain on anyone's parade"—I pointed at Thorin—"but I need to borrow your training dummy for a minute."

Siobhan snickered. Naomi stepped aside, allowing room for Thorin to pass. The heat of his stare burned on my neck as I led him outside to the patio.

"They can't fight Helen's army with fists," I said after he slid the door shut behind him. "Their knuckles will break long before those golems do."

He pressed his lips together, folded his arms over his chest, and leaned against a column supporting the porch roof. "They're just burning off steam."

I nodded. "There's a lot of that going around."

"What do you want, Sunshine?"

"World peace and an end to hunger and poverty."

He huffed.

"No?" I clucked my tongue. "I can always hope."

"Is this more of you being flippant because that's how you cope with stress?"

My eyebrows flickered up. *He knows me so well, does he?* "Better than a firebomb, amiright?"

"Sunshine…" he rumbled.

"Okay, okay." I waved off his censure. "This is hard for me. I need a second to work up to it."

Thorin's brow furrowed, and he tilted his head, clearly interested.

I bit my lip, turned my back to him, and stepped away, moving into our private courtyard's grassy lawn. "You were right."

Silence. "I'm sorry. Could you say that again? I think I misunderstood."

I whirled around and shoved a hand on my hip. "You heard me."

He bit back a smile, but humor danced in his eyes. "I'd like to hear it again."

"Don't press your luck."

"I was right about what, specifically?"

I bunched my hands in my jeans pockets and kicked the grass at my feet. "This doesn't have to be my fight. I can let the Valkyries go on their own. My fire is no good against those things, and I don't know how to shoot or throw hand grenades or whatever it is the Valkyries do. I'm sorry for being bullheaded."

Thorin sucked in a breath and stood up straighter. He unfolded his arms, strolled over to my side, and snatched something from the air. He rubbed it against the hem of his T-shirt and grinned as he presented the imaginary offering. "That was a real gem of an apology."

"You're going to polish it up, get a setting made, and wear it around to make everyone jealous?" It was our old joke. *Huh. We have a joke. Next thing you know, we'll have a song.*

"Yup. We'll have a matching set."

I snorted. "Whatever. Maybe it's good if I stay behind, in case Baldur's network inadvertently comes up with another lead for me to look into while you're gone."

"No, Sunshine, I'm staying here with you. We'll ask Skyla to arrange for a Valkyrie to stay with us, too."

I blinked at him. "You're not going?"

He pointed to himself. "Wall that everyone has to go through to get to you, remember?"

CHAPTER 4

"MAYBE I SHOULD STAY, TOO," Skyla said, when I broke the news that I intended to let the Valkyries go to Helen's warehouses without me. She had found Thorin and me outside on the patio. Probably, she had come to see if I was going to burn down the hotel, or if he was going to demolish any more walls.

"No." He jabbed a finger at her. "I want you in that warehouse. You're the only one I trust to bring back a truthful response."

"What would the others have to hide?"

"If I have my way, I'll never know because you'll be there to prevent them from covering anything up. The Valkyries are unstable, Skyla. Their loyalties are uncertain."

Her eyes blazed, but she said nothing.

"Skyla," I said. "He's right."

"I know he is," she spat. "Doesn't mean I have to like it."

"But we all trust *you*."

Her expression softened. "I'll see if Amala will stay behind, then. I think she's on the up and up."

Thorin nodded. "Better to be safe than sorry."

―――――――◈―――――――

A few minutes after sundown, Thorin teleported out to Helen's warehouses, found them fortified by a small army of security guards, and transported back. "She's certainly protecting *something* out there," he said upon his return.

"Couldn't you get a look inside?" I asked. Skyla and I sat with Thorin in the living room. The Valkyries stood sentry around us, listening to his report. He had sunk onto the loveseat across from me and stretched his

26

arms along the back. Although it was meant to seat two, Thorin made the chair look like a throne built for a king. "You had Nate's key card."

"It didn't work," he grumbled.

"You could blip around from place to place, inside and out, couldn't you?"

His lips thinned. His voice lowered. "If you'll recall, I didn't have complete control of my faculties the last time I was there. It's difficult to 'blip' inside a place I've never seen before, not without making a commotion or drawing a lot of unwanted attention, which would have negated the purpose of me going there, right? You wanted to know if the place had been abandoned. It hasn't."

Val had explained the look-before-you-leap rule when we had attempted to break into the Valkyries' library. Magic came with more restrictions than I'd expected. "Sorry." I shrugged.

He waved aside my apology. "I did manage to get a look at the building that houses those shipping containers you described. Several stone men patrolled the exterior."

"They were?"

He nodded.

"How long do you suppose it would take the Valkyries to tear that army apart?"

Skyla's lips split into a devious smile. "I don't know. Why don't you give me a chance to time them?"

Thorin nodded and rose to his feet. "There's no reason to wait. Call them together. You'll head out tonight."

"How are you going to get a dozen women out to Laughlin in the middle of the night?" I asked.

Skyla tapped a finger against her bottom lip as she thought it over. Inspiration struck, and she grinned. "You know those big black buses that go around town, hauling bachelor parties back and forth?"

"A party bus?" I said.

She nodded and jabbed a finger at Thorin. "Make sure to get us one with a disco ball."

Thorin made Skyla show him her cell phone before she left, proving she had it powered on and close at hand. "If anything happens, *anything*, if you get a sore throat or an itchy nose, you call me."

She rolled her eyes. "The last time you said something like that, you ran off after Baldur, and your asshole brother tried to freeze Solina to death in an ice cave."

He growled—an actual angry lion sound rumbled from this throat.

"Okay, okay..." Skyla waved him away. "Overprotective much, Dad?"

He scowled and blipped away without a word. My ears popped as an afterthought. "Ugh," I said to Skyla. "I hate it when he does that."

Back in our bedroom, Skyla finished fastening her sword sheath to her side, securing it tightly to her thigh using military-grade Velcro strapping. Calling her weapon a sword was a bit grandiose. "Great big knife" or "fancy machete" described it better. I'm sure there was some official name for it, but why did I need to know? I had fire, and that was weapon enough for me. Skyla wiped a rag over her blade and tossed the cloth into her suitcase. She silently slid the sword into its nylon scabbard, an anticlimactic gesture. "Yeah, I know. It's not as cool as they make it sound in the movies."

"Things rarely are."

"Says the girl who can create CGI fire from thin air."

"I didn't say there were no exceptions. Now, do you have everything you need? Clean undies, a change of socks, a full charge on your cell phone in case you need to call me to come pick you up? Don't go anywhere with any strange men. Don't drink and drive—"

Skyla laughed and threw her arms around me. "You're such a weirdo."

I returned her hug. "You love me anyway?"

"Always. We'll be back shortly. I'm going to keep a golem head for my collection."

After the Valkyries left, I tried settling down in the living room with Thorin's laptop, intending to research my theories about the existence of others like me, others with more knowledge and experience who could train me to develop my premonitions. But my muscles thrummed with a need to move, to act, to do *something*. I couldn't dismiss the feeling that killing Nate equated to kicking a hornets' nest filled with angry, volatile reciprocation, and what the Valkyries were about to do would only make it worse. *Which is what you wanted, right?*

I replayed all that had happened earlier in the day: the horror of Nate's death and the cold efficiency of its execution—Embla's remorseless commands and Amala's unhesitant responses. Their detachment chilled me. Not that I minded Nate's demise. Someone with higher moral standards might have protested the lack of proper judicial procedure, but those people had never transmuted into a star or stood face to face with the ruler of the underworld or awaited death in a glacial cave because of a bad case of sibling rivalry. Theories of jurisprudence more or less escaped the Aesir, and their revenge cycle was never ending.

I clicked around on a few Wikipedia pages and quickly found an article about a legendary, shamanic seeress in Norse paganism called a *völva*, who practiced an ancient oracular art called *seiðr*. But every time I tried to focus on the words, my mind drifted, and I found myself skimming without comprehension. After reading the same paragraph a couple of times without retaining any information, I shoved the laptop away, closed it, and rubbed my eyes. *Not tonight. I'm not in the right mood for research.*

I stood, crossed the room, and stopped before the glass wall overlooking the patio and private pool. The harsh desert sun had set, allowing for the birth of a clear, starry night. Lights under the pool's surface cast a rippling glow on the landscaped courtyard. Something about that undulating light mirrored my mood, and it beckoned to me. I slid open the patio door and stepped into the chilly air.

My mind wandered untraceable paths that my consciousness declined to follow. Zoned out, unaware, oblivious, I never heard Thorin follow me outside, but he drew me back to reality when he said my name.

"Solina?"

I flinched and spun around to face him. He had changed into a long-sleeved shirt, blue like a southern sky. He wore his usual jeans and scuffed boots. Without thinking, without succumbing to the hesitation and doubt that always stopped me, I stepped closer and twisted two fingertips into the strands of pale hair trailing over his shoulder. He stiffened, and his breath stilled.

His hair was as soft as I thought it would be. Softer.

He caught my hand and held it over his heart. Confusion flittered over his face, but not the harsh kind that proceeded his condescension. If I had to guess his thoughts, based on the look in his eyes, I suspected he wondered what had come over me. What was this reaching out, when I was usually quick to pull away?

"What is it?" he asked, his voice husky and thick—even lower than its usual burly rumble. "What's bothering you?"

"The waiting. The doing nothing. It's killing me." I tugged, and he released my hand. I breathed in, exhaled, and plastered a smile on my face. "I don't want to think or worry about it anymore right now. I need a distraction."

"You have any ideas?" Thorin asked.

"I don't know. Maybe some fresh air. A walk or something."

"Why don't we go to dinner?"

"You don't eat."

He shoved his hands into his pockets and hunched his shoulders. "I'll make an exception."

I glanced down at my attire: jeans, tunic shirt, scruffy boots. "I'm not dressed for dinner."

He gestured at his own casual appearance. "Burgers?"

"What about Amala?" The Valkyrie sat in the living room, scrolling through movie channels.

He rolled a shoulder. "Let her order room service."

After the day's traumatic and trying events, maybe I deserved to let my walls down for a few hours. I'd earned the right to enjoy Thorin's company and leave the baggage behind. "Burgers and a stroll down Las Vegas Boulevard like normal people?"

"Normal?" He smiled. "Us?"

"Hey, we can pretend, right?"

He took my hand and led me inside, and I didn't resist or pull away. *Just for a few hours. For a few precious hours, I will enjoy him and not worry about right or wrong, good or bad, eternity or mortality. I won't worry about heartbreak or sadness or regret.*

"Amala," Thorin said as we entered the living room. "We're going to grab dinner. You hold the fort until we get back, okay?"

Amala glanced at our clasped hands. She shrugged and turned to the TV. "Yeah, whatever."

"Let me grab my jacket," I said. "Then we'll go."

My aversion to catching a chill saved me. Otherwise, I would have been standing at the front door when it blew open. Three men in dark military-style clothing burst in, followed by another four or five of the stone men I'd last seen in a field somewhere outside Portland—the same stone men Skyla and the Valkyries were on their way to investigate and potentially terminate.

The first man drew a gun from his hip holster and pointed the barrel at us. Thorin grabbed my shoulder, shoved me into the bedroom, and barred the doorway with his massive frame. Amala must have taken her own action, because the intruder ordered her to stop. Then he fired.

Thorin brought out Mjölnir and threw the enormous hammer. I couldn't see much from my position, but rock exploded, and rubble sprayed over his shoulder into the bedroom. "Get your fire ready," he said.

"You don't have to tell me." I let my flames out, fisting two fireballs in my hands. I held the fire, not releasing it, but having it ready in an instant if I needed it. Another gunshot exploded, once, twice. I backed away from Thorin. He stepped into the living room and threw his hammer again. Furniture crashed. Amala yelled something.

More gunshots.

Amala yelped and cursed.

I turned away, heading for the sliding glass door in my bedroom that exited to our courtyard. Before I made it across the room, though, three figures—three more stone men—crashed through the glass and cleared the way for another, a human, to enter. He stood in the demolished doorway and aimed a weapon at me. Not a gun or a Taser... But what was it?

No time to wonder. Only time to act.

The flames in my palms erupted, burning everything until I was a creature composed of fire and light. Unlike that morning, I *wanted* this release, and it felt so very good. The power coursing through me was a seductive demon, convincing me of my invincibility. I lunged, a running leap that took me past the golems, and threw myself toward the human, toward the exit blocked by his fragile, fleshy body. He yelped and tried to dodge aside, but I tackled him, and we rolled through the broken doors onto the patio. He screamed, released his hold on me, and dropped his weapon.

"Is that a dart gun?" I asked. "What am I, a rabid animal?"

He tried to stand but only made it to his knees, huffing and gritting his teeth. With each passing second, the red tones in his skin deepened. I had burned him. Badly. Either he hyperventilated or the shock from his injuries overwhelmed him, because his eyes rolled back in his head, and he slumped to the ground.

I stood and backed over the grass, moving farther into the courtyard. The golem trio offered no assistance to their fallen human comrade. They paused in the doorway, watching and silent.

"What use are you?" I yelled at them. "You're a waste of perfectly good mud."

One stone man stepped forward—in response to my taunting or some silent command? Another shifted behind him, and they rushed for me. I dodged aside, avoiding them both, but the third golem blew through the courtyard, crossing the space between us in a burst of unexpected speed. He latched onto my arm, moving surprisingly fast for a figure of such dense construction.

"Thorin!" I screamed—not so much a cry for his help, although it was certainly welcome, but to alert him to the presence of trouble beyond the villa's interior.

The stone man who held my arm cinched an unforgiving embrace around my waist. His partner reached for me, but before he could complete his objective, his head exploded. Thorin stepped through the bedroom doorway into the courtyard and recalled his hammer to his outstretched hand. The old sagas and texts had said Mjölnir would "... *never fly so far as not to return to his hand.*" That trick was one of the few things the Marvel comics had gotten right.

The third golem, the one not occupied with holding me in place, stalked toward Thorin, heedless of the hammer's threat. Thorin swung, reducing the golem to a rubble pile. Then he shifted his attention to my captor and me.

He raised Mjölnir again, taking aim. "Duck, Solina." Before he could release the hammer, a gun barked, and he jerked and dropped the hammer. A bloodred rose bloomed on his shoulder.

I screamed and reached deeper into my well, seeking the starlight within—anything to save us. To save *him.*

Thorin reached for me. "No, Solina. Don't."

He swept up Mjölnir and flung the massive hammer toward me. I ducked. The golem's head, mere inches from my own, disintegrated in an explosive burst of dust. Thorin stretched out a hand, calling for his weapon, but another gunshot ripped through his chest. Another bloody floret spilled across the center of his shirt, and he fell to his knees. In the low light, the stain appeared dark, almost black.

Had I thought only rain and thunder pumped through his veins?

He coughed and slumped onto his side. A man, a human, stepped forward, brandishing a knife. He crouched over Thorin, slashed his shirt open, and drew the blade in flickering movements across Thorin's chest. I screamed for him to stop, and the intruder looked up at me, wearing the kind of smile that issued a challenge.

The golem had not let go of me, but the loss of his head made him clumsier, off balance, slow to react. After a brief struggle, I freed myself from the golem's grip, but by then Thorin's attacker had disappeared, leaving the thunder god prone on the floor in a bloody pool. That last gunshot had torn through the center of his chest, through vital organs. But he was immortal, right? Did he have lungs and a heart? His wounds proved he had blood, though, and that realization chilled me to my core.

I backtracked to the bedroom's shattered doorway and crouched beside him. He lay across the entrance, Mjölnir in hand, his breathing shallow but evident. Blood trickled from the corner of his mouth. I retracted my flames and stroked his temple, pushing his hair off his face.

His eyes fluttered open. He smiled, revealing bloodstained teeth. "Sunshine," he croaked.

I choked down a whimper. "God of Thunder, you gonna die on me?"

"Wasn't planning on it."

"Good. This would be a bad time for you to leave me on my own after all the bravado you've been selling so hard."

"Bring it on." He winced.

Heedless of my nudity, the broken glass, and my scraped and bruised skin, I knelt beside him, intending to help him to his feet, but at that same moment, the wolf of my worst dreams bounded through the doorway at the opposite side of the room. His amber eyes fell on me... and slid away. His gaze settled on Thorin, and he hunkered low,

His muscles bunched, his teeth gleamed, and he snarled and coiled for a leap.

Something's not right about this. Something's not right about the wolf…

I once saw an Internet video of sun flare—lavalike whips and arcs of plasma exploding from the sun's molten body. Holding that image at the forefront of my mind, I called out my fire again. The previous fight had drained my stores, leaving me little to use against the wolf, but I intended to make the most of what remained.

Leaping forward, I grabbed at the beast of my nightmares. He yelped and slipped away, fast and sleek. *I've got to stop underestimating his speed.*

Thorin grunted something unintelligible. A dull sound thudded behind me followed by a squall of mortal pain. A brief look behind me revealed that Thorin, still seated and bleeding, had taken down another attacker. A flesh-and-bone man lay on the floor in the doorway, blood pooling around his head. That distraction had invited the wolf's attack. He came for me, teeth bared. I raised my flames again—one last effort—and met him, catching the beast in a fiery embrace. He squealed, applied his claws and teeth to my softest parts, and tore his way free.

I grabbed at the wolf again, but he evaded me. His attention flicked to something behind me. His ears lowered and drew against his skull. His tail tucked under his belly. He bared his teeth, leapt through the patio doorway, and dashed across the courtyard. Then he jumped over a short row of privacy hedges and raced into an alleyway.

I spun around, searching for whatever had frightened him away. Thorin, still slumped on the floor, had drawn back and held Mjölnir positioned for a throw. "Too slow," he panted. "I was too damned slow."

I dropped my flames and reached for a dirty shirt on the floor by Skyla's side of the bed. The T-shirt barely covered everything once I shrugged it on, but it would serve for chasing a wolf. "I'm going after him."

"No," Thorin said, his voice weak and raspy. "Let him go."

"Hell, no. We might not get this chance again."

"*Solina*—" He started another protest, but I ignored him and sprinted through the doorway, across the small lawn, hurdled the privacy hedge, caught my foot in a branch, and fell on my outstretched hands. I screamed a few choice words, rolled over, stumbled to my feet, and took off in the direction I had last seen the wolf's disappearing backside.

CHAPTER 5

EVERY STEP SENT PAIN STABBING up from my heel, through my ankle, into my knee. I could have stepped on any number of things: broken glass, rubble, shrubbery. Ignoring my physical complaints, I kept going, single minded and intent on the wolf.

The alleyway ended at an access street leading to hotel parking in one direction and Las Vegas Boulevard in the other. A wolf running pell-mell down the main drag should have stirred some kind of interest—shrieking tourists or honking horns—but the night was relatively quiet. Maybe the wolf had changed into human form. In a town nicknamed Sin City, a naked man streaking down the sidewalk was much less likely to incite a riot than a wild wolf. He could have also hidden himself among the parking deck's shadows, intending to lure me into a surprise attack. My gut clenched at the thought of playing hide-and-seek in the garage's dark interior.

To Las Vegas Boulevard it is.

I scampered down the hotel's access road, sticking close to the darkest shadows of a building. Cars rolled past me, oblivious or simply uninterested. My heel protested louder, and I skip-hopped on tiptoe, limping forward until I reached the sidewalk.

A group of casually dressed sightseers crossed in front of me. A few noticed me and turned around as if to inquire about my situation, possibly even ask if I needed help. Or maybe they simply wanted to ridicule my strange and bedraggled appearance.

"Um, ma'am?" said one of the young men. I guessed he was Southern by his accent, inclined to help a woman in distress by his upbringing, and an Atlanta Braves fan by the logo on his ball cap. *Bless his heart.*

I interrupted him before he could finish his thought. "Did you see a wolf come from this direction?"

He frowned and recoiled. "A wolf?"

"Or a large dog that looked like a wolf?"

"Is that what happened to you?" asked a young woman standing beside the Braves fan. She studied my disheveled appearance. "You get attacked by a dog or something?"

"Did you see it?" I asked.

She shook her head. "Nope. No dogs. Or wolves."

"How about a naked man?"

She cut her eyes to the Braves fan. "Saw *him* naked this morning. Does that count?"

Despite my anxiety, I smiled. "No, but good for you."

She smiled back. "Yes, it *was* pretty good for me."

"You sure you're all right?" asked the Braves fan, whose cheeks had flushed a deep shade of pink.

Really? Blushing? I thought that was illegal in Vegas.

"I will be," I assured him and pushed past the group so I could peer down the sidewalk. A scream rose above the traffic noise. The tourists and I turned toward the outcry.

"There goes your dog," said my blushing knight-in-dingy-baseball-cap. He pointed at a shaggy, four-legged figure, crossing Las Vegas Boulevard among a crowd of pedestrians. A few had stopped and pointed at the lupine figure dashing toward the sidewalk on the highway's opposite side.

Someone else saw him and screamed. Terror spread, and people dodged aside, making way for the wild beast. I took off after him, following not by sight but by the shouts and parting waves of people. As if sensing my presence, the wolf slowed and stopped under a streetlight. He turned and looked back at me.

He's not red. That's what's different. He's browner, tawny colored. What the hell? But if the wolf wasn't Skoll, who was he? An answer flared in the depths of my mind, but I shoved it away. Acknowledging that possibility was too painful.

The wolf huffed, put his head down, and trotted forward again. Barefoot, half naked, nearly bankrupt of superpowers, and exhausted from fighting mythological creatures, I should have let the wolf go. If I'd had an ounce of sense, I would have returned to Thorin's side. In my imagination, I heard him and Skyla screaming at me, begging me not to do this. I shut those voices out.

If the wolf veered off into an unpopulated area or tried to lead me into an enclosed area, I would go back, but until then, I'd follow him through the crowds. I needed to find out who he was and what he wanted with me.

No, not me. Thorin. Before I had intervened, the wolf's attention had been focused on Thorin. *If that wolf is who I think he is, his interest in Thorin over me would make sense.*

The people around us had stopped screaming. Those who'd parted to allow the wolf's progress stared back and forth between us, probably wondering if they'd happened upon a reality TV show filming live on location or maybe a shocking new street-magician performance. I had Hollywood to thank for creating a culture in which the average Joe accepted special effects trickery as an explanation for paranormal activity. In fact, several people had pulled out cell phones to record the encounter.

Someone stepped out of the crowd beside me and put a hand on my shoulder. "Solina."

I flinched and spun around to face a man I hadn't expected to see but was rather glad to have at my side. "Baldur? Where did you come from?"

"Thorin called. He told me which way you had gone, and you weren't hard to follow. What do you think you're doing out here on your own?"

I turned to the wolf, but he was gone. I stumbled forward, intending to run after him, but Baldur drew me back. "Come with me. Help me... *please?*" I tugged on him, urging him to follow me. The stern expression on his face softened. "Please?"

"You're in no state to be chasing wolves." He frowned at me, but then he glanced down at the sidewalk as if searching for the wolf. "Go back to the hotel, and help Thorin. You need to get him out before Helen sends reinforcements or the mortal authorities arrive. Call the Valkyries; tell them what happened. I'll see if I can track down this wolf. I'll catch up with you again in a little while."

My ears popped, and Baldur vanished before I could say anything.

If people around me noticed Baldur's disappearance, they kept it to themselves. When the wolf had moved on, so did their attention. A few curious types glanced at my disheveled appearance, but when I turned on my heel and limped to the hotel, most avoided eye contact and pretended not to see me.

When I reached the hotel room, I found Thorin in the same place I'd left him, sitting near the patio doorway in a puddle of blood and broken glass, keeping the company of several shattered stone men and one badly charred human—still breathing, but for how long? I gulped and looked away, not allowing myself to contemplate my own guilt or moral failings.

Kill or be killed. That's the world I live in now. Maybe that was the world Sol had always lived in. And Thorin lived there, too. Maybe it was time to cut him some slack.

I stepped over broken glass, found a pair of jeans, and slid them on. I shoved my feet into a pair of Adidas slides I found by the side of the bed—Skyla's, I presumed. Then I knelt beside the bruised and beaten God of Thunder.

He peeled open his eyes and peered at me. A flurry of expressions passed over his face: relief, anger, pain. "Baldur says I need to get you out of here," I said. "I tend to agree. Who knows what's coming for us next?"

"Where *is* Baldur?"

"Chasing that wolf. He said he'd catch up with us later."

"That wasn't Skoll."

"I know." Neither of us seemed to want to explore the wolf's identity.

He shook his head and closed his eyes. His head fell back against the wall. "We'll let Baldur deal with it. You and I need to get moving."

"What about—" I stopped and swallowed. "What about Amala? Is she... "

He rolled his shoulder—the one not covered in blood. "I haven't heard anything from the other room. That headless golem stumbled over here a few minutes ago." He pointed into the courtyard. Another stone body, crumbled to gravel, lay several yards away. "I finished him off."

I caught my lip between my teeth and bit down, hard, using the pain to chase away my tears. I rose to my feet. "I'll be right back."

Thorin said nothing but closed his eyes again and nodded.

I stepped over another corpse into the living room, into a showcase of horrors. Rubble, demolished furniture, bodies, blood. Everywhere, blood. *Detachment*, I told myself. *Compartmentalize. Focus on Amala.*

I found the Valkyrie lying behind the sofa in a dark, sticky puddle. Black holes—bullet wounds, I supposed—riddled her chest. Another shot had gouged a hole in her cheek. Empty eyed and motionless, Amala stared up at the ceiling. I touched her neck in a hopeful gesture, but her skin was as cold as the marble floor. Bile rose up in my throat. I turned aside and vomited. Why try to fight it? What did it matter if I added to the gore?

When my legs allowed for it, I rose and stepped away from Amala, rubbing my mouth and urging my stomach to settle. Setting my gaze on the doorway of my bedroom, I stumbled to Thorin's side. "We've got to get moving. Please tell me you have one magical mystery tour left in you."

He peeled his eyes open. "What?"

"Can you blip us to the 4Runner?"

"Amala?"

I shook my head and looked away.

"Okay, get an arm around me." He struggled to get to his feet. "We'll see how much gas is left in my tank."

Turned out his gas tank was on E. He shifted us only as far as the edge of the courtyard. I tugged on him and shoved my shoulder into his armpit. He grunted and lumbered forward. "C'mon, Holy Thunder," I urged. "You can move faster than that."

He grimaced. "Holy Thunder? That's the best you can do?"

Half jogging, half limping, we rounded the corner of our private yard and stumbled into the alleyway. I turned us, and we staggered toward the parking deck. "Please tell me you have the keys in your pocket."

He grunted again and tried to stand up straighter. He pulled me close, and we blipped again and arrived at the parking deck entrance.

"I thought you were empty."

"Second wind." His eyes rolled up into his head. He nearly fell face first onto the asphalt, taking me down with him.

"Thorin." I wheezed and braced my legs against the pull of his weight. "No time for this. You're a freaking giant. I can't carry you."

He shook off his dizziness and wobbled onto his feet. Blood coated his shirt and covered me in warm, gummy red. "You love it," he muttered. "Finally, an excuse to get your hands all over me."

"You're right. I *can* do better. Move your ass, Your Royal Norseness. Boy Thunder. Lord of the Rain Dance..." By employing a steady stream of sarcasm and a weary shoulder, I managed to guide him through the parking deck gate and into the elevator. We collapsed into a bloody pile on the floor. "Where's the SUV?"

"The valet parked it."

"How are we going to find it?"

He pulled the key fob from his pocket. "Open the door again."

"What?"

"Just do it."

I pressed the arrow button, and the elevator's sliding doors parted. Thorin thumbed a button on the key ring, and we listened for car alarms. Nothing. "Second floor," he said.

We repeated the routine until we found the racket of honking horn and electronic bells and whistles on the fourth floor. I helped him to his feet, and we struggled across the concrete parking deck, following our ears until we located the SUV. He handed me the keychain. I stared at him, mouth agape. "You deign to let me drive?"

"Only on my deathbed."

"That better not be true." After settling Thorin in his seat, I slammed the door, jogged around to the driver's side, and slid into place behind the wheel. Even though I doubted it offered much protection, I pressed the door lock, and the *ka-chunk* of the mechanisms engaging was a sweet, sweet sound.

"Back to New Breidablick?" I reversed from the parking space.

He nodded. "It's the only safe place I can think of right now."

"What about the Valkyries?"

"They can fend for themselves."

"How do I get to New Breidablick from here?" I had only made the trek via Thorin's magical means, and while I knew Lake Tahoe's general direction, getting there required a more specific knowledge of highway navigation.

He fiddled with the GPS system. A pleasant English lady's voice instructed me to travel north on Las Vegas boulevard. He slumped against his window and closed his eyes.

"Promise me you're not about to die over there."

"You worried about me, Sunshine? Takes more than a couple bullets to put me out of my misery."

I wheeled us out of the parking lot and followed the hotel drive to the main drag. The lady in the GPS reminded me which way to turn. I checked my rearview for signs of pursuit but saw nothing beyond the ordinary.

"You lost a lot of blood," I said. He needed rest, maybe sleep, if not total oblivion. I also desperately wanted to clean him up and feed him something. Whether he usually ate or not, losing that much blood, even for an immortal, had to be rough on the system.

"Didn't say I felt particularly chipper," he said, "but I promise not to die."

After retrieving his cell phone from Thorin's pocket, I used it to call Skyla. Despite Thorin's demands that she stay in contact, the call went directly to her voicemail. I left her a message telling her what to expect if and when she and the Valkyries returned to the hotel. "Tell Embla to warm up her runes. She's going to need them if she's going to clean up that disaster."

I drove north from Vegas until the car lights in front of me blurred. My eyelids had gained so much weight I could barely hold them open anymore. Just over the Utah border, in the town of St. George, I pulled over at a decent-looking motel and reserved a room.

"Zombie movie extra," I told the motel clerk as he eyed my bloody clothing.

He shrugged, swiped Thorin's credit card, and passed me the receipt to sign. He handed me a set of key cards and motioned in our room's general direction, all without uttering more than four or five words.

"Why are we stopping?" Thorin grumbled when I opened his door to help him out.

"I can't hold my eyes open anymore. We need sleep and food, and I want to clean you up and make sure the bleeding has stopped."

"You want to get me out of my clothes?" He grinned.

I slapped his unwounded shoulder. "Blood loss makes you loopy. No more talking until you feel better."

After opening the door and flicking on a light, I pushed him into the room and shut the door behind us. After turning the deadbolt, I flipped the swing latch into place. Not that it would keep out mythological beasts, but we had seen that even mundane intruders could prove problematic, and an extra lock might buy us some time. Also, habits.

"Get in the shower. I'm going to run out and get some food." I eyeballed his bloodstained shirt. "I'll see if I can find you something clean to wear, too."

Not waiting for his reply, I turned and started for the door. Thorin snagged my wrist and towed me back. "You don't need to go anywhere looking like you just butchered a deer. I've got a bag in the rear of the truck. It has some clean clothes in it. It'll get us by for now. Why don't you take a shower first, and I'll get the clothes?"

"I'm not the one who got shot. Quit being a hero, and go clean up. *I'll* go get the bag."

He nodded and released my wrist. No arguments and following my commands? This compliant side of him worried me even more than all the blood.

"Solina?"

"Yes?" I turned to look at him.

He met my stare and dropped his tough exterior. He let me see his pain and fear and something more... something I refused to name. His openness stole my breath. "I—"

I waved a hand, cutting him off. No matter what he was about to say, it would have been too much. It would have wrecked me, and I wasn't ready to be undone by him. Not yet. Not in some cheap roadside motel halfway between Vegas and Tahoe. "Whatever it is, it can wait. We're both worn out. Exhaustion tends to make people maudlin."

He arched an eyebrow. "Maudlin? You?"

In reply, I rolled my eyes, unlocked the door, and ducked into the night.

When I returned a few minutes later, the hiss of spraying water told me Thorin was in the shower. I set his bag on one bed and stretched out on the other. I meant to watch TV and wait for my turn in the bathroom, but I passed out the moment my head hit the pillow.

A warm hand on my shoulder woke me. "Sunshine. You can't sleep in bloody clothes."

I rolled over and rubbed my eyes until my vision cleared. Thorin stood over me, wearing nothing but his jeans, his iron *Járngreipr* bracelets, his *Memegingjörð* torc, and a few tantalizing water drops. I turned away as if it would help, as if not looking at him could stop the wanting.

"Okay, yeah, thanks," I muttered.

I dropped my feet to the floor and trained my eyes on the carpet—utilitarian, boring, safe hotel carpet. I stood and started toward the bathroom. He moved, barring my way. I must have looked like an idiot, standing there, blood crusted and stubbornly staring at the floor.

"What are you doing?" I asked.

"Waiting for you to look at me."

"Why?"

"Because you're trying so damned hard not to."

I did look at him then, irritation diluting my desire. He was perfect, lovely, golden skinned, and unbelievable. No bullet holes, no blood—only a few ancient scars that spoke of another time and another world. He took my hand and set it over his heart, over the place where I had seen a bullet explode from his chest. Warm flesh, the opposite of Amala's.

"Not even a mark?"

He shook his head. "I'm perfectly whole and still very much alive."

"One of those men carved something in your chest with a knife. After you'd been shot. Twice."

He shrugged. "I vaguely remember that."

"But you don't know what he was doing?"

"It doesn't matter, does it? My wounds are healed."

"It's good to be you, isn't it?"

He pulled my hand away from his heart and pressed his lips to the heel of my palm. I gasped and tried to wrench myself free, but he wouldn't allow it. "I'm trying to say, 'Thank you.'"

43

"I-I owed you one," I stuttered. My mouth had gone dry.

"Can't you just say, 'you're welcome'?"

"Would you have been all right if I had left? Would you have recovered on your own anyway?"

"Probably. Or maybe they would have come with a weapon that would have destroyed me. Maybe they would have drugged me and kept me in captivity the way they did before."

"I'm never going to leave you behind, Thorin. I've lost too much already."

His brown eyes gazed into mine, trapping me. I might have stood there all night, enthralled, but he released me. "Go take a shower. You stink of wolf and dried blood."

I lacked the energy to form a proper retort.

Using the motel's complimentary shampoo and soap, I scrubbed grime and filth and blood from my hair. The spray ran in pink rivulets down my body and disappeared in the drain. The hot water worked miracles on my tired and achy muscles, restoring my sense of well-being. I reached to turn off the shower, but then I thought about the man—god, deity, divine being—on the other side of the bathroom door. What did he expect from me? What did I expect from him?

More importantly, could I sleep in the shower?

You're a grown woman, I told myself. *Start acting like one.* I turned off the water, patted down with a towel, slipped into Thorin's huge T-shirt, and wrapped another towel around my hair. The T-shirt did little to protect my modesty, but he had seen me wearing less. *So much less.*

I stepped into the bedroom. Only the TV's glow illuminated the room. The comforting aroma of burgers and fries greeted me, so I followed my nose to the table where Thorin had laid out a beautiful fast-food dinner. I forgot all about the uncomfortable immodesty of sharing a hotel room with the most desirable man in the world. French fries called to me, seducing with their salty siren song. I grabbed the carton and stuffed a handful of fries in my mouth before turning to face him.

"Grmm." I groaned through the food. I finished chewing and swallowed. "These may be the best fries I've ever had."

"I promised you burgers." He grinned. "I'm a man of my word."

I sank into the chair and unwrapped the massive cheeseburger. Sighing a sound of infinite pleasure, I licked salt and ketchup from my fingers. "Thank you." I shoved another pile of fries into my mouth.

"You're welcome."

I paused, mid-chew, my cheeks bulging with food, and glanced over at Thorin, who was stretched out on the bed, dressed—thank heavens—in jeans and a T-shirt. He stared at the ceiling as though he might find the answer to all the universe's questions in its swirly textures.

"You lost a lot of blood," I said.

"It's not the first time. Probably won't be the last."

"You're sure you don't need something to eat?"

He rolled up on an elbow and met my gaze. Then he shook his head. "No food. Just rest. You know I'm a quick healer."

I screwed my lips into a sideways smirk and concentrated on finishing my dinner. *Fast healer, indeed.* Short-term memory loss or bullet wounds to the chest, he had repeatedly proven his invincibility, at least to human calamities. *Wish the same was true for me.*

I finished my meal in silence and cleaned up my trash without further comment from Thorin, but the tension between us needed no words. Light a match and the room would explode. *Who needs a match? One touch and I'd probably go up like a roman candle.*

After discarding my trash, I returned to the bathroom and splashed cold water on my face until the blush drained from my cheeks. I washed my hands and finger-combed knots from my damp hair. Thorin had turned off the TV, and a heavy, dark silence fell over the room. I returned and eased under my bedcovers. "Don't turn the TV off on account of me," I said. "I could sleep through a hurricane right now."

"Oh yeah?" He chuckled, and thunder rumbled in the distance. "Want to prove it?"

"Could you do that? Here? This far from an ocean?"

"Maybe. Would you like me to try?"

"I think it would freak out the locals, but no. After what we've been through today, you should rest. You should sleep, but you don't sleep. So you should meditate, or do whatever it is you do to relax."

"I sleep sometimes," he said, soft and low.

"Do you? Do you dream?"

"On occasion."

"What does the God of Thunder dream of?"

He hesitated. "Sometimes, I dream of fire."

Sometimes, I dreamed of fire, too. That night, after drifting to sleep, comforted by Thorin's steady breathing, I dreamed of roaring rivers and runes. I dreamed of echoing darkness and teeth. I dreamed of exploding suns and broken hearts.

CHAPTER 6

T HE RUMBLING OF BALDUR AND Thorin's voices engaged in quiet conversation woke me before sunrise. The bedside clock showed I had slept for three hours, give or take. *Not enough time. Not nearly enough.*

"Solina," Baldur said when I sat up and rubbed my eyes. "Sorry for waking you." A dim light shone from the overhead fixture, but the rest of the room remained in shadows. Thorin sat across from Baldur, sipping from a takeout coffee cup, and his dark eyes were locked on me in silent contemplation.

I waved off Baldur's apology. "What's the news?"

"I was telling Thorin I followed your wolf a ways. A black car stopped and picked him up. Followed it to a private home in a gated community on the outskirts of Vegas. It wasn't the wolf that got out, though." Baldur swallowed and looked away. "It was Rolf."

Silence fell over the room like an avalanche, sudden, suffocating, and cold.

I cleared my throat. "You mean Val?"

Perhaps the revelation of Val's shape-changing abilities should have surprised me, but I had guessed as much already. The Aesir had forced Val to transform into such a beast thousands of years ago. Apparently, he still retained that ability. He *was* the son of Loki, the master trickster, after all.

"Do you think he knows you followed him?" I asked.

"He has the ravens," Thorin said. "He knows everything, remember?"

"So what does he want? He must expect us to come looking for—"

Thorin's phone rang. He tugged it from his pocket, read the caller

47

ID, and brushed his thumb over the screen. He laid the phone on the table. "What's the news, Ramirez?"

Skyla's anxious voice projected from the speaker. "Boss Man, what the hell happened?"

"Where are you?"

"Outside the Bellestrella. I got Solina's voicemail. We came back to see what we could do about Amala, but the police are already swarming the place. Embla is talking to someone official. You stirred up a shit storm."

"Not us," I said. *But why? What's Val up to now?*

"You know what I mean," Skyla said.

"Tell us about the warehouses," Thorin said. "What did you find?"

"The guards and the golems you saw were decoys. The containers were all empty."

He swore and pounded a fist on the table. The sensation of holding my breath and being on the verge of suffocation returned. I fell against my pillows and covered my eyes. *One break. Just one break, it's all I ask for.*

"We questioned one of the guards," Skyla said. "Embla, uh, *ensured* he was telling the truth."

"More rune carving?" I asked.

"Yes. He said the contents of the containers were moved a couple days ago."

"Where'd they go?" Thorin asked.

"He didn't know, and considering the conditions of his interrogation, we were inclined to believe him. He said a bunch of eighteen wheelers showed up. They transferred the cargo, and the trucks left." Skyla inhaled a deep breath and let it out in a rush. "But we have a working theory about where she may have taken them. It's not great, but it's something."

"Not great is certainly better than nothing," Baldur said. "What's your guess?"

"Okay, Hela used the spirits of the dead at a final battle which took place... *where?*"

"On Vigrid's plain," Thorin said. "It's also called Oskopnir."

"Vigrid is the place where the Aesir fought Hela, Loki, and everyone else," Skyla said. "Legend said it measured a hundred miles each way.

48

The hundred miles is considered to be a phrase generally indicating a vast distance—sort of like how forty days and forty nights meant a really long time in the Bible."

"Seemed a pretty accurate measurement at the time." Thorin rose from his seat and paced the open space between the table in the bathroom door. "But Vigrid existed in Asgard. That's going to be a problem for Helen if she's sticking to history."

"But what is the literal translation of Vigrid?" Skyla asked.

"Battle-surge," Baldur said. "Or a place on which battle surges. And Oskopnir means the not yet created or not made."

"If we're being literal," Skyla said, "then Vigrid can be any place where the battle will surge, and it may even be a place that is not yet created but will exist when Helen names it and sets the battle there."

I rubbed my face and shook my head. "If I'd had a full night of sleep, I might be able to process the meaning of what you just said."

"All I said was that Vigrid is a self-fulfilling prophecy."

"Nope. I'm sure you said a lot more than that."

"That is a wonderful theory." Sarcasm saturated Thorin's tone. "But you can't plot the not-yet-created-battle-surge on a map, can you, Skyla?"

"Don't get your undies in a wad, Boss Man. I'm not finished. That guard gave us one more useful bit of information before Embla, uh, eliminated him. The trucks all have GPS tracking. The guard said if we could find Helen's tracking program, we might locate the trucks."

He stopped pacing and folded his arms over his chest. "And?"

"We left some of our techie types at the warehouse office. They're trying to hack into Helen's network, but even if we find the tracking program, who knows if the GPS trackers are on or if the trucks made a delivery and moved on to somewhere else?"

A very dull light bulb clicked on over my head. I shifted and sat up on my knees. "You've got to see if the trucks travelled somewhere that might serve as a modern-day Vigrid. And if we're lucky, the trucks might still be there like a giant flashing sign—future site of Vigrid's Plain, coming soon."

Skyla snorted. "Yes, something like that."

"You got your work cut out for you. And in the meantime, we have a new wolf problem to solve."

"You said something about that in your message. It didn't make any sense."

I told Skyla about the new wolf, about our fight, my chase, and Baldur's discovery of Val's involvement.

"I think we should get over to that house and see what Val's up to," she said.

Baldur leaned forward toward the phone. "I can meet you at the Bellestrella and show you the way."

"Val will know if you're coming for him," I said. "It's probably what he wants."

"You're probably right," she said.

"Be careful."

"Always. Baldur, we'll wait here until you show up."

Skyla ended the call, and Baldur stood and looked at Thorin and me. "What are you two going to do?"

"We're going to keep heading to New Breidablick," I said. "Neither of us are in the best condition to fight right now."

Baldur nodded. "Okay. I'll meet you there as soon as possible." My ears popped, and Baldur disappeared.

Thorin looked at me and arched an eyebrow. "Really? No insisting on going back to Vegas to confront Val?"

I gave him an are-you-kidding-me look. "My fire is bankrupt. I'm exhausted and in no state to fight wolves or face Val... Rolf... whoever." My stomach turned over at the thought of seeing him again. My brain still tended to reject the truth—that Rolf and Val were the same, and when I forced the question, things inside me went cold and dizzy. "I have a feeling going to Val plays into his scheme, whatever it is. If he wants something from us, I don't plan to make it easy for him. And maybe, just maybe, Skyla and Baldur will get lucky."

He nodded. "I won't argue. I think you're making the right decision. And if you agree to go my way, we can be at New Breidablick in a blink."

"Your way makes me seasick."

"It's another hour and a half by car."

I motioned toward the parking lot. "What about the bloody truck outside?"

"The rental company will take care of it. Discreet, remember?"

"Is your rental company owned by the mob?"

"No, I own the rental company. The mob rents from me."

I studied his face, looking for a clue as to whether he was teasing me or not. I rolled my eyes and snorted. He grinned, knowing he had won the argument.

Baldur had established New Breidablick as a fortress of runes, wards, and inexplicable magic that shouldn't exist in the human world. It was safe and probably the only place I could relax. "You guys with your lakes and mountains and predilections for snow." I slid out of bed, intending to retrieve my jeans from where I had left them folded in the bathroom. "You're all so much alike and still so completely different. Take you and your brother, for example. What happened to make you two hate each other so much?"

I had meant the question rhetorically, not expecting an answer. Thorin and personal questions were anathema. Instead of ignoring me or changing the subject, he answered. "I don't hate Grim."

I paused at the bathroom doorway. "Could have fooled me."

"Our history is too extensive for hate."

"Well, I have enough hate for him to cover the both of us."

He gave no reply but picked up his coffee cup and scrutinized the lid as if he had discovered an alien artifact.

I let him suffer the discomfort of my prickly glare a few seconds. "What do you think happened to Grim after the fight at Rainier? You never said, and I've been too distracted to ask."

He shook his head and looked away. "I don't know what happened to him. I assume the cave-in buried him. I... I've been back to check, but there was no sign of him."

"He's a wild card again. Another unpredictable factor we don't know how to account for?"

He raised a shoulder and dropped it. "I'm sorry, Solina. I wish I could tell you something more definite."

"Do you regret it?"

His gaze cut to me, and his lips thinned. "Regret what?"

"Fighting him. He's your brother, after all."

His throat worked. A muscle flexed in his jaw. "At the time, I was willing to do whatever it took to bring him down..."

"But now that you're no longer in the heat of the moment?"

He pressed his lips together and avoided my stare. How many times had Mani and I fought? How many times had we said and done things to hurt each other in moments of extreme anger? Of course, Mani had never tried to kill anyone under my protection and care. I still hated Grim, but then again, he wasn't my own flesh and blood.

Time for a change of subject. "Hey, Thorin?"

He set down his coffee cup and looked up at me. "Yes?"

"Where are my jeans? I thought I left them on the counter after my shower."

"They were bloody. I hope you don't mind, but..." He bent, grabbed something from the floor near his bed, and tossed it at me.

I caught the bundle, recognizing it as a shopping bag from a national chain. Peeking inside, I found a pair of jeans in the same size and style as my previous pair, generic sneakers and socks, a long-sleeved shirt and a tank top—the kind that came with built-in support—and a plain gray hoodie. As if I needed further evidence of my exhaustion and strained nerves, embarrassing tears welled up in my eyes. The smallest gestures and a little kindness—those things meant the most in difficult times. A couple of deep breaths got my swirly emotions under control. I cleared my throat and squared my shoulders, but I kept my gaze pinned on the floor.

"Thank you."

"I got you a toothbrush, too. I would have gotten you some, ah, *other* things to wear, but I was afraid you would think it was presumptuous of me."

"No, this will do fine. It's perfect, actually."

"When I promised to protect you, I meant more than just keeping you alive."

I swallowed and met his eyes. "You don't have to do that."

A brief grin played across his lips. "But I *want* to."

"Why?"

"Because maybe I think you're worth it."

My knees nearly buckled, and I retreated into the bathroom. My brain short-circuited on forming a reply. "I, uh..."

"Solina lost for a smartass retort? I never thought I'd see the day."

I closed the bathroom door, slumped against the counter, and exhaled a long sigh. A being like him was never intended for a mortal woman like me, one who aged and died. *I can't ever be more than a fruit fly to him, a passing whim. If only he would stop making it so hard to believe that.*

After I dressed, I splashed water on my face and tied back my hair. I sucked in a deep breath and opened the door.

Thorin leaned against the wall across from me. He glanced up from his phone. "Ready to go?"

"Ready as I'll ever be."

In a flash, he crossed the space between us, and with a gentle touch, he drew me close, filling my senses with his scent of storms and ozone. I reached around his neck, preparing to secure myself for the ride through the ther, but then I paused and pulled back.

He frowned. "What is it?"

"Turn off your thoughts."

His scowl deepened. "What do you mean?"

"Whatever's in your head right now, I don't want to know about it. There's something there. I feel it crackling around you like static electricity."

"What are you so afraid of seeing?"

"A whole lot of things. It might not be wolves or monsters, but I have a feeling it could hurt me just as badly."

He gasped and tightened his hold. His eyes darkened. "Sunshine, I'd never—"

"Please," I implored. "Later. When things are... not like they are now. So uncertain and volatile."

Chicken shit, said my inner critic, the little devil on my shoulder.

"We may never get that chance. Is that a risk you want to take? The regrets might be worse than reality. I thought you wanted to be more like your brother. He wouldn't hesitate or deny himself."

I sucked a sharp breath through my teeth. "That's a cheap shot."

"Doesn't mean it isn't true."

"You're right." I raised my chin and tried my best to stare down my nose at him. "My brother wouldn't hesitate. He was impetuous and pleasure seeking to a fault sometimes. And that part of his nature might have been a factor in his death. I *do* want to be more like him, but not to my own detriment."

He stiffened. "And you think I'm a detriment to you?"

I inhaled a slow breath and held it. Then I shook my head and let it out. "I think... I think immortality and humanity are like oil and water. They don't mix."

"I thought you said you believed in me."

Not understanding his point, I frowned. "I do."

He shook his head and grimaced. "No, you don't. Or you wouldn't have these doubts. You should know me better by now. I'm patient, persistent, and don't easily surrender." And with that, my ears popped, and the hotel room blurred away.

Either he guarded himself as I had asked, or the distraction of space and time screaming past us disrupted our connection. He held me close—so close my ribs creaked, and although I had thrown my arms around his neck and pressed myself against him, I sensed none of his thoughts. And for a moment, I regretted it.

⊰•──◆──•⊱

We fell from the æther with a bone-crunching suddenness. I squeaked, and Thorin grunted.

"I've got you." He held me steady until the room stopped swirling and my stomach settled.

After peeling open one eye, I peeked at my surroundings: dark stone floors, timber beams crisscrossing a high ceiling, colorful, plush carpets, a massive rock fireplace, sturdy furniture that invited visitors to sit but still managed to look regal. An artwork collection from innumerable periods, regions, and styles hung in a hodgepodge on the wall behind Thorin. And everywhere books, books, and more books. The style was eclectic, just like its owner.

Welcome back to New Breidablick.

I let go of Thorin, stepped back, and let loose a jaw-popping yawn. I groaned. "Why do I think going to sleep won't be easy?"

"I'm sure you're as anxious to hear from Skyla and Baldur as I am."

"Val wants something from us, from *you*. Until I know what it is, I won't be able to really relax."

He nodded and took my hand. Still, no flashes of insight, no visions—he had respected my request to keep his mental walls raised. He towed me down the hall and stopped us in the doorway to the bedroom Baldur had assigned me. The huge bed beckoned. Its mountains of pillows and filmy curtains promised to lull me into a deep and restorative sleep.

"Try to get some rest," he said. "Not just for yourself, but for me."

I arched an eyebrow. "For you?"

"I'll put myself in harm's way for you without batting an eye, but I'd feel a lot better knowing you weren't completely defenseless. Sleep, restore your fire, recover your strength. Then when the time comes"—he winked—"you'll be ready, and I won't have to save the world all by myself."

I chuckled. "But you could, right?"

"I wouldn't even break a sweat."

"Promise you'll wake me up if something happens."

He squeezed my hand and let go. "I promise."

Thorin closed the door behind him as he left. I crossed the room, drew back the thick down comforter, shoved aside a mountain of pillows, and climbed in. But of course I couldn't fall asleep. My mind dwelled on the moral quandaries of Nate and Val. Like a movie camera, my memories focused on Nate's face—close-up shots emphasizing the proud tilt in his jaw, the clarity in his eyes. No insanity there, only conviction.

I had participated in Nate's death, and while I hadn't drawn the blade across his neck, I couldn't say I hadn't known the outcome of that meeting. As if Thorin would have let Nate live if the Valkyries hadn't finished him off. As if I hadn't wanted to kill him myself for what he had done to my brother. But the Aesir had killed Narfi—Nate's father and Val's brother. The gods had used Narfi's death as a tool to torture Loki as punishment for his hand in killing Baldur. But Narfi had been an innocent, as much of an innocent as my brother. Were Val and Nate not due as much vengeance as I?

Justice. Revenge. Two sides of a thin coin.

Everyone's offenses against each other and claims to righteousness seemed equivalent on their surfaces, equally valued, equally conflicting. Did anyone's pain truly take priority over another's? Was anyone's anguish purer? And when a situation called for a clear, quick decision, would I act, or would my empathy make me hesitate? Hesitation was deadly.

I gritted my teeth and groaned. Although my bones and muscles felt as though they had gained an extra hundred pounds, and my eyelids rasped like sandpaper every time I blinked, sleep remained elusive. Instead of drowning in useless, circular worrying, I rolled out of bed and crossed the room on tiptoes, trying not to alert anyone to my movements. *If I'm going to be awake, might as well do something useful.*

Thorin would probably lecture me about the dangers of exhaustion if he found me traipsing around the house, and I wanted to avoid explaining my actions, at least until I had something worth explaining. Investigating ancient Norse shaman practices sounded like a stupid idea when I ran it through my common-sense filter, but I had no other leads to follow.

I drew open the bedroom door and stepped into the hallway, ears tuned for voices or movement. During my previous, short visit, I had seen Nina using a tablet computer, and she kept it stashed in a desk in the living room. And who knew? Maybe Baldur had an *Encyclopedia of the Völva* on one of his ubiquitous bookshelves.

The plush rugs underfoot dampened my footsteps, and Baldur's house remained quiet as I prowled. I found Nina's tablet in a bottom desk drawer, and as it powered on and booted up, I sank onto Baldur's sofa and curled up beneath a warm chenille throw. *If Nina has a passcode on this thing, I'm screwed.* But the tablet's home screen came up without a log-in request, and I breathed a quiet sigh. Of course, a woman who openly admitted Helen Locke was her foster mother probably had nothing to hide.

This time, as I researched, the information sank in, and a little flame of hope flickered to life inside me. The term *völva* came from a Norse word meaning "wand carrier" or "carrier of a magic staff," and they tended to be women. The term *spákona* was used almost interchangeably with *völva*, but it also seemed to refer more specifically to a woman with prophetic abilities—a seer. These women had their own saga in the Prose Edda, much the same as the Valkyries. *And if the Valkyries are real, does that mean these women are? And if so, how do I go about finding them?*

A quick search of the online white pages turned up nothing. No Vlva

Union Local 113, Lake Tahoe branch. After skimming through another set of search results, I stumbled onto an online forum full of postings by academic types, arguing the minutiae of ancient religions. One thread discussed *völvur* mystical practices. With no better idea about how to make a connection, if such a connection existed, I registered for access to the message board under a fake name and left a note asking anyone familiar with ancient Norse shamanic practices to leave a note or call Thorin's cell phone.

I read my message a few more times, snorted at the ridiculousness of it, and logged out. As much as I doubted the likelihood of finding them, I hoped if the *völvur* were real, perhaps they knew about the existence of the Aesir in this modern world. The mystical forces that brought me my visions might reach out to these seers on my behalf. Perhaps I had rung a cosmic doorbell. Now I had to wait for someone to answer.

My eyes felt as though they had rolled across a hot, dry desert. My tired brain begged for a reprieve, so I shut down Nina's tablet, set it on Baldur's coffee table, and snuggled deeper into my blanket. Sleep had evaded me before, but now it bloomed like a thick, viscous fog. I turned on my side, curled into a ball, and sank into the mists.

⎯⎯◈⎯⎯

In darkness, the roar of rushing water drowned out everything. I stepped toward a distant pinprick of light. Rocky and uneven ground threatened to roll my ankles and challenged each step. I moved slowly, bracing a hand against the jagged wall beside me, and worked my way toward the light. The pinprick widened into the uneven, serrated mouth of a cave. Light diluted the darkness and revealed the rocky floors, walls, and ceiling of a massive cavern.

A river rushed beside me, pouring out from the cave mouth, cascading down a series of stone steps, and pooling into a rock basin several yards below. Silver scales flashed in the sunlight as a fish jumped and landed with a splash. The fish darted away downstream and disappeared.

I headed for the light, but before I reached the exit, someone called to me from within the cave. His hollow voice echoed against the walls. "Solina?"

Spinning on my heel, I lurched into the cave, chasing the familiar voice through that unfamiliar, dark space. A cold finger of ice stroked my spine, and a chill settled over my shoulders like a shawl made from frost. "Dad? Is that you?"

Relentless and driven, I searched that cave, following its endless twisting corridors, but I never found him. The dream faded away.

CHAPTER 7

L ATE IN THE AFTERNOON, I stumbled into Baldur's kitchen, groggy and famished. Coffee warmed in a pot on the counter, and Nina stood before the oven, back facing me. Her presence startled me, but I calmed myself. *Can't avoid her in her own house.*

New Breidablick was her own house, although she hadn't claimed it—although she couldn't remember it. A sympathy pang tugged at my heart. Nina had warned me, not long ago, that she would throw me to the wolf if it worked in her favor, but she had also been kind to me while I was lost in a fog and grieving for Val. She had defied my icy disposition those first few days, bringing me coffee and microwaved bowls of canned chicken soup. She never mentioned Helen—never made a threat. In fact, she'd rarely said a word.

Baldur's love and attention were healing her. I had to believe that.

I sniffed and recognized vanilla, brown sugar, citrus, and something else... something salty? Bitter?

"Muffins," she said, as if reading my mind. She had pulled her dark hair into a neat knot, and she wore comfortable loungewear—a draping sweater and soft knit pants. Not invalid clothes, but close. She glanced at me over her shoulder. "Thorin said you might be hungry when you woke up, which is pretty thoughtful for a guy who doesn't eat. None of them eat. Did you know that?"

So far she had mostly managed soup and simple sandwiches. Venturing into baking seemed like a big step, one for which I wasn't sure she was ready. "You bake?"

"No, but I got bored, and it was something to do."

I eased closer to the oven, still trying to discern the ingredients based on smell. Muffins were innocuous—easy to make, easy to screw up with too much mixing, subpar ingredients, old stale flour. The smallest thing made the difference between fluffy, moist perfection and dry, crumbly *blech*. I sniffed again. "Orange?" Orange and cranberry was a classic combination. *Orange spice?*

She grinned, her eyes lit up, and she nodded. "Orange zest."

"And what else? I smell another ingredient."

Her smile turned cagey. "It's a secret."

I arched an eyebrow. "Oh?"

"Maybe you'll guess it."

Mystery muffins, my favorite. I didn't roll my eyes because Nina was being nice and not too crazy, and I wanted to encourage that behavior. Call it positive reinforcement.

"You were a baker, weren't you?" she asked.

"When you talk about it in past tense like that..." I smiled sadly at her. "It's like talking about someone who died."

"You think you'll ever go back to it?"

"I'm not sure there is such a thing as going back anymore. But I'll always be a baker in my bones."

A timer dinged. Nina turned and slid on an oven mitt. She opened the door, pulled out two pans, and set them on the counter. She gestured to the tins. "Be my guest."

Gingerly, I plucked a hot muffin from the pan and juggled it until it cooled. After peeling away the paper, I broke the muffin in half, and steam seeped from the center, bringing out a strong orange aroma. Dark bits peppered the muffin's interior. *Not chocolate. I'd smell that.*

She leaned forward, watching, obviously eager for my opinion. I bit in, chewed once, and froze as the flavor combination spilled over my tongue. Orange, definitely, and an incongruent saltiness. Still holding a partially chewed bit in my mouth, I said, "Olives?"

She grinned, a purely childlike, innocent expression without a spark of malice. "Like it?"

I gulped, and the muffin slid down my throat like a rock. "Mmmm." I forced a smile. "That's... unique."

"Baldur doesn't have much in his kitchen. I had to be creative."

Creative. Riiiight. "Well, I think you nailed it." I set down the rest of my muffin and hoped Nina wouldn't notice if I didn't finish it.

She waved at the muffin tins. "Have as many as you want. I don't have much of an appetite."

"I think I'll get coffee first. I usually need caffeine as soon as I wake up."

She nodded. "Yeah, me too."

I paused as I reached for the coffee pot handle. "Did you make the coffee?"

"Nuh-uh. Baldur made it."

Relieved, I grabbed the pot and poured a cup. "Speaking of... Where are the guys?"

She shrugged. "Haven't seen them in a while."

"Did they say anything about leaving?"

"Maybe they did, and I wasn't listening. It's not like they would take me with them."

I finished doctoring my coffee and sipped. No surprises—just the way I liked it. Since Nina and I had successfully conquered small talk, I attempted a weightier subject. "I have what may seem like a strange question for you."

She leaned against the counter and stared at me, both eyebrows raised, and motioned for me to continue.

"Before Baldur found you in the hospital, he followed a rumor that said Helen was holding you in some warehouses in the desert near the border of Arizona and Nevada. We all went there looking for you, but instead, we found Skyla and several dozen cargo containers full of stone statues. But they weren't really statues. Helen used her magic to animate them and turn them into soldiers." I watched Nina's face and searched for signs of understanding or recognition, but her expression remained impassive. "Do you know what I'm talking about?"

She shook her head. "I don't know anything specific. Helen was involved in a lot of business, and she kept me out of most of it. All I know is what Baldur has told me."

I believed her. Why would Helen give all her secrets away to a foster daughter she planned to send to Baldur? She wouldn't risk Nina sympathizing with us and giving us insider information. Still, I had to ask. "Do you know if Helen has any more places like the one in Nevada? Any more warehouses or big tracts of land."

She shrugged. "I'm sure she has dozens. That woman has more money than God. But do I know of anything specifically?" Her shoulders slumped. "Helen kept me in the dark about many things and made it clear that she'd cut me off if I didn't obey her implicitly." She raised her dark eyes and met mine, staring at me unwaveringly. "She was a cold bitch, but I never went hungry or homeless thanks to her. I also never learned how to take care of myself. She enabled my helplessness because she knew it would keep me loyal and dependent. She certainly never held me in enough regard to tell me her secrets. And I didn't ask. The guarantee of a warm bed and a full stomach, as well as the threat of losing them, can be powerful motivators sometimes."

I returned her stare, studying, evaluating. Then I turned away, dismissing the subject and accepting Nina's explanation as truth. "Do you know if any of the Valkyries have called?"

She shrugged again. "No idea."

The muffins had stopped steaming, so I plucked them from the tins and set them on the counter to finish cooling, even though I planned never to eat another one. The task kept my hands busy and gave me something to do other than stare at Nina. "You've been with Baldur around the clock. Anything seem familiar yet?"

Her nose wrinkled, and she shook her head. "Not familiar. But not bad either. Baldur's..." A smile snuck onto her lips. "He's all right, I guess."

"Does that mean you'll stay with him?"

"I don't have anywhere else to go." Nina leaned a hip against the counter and folded her arms across her chest. She stared into the distance, eyes unfocused. "If I stay, I get luxury and a good-looking man who sees to my every need." She waggled her eyebrows at me. "I'd be an idiot to leave."

I peered into my coffee mug. "He loves you. A lot."

"He loves a memory."

"Maybe." I had thought something similar on occasion. But Nina and Baldur had come together countless times throughout the ages. They always found each other. They made a family. They stayed together until she died, again and again. On the one hand: romantic. On the other: tragic and disheartening. It was a wonder either managed to function on any level of sanity. If I had been subjected to that fate, I would have made a padded room my permanent residence. "But he's damned committed to that memory."

I drained the rest of my coffee, rinsed my mug, checked the dishwasher, found it mostly empty, and set my cup in the top rack. "He's a good man. He's saved my life more than once. And he's spent so much time looking for you. You should give him a chance."

Nina waved, a gesture encompassing the whole room. "I'm still here, aren't I?"

I nodded, not knowing what else to say. Baldur deserved greater advocacy from me, but relationship advice required more experience and sensitivity than I could offer. Who was I to advise Nina when I didn't know how to handle my own personal interactions? "I'm going to look around for the guys. See if they've found out anything."

She nodded, grabbed a muffin, and tossed it at me. I caught it. "Take one for the road."

Clutching the muffin like a sweaty sock, I scurried out of the kitchen. *Maybe the birds will eat it.*

I wandered around inside, calling for Thorin and Baldur, but no one answered. The massive house swallowed my voice, and I felt miniscule and insignificant. New Breidablick personified regality in its own distinct style—a combination of hunting lodge and elegant country estate, modern, yet rustic. Baldur had created a home for both a Viking god and a twenty-first-century man who enjoyed air conditioning and flat-panel TVs.

When I found neither Thorin nor Baldur inside, I extended my search to the grounds. I stepped out onto the stone patio and braced against the biting temperatures. Standing at the railing, gazing into the expansive views of the peaks and valleys composing Carson Range, I felt I could jump and fly away.

But I don't fly. I only burn.

Baldur cultivated a vineyard and kept bees. His small horse herd grazed in the pasture at the bottom of the ridge. He also raised sheep and goats. And dogs. His two Great Danes, Geri and Freki, must have caught my scent or heard the opening door. They bounded around the corner of the house and ran up to me, tongues lolling, jowls flapping, drool dripping.

As they crowded around me, pressing their huge, heavy bodies against my thighs, I rubbed their velvet ears and crooned at them. "Good boys... Who's a bunch of good boys?" They panted and pushed each other aside, both eager for my attention. "Want a muffin? Who wants a muffin?"

I raised Nina's baking atrocity and waggled it as if it were an enticing treat. Maybe to them it was. Both dogs' rear ends plopped down. They sat up, chests out, ears perked, tails whapping a steady beat against the patio's stone flooring. I broke the muffin in half and tossed it to them. Geri and Freki lunged, caught their treats, and swallowed the muffin halves in a single gulp. They both sat again and stared at me, doe eyed and pleading.

I brushed my hands together and showed them my palms, fingers splayed. "That's all I have. If you want more, you'll have to talk to Nina."

Freki, the spotted harlequin to my left, cocked his head as if considering.

Geri, the blue with the silvery coat, woofed, an imploring sound resounding from deep within his chest.

"That's all." I waved my hands.

Freki huffed, his jowls billowing. He stood and trotted away. Geri eyed me once more before he turned and followed his buddy. I stepped into the yard behind them, but they turned to adventure somewhere down the hillside. I set a path straight across the yard toward the barn.

The smell of livestock greeted me when I stepped through the door: a mixture of feed, fur, manure, tangy hay, and the sharp astringency of cedar chips. Baldur, or one of his part-time workers, kept the barn pristine and orderly. The goats and sheep bleated in a pen outside, alert to movement on the inside. They probably expected me to come feed them something.

"Baldur?" I said, although I expected no reply. "Thorin?"

The barn was obviously empty. I turned on my heel, intending to go out, but a ruffle of movement called my attention to the rafters. A shadowy shape peered at me from a beam above my head. The silhouette leapt from the rafter and spread wider. I squealed, stepped back, and reached for my fire.

A ray of sunlight illuminated the figure, revealing a familiar shape: a raven. The shadow expanded again, growing into something too big for a bird. The transforming figure sailed toward the floor, and as it touched down, the silhouette settled into its final form: a man, a rather familiar one, and he was very, very naked.

"Hugh?" I backed away again as my heart tapped a fast jig, and my pulse thudded against my ear drums. *What is this?*

He doffed an imaginary cap and bowed. "At your service."

Until that moment, I had never noticed how much Hugh's features resembled a bird's—black hair cut in a shag that looked like feathers in certain light, a beaky nose, and glittering black eyes. I trained my eyes on his face, not daring to look lower than his clavicle.

Another squawk echoed in the rafters. Something moved and caught the light: another raven. I looked at Hugh, raised a pointer finger, and gestured at the darkness. "Joe?"

Hugh cocked a smug grin. "He prefers Munin."

"Kind of shy, isn't he?"

He nodded. "He's a *very* good listener, though."

"What are you doing here?"

"Straight to the point, eh?"

"You'd rather play games?"

"Well..." He looked down at his feet and shrugged. "I *am* a raven."

"I thought you were an aggressively flirtatious outdoor guide."

He met my stare and grinned again. "I'm multidimensional. Who likes a shallow guy?"

"Baldur thought his runes could keep you out."

"He's not entirely wrong. We can cross his wards physically, but your thoughts and memories are well protected. Don't worry."

I harrumphed and folded my arms across my chest. "Then I'll ask you again. What are you doing here? Is Val with you?"

Hugh waved me off. "He's otherwise occupied."

"He let Baldur follow him in Vegas, didn't he? He wanted us to know where he was. What does he want?"

He flapped his hands again, plainly the gesture of an anxious bird. "Solina. Stop. That's not why I came."

I uncrossed my arms, balled my fists, and stepped toward him. "Okay, so why are you here?"

"To make a proposition."

Proposition? I cocked my head and arched an eyebrow.

Hugh grinned again. "Speechless? You?"

"What do you know about me?"

"You forget who I am. *What* I am."

I pursed my lips and huffed. "Yes, yes... You know *everything*."

"I am Thought. My brother is Memory."

"Pretty damn near omniscient to me."

"You're right." He nodded, and his dark hair fluttered over his eyes. "But we're not omnipotent. We can't fight or defend ourselves. We, my brother and I, have been slaves pretty much since our conception. We didn't mind it so much when Odin was our master, but Val..."

"He's not the type to inspire your fealty?"

Hugh waggled his shoulders and arched his neck. On a bird, the motion might have ruffled neck plumage and puffed out breast feathers. My question had clearly agitated him. "Ravens are opportunists, Solina. Munin and I see an opportunity in you, something heretofore unavailable to us."

"Oh?" I said, curiosity piqued.

"You were curious, weren't you, about how Val came to have control over us? How he took us from Vali Odinson?"

"Sure, I'm curious. But I don't see how it matters in the larger scheme of things."

"It wouldn't matter if I weren't about to make this offer to you. But this proposal hinges on your ability to do to Vali Lokison what he did to Vali Odinson so many years ago."

My breath caught, and my blood chilled as Hugh's meaning sank in. "You want me to kill Val?"

Slowly, he nodded. "Not just kill him. Decimate him. Wipe him from existence. Only then can you take control of us."

Hugh's words hit me like a three-punch combo—*jab, cross, hook.* I gasped. "Decimate? What are you talking about?"

He twined his fingers behind his back and turned to pace a short track. "The gods go on and on about their immortality, and in some ways, it's true. Their essence, their godhood, the thing that makes them divine... That part of them is nearly impossible to destroy. The Aesir's bodies and flesh are more durable than humans, but it *can* be annihilated." He ruffled his imaginary feathers again. "There are a few weapons that can destroy even their divinity. Their essence."

"Gungir and Mjölnir," I said.

He nodded and narrowed his beady eyes at me. "Your fire is another one of those ultimate weapons. It can destroy Val to the point where he'll never come back."

"Don't get me wrong. There's no love lost between Val and me. And I sympathize with your situation, Hugh. But what you're asking me to do... Annihilate someone, just to free you?"

"It won't free us."

I threw up my hands and groused. "Then what would be the point?"

"By killing Val, our bonds would transfer to you. With our knowledge, you could end this. Everything. You can find Skoll anytime you want. You can kill him and be free."

Everything stopped—a total freeze-frame moment. My awareness narrowed to a pinprick of light. Then a synapse fired in my brain and brought everything online again. "Why...?" I wheezed. "Why would you help me like that?"

"Because I want a favor in return." Hugh glanced at the rafters, presumably at his brother. "*We* want a favor. You break our bonds and let us go, and we'll make sure you always know where the wolf is."

"Break the bonds, how? By killing myself?"

"Other than Val, no one has to die. It won't even hurt. Well..." He pursed his lips in a coy grin. "Maybe a little."

I ran the toe of my boot through a scattering of hay on the barn floor, clearing a thin trail. "Assuming what you say is true... How could I trust you? How do I know this isn't some scheme Val came up with?"

"How would *we* trust *you*? Our power is addictive. Why do you think no one has ever let us go?"

"Why ask this of me? Why not Thorin or Baldur?"

Hugh huffed. "Do you really think either of them would give us up?

Baldur could dismantle his information network if he had us. He could find each of Nanna's reincarnations in an instant. And Thorin... The strongest god would become the most omniscient? You actually think he'd resist that temptation?"

"He's honorable." I shrugged. "To a fault."

"Honorable to you, maybe. He wants you so badly, he can hardly see straight."

I looked up from the hay-strewn floor, snorted, and rolled my eyes. "As if."

He tapped his temple. "I am Thought, remember? I've read his mind." He clicked his tongue. "You humans. So blind. Refusing to see what's right in front of your face."

"Never mind all that." I waved aside his disturbing revelations. "Tell me about Val's plan—" Before I could finish, Hugh's eyes went wide and round. He stumbled back and glanced overhead. He said nothing but crouched and leapt up, jumping unnaturally high. By the time he reached the rafters, he was a bird again. I gasped, overwhelmed by the surrealism of it.

The barn door opened, and Baldur and Thorin stepped in. The two ravens dove from their perch and streaked through the opening. Baldur and Thorin flinched but recovered in an instant. Thorin dropped into a fighting stance, Mjölnir at his side. When the ravens failed to engage, he stepped back and watched Hugin and Munin fade into the distance.

I stepped outside and blinked until my eyes adjusted to the sunlight.

"What were they doing here?" Thorin spun on his heel and stalked toward me.

"Negotiating."

He started. "What?"

"Let's go inside." I motioned to the house. "I'll tell you everything. But I need another coffee first."

"Allfather, how did they get in?" Thorin asked. "I thought your runes—"

"The runes worked," I said. "Hugh said our thoughts and memories were still safe."

Baldur grunted but said nothing to contradict me.

Thorin flanked me as I started toward the house. "What did they want with you?"

"Coffee first." Not that I needed the caffeine. Mostly, I needed a moment to process, time for the magnitude of Hugh's proposal to fully sink in.

CHAPTER 8

IN THE KITCHEN, I POURED another cup of coffee and caught Thorin eyeing the muffins, his brows drawn together, mouth turned down. He reached for one of the devious confections, but I pushed his hand away. "I wouldn't if I were you," I whispered in case Nina lingered somewhere within hearing range.

"What's in them? They smell..." He stopped and sniffed. His nose wrinkled.

"Don't ask," I whispered. "If Nina gives you one, take it and smile. Then feed it to the dogs. They liked them."

Baldur narrowed his eyes at the muffins and scowled.

I set my mug on the counter, letting it clatter like a gavel, bringing our meeting to order. "Where have the two of you been?" I cut my eyes between Baldur and Thorin. "I've been looking all over for you."

Thorin arched a brow. "All over? We were in the basement."

"In my office," Baldur said.

"I didn't know there *was* a basement." Not knowing the house's layout was my fault for spending so much time hiding in my room and in my own head the last time I was here.

Baldur shrugged. "C'mon. I'll show you. And I'll show you what we were looking at."

"You can tell us about the birds on the way," Thorin said.

As I rehashed my conversation with Hugh, the guys led me from the kitchen, down a hallway, and stopped before a door set in the wall beneath the stairs to the second floor. I snickered, imagining the door would open to reveal the living quarters of a small boy with a lightning-bolt scar on his forehead.

Instead of a cubbyhole, the doorway led to stairs, and Baldur ushered

70

us down to an open space lined in warm wood paneling. Recessed lights lent the windowless space a theatrical quality. Another massive TV screen covered most of the wall on one end of the room, and cozy, worn furniture squatted before it. This looked like a space in which Baldur probably spent most of his time, when he wasn't outdoors with his animals.

In the room's rear, several bookcases towered over a massive mahogany desk. A slim computer screen sat to one side, its modern sleekness contrasting with the considerable weight and age of the furniture supporting it.

Baldur motioned to the seating in front of the TV. I sank onto the loveseat, and Thorin sat beside me. Warmth radiated from him along with his scent of rain and storms. Hugh's words flashed through my mind again, his insistence about Thorin's feelings for me. I pushed the thought away and focused on the immediate issue.

"I can't do it, you know." I leaned forward, bracing my elbows on my knees, and buried my face in my hands. "I can't just march up to Val and light him up like kindling."

Beside me, Thorin shifted his weight. He grasped my wrists and tugged my hands away from my face. I inhaled, let out the breath, and brought my eyes up to meet his. "No one's asking you to, no one other than those birds. Besides the fact that it's too great a risk, you aren't a killer. Not like this."

My shoulders slumped, and his absolution washed over me. Until he said it, I'd half feared he would ask me to do what the birds wanted. I would have either hated him for it, or I would have considered doing it and hated myself.

"It would solve a lot of our problems." I played the devil's advocate.

"Or make them worse," Baldur said. "Val is not your enemy, Solina. He doesn't hate you or seek any kind of revenge against you. But doing this would change that, and you don't need any more enemies."

"You know the secret now," I said. "With Mjölnir, you could kill Val and take the birds. They were afraid of that, you know. That's why they asked me to do it. Hugh said if either of you had them, it would be too much temptation. You wouldn't let them go."

Thorin blew out. "He's probably right. I can't say the idea isn't appealing."

"But you're not going to take the bait?"

"Not today." He captured my gaze again. "But I can't say if the opportunity presents itself, I won't take advantage. If having those birds could end this, save us all..." He took my hand and squeezed my fingers. "If it would save *you*, I'd kill Val and take control of those birds without hesitation. Skoll could never hide from us again."

Biting my lip, I nodded and turned to Baldur. "And you, Allfather? Would you do anything to have those birds?"

He shook his head. "I don't have any of the weapons it would take."

"You couldn't kill Val with your runes?"

His face flushed, and he looked away. "Using them that way... It's a perversion."

"The Valkyries use runes to get what they want. They've killed with them."

"Their runes were gifted from Odin. They chose to use them as they see fit. I use mine as I see fit."

"One more question, then I'll leave you alone."

Baldur raised his chin then dropped it once in a quick nod.

"Why didn't you use the runes to get away from Helen, when you were her captive?"

His jaw worked as he gritted his teeth. "I *did* use the runes to escape Hela. But the sacrifice I had to make to gain their power took a lot more than Odin's nine days."

A sacrifice made to gain wisdom—it was what Hugin and Munin had asked of me. Make Val the sacrifice. Gain near omniscience at the cost of my self-respect and virtue. "I'm no Allfather. I'm a woman with a goddess bottled up inside. I'm not even the genie, just the lantern. Even if I could do what the ravens asked me, how could I handle that kind of knowledge and power? I don't think I could."

Thorin shifted closer. His knee pressed into mine. "You don't give yourself enough credit. But I think your reluctance is wise for now. Forget the birds. Forget Val. Stay focused on the goal."

"Skoll," I said.

Thorin nodded. "Yes."

"Where the hell is he?"

He shrugged. "Your guess is as good as mine."

I shifted my attention to Baldur. "What happened when you went to confront Val with the Valkyries? And where is Skyla?"

"I was wondering when you were going to ask," Baldur said.

I gave him a half smile. "Sorry. I was a little distracted."

He waved aside my apology. "The house, the one I followed the wolf to, was deserted. We checked it out. The Valkyries went back to the hotel to await word from the women trying to hack Helen's GPS network."

"Why would Val lead you to a deserted house?"

"Because he wanted us to find this." Thorin leaned back and fumbled for his pocket. He withdrew his fist, held it over the coffee table, and unclenched his fingers. Something metallic clinked against the tabletop.

I leaned forward to get a better look. *A ring?*

"May I?" No one stopped me as I retrieved the bit of rusty metal and examined it. Worn and brittle, it appeared old, maybe ancient. The large band, larger than the circumference of my thumb, bore a roughly hewn shape resembling... "A bear? I don't get it. What does this mean?"

Thorin cleared his throat. "When my father died, his essence was split between his two offspring. I got his strength. Modi got his anger, his battle rage, I guess you could say." He paused long enough that I wondered if he would say more. "Have you ever heard the term 'berserk'?"

"Sure. I mean, in a general way, to imply someone has gone crazy."

He nodded. "It was also a term for a certain kind of fighter, well known among the Vikings. A berserker fought in a trance-like fury. They were like beasts or monsters, and they fought until they were killed or until everyone else was dead. The word for berserk comes from their habit of wearing a bear pelt during fighting. It literally means 'bear shirt.'"

"I know you're going somewhere with this," I said dryly, "but the anticipation is killing me." Val had mentioned something about berserkers in relation to Thorin's brother when we had been preparing to confront him at Mineral Lake. Grim's personal history had mattered less to me at that time than his potential threat to my future welfare, so Val's brief history lesson had failed to make the transition into my long-term memory.

Thorin sniffed. "My brother was the Viking berserkers' god. He was the one they beseeched before going into battle. Hundreds of years ago, they gave Grim this ring, a token of their praise and admiration. Grim never goes without it."

A desert rolled across my mouth. I swallowed. "This... this is Grim's ring?" Thorin's head bobbed. "And the fact Val has it means what? He has your brother?"

"Or that he's dead," he said in almost a whisper. His eyes turned up to mine, dark and bottomless. "Have you... *seen* anything, Solina? Bears? Strange wolves? Anything?"

"I haven't had many coherent dreams lately. They've been a swirl of things. Impressions. Images." I stood and ambled to the pool table squatting in the center of the room beneath an elegant stained-glass light fixture. As I made my way around the table, gathering balls from the netted pockets, I recounted my latest dream about the cave, the roaring river, the waterfall, and jumping fish.

And someone calling for me. Someone who sounded very much like my father.

The only reason I hadn't gone running home to check on them already was because Baldur's men had verified everything was fine and dandy in North Carolina. I operated under the assumption that staying far away from them was the best thing I could do to keep my parents safe.

"There haven't been any bears," I said. "Nothing I can relate to Grim."

Thorin's skeptical expression turned resigned. He scraped a hand through his hair and tucked the long strands behind his ear. He stood and approached the pool table where I had finished racking the balls. "Your dreams are never just coincidences."

"Does it mean anything to you? The fish and the cave. My father's voice?"

He rearranged several balls in the triangle configuration, changing out stripes for solids. The eight ball went in the center; I knew that much. Not like I had played a lot. Not like I had the time.

"It could," he said. "But I can't see what point Val's trying to make with it. Or what could happen to lead us there again."

"The cave is real?" I lifted the rack from the table and replaced it in its holder. I selected a cue stick from the rack on the wall and positioned the white ball on the table.

Thorin looked at Baldur. Baldur blinked like a tired old owl. "Loki," Baldur said.

Thorin nodded. He grabbed a cue stick and chalked the tip. I held out my hand, and he slapped the chalk in my palm. I readied my stick, bent over the table, and lined up my opening shot. My brother had been a pool-playing phenomenon. Anything he set his mind to, he could do and do well. In college, he had funded his social life by hustling in the local bar circuit. He taught me a few things, but that was a long time ago, and I was sorely out of practice. *Here goes nothing.*

I drew in a breath, exhaled, and made the opening break without skidding my stick across the felt or slipping on the cue ball. The yellow-striped nine ricocheted off the end of the table, rolled back, and sank in the corner pocket to my right. Good beginning.

"Loki. The salmon. I should have put it together." But the legends were all still rather new, and I tended to forget the details until something jogged my memory.

After killing Baldur, Loki had tried escaping retribution by hiding out as a salmon in a stream. But the gods had found him, fished him out with a net, and carried him to a cave where they bound and tortured him. The rest was history. Val's history. Val was turned into a wolf and forced to kill his brother, Narfi, whose entrails the gods had used to bind Loki.

I bent and lined up another shot, aiming to sink the red-striped eleven into the far left corner. The shot carried through, and the ball fell in. Leaning heavily on my luck, I repeated that same performance twice more.

Thorin whistled low between his teeth. "All right, Fast Eddie."

"You can be Fast Eddie," I said. "I'll be Vincent because I'm younger and cuter."

My next shot flopped, banking too hard off the rail. The violet twelve ping-ponged down the table, and I nearly lost the cue ball in a side pocket. I scowled. "You jinxed me."

Grinning, he leaned over, steadied his stick, and made quick work of clearing the table until only the shiny black eight ball and two of my stripes remained. He straightened, crossed his arms over his chest, and winked at me.

"So." I rolled my eyes. "I'm dreaming about Loki's cave, and Val is leaving clues about your brother. Do we think the two are related?"

Thorin said nothing until after he'd made his shot. The eight ball strolled the length of the table before teetering into a corner pocket. He cocked his head and studied my face before answering. "I think it's too soon to know. But I don't like that you're dreaming about your father. That makes things more... *complicated*."

Cold shivers trembled down my spine. "What would Val want with them? I understand Helen using them as leverage to get to me, but Val? His schemes have never involved me, except as a means of getting to you. How would using my parents get to you?"

He set down his pool cue, took my hand, and drew me close. An undercurrent of energy ran beneath the surface of his touch, but it remained vague, never formulating into an image or impression. Still, it felt like... *longing*? Unbidden, Hugh's words about Thorin's feelings popped into my mind again.

"If it hurts you, Solina, it hurts me."

I met his warm brown stare. "Do you know where the cave is? I mean, wasn't that eons ago? And it's here, on earth. Not in Asgard?"

He shook his head. "Midgard was less familiar to us. Loki thought he could lose us here. He underestimated Odin. He underestimated the Ravens."

"Could you find it again? The cave?"

"Perhaps. If there's enough incentive."

I frowned and pulled my hand free. "I'm sure, given enough time, Val will present us with plenty of incentive." Would he use my father as bait to lure me, and thereby Thorin, into his scheme?

"I'm sure, too." He motioned to the pool table. "Now, are we going to bet or what?"

"I always lose when I bet against you. I learned my lesson after that game of rummy in the desert."

He grinned. "Smart woman."

"Just out of curiosity, what would the stakes be?"

"Anything you want." His smile widened. Totally Cheshire Cat. "And anything you're willing to give. *Give* being the operative word."

My attention flickered to the empty space behind Thorin. Baldur had disappeared, silent as a ghost. My heart fluttered, and my breath turned to insubstantial mist. I coughed, clearing my throat. "What happened to the thunder god who demanded and bullied to get his way?"

He scrubbed a hand across his jaw and lowered his gaze. "It's still my nature to be that way, Sunshine. Perhaps I realized you deserve better."

"I thought you didn't play games with naïve little blondes."

"It's no game to me."

"Yes, it is. It's called eight ball. And you're going to lose."

He raised his chin and issued a smug smile. "I'm willing to risk it. No tricks. We play clean and honest."

"I'll run the table." Full of false bravado, I smirked at him and chalked my cue stick, giving my shaking hands something to do. "There'll be nothing left for you. Wait and see."

But I never made the first shot. Baldur jogged down the basement steps, loud and heavy footed, and interrupted. "I've got news."

Thorin huffed, and his nostrils flared. The muscles around his eyes tensed. His reply was for Baldur, but he kept his attention focused on me. "What is it?"

"The Valkyries hacked Helen's network. They found something. Might be one of Helen's trucks."

I blinked and shook myself as if the gesture might scatter the tension between Thorin and me. "Time to hit the road again?"

"The game will still be here when we get back," Thorin said, and I suspected he meant more than just a round of eight ball.

I looked away, unable to bear his gaze any longer.

"You coming with us?" he asked Baldur.

The Allfather shook his head and offered a sheepish grin. "But call me if there's an emergency."

"Where are the Valkyries now?" I asked.

"GPS pinged something at the Nevada and Oregon border, near a small town called Winnemucca. The Valkyries are nearly there."

Thorin rounded the edge of the table, stepped close, and held out his hand. When I took it, he drew my arm around his neck, and his hands slid to my hips.

"Couldn't talk you into taking the jet, could I?" I asked.

He frowned. "Does it really bother you that much?"

"Maybe I should make Dramamine a permanent part of my daily regimen."

He tightened his grip. "You'll get used to it."

My ears popped.

My vision swirled.

The world dropped from beneath me.

CHAPTER 9

THORIN AND I REGROUPED WITH the Valkyries in the rear parking lot of an ancient motel set on the side of a two-lane highway on the outskirts of Winnemucca, Nevada. I dropped to a knee, closed my eyes, and urged my stomach to settle. When I belched, the worst of my nausea drained away. "'You'll get used to it,' he says."

A footstep fell beside me, and a warm hand settled on my back. "You gonna be all right, girlfriend?"

"Skyla." I rose to my feet and rubbed my wrist across my mouth, wishing for a bottle of water. "I'd hug you, but I don't want to puke on you."

"That bad, huh?"

"I don't do the spinny rides. The Gravitron, the Scrambler, the Himalaya, they all make me sick."

She chuckled. "Are you comparing Thorin to a cheap carnival ride?"

"If the shoe fits..." I scowled at the subject of my analogy, but he was focused on the single eighteen wheeler parked at the rear of the motel: a huge black Kenworth tractor attached to a plain white shipping container, same as the ones from Helen's warehouse. "Have you checked it out yet?"

"No. We just got here."

I glanced around at the Valkyries—fifteen women of varying ages and ethnicities, most wearing what amounted to tactical gear: heavy-duty boots and pants that had been most likely purchased from law enforcement or army surplus stores. For accessories, they wore utilitarian gun holsters, sword and knife sheaths, belts loaded with extra ammo, even a couple of pairs of handcuffs here and there. Everyone kept their hair cut short or tucked it up in tight braids or under caps.

I eyed my cheap sneakers, jeans, and hoodie sweatshirt and frowned. Upgrading my wardrobe would have wasted time and money. Everything I wore burned away whenever it came to a fight. *What do they make Johnny Storm's uniforms out of, anyway?*

"Seems a little strange for it to be sitting here, all on its own, at a roadside motel," I said. A mostly abandoned motel at that. Judging by the parking spaces in front of the rooms, the truck and its driver were the sole occupants of Finney's Roadside Retreat. No surprise. Sleeping in the backseat of a car appealed to me more than this broken-down motel with its peeling pink paint and bleached-out signs. Even the fading sunlight failed to mask the motel's worn and weary appearance.

Skyla nodded. "This was the only one with an active GPS signal. The other trucks are still dark. We have no idea where they are or where they went."

"I know I think everything is a trap. And it pretty much has turned out to be, so why should things be different this time? Maybe Helen wanted us to find this truck."

She shrugged. "And what have you done each time you faced this situation?"

I grimaced. "I stepped in the trap."

"Your survival record is pretty great, so far."

"No one has a perfect score forever."

"So what are you going to do?"

I exhaled and stepped forward, heading for the rear of the truck. "What I always do. Take the bait."

Our whole cadre—fifteen Valkyries, Thorin, and me—grouped around the back of the truck and eyed the doors as if they might open on their own.

"Has anyone ever seen *Maximum Overdrive*?" I asked.

Standing beside me, Naomi turned and slapped my shoulder. "Don't go there. This is creeping me out enough already."

"Siobhan. Keisha." Embla pointed. "Start knocking on doors. We need to talk to the driver."

I sucked in a breath, steeled my nerves, and hopped onto the bumper without a second thought. *I always take the bait.* Before I could fully grasp the handle, the door blew open, knocking me from my perch. I yelled as I fell back, and Thorin caught me. He set me down and rose again in one fluid motion, Mjölnir already in his hand, ready to go.

Stone men streamed from the cargo hold, and Thorin stepped up to the plate, a regular Casey Jones. Heads rocketed into the air like pop-fly baseballs. Torsos exploded. The Valkyries streamed in around me, weapons drawn, blades flashing, booted feet kicking and striking.

Skyla scooted up beside me. "This is the worst Easter egg hunt ever."

"I was thinking it was more like the worst piñata."

"Same idea, though." She drew a big black gun from a holster under her armpit and fired into the head of a grabbing monster. His skull exploded, but he kept reaching for us. I put a foot to his abdomen and shoved. He stumbled, lost his balance, and fell onto his back, where he lay scrabbling like an overturned turtle.

"Why were we scared of these things again?" she asked. "They're ridiculously stupid. Like zombies, but without the bite, and none of those pesky cravings for brains."

"You know how you lose in a zombie movie?" I asked. Another golem stumbled close. Skyla blew him away in two shots, point blank. "Numbers. When there's too many for one person to overcome, it doesn't matter if they're slow and stupid. And these guys aren't slow."

Thorin pressed in beside me and made rubble of another stone man. "Hanging in there, Sunshine?"

From the corner of my eye, I spotted a stony arm reaching for me. I ducked under it, shoved my shoulder into the golem's pelvis, and knocked him off center. He teetered, and I swiped his leg out from under him. When he crashed to the ground, Thorin casually dropped Mjölnir to the golem's chest, shattering him to bits.

I rolled my eyes. "Showoff."

Piles of rubble lay around us, and the Valkyries made short work of destroying the few remaining stone men. Naomi shoved her short sword into the juncture of a golem's neck and shoulder, in a place like soft mortar between bricks. Careful to stay at his side, beyond the stone man's reach, Naomi separated head from shoulder, using her sword like a pry bar. She grunted and heaved, and his head came loose with a gritty crunch. She shoved him to the ground, and Skyla fired a round into his chest, blowing a crater into his ribcage. If he had a ribcage.

"Okay, Dirty Harry," I said.

Skyla slipped the pistol into its holster. "This isn't a Dirty Harry gun. It's a Desert Eagle. Point five-oh."

Naomi grinned. "Go on, girl. I like it when you talk dirty to me."

Voices rose in the distance, loud protests and shouts. We spun around, searching for the source. Siobhan and Keisha approached, dragging a reluctant man between them. A bruise had already started forming around his eye. Blood dribbled from his nose.

"Did we miss all the fun?" Siobhan eyed the rubble.

Keisha shoved her captive forward. He stumbled, caught himself, and stopped, chin raised in a defiant posture. "He's the only one here," she said.

Embla stepped to the front of the crowd and appraised the truck driver. Her gaze scraped from his dingy sneakers up to his balding head and back down again. She slipped her knife from a sheath at her waist. "Open his shirt."

As Siobhan reached for the man, flashbacks of Nate's horrible interrogation assaulted me. I pushed my way forward and raised my voice. "Wait. Maybe you could just ask him."

Embla peered down her nose at me. "My way is more efficient."

"Your way is torture. It's a last-ditch effort, not the opening bid." I turned to the driver and met his eyes. Well, his one good eye, anyway. The other had mostly swollen shut. "What's your name?"

The driver's good eye blinked, and his eyebrow quivered on his wrinkly forehead. "What's it matter to you?"

"Better than 'hey fella,' right?"

He shrugged. "Kowalski. Andy Kowalski."

I winked at Skyla. *See? Progress already.* "Mr. Kowalski, where are the other drivers?"

He sniffed and jerked his chin toward the highway. "Ain't seen them in days. We stopped for fuel outside of Portland, and curiosity got the best of me. Got one look at the cargo and lit out like my ass was on fire."

I snorted. "If you were so afraid, what are you still doing here with your truck and a full load?"

Kowalski scratched his chin. "Well, I got to thinking… Someone paid me a ton of money to show up with my truck at a warehouse out in East Jesus, Arizona, in the middle of the night. They put armed guards on all us drivers and wouldn't let us get out of our rigs. They just loaded us up, gave us a preprogrammed navi-system, and told us to hit the road. I figured whatever was worth all that money and all that secrecy might be worth even more to the right buyer."

"Mr. Kowalski…" Embla shook her head the same way one shakes her head at a bad car accident in which it was obvious there were no survivors. "You have no idea the trouble you're facing. As soon as your employer discovers what you've done—"

Kowalski cleared his throat in a long, wracking cough and spit a wad of phlegm at Embla's feet. Dismissing her altogether, he raised his watery blue eye up to meet my gaze. My hackles rose, hairs standing on the nape of my neck. My reluctance for the use of Embla's knife was quickly waning.

"What are them things, anyway?" He glanced around at the piles of rubble strewn about the motel parking lot. "I thought they might be some kind of antique statues or something, but the way they moved… Was they robots?"

I grimaced at him. "You can believe me when I say you don't really want to know."

He hacked and cleared his throat again but refrained from spitting. "The way I see it, you all destroyed the merchandise. If anyone's got to answer for that, it's you."

I laughed, a bitter, wry sound. "Keep telling yourself that, and maybe you'll be able to sleep tonight. But if I were you, I'd start running, and I'd never stop."

Thorin stepped up to my side and loomed over our witness. "Where were you headed with that truck?"

Kowalski leaned back, trying to take in Thorin's remarkable stature. His lips thinned. His good eye narrowed. "Don't know for sure."

Thorin stepped closer, jaw clenched, the threat of physical harm obvious. Kowalski flapped a hand at him. "You ain't got to get all hostile like that. I'm telling you the truth. We were headed north. That's all I know. Check the navi on my truck, and you'll see."

Embla motioned to the Valkyries. "Feryal, go take a look at his navigation system. Siobhan, take Mr. Kowalski to his room, and don't let him leave."

A dark-skinned woman wearing an olive-colored hijab separated from the group and headed toward the truck's cab. Siobhan winked at Kowalski and tugged his arm. "Let's go, sugar."

Skyla, Thorin, and I huddled with the rest of the group, waiting for Feryal's findings. "Port of Portland," she announced from her seat inside the truck cab a few moments later.

Thorin shifted and made a sound in his throat. Irritation? Acknowledgement?

"What is it?" I asked.

"If she's right, those containers could be miles from here by now. They could be anywhere."

"All we can do is follow the trail. And hope for another lead."

"How far is Portland from here?" Skyla raised her voice for Feryal's benefit.

"Seven hours," Feryal said from her seat in the truck cab. "Give or take."

"If we leave now, we'll be there by sunup," Embla said.

Skyla groaned beside me. "I'm getting sores on my ass from all the riding."

I bumped my elbow against her ribs, a playful shove. "You got some fighting action." I waved at the piles of stone. "A little exercise to brighten your day."

"What, this?" She scowled. "This is nothing. I didn't even break a sweat."

"Just think, though, there's hundreds more out there somewhere, waiting for you. The sooner you find 'em, the sooner you break 'em."

"You gonna ride with us? We've got an extra seat in my truck." Skyla motioned to the row of black SUVs parked at the shoulder along the front of Finney's Roadside Retreat. Riding in the SUV was tempting compared to the seasick sensations of travelling with Thorin. The comfort of female camaraderie also appealed to me, especially after I had been away from it for so long.

As if reading my thoughts, Thorin stepped closer to my side. I heard his teeth grinding. But if he could read my thoughts, I could read his too, and he was right. We couldn't afford to waste the time.

"No." I exhaled the word on a sigh. "Chances are, if Helen shipped those containers out, they're probably long gone. But either way, we have to go ahead while there's a chance the trail's still warm."

Skyla nodded and watched as the Valkyries dispersed, heading for their convoy. "We'll meet up again tomorrow, first thing. Pay attention, Blondie. I want a full report." She raised her eyes to Thorin. "Keep her safe, Boss Man."

He merely arched an eyebrow in reply.

She threw her hand to her brow in a lazy salute. Then she turned on her heel and marched toward her SUV.

Thorin slipped a hand around my shoulder, preparing to draw me in and make the jump to Portland, but I stepped out of his grasp. "Wait. Don't you find it a little odd that Embla was so easily satisfied with Kowalski's answer?" I snapped my fingers. "Just like that, she's ready to roll out to Portland."

He tilted his head like a curious dog. "But, Sunshine, navi-systems don't lie." His tone suggested he was playing the devil's advocate rather than arguing.

I turned and started toward Kowalski's room. "You're right. They say exactly what their programmer tells them to say."

"And the programmer is quite capable of lying." Thorin's heavy footsteps echoed off the pavement behind me. In the dying light, the parking lot seemed extra quiet, extra empty. "You think Helen planted Kowalski on purpose? Had him feed us a bogus lead?"

"I think we need to find out for sure, either way."

"How are you going to make him talk? You don't have the Valkyries' runes or the authority to use them if you did."

I stopped, looked over my shoulder at him, and smiled. "Then we'll have to play good cop, bad cop. Guess which one you get to be."

CHAPTER 10

AFTER WE PUT ANDY KOWALSKI to the test—Mjölnir in the fist of a thunder god could be mighty persuasive—he had admitted someone—a nameless, nondescript man—had paid him to exit the truck convoy and find an out-of-the-way place to hang out. The truck driver insisted he knew nothing more than that, and I was inclined to believe him. Helen had planted Kowalski there for us to find—a big, fat red herring. Why Embla and the Valkyries hadn't pressed Kowalski further posed an even more problematic question. Why were they so eager to swallow Helen's hook?

Satisfied with the results of our interrogation, Thorin and I set our sights on Portland. He whipped us away on another whirlwind journey, and we set down in Port of Portland's dark parking lot adjacent to the commercial shipping terminals at the edge of the Columbia River. A frigid breeze blew in off the water, gathering my hair and twirling it around my face, poking chilly tendrils down the neck of my hoodie. The wind caught and dispersed diesel fumes and the faintly fishy, mildew, sour-milk odor of the river water that had collected in the crevices around the docks.

Thorin's huge frame shielded me from the worst of the breeze, and despite the way the air currents tossed his own hair about, he seemed oblivious to the weather.

"Is imperviousness to the elements another one of your superpowers?"

"I'm aware of the cold." A small smile curled at the corner of his mouth. "It simply doesn't bother me."

I turned my attention to the shipping terminal and studied the scene. "I don't see any golems hanging around waiting for someone to give them a lift."

He stared across the parking lot. "This once, I hoped we might get a break, that it might be that easy."

"It's a shame Kowalski was so useless. I can't help feeling this is going to be a huge waste of time. We're going to find out Helen's already shipped these things to Russia or something. Wait and see."

The *Savannah*, the only ship in port, loomed before us, a hulking feat of maritime engineering, and it more closely resembled a cityscape than an ocean vessel. Stacks of shipping containers rose from the deck like multicolored high-rise buildings, and the control tower housing the captain and crew loomed above it all like some nautical Empire State Building.

The *Savannah* floated next to a massive crane, an iron assemblage of beams and posts arranged in a way that formed a skeletal camel or one of those Imperial AT-AT walkers from *Star Wars*. An eighteen wheeler pulled up beneath the crane's belly. The machine extended a long, ropy tongue and latched onto the truck's cargo, a white metal container the same size and shape as the hundreds of others already loaded aboard the *Savannah*. The tongue retracted, hoisting the container up and forward along its belly and neck. When the container reached the end of its track, the crane's cable extended again and deposited the box on the ship's deck like a dog setting a newspaper at its owner's feet.

"Do you think any of those containers belong to Helen?" I asked, although I doubted it.

"We'd be very, very lucky if they are."

"What are we waiting for?"

The orange glow of the parking lot lights illuminated Thorin as he winked. "A sign from God."

I snorted and rolled my eyes as he cinched his arms around me. My ears popped, and in a blink, we had moved from the Port of Portland parking lot into the shadows at the base of the tower housing the *Savannah's* control center. Crew members in hard hats bustled about the ship's deck, but the darkness kept us camouflaged.

"There must be thousands of those containers on this ship," I whispered. "Where do we start?"

Thorin's body heat radiated beside me, but the shadows concealed his expression and gestures. "Start with the closest one." He stepped into the spotlights affixed to the ship's towering bridge and motioned for me to follow. "Stay close. I don't want to have to find you if we need to make an emergency exit."

A rust-red container formed the foundation of the nearest stack. Thorin tugged the door latch, but the mechanism resisted. He motioned to a panel attached over the seam between the container's two doors. "Locked. But not for long."

He reached beneath the panel, and after a brief metallic crunch that sounded like the wadding of industrial-strength aluminum foil, the remnants of the padlock crumbled to the floor at our feet. "What grand prize is waiting for us behind door number one?" He tugged the latch again.

The door swung open on squeaky hinges, and I gritted my teeth. The squeal sounded like the trumpeting of alarms, but the rumble of the crane and the ship's engines had probably drowned out the worst of it. When none of the ship's workers came to investigate, I let out my pent-up breath.

"Tell us what they've won, Bob." I waved, mimicking a game show host. Stepping forward, I raised my hand, allowing a soft glow to fill my palm and illuminate the scene. "A lifetime supply of..." I stooped and read the words stamped on the sides of the barrels packed inside the crate. "Soda ash. Hooray."

Thorin grunted and shoved the door into place. "You ready for the next one?"

I eyed the countless stacks of containers. Hopelessness accumulated inside me like hourglass sand, abrasive and suffocating. "This could take all night."

"It could, but we'll do this in fast-forward mode and have it done before we know it." He threw his arms around me. My ears popped, and we teleported to the ship's far end, to an area fully stocked, loaded, and free from potential observation. We worked like a machine, utilizing my light and his strength and unnatural ability to cut through space. By the time the crane had shut down and the last box had settled into place, we had searched most of the ship, leaving a trail of crushed padlocks in our wake.

I'd hate to be the one who has to explain that in the morning.

Serving as Thorin's personal flashlight had expended a good portion of my energy. I sagged on my feet but kept my complaints to myself. A horn blared out from the bridge, and the steady vibration beneath our feet intensified, as if the engines had woken from hibernation and their subtle snoring turned to gruff, hungry roars.

"Time to surrender," Thorin said.

My shoulders slumped. "It's what I expected all along. Why am I so disappointed?"

He hung his head. "I'm disappointed, too, Sunshine, but not defeated. Not yet. Let's get a room, get you something to eat and some sleep, and then we'll talk to Baldur. Maybe he can ramp up his information network again. Not that it isn't ramped up already. In the morning, we'll send someone back here to ask questions. If we can get our hands on the shipping records, we can see if there's anything that looks like it's had Helen's touch on it."

"It would be handy to have those ravens in our pockets right now." *Or one of those* völva *seers.* I hadn't had time to check the message board where I'd posted my vague solicitation, and if he'd checked the voicemail at his store, Thorin hadn't indicated anyone had left a message for me. In fact, if someone *had* left me a message, he would have probably subjected me to an intense session of *Who? What? When? Where? and Why?* Not that I meant to keep it from him, but I preferred to give him the news when I had something useful to offer—something other than more speculation.

His jaw muscle worked as he stared into the darkness over my shoulder. "The cost of having those birds might break you, and that's not something I'm willing to risk."

"Could you kill Val without it bothering your conscience? Not that I'm asking you to."

His gaze hardened, his expression settling into a cool mask. "Before our last fight, before Val revealed the truth of his identity, before he took my brother and threatened the security of my world, I would have said no, but now... I've done worse and lived with the guilt. I could kill him, Solina, but I couldn't let the ravens go afterward. They know me too well, and I'm sure they'd never let me get close enough to Val to try."

"Which leaves it up to me."

Thorin looked at me. "You're honestly considering it?"

My gaze fell, and I turned away from him. "I-I don't know. I'm not a murderer, and that's what this feels like. I'm contemplating murder." The wind kicked up again, and the harsh cold on my cheeks felt like a slap of judgment. I shook my head and wrapped my arms around myself, bracing against the frigid air. "He would have to provoke me at least. He would have to threaten my life. Otherwise..." A soft whimper escaped my throat before I could choke it back.

"Enough." He stepped closer and cupped my face in his hands, flooding my cheeks with warmth and ridding them of the wind's bitter sting. His dark eyes peered into mine and warmed me from within. "We're in the worst conditions to be having this discussion. The world won't end tonight. I won't let it. Let's talk about this somewhere else. Some*time* else."

I nodded and let myself sink against him, soaking up his warmth. "You're right. Let's get out of here."

⋖━◆━⋗

Half an hour later, I stood in another indistinct and posh bedroom, stationed before a panoramic window at the River's Edge Hotel. *At least it isn't Finney's Roadside Retreat.* My life had become a series of temporary living situations, and it chafed. I missed my old bedroom, its personalized clutter and familiarity. I craved the comfort of dependable, mundane routine.

Room service had come and gone after delivering a sandwich and a pile of fries. I ate on autopilot, gobbling turkey on rye, oil and vinegar dribbling down my fingers while I stared into the inky waters of the Columbia River, five stories below. The dark water served as a backdrop, a blank movie screen onto which I projected my thoughts. The images played on repeat like a .gif file. Over and over, I saw Hugh in Baldur's barn as he told me how this whole nightmare could end, if only I'd obliterate Val. *There's got to be another way.*

Behind me, in the sitting room, Thorin debriefed Baldur on the evening's events. "There's got to be some way we can trigger more specific visions from her," Thorin said as if echoing my thoughts. His words sank through the static haze in my brain and woke me from my trance.

I blinked and turned away from the window, clutching my half-eaten sandwich. "I don't see any World Trees standing around, waiting for me to hang myself from their branches. And I'll be keeping my head connected to my shoulders, thank you very much. Don't think I haven't read about that Mimir guy. If you carry *my* severed head around with you, it won't be words of wisdom I whisper in your ear."

Thorin chuckled. "I like your head best right where it is, Sunshine. No, I was mostly thinking out loud."

"The Greek oracles used hallucinogens sometimes, didn't they? Or was that just in a movie?" I drank alcohol only on rare occasions, so the thought of heavy-duty drugs turned my stomach. But not as much as killing Val, so... *Psychedelic mushrooms, anyone?*

I crossed the room and joined the men in the suite's seating area. I tossed the remnants of my sandwich in a nearby trashcan before taking a seat in one of the empty club chairs. Thorin sat parallel to me in the other chair, and like defense and prosecution before the judge in the courtroom, we faced Baldur, who managed to look lordly, even as he sprawled across the sofa.

"I think acid-induced delusions don't count as reliable," Baldur said.

"It's about thinning the walls between realms so the spirit can travel or some such, isn't it? If you guys can exist and do the things you do, why couldn't I have an out-of-body experience?"

Thorin grunted. "Are we really having a discussion about taking drugs?"

"We need something concrete," Baldur said. "And right now, that's my network. I've already put them on the lookout, searching for anything out of place, listening to the internet and social chatter. If Helen slips up, makes one little mistake, we'll find her."

"And what if she doesn't?" I took a deep breath, steeling myself with the courage to broach a sensitive subject, something Thorin certainly wouldn't like. "I think the idea of refining my visions has merit. We've proved I can reach into people's thoughts with more purpose and intention than I'd thought was possible. Why not put some purpose and intention into my visions?"

Thorin's face reddened, and his jaw clenched. "The last time we experimented with your gifts, it nearly killed you."

"Aw, pshaw." My lips spluttered. I waved my hand in a dismissive gesture. "Don't be so dramatic."

He had stated things accurately, though, and the recollection of that experience, of reaching into his mind and drowning in the immensity of his memories, still chilled me. But giving in to fear never got me anywhere. Putting on a false front of bravado might not fool Thorin, but it might fool my own inner doubts. "It's like learning to ride a bike. I have to crash a few times before I get the hang of it."

He leaned toward me and lowered his voice. "It is *not* like riding a bike. It was not a scuffed knee or a sprained wrist. You almost *died*."

I replied through gritted teeth. "And you said you wouldn't stop me from learning to use my abilities. All of them. You said you'd be there, be my lifeguard, pull me out of the deep if I needed it. You're taking that back now?"

His nostrils flared, and he exhaled like an angry bull. "I ought to." He scrubbed a hand across his face and leaned back in his chair, eyes closed. "But I gave you my word. If you want to pursue this..."

"I'm scared," I admitted, letting Thorin hear the uncertainty in my voice and trusting him not to use my vulnerability against me. "But it's a lot less risky than some of our other options, don't you think?"

"What are you getting at? It sounds as if you have something already in mind."

"I sort of do." I looked away, wrapping a strand of hair around my finger as I fidgeted with my split ends. "I've been thinking about this for a while, and I did some research." I paused.

He sat like a rigid statue, shoulders square, back straight, eyes hard, attention narrowed on me like a sniper sighting his target. "And?"

"And I found something about *völvur* and *spákonas*."

"Witches," he said in the tone one used to discuss bitter and rotten things.

"And that"—I pointed at his scowl—"is why I've been reluctant to say anything. I was sure you'd be dismissive."

Baldur put a fist to his mouth and coughed politely. "They were mostly charlatans, Solina. Scammers with strong cults of personality."

I frowned. "I guessed as much, but I still think it's worth a try. My visions are real. I can't be the only one who has them."

Baldur shifted in his seat, sitting up straighter. "Maybe. But I wouldn't get my hopes up. I've met modern women calling themselves seers. At the time, I thought they'd make a useful addition to my network. None of them ever panned out though. None of them foresaw anything that ever came true."

I shrugged. "It's not as though I would know how to get in touch with one if they *were* real."

He leaned back, stretching until his joints popped. Then he stood and tugged his cell phone from his pocket. "I'll make a couple calls. Send out some feelers. Just because I had no luck doesn't mean you won't. But you have to do something for me first."

My eyebrows arched, and I sat up straighter. What favor could I do for the Allfather, Master of the Runes? "Of course. Anything."

"Go to bed. Don't take this the wrong way, but you look wrung out."

Short on sleep and burning through my fire the way I had been, I couldn't disagree. I felt like, and probably looked like, a thrift store rag doll, all dingy and frayed. Baldur's words worked like magic, and maybe they were—one of his Allfatherly imperatives influencing me. My bones gained weight, and lead shot filled my muscles. My heavy eyelids fluttered.

"Okay..." I yawned and somehow managed to stumble to my feet and into the bedroom. "But don't let me sleep too long. We've wasted so much time already."

"All of our problems will still be here in the morning," Baldur said. "Sleep and try not to worry."

The command in his voice held sway, and I slept.

I came awake with a screech, the burn of a sharp smack throbbing on my rear end. "Wake up and scooch over, girlfriend," Skyla said.

She shoved at my shoulder, and when I made room for her, she sank into the mattress beside me. I propped up on one elbow and rubbed my eyes, trying to distinguish her form in the darkness of the hotel room. "When did you get here?"

She scraped her fingers through her wild curls. "Just now. And I can hardly hold my eyes open another minute."

"Where's everyone else?"

"Baldur's finding rooms for them. I told him I'm bunking with you. I'm tired of those women. I've been cooped up in a car with them for almost twenty-four hours, and I can't take it anymore. Did you know women can smell just as bad as men? And Siobhan farts. Like a horse. Not like a regular horse, either. Like a Clydesdale. How can someone so tiny be so toxic?"

I giggled, slumped down on the mattress, and yawned. "Did the guys tell you everything?"

"Yup. No luck at the shipping terminal. And now you're trying to meet up with some modern soothsayers?"

"If I can find them. If they're even real. I'm hoping they can help me refine my visions." I hadn't told Skyla about the ravens or their offer yet. I should have, but there hadn't been time. And Baldur still hadn't talked to her either. My patience for his hesitancy was wearing thin.

"That's what Baldur said. I want to go with when you meet them."

Skyla's words swept the last cobwebs of sleep from my mind. Alert, I sat up again. "You do?"

The bed bounced as she rolled over and kicked off her boots. "Nothing else more interesting is going on."

I huffed. "Tell me about it."

"What visions have you been having? You haven't said anything."

"There's a lot I haven't told you, and none of it's going to be a short story. You want it all now, or you want to sleep first?"

Skyla groaned and fell against the pillows, landing with an "oomph." She threw an arm across her eyes and sighed. "I'm so tired I can hardly see straight, but I'm afraid if you don't tell me everything now, something will happen before you get another chance."

"You sure?"

Her dark silhouette nodded. "Just poke me if I start to snore."

I summarized everything as best I could—my random dreams, Hugh's offer, the likelihood Val had done something with Thorin's brother. By the time I finished talking, I had curled into a ball beside

Skyla. Her fingers stroked through my hair, nails scraping my scalp. My inner cat purred.

"Jeez." She blew the word out on a breath. "Maybe I should have told you to wait until tomorrow. That's a lot to digest in one bite."

"I know." *And the biggest bomb is still waiting to be dropped on you.*

"It's like... where do we even start?"

"You'd have no problem doing what the ravens asked, would you?"

She hesitated before answering. "I'm not saying it would be easy, but yes. I think I would have to accept that offer."

"There was a time when I thought I could fall in love with Val. I know the man he is isn't the man I thought he was. I don't owe him anything..."

"But you're not a murderer."

"I killed Hati."

"Not the same thing. He was never really a man, and he was absolutely going to kill you. Val hasn't ever truly threatened your life, though he might not go out of his way to protect it either. I understand your issues, girlfriend. It's not a problem we have to solve today. Let's find these *vo—völvur*, right? Maybe we won't even need the ravens."

"Thank you, Skyla."

"For what?" she asked through a sleepy yawn.

I shifted, threw my arm around her, and snuggled into her warmth. "For being my best friend."

CHAPTER 11

S ITTING AROUND, DOING NOTHING—THE INACTIVITY irritated me, rubbing me like the worst kind of T-shirt tag. As though he could read my mind, Baldur suggested we discuss our options over an extremely late breakfast in the River's Edge dining room, and I agreed. At least eating would keep me occupied.

"Have you gotten any more updates on my parents?" I asked Baldur, who studied his complementary *USA Today* while stirring his coffee. Skyla poked at her egg-white-and-spinach omelet, and Thorin sipped coffee and thumbed his phone screen. *Ancient god addicted to technology just like the rest of us.* I twirled a spoon around my half-eaten bowl of organic, steel-cut oatmeal and tried not to laugh at the scowl on Skyla's face as she contemplated her low-fat, low-carb, low-everything breakfast.

Baldur set down his paper and wrapped both hands around his coffee cup as he leaned forward, elbows planted on the tabletop. His auburn hair lay in a mess of cowlicks and swirls, but he made it look artful, like an advertisement for men's hair products. But it had to be accidental. I couldn't picture Baldur standing before a bathroom mirror combing his hair or caring about his appearance at all. Sitting there beside his unassuming granddaughter, none of Baldur's pale, auburn looks much resembled Skyla's darker ones.

Tell her, I urged him in my head. *Tell her, tell her, tell her.* Reading the thoughts of others, I could sometimes do, but broadcasting my own thoughts... Not so much.

"I have two men on your house," Baldur said. "Two more on the bakery. One who follows them wherever they drive. Your parents are safe."

I paused, spoon hovering over my bowl. "You've seen them?"

He shook his head. "I haven't. But my men have texted me photos of them coming and going on their daily routines."

"You think that's enough? A few men here and there?"

His eyebrows rose. "I could surround them with an army, but they might notice. Are you prepared to come back from the dead and explain to them what's going on?"

"I don't know..." I eyed Skyla's plate again: unnaturally white eggs, limp spinach, gluten-free toast. I missed my mom's sausage gravy and biscuits. A wave of homesickness washed over me. "It might be worth it, if it kept them safe."

Thorin set his phone on the table and pushed it toward me. "Anytime you want to break the news to them..."

I stared at the phone and considered the cold swirling in my gut. "How can I face down wolves and gods and stone warriors, but I'm too afraid to call my parents?"

"My men understand what's at risk," Baldur said. "They understand there's more to this world than meets the eye. They are not infallible, but they will serve. Your parents are under the best protection I can offer, unless you want me to take them to New Breidablick. I'm perfectly willing to host them, but you know you'll have to be the one to make the invitation."

I dropped my spoon, and it clattered against the edge of the bowl. "Okay. That's what I'll do. Thorin and I will head to North Carolina. I'll talk to my parents, tell them everything. I'll convince them to come to New Breidablick."

"I think we'll all rest easier," Baldur said. "And I think you should consider going to them sooner than later, especially if getting in touch with a real *völva* is going to be as difficult as I think it..." Baldur trailed off as his gaze settled somewhere behind me. His face hardened, and he clamped his mouth shut.

Curious, I turned to look behind me, searching for whatever had upset him. There, in the dining room doorway, stood a pale woman, wrinkled and white as winter snow in every way except for her eyes, which, even from this distance, burned a feverish green. She wore ripped jeans, a hot-pink T-shirt that said "SASSY!" in fluorescent colors, and black Chuck Taylors. I had expected someone more like Professor

McGonagall and less like Punk Barbie's grandmother, but if *völvur* were in short supply, I'd take what I could get.

Having spotted Baldur, the old woman raised her chin and peered down her nose at our group. She lifted a knobby, gnarled finger and pointed in my direction. "I'll talk to the girl."

My attention swung to Baldur, and I gaped at him, silently asking for an explanation. "Solina," he said, without meeting my gaze. "I'm making an educated guess, here, but it appears the *völva* you've been looking for has found you."

Still stunned and mostly speechless, I rose from my chair and crossed the room.

The wrinkles in the old woman's face deepened as she scowled. Her hair stood out around her head in cotton-candy puffs, and she leaned against a slim, knobby cane carved with intricate patterns. "Only her."

I glanced over my shoulder. Skyla and Thorin had stood up behind me, obviously intending to follow. I waved them back. "Do what she asks, please. I can't afford for her to change her mind before we know if she can help me or not."

Before I reached her, the old woman turned out of the dining room and crossed the lobby, heading toward the hotel's main entrance, moving faster than her cane would have suggested. *But it's not really a cane, is it? If she's who I think she is, that's her wand or magic stick or whatever...* Even if my lame publicity attempts had somehow caught her attention, I wondered how she had known exactly where to find me. Perhaps she was truly clairvoyant.

How do you know Helen or Val didn't send her?

That thought stopped me in my tracks. "Um, ma'am." I raised my voice to carry across the lobby. "I can't just follow you out that door. I don't know if I can trust you."

The wizened woman stopped and turned on her heel, graceful despite her apparent age, spiderweb hair bobbing as she moved. Her expression seemed critical, green eyes cold and hard, deep parentheses forming around her mouth, but she smiled and transformed her face into something radiant and bright. "It's good to know you aren't a complete idiot. I can work with that."

She had stopped near the doors leading outside, and I approached her with hesitant footsteps. "Let's start with names," I said.

Close enough to touch now, I held out my hand, offering to shake. Her lips puckered, and she eyed my hand as if I had offered her something unseemly. Instead of taking it, she folded her arms across her chest, hands tucked firmly beneath her armpits. "You're Solina Mundy."

My eyes popped wide, and I stifled a laugh. "Well, yeah, but I already knew that."

"But you didn't know *I* knew it."

"I guessed as much. Or why else would you be here?"

"You're looking for a *völva* to train you."

My heart fluttered like a butterfly in a strong storm. Had I found her, whoever she was, so easily, after all? "And you are a *völva*, I take it?"

She narrowed her eyes again and thinned her lips but said nothing.

The butterfly sensations settled, and my humor drained away. "Are you always like this?"

"If you are to be a seer, you will have to learn how to find your own answers."

I stifled an irritated groan. "I think I've seen this movie or read this book or played this video game before. Now enters the frustratingly vague fortune teller."

The lines between her brows deepened. "Are you accusing me of being a cliché?"

I bit my lip and offered an apologetic grimace because, yeah, I had sort of accused her of that. "Sorry?"

Her face brightened again as she laughed. "My name's Gróa, and I'm just messing with you. My Winnebago's outside, double parked. We gotta go before I get towed. Getting that thing out of impound always costs a fortune."

I glanced at the dining room doorway and wasn't surprised to find Skyla and Thorin there, wearing matching scowls. I turned to Gróa and chucked a thumb over my shoulder toward my loyal companions. "I'm not sure those two are going to let me go anywhere on my own. I'm not sure I *want* to go anywhere on my own. Not until I know if I can trust you."

She leaned around me, narrowed her eyes, and grunted. "You'll be perfectly safe with me, you know. I'm not afraid of those ravens. Or the wolves." She tapped her temple as she widened her eyes into a kooky stare. "Can see 'em coming from a mile away."

I gave her an uneasy smile. "Really?"

She blinked at me, wide eyed and grinning. "Wouldn't be worth my salt if I didn't."

"Sunshine?" Thorin asked, having moved up behind me in his usual silent way. Surprised, I flinched and spun around to face him. He narrowed his eyes at my strange new companion. "Aren't you going to introduce us?"

Gróa stopped leaning on her cane. She stood up straighter and patted her flyaway hair. She cut her eyes to me, batted her lashes, and waggled her eyebrows. It was almost... *flirtatious*? Gesturing to Thorin, I said "Um, Gróa, this is—"

"Magni, Son of Thor," she said. "I'd recognize those cheekbones anywhere. And that nose. The hair too. Shoulders, and..." She scraped her gaze down Thorin, head to toe and back up. She waggled her eyebrows again. I nearly choked trying to hold in my laugh. He shot me a dark look. "Looks a lot like his old man."

Thorin's eyebrow arched. "You knew my father?"

She shook her head and waved him off. "Never in person. But I've *seen* him."

His lips thinned. "Really?"

"Look, I was telling Solina my home is about to get hauled away. I wasn't looking for a lot of company, but I can see the two of you"—she pointed between Thorin and Skyla, who had made her way across the lobby to join our party—"are willing to make things difficult, and we don't have time for that." She turned on her heel and marched toward the exit. "So come on, then, if you're coming."

"What about the others? Baldur and the Valkyries?" I asked Thorin as we followed Gróa out to the street.

"Baldur will have to take care of himself. That's what we all agreed, right?"

Skyla slipped a phone from her rear pocket. "I'll text Embla and let her know we'll be in touch. She and Naomi and a couple others were going to head over to Port of Portland and sniff around a little."

She pushed a stray curl out of her eyes and shrugged. "Does it look like I give a damn?"

I turned to Gróa, who stared at me, eyes wide, mouth slightly agape. "That's some kind of loyalty," she said. "You do anything to deserve it?"

I dropped my gaze and shoved my hands in my jeans pockets. "I ask myself that question all the time. Still pretty sure the answer is no. But they don't seem to agree."

The old seer picked up her pace. "The Honeywagon's still here. Good. Let's get this baby on the road, and then we'll talk."

Lo and behold, she had stenciled "Honeywagon" across the back and beneath the Winnebago's passenger window. When she'd first mentioned her mobile home, I had envisioned something older and more decrepit: a square, lumbering beast on whitewall tires, trimmed in avocado-green paint and lots of rust. This current incarnation, however, was classy with sleek lines and muted colors. She obviously appreciated her comfort.

"We could get you a spot in the parking lot, couldn't we?" I asked as we trundled up the steps and into the plush interior.

Gróa swung herself into the driver's seat and fastened her seatbelt. "Nope. A *völva* never stays in one place too long, honey. I've been in Portland for two weeks waiting for you to get here. I've nearly worn out my welcome."

"Two weeks?"

"Didn't want to miss you. I knew you were coming, just wasn't sure about the date."

"Where are you taking us?" I asked as Skyla and I settled across from each other at the little table where Gróa probably ate all her meals. Thorin eased his huge frame into the front of the RV and slumped into the passenger seat. He wore an expression I couldn't interpret. Irritation? Confusion? Dread? Curiosity?

"Nowhere important right now." Gróa shifted into drive. The motor home lurched forward, and Skyla grabbed at the table in front of her, her knuckles going white. "We just gotta move."

Thorin glanced at me before returning his attention to Gróa. "Is someone chasing us?"

She yanked the steering wheel and weaved through traffic. Someone honked. Skyla groaned and bit into her bottom lip. "Not us," the seer said. "Just me."

"Why?" He growled.

"Being a seer doesn't always pay very well. I might have missed a couple of payments on the old Honeywagon." She patted her dashboard and fluttered her eyelashes at him.

"We're running from the repo man?" Skyla asked, her voice high and squeaky.

Gróa laughed and jerked the steering wheel again. The Winnebago lurched and recovered its balance. "Better than running from the wolf, though, isn't it?"

She followed the highway for a while before turning into the driveway for the Rolling Hills RV park, a few miles outside the city. She twiddled her fingers at the front gate guard, and he waved her by.

"Is this where you've been staying?" I asked. "Won't the repo man look for you here?"

"Nah," Gróa said. "That's Nathaniel on the gate. We go way back. If anyone comes looking for me, he'll throw them off my trail."

She slowed, bumped over one speed bump and another before she pulled into an empty campsite and killed the engine. Thorin unhooked his seatbelt, rose, and squeezed through the narrow passage between his seat and the driver's. A frown sat heavy on his face, and I nearly choked on the urge to laugh. How could I not? The whole thing was the setup for a cheesy joke: a fortuneteller, a Viking god, a Valkyrie, and a reincarnated sun goddess are riding in a Winnebago...

He motioned for me to move over, and I made space for his big frame. He said nothing but set his fisted hands on the tabletop and cracked his knuckles. Gróa climbed from behind the wheel and joined us at the table, but she didn't sit. After several tense seconds of listening to Thorin's knuckle popping, she reached out and laid her withered hand over his massive fists. He stopped and sat still, although his bunched shoulders and clenched jaw indicated his annoyance.

"I understand you're out of your element," Gróa said, "and it's probably doing funny things to your nerves, judging by those rain clouds that have been following us since we left the city."

I glanced out the window beside us and noticed, for the first time, the ominous darkness blanketing the sky. Thorin exhaled and rubbed a hand over his face. "Until I'm certain of you and your intentions, the storms will stay."

She sniffed and rolled her eyes. She turned from the table and stepped into her compact little kitchen, where she pulled a teapot from a cabinet and filled it with bottled water retrieved from another cabinet. "Good thing I don't mind the rain. Sets the right kind of atmosphere for what we've got to do anyway."

"And what's that?" I asked.

"Accessing the energies fueling our visions requires concentration, focus, calmness and complete self-control. A *gentle* storm"—Gróa arched a meaningful eyebrow at Thorin—"can put me in the right mood for divination." She set the teapot on the stove and turned on the flame.

Skyla snickered. "Did you hear that, Boss Man? Gentle." Thorin frowned at her, but Skyla returned his stare with a wide-eyed look of obstinacy until he snorted and turned away. To Gróa, she said, "This sounds a lot like the sort of things I had to do to invoke a spirit once."

She was referencing the time she contacted the spirit of one of the Valkyries who had perished in the fire at the Aerie. The information from that spirit had led us to the recovery of Surtalogi, the fire sword. It had also led us to Thorin's brother, Grim, and his ice cave on Mount Rainier. Ultimately, that confrontation had all worked out to our benefit, but not before we all waded through a flood of pain, heartache, and betrayal. Should I expect this experience to be any different?

Probably not.

"That was all about control and focus, too," Skyla said.

"And innate ability." Gróa searched her cabinets again until she came up with a box of tea and a canister of sugar. "Solina, you have the ability, but you lack experience. I can help you with that."

"When do we get started?" I asked.

The seer's gaze flickered around the table to Thorin then Skyla and back to me. Her shoulders bobbed once. "Now, I guess."

"One more question, first. How did you find me?"

Her shoulders bobbed again, a dainty shrug. "I *saw* you."

Skeptical, I arched an eyebrow. "You had a vision specific enough to lead you to the River's Edge Hotel on the right day at the right time?"

"*Wellll...*" Her nose wrinkled, and her green eyes sparkled. "So maybe someone told me about the message on that bulletin board on the Interwebz or whatever you call it."

"I didn't leave my real name in that message."

Gróa rifled through her dishes until she found four mugs, none of them matching. "I had seen enough to know I needed to be in Portland for some reason. After I got that call about your message, a lot of things became clearer, including your identity."

If I believed her, it seemed ringing that cosmic doorbell had worked after all. "So it's still a guessing game? Even with experience and guidance, I still won't know everything."

Her face crinkled into a diffident smile. "The future is a puzzle. With our abilities, we get a lot more pieces of that puzzle than the average person. With training, you'll get almost a complete picture."

"Almost."

She nodded. "Almost. We are not omniscient. That's too much for any one person to handle."

"Not for the ravens," Thorin said.

The old woman glanced at the RV ceiling as if she could peer through the aluminum roof and look into the sky, as if she expected to see the ravens circling above us right that minute. Maybe they *were* up there. Not that it mattered. It might have been good for them to know I didn't need their help, after all.

"Hugin and Munin are a powerful force, for sure," she said, "but they can't know the future. They can only know what *has been* done or is currently *being* done."

The teakettle whistled, and steam erupted from the spout. Gróa flinched. She laughed at herself and turned off the flame under the pot. Using a rooster-shaped potholder, she pulled the kettle from the stove and poured water in four mugs. "The ravens can only know a thought once it's been made, and not a moment before. The ravens' lack of precognition is their greatest weakness, their fatal flaw, so to speak."

She passed out mugs and set the tea box on the table along with a sugar canister painted with scenery from the Grand Canyon. She slid into the seat next to Skyla and fished teabags from the box. "Afraid

I only have chamomile, but I was raised to offer refreshments to my guests, so there you are. Take it or leave it."

I took one of the offered teabags and dunked it in my Niagara Falls mug. Skyla also accepted the tea and added it to her Wild Wonderful West Virginia! cup.

"You travel a lot, huh?" I motioned to the mugs.

"That's the life of the *völva*," Gróa said. "Go where the visions take you."

"From what I've read, the *völvur* were once treated like queens, given the best accommodations in the village, food and drink. People generally didn't bother them when they were on the road but respected their autonomy."

She smiled wistfully and leaned against the counter. "Those were the good old days. Now, I'm mostly treated like a roaming sideshow. I have some regular clients who keep me going, but I have to eke out a living wherever and whenever I can."

Skyla finished shoveling sugar in her cup and passed the canister to me. I spooned in a heap and stirred until it dissolved. "Why do you do it? You could live a more conventional life if you wanted to, right?"

Gróa shrugged. "Never wanted a conventional life, honey. Besides, the visions are my calling. Things get... *uncomfortable* for me if I try to ignore them."

"Uncomfortable? How?"

"Headaches, problems with my regular day-to-day vision. I haven't tried to deny what I am since I was a kid, so it's mostly not a problem."

I had run out of questions, and stilted silence filled the Winnebago's cramped interior. I blinked at Skyla. She blinked at me. Thorin popped his knuckles again. Gróa sat up straighter and exhaled a breathy, dramatic sigh. She jabbed a knobby finger at Skyla and Thorin. "If you're going to be here, you're going to help. You don't get to ask questions, and you don't get to be cynics. If you don't like it, you're free to leave anytime, understand?"

Skyla nodded. Beside me, Thorin huffed. I elbowed him, and he shot me a dark look.

"I'm not going anywhere," he said. "And I won't interfere unless you do something that jeopardizes Solina."

The seer's face crinkled into an ocean of wrinkles as she smiled. "You got nothing to worry about, hot stuff." She clapped her hands, and the gust of air generated by the gesture set her frothy hair atwitter. "Now, finish your tea so we can get this show on the road."

CHAPTER 12

"THIS IS MOSTLY A MIND game." Gróa had arranged a ceremonial spot for me in the center of her cramped little RV after folding away her dining room table. I perched on a stool atop an uncomfortable cushion stuffed with hen feathers that crackled whenever I shifted. The seer had unearthed the pillow from a closet in her bedroom and swore she used it whenever she undertook particularly difficult divinations. She had also dressed me up in a ridiculous costume: a blue velvet robe trimmed in rough-cut stones. On my head, she'd set a soft, furred hat, and I refused to ask what animal had sacrificed its life to make it. As she dressed me, she vaguely explained that the costume had something to do with honoring the goddess Freya, who was the first *völva*.

"All of this ceremony is symbolic," she said. "But symbols exist for a reason. They have an uncanny ability to accumulate power. And when they are evoked under the proper conditions, they can unleash that power and bring chaos and destruction, *or* unity and peace. I think you can guess which effect we're going for here."

Outside the Winnebago, rain fell in a steady, calming patter, and the clouds filtered the afternoon's thin sunlight, turning the atmosphere gray and ghostly. If I dismissed the absurdity, I had to admit I felt something—possibility or portent, maybe. Thorin and Skyla stood on either side of me, close enough to touch, and I refused to look at them in case I started giggling and ruined the mood.

Skyla shifted her weight and cleared her throat. Thorin stood still and stolid as a statue. He had adopted a similar stance when he meditated in the moments before his fight with Rolf in the field outside Portland. Perhaps he had more faith in what was about to happen than the rest of us. He was a magical being of sorts, after all. This was probably all run of the mill to him, or maybe he was just trying hard not to laugh.

"Now," Gróa said. "This is the part where it gets really weird, but you've got to go with it if you want this to work."

"Gets weird?" Skyla said. "Lady, it's been nothing *but* weird since you showed up at the hotel."

Gróa made a hacking, cynical sound in the back of her throat. "I said you could leave, remember?"

Skyla clamped her lips together, and the muscles around her eyes tightened, but she held her place at my side, demonstrating the loyalty Gróa had questioned whether I deserved. And no, I didn't deserve it, but, boy, was I thankful to have it.

"I'm going to start with a chant. Don't ask questions, don't laugh, and most importantly, don't interrupt. While I'm chanting, the three of us will form a ring, hand in hand, encircling Solina. We won't break the ring until I say so." The seer narrowed her eyes and looked pointedly at Skyla and Thorin. "Now's your last chance to leave. After this, you risk hurting Solina *and* me if you don't follow my directions implicitly. You don't have to like it. You don't have to believe in it. You do have to obey me. Any problems with that, Valkyrie?"

Skyla shook her head.

"How about you, O Thunderous One?"

I bit my lip, trying not to laugh out loud when Thorin scowled.

"No problems," he said. "Let's just get on with it." A distant clap of thunder rolled over us, still neutral but bordering on ominous and threatening. The God of Thunder was playing nice for my benefit, I suspected, but the storm outside suggested his nerves had worn thin.

"When I start the chant," Gróa said, "I want you to picture yourself walking on a pathway. Any pathway. Put yourself on a trail, and stay on it. Don't leave the path you make for yourself. It's imperative, okay? Wherever it leads you, follow it. If it brings you to a doorway, a bridge, or a gate, keep going. Just don't leave the path."

"Don't leave the path." I nodded. "Got it." I had almost drowned in a similar exercise with Thorin. If Gróa thought I could somehow lose my way in a mental forest, I would take her advice, and I would not stray. I peered at the Viking god beside me. "It'll be all right. You're my lifeguard, remember?"

"Vividly." Thorin's gaze pierced me until I felt it in my toes. I took his big, warm hand in mine and squeezed. His eyebrows rose, and he blinked, probably surprised by my gesture. He turned to Gróa. "It won't go well for you if something bad happens to her."

A crimson stain crept into the old woman's cheeks, and her green eyes glittered like chips of cold emerald. "I know my business, Aesir. Don't get in the way of it." She turned to Skyla. "Light the candle, and hit the lights."

Skyla snatched a lighter from the counter. At the same time, she brushed the switch on the wall, and the overhead light went dark. A moment later, the moody glow from the flame of a single fat white candle filled the tiny room. Gróa held her hands out at her side, palms up, and gestured to Thorin and Skyla. The three joined together, forming a ring around me.

"A circle like this usually acts like an electrical circuit," Gróa said. "It amps up the energy, gives the *völva* in the middle more bang for her buck. But with two beings who already carry a great deal of otherworldly energy... I'm excited to see where this will take us."

Excited, yeah, that's the word for it. The cold ice ball in my stomach disagreed. "Let's get going before I change my mind."

"You don't have to do this, Sunshine," Thorin said.

I closed my eyes and exhaled. "Yes. I do."

Gróa cleared her throat. "Imagine your path, Solina. Something familiar, but not too familiar. You need to provide the construct, but the vision will provide the details. Now, I apologize in advance. I can't carry a tune in a bucket."

She inhaled and exhaled a long, low syllable, an unrecognizable word. She inhaled and let the sound out again, an eerie human-and-bagpipe-hybrid noise exited her throat. She repeated the sound again and again, increasing the tempo until the rhythm developed into a steady patter, like a drum beat.

I focused on bringing up an image, a forest pathway, but the collar of my robe scratched my neck. The fur hat had slipped and sat low on my forehead. The hen feathers in my seat cushion had bunched into irritating little lumps. Skyla shifted her weight and exhaled, and it sounded annoyed and skeptical. Or maybe I was projecting.

Gróa stopped singing, and I opened my eyes, meeting her perturbed glare. "What's the matter?" she asked, her tone flat.

"I feel ridiculous." I shoved the fur hat higher on my head, but it slid over my eyebrows again. Skyla coughed, but it sounded suspiciously like a laugh. Beside me, Thorin rolled his head on his neck and flexed his shoulders. Awkwardness and tension fell over the Winnebago's interior, as palpable as the rain falling outside.

"Maybe I should have had a drink first," I said. "Something stronger than tea... to help me relax."

The seer's face brightened. She released Thorin and Skyla's hands and jabbed her index finger in the air like an exclamation point. "Great idea."

She marched to her cabinets, threw open a door, and pulled down a square glass bottle half full of amber liquid. She took down a collection of shot glasses, enough for the four of us. She unstoppered the bottle, poured four healthy dollops, and passed the glasses around. "Bottoms up." She sucked down her shot.

I peered into my glass. When I said I needed a drink, I'd mostly been joking. "What is this?"

"Scotch," Gróa said. "Don't question it. Just drink. All of you."

I shrugged, tossed back my head, and swallowed the whiskey. It burned all the way down, and I coughed and gagged. Skyla and Thorin drank theirs with less dramatics. Gróa took our glasses, refilled them, and passed them out again. "One more time."

"Really?" I asked, but I drank it down. The second helping slid down my throat, putting up less resistance, and the scotch lit a contented little fire in my stomach.

"Is that enough, or do you need one more?"

I turned to look at her, and the room spun. I wobbled on my perch. "Ah, I think that'll do."

She removed our glassware and, without a word, prompted Skyla and Thorin to take her hands again. "Eyes closed, visualization on, Solina."

Without protest, I followed her orders. This time, as she sang, my self-consciousness drifted away. An image rose from the depths of my memory, sharpening into a specific place, a familiar pathway.

Mani's favorite hike was a stretch in Grayson Highlands State Park in southwestern Virginia, from Massie Gap to Mount Rodgers and back again—about eight miles round trip. The hike ran over two bald peaks and delivered exceptional views of the Blue Ridge Mountains, rippling in blue-gray waves out toward the horizon. My brother had loved the hike for the terrain and vistas. I had loved the wild ponies roaming the glades.

I had taken that hike with him only once, and a half hour into it, clouds rolled in, rushing toward us like angry giants intent on making war. Mani refused to go back, said we'd make it to the Thomas Knob shelter before the storm caught up. He was wrong. Those black clouds had torn apart and dumped torrents of chilly rain over us. Mani and I humped through boot-sucking mud, slippery rocks, and a general state of soggy discomfort despite the best efforts of our ponchos. Eventually, we reached the shelter and hunkered down with several other unfortunate hikers waiting for the storm to pass.

When the clouds had dispersed, the sun turned the sky an unbelievable, ethereal blue, as if Mother Nature meant to apologize for ruining our day. For the remainder of our hike, the day came as close to perfect as possible. Wild ponies greeted us in the meadows, and the peaceable light filtering through the spruce forest—the trees so tall and proud and serene—restored my spirit. The wonder of it stole my breath, and for once, I understood Mani's wilderness obsession. The hike was a holy and divine experience, a brush with the Creator God more spiritual and intimate than anything I had experienced inside the four walls of a church.

It was that day and that hike I recreated in my mind, there in the Winnebago's tiny living space. Gróa's chant, rhythmic and hypnotic, lured me further into the fantasy, until it all fell away: Skyla, Thorin, Gróa, the Honeywagon, Portland, and the rest of the real world. The chanting faded, replaced by chirping birds, susurrating winds, and the musical beat of my heart.

The imaginary day mimicked the one from my memory: the vivid emerald of trees and brush complemented skies as blue and crystalline as the old Ball jars my grandmother used for canning. The air smelled of growing things, clean and herby. A small herd of ponies grazed in the distance, where details faded into a ghostly blur of a dark spruce forest. The rise and fall of my chest as I breathed matched the rise and fall of my feet, marking my progress in a steady cadence.

A shadow brushed over me, and I looked up. A hawk had caught a thermal updraft and spiraled in lazy circles. I turned my attention back to the trail. Fear of losing my way kept me focused and intent. The path carried me into a wooded area, and the loamy smell of decaying leaves infused the air as it condensed into cool mist. Sunlight dimmed into a dreamy gloom, and the pathway descended on a steady slope, as if approaching a river or a creek bed.

I had guessed right. The trail bottomed out in a wooded ravine bisected by a shallow, rocky stream. Across from the creek, the path disappeared into a dark cave mouth. I was pretty sure none of the trails in Greyson Highlands State Park led to a cave, so my imagination, or the power of the vision quest, must have constructed it.

The cavern's gaping maw beckoned, but my feet remained rooted in place at the creek's edge. Goosebumps broke over my arms, and the fine hairs on the nape of my neck stirred in a prickly way. My stomach grumbled, voicing a protest echoed by my survival instincts.

Don't go in there.

But Gróa had said no matter where the path led, I had to follow. Perhaps all the answers I needed lay somewhere in the cave's depths, or maybe a nightmare lived in there. *Or a little white rabbit with nasty, big, pointy teeth.* If I turned back, it meant never knowing and giving in to doubt. It meant denying a chance to fully recognize an aspect of myself that had been a mystery for most of my life.

Would my fire work in this dream world? I examined my internal power source and felt it burning, as constant as ever. I cupped my hand, and a reassuring pool of fire filled my palm.

"Well then..." I plopped onto the bank to remove my boots and roll up the cuffs of my jeans. "What are we waiting for?"

After taking a steadying breath, I plunged into the creek. Stinging cold currents rose to my shins. I sucked in another breath, bit my lip, and forged through the frigid waters, ignoring how the arches of my feet cramped, protesting the cold. Once I reached the other side, I shook my feet mostly dry, unrolled my cuffs, tugged my socks onto my still-damp feet, stepped into my boots, and continued on before I could talk myself out of it.

The moment I stepped into the cave mouth, the air changed, dropping several degrees and collecting odorous notes of damp earth and minerals. Light dimmed, and the path led downward, steadily descending into murky darkness. *Good thing I brought a light.* I paused to center myself and focus on separating my light from my heat—fire without the burn. A phosphorescent glow lit my skin, providing enough illumination to move forward over rocky and uneven terrain.

Maybe we got it wrong. Maybe the dreams I had about caves and rivers had nothing to do with Loki and Val and Grim. Maybe I was foreseeing this moment. But it seemed redundant to have a premonition about a vision quest.

My light reflected off shimmering minerals and lit elegant swaths of stalagmites and stalactites dripping from the walls in ruffled curtains and lumpy, waxen mounds. But after a while, the formations became redundant, and monotony chipped away at my enthusiasm. Darkness pressed in, cloying in its prevalence. The cave went on and on, winding endlessly down. Would I walk to the center of the world before I found what I was looking for?

With no way to account for time—and what was time on an imaginary journey?—I couldn't measure the length of my trip, but it felt endless. I questioned my progress or the lack thereof. My uncertainty deepened, and each step fell heavier and slower, leading me closer to defeat. This exercise was futile, and I wouldn't learn anything from it other than a couple of shots of whiskey and some chanting could make a very vivid, but pointless, dreamscape.

Dante's sign should have hung at the mouth of this cave: *Abandon hope, all ye who enter here.*

I stopped and let my light go out. Absolute blackness fell over me, thick, viscous as crude oil, dense as volcanic rock. It seeped into my lungs and stifled my breathing. It not only felt like despair but tasted like it, too—as cold and bitter as old coffee grounds. My shoulders slumped, and my chin fell to my chest. My knees wobbled, and I dropped into a crouch, burying my face in my lap. With my eyes closed, the darkness's oppression eased, and I inhaled several times, blowing each lungful out in an emptying rush.

My heartbeat throbbed against my eardrums. In the silence, my breathing crashed as loud as ocean waves on a rocky shore. I inhaled and held it in. Tears burned against my eyelids, but I gritted my teeth and growled, chasing away the frustration. *Focus, Solina. Don't leave the path. Don't turn around. Don't go back. You can do this.*

Wolves and gods hadn't defeated me. Neither would a stupid dream cave.

I stood and brought my light out again, more brazen and brighter than before, defying the darkness. One step at a time, I inched forward, still heading down, still uncertain where all my efforts would lead, but I was determined to see it to the end.

The powers that be must have taken mercy on me, or perhaps I had proven something—my worthiness, perhaps. Whatever the reason, I had only to walk a few more steps before the glimmer of a distant light reached me. The descending slope leveled out, and the narrow cave passage opened into a magnificent cavern whose walls vaulted so high that the darkness camouflaged the ceiling's true elevation. When I looked up, I might as well have been staring into an endless night sky devoid of stars.

Cutting through the cavern's floor, a quiet stream trickled like a silvery ribbon rippling in the wind. A simple arching footbridge spanned the water, but it seemed superfluous, considering I could have stepped over the stream at its narrowest places. The bridge, however, provided the only suggestion of a pathway. I started toward it but hesitated before setting foot on the first slat. An undulating light stood at the bridge's apex, occupying a space roughly the shape and size of a person, a grown man.

The figure of light waved, as if beckoning me, and something about the being seemed familiar. As I stepped forward, the light solidified into a rigid shape and form. The suggestion of a man became more pronounced, more real, more unmistakable.

Shimmering hair darkened into a shaggy black mop. Luminescent eyes dimmed to silvery gray, the same silvery-gray eyes I had looked into almost every day of my life. My heart stopped, and my breath froze. *It can't be. How the hell* could *it be?*

My light guttered and died.

I choked when I said his name. "*M-Mani?*"

CHAPTER 13

THAT SMILE. OH, THE GODS, that smile.

My memory of his brilliance was a dulled photograph of a sunny day viewed in a dark room. The real thing was like standing outside in an open field under a cloudless sky in the middle of July. I had forgotten... How could I have forgotten?

My lip quivered. My knees wobbled. A sob scrabbled its way out from my throat, but before I dissolved into a puddle of tears, my brother caught me and locked me in his embrace. His arms were strong and solid and *real*, and any thought of this being imaginary or only in my head drained away.

He smelled crisp and sharp like a snowy winter day, but his warm breath stirred the fine hairs at my temple. His cheek pressed against mine. He held me, and I held him, and perhaps the world could go to hell, as long as I could stay forever like that, wrapped up in the one person I had always considered my other half.

I never denied my brother's death had carved a hole in me, but there, in that moment, I fully comprehended the vastness of my emptiness. Only after Mani's presence filled it did I realize how much of me the hollowness had consumed. Not only had I forgotten the wonder of his smile, I had forgotten what it felt like to be whole—wondrously and completely whole.

At some point, my voice returned, and a million questions flooded my tongue, stumbling over each other for a chance to be spoken. But one word broke through all the others, and I said it over and over. "Mani, Mani, Mani..."

He chuckled, raised his head, and leaned back to peer in my eyes. "Solina, Solina, Solina," he teased. The repetition of my name ignited a memory. Had he always sounded so much like our father? Had I heard Mani's voice in my vision and mistook it for our dad's?

His teasing didn't bother me. In fact, I welcomed it. A man dying of dehydration in the desert never tasted anything sweeter than his first drink of water; and a grieving sister never heard anything more beautiful than her name spoken by her beloved brother.

"How can this be? Is it real?"

Mani's smile dimmed. Others might not have noticed, but his every molecule and each of his atoms were familiar to me. "It's... *complicated.*"

I huffed and rolled my eyes. "Tell me something I couldn't figure out for myself."

"I don't know how this is happening." Mani's arms relaxed, and he released me from his hug, but he took both of my hands in his, maintaining our connection. "Your being here is as much of a wonder to me as it is to you."

I looked up at the darkness and let my gaze fall to the cavern walls. "What is this place? Where are we?"

"The others here call it the *helgafjell.*" Mani waved as if shooing a fly. "It's not important. It's a lot to explain and comprehend, and I get the feeling we don't have much time together. Let's focus on what you came here to do and not waste our time on sadness, grief, or useless questions, okay?"

"Okay?" I blinked at him dumbly. "How can any of this be *okay?*"

"I know it's not." Mani squeezed my hands. "But you have to trust me."

"I've *always* trusted you."

He nodded. "And it's one of the million reasons why I love you. But we have to get going." Still holding my hand in his, my brother turned and tugged me forward, leading me over the bridge. Urgency seemed to fuel his footsteps, and as I followed him, my mind reeled. An abundance of unanswered questions slowed my thought process like a computer running too many software applications at once.

How? That was the main question nagging me. How could this be? I shook my head as if I could shake away my confusion. "How did you find me?"

Mani led us into an area that looked less like a cave and more like some ancient dwelling carved of stone blocks. Iron sconces supported torches burning on the walls, spilling yellow light along our path. He glanced at me but didn't slow his pace. "A messenger came and told me to meet you and lead you to the well."

"Well?" Goose bumps shivered over my arms. "What well?"

"You'll see soon enough." He tugged me again, and I stumbled forward. Our path wound in a tight corkscrew, sloping at a steady decline. After my long descent from the mouth of the cavern, I should have dreaded going any further down, but Mani could have led me into a fiery lake or jumped off a cliff, and I would have happily followed him.

The winding corridor leveled out in another vast, cavernous opening. Darkness obscured the far walls, and shadows expanded infinitely. Instead of a high ceiling veiled in gloom, a woven tapestry of gnarled tree roots crisscrossed overhead, branching and dividing like blood vessels. Knotty, twisted lianas trailed down the nearest wall and along the floors until they converged and spilled over the rim of an inky pool set in the ground like a black mirror. Warmth, mustiness, mildew, and decaying wood permeated the air.

Mani pulled on my hand, urging me forward, but I stopped and held my place. "Is this…"

I paused and scanned the space again, taking in the details. Gears in my brain chugged to life, processing the clues and delivering a result. "Are we beneath Yggdrasil? Is this the well at the base of the World Tree?" Was I looking at the legendary home of the Norns: divinities of fortune, fate, and destiny? *Impossible.*

I wobbled as my knees weakened, but Mani grabbed my shoulders and held me steady.

"Don't lose your grip." Wrinkles puckered his forehead as his brows drew together. "This is the whole reason you came here, isn't it?"

"Is it? I came looking for answers, for better control of my visions."

He nodded. He turned and pointed toward the murky black waters. "That's the last step in your journey. Your answers are in that well."

My jaw fell open, and I gaped at him, wide-eyed and unblinking. "In there?" I crinkled my nose and grimaced. "I have to go *in* the well?"

"Either that or turn around and go back. But you didn't come all this way to give up, did you?"

I took his hand and squeezed it. "I could stay here with you." It was tempting. *Mighty* tempting.

A dark expression fell over his face, and he recoiled. "This is no place for a living person. You have an entire life ahead of you. What would make you think I'd ever be okay with letting you give that up?"

"It hurts. Living without you is the worst pain I've ever known."

His eyes flashed. "Pain exists to remind you you're alive and have a soul. You've come all this way because you're fighting for something, not because you're looking for an excuse to give up."

I shoved him, but he held his place and braced himself as if I might attack again, a smart move because I wanted to hit him and kick him and scratch him, inflict some of the pain his death had brought on me. So he would understand, so he would know what it was like for me. Instead, I sank to the floor, hugged my knees, and stared into the well's murky waters.

"I didn't stop to think." He lowered to a crouch beside me. Dark hair fell over his forehead, nearly covering his eyes. I reached out, brushed it back, and savored the feel of those silky strands beneath my fingertips. How many times had I touched him like that and taken it for granted? "The messenger said to come and get you. I never stopped to think what it would be like for you."

"What about what it's like for you? You'd let go of me so easily?"

Thin lines formed around Mani's eyes and mouth as he frowned. "Easy? It wouldn't be *easy*, Solina. I could cut my heart out, and it would hurt less. But this place..." He glanced up at the dark ceiling. "It's like anesthesia. It numbs and dulls and makes you kind of stupid, if you don't watch it. It's deadening. And you are alive, and vivid, and bright, and why the hell do you think I'd want you in this place that would take all that away?"

"Isn't having a dull me better than having none of me?" I asked, trying for a joke. It fell flat, and he didn't smile. "How do I walk away from you? Losing you before... I didn't let you go—you were taken from me. But now you're asking me to just give you up. This time it will be my choice. My fault."

"This isn't real for you. You can't stay in a dream."

I rose to my knees and scooched closer to him. He let me take his hand and hold it against my chest, over my heart. "I've done something like this before. I'm not dreaming."

His eyebrow arched. "You've done this before?"

"Not this exactly. But I have separated myself and visited another realm."

He sat back and blinked. "What other realm?"

"Asgard. I've been there. I've seen the city."

"Asgard?" The corner of his mouth twitched. "Huh. I guess if this place exists, then why not that one? What was it like?"

"A burnt-out wreck, mostly. Parts of it are growing back though." I smiled as I thought about my orchard.

Mani gave me a curious look before he rolled to his feet, stood, and tugged me up beside him. He pulled me into another hug.

"This isn't making it easier to leave," I mumbled into his shoulder.

He chuckled and squeezed me once before letting go. "We'll be together again, one day, I promise—unless you figure out how to live forever."

I kicked a loose stone in the floor. It plopped into the well, and ripples spread across the glassy surface. I shook my head. "I don't know if I want immortality. I want..." After recovering from the shock of reuniting with Mani, I had to admit staying here meant surrendering. It meant abandoning everyone and everything I had fought wolves and manipulative gods to keep. Nothing I had done before would matter— the sacrifices I had made as well as those made by others on my behalf. It meant deserting Skyla, and Thorin, and my parents, and a lifetime of possibilities. It meant letting Helen get away with murder. "I want a life. One time around is enough, but I want it. The whole thing, beginning to end."

Mani smiled. "Your eyes are burning the way they do when you're fired up about something. I didn't believe my sister was a quitter. Good to know I was right."

I studied the well's black waters, ominous and foreboding, and I shivered. "You're *sure* I've got to go in there?"

"Yup."

"Then what?"

He shrugged. "I dunno. I'm not the one with the freaky premonitions."

I swatted his shoulder. "It's not freaky."

He blinked at me and twisted his lips into a wry grin.

"Yeah, okay." I bobbed my head. "It's a *little* freaky." When I stepped closer and toed the water, it coated my foot in oily, wet warmth. "You'll be all right here?"

I kept my gaze fastened on the well. If Mani's eyes gave anything away—sadness, pain, regret—I might have stayed and said to hell with everything else.

"I'll be all right," he said. "This place is comfort and warmth. It's easy."

"What about happiness?"

"It has its moments. Maybe there's no great joy, but there's no pain or sadness either. When they call it 'eternal rest,' they aren't kidding."

I stepped forward, drifting further into the well. The water rose to my knees. "You're the most nonrestful person I've ever known." In fact, my family had regularly joked that Mani was short for "manic." "You're okay with being suspended in eternal rest?"

"Just because it's not stressful doesn't mean I'm going stale. I've got projects."

"Projects?" I turned to him, to memorize his face, to ingrain that smile a little deeper in my memory. Mani stood at the edge of the well, not close enough to touch the water, but almost. What if I pulled him in with me, pulled him back into reality? But that probably wouldn't have worked. *Would it?*

"I'm not alone here, Solina. There are generations of Mundys in this place. I'm helping one of our great-great-great-uncles on a mapping and exploration project."

I gaped at him. "Are you serious?"

He swiped a lock of dark hair from his eyes and grinned in his charming way. Girls across the world, and more than a few guys, had gone weak kneed at the sight of that smile. "This place has more secrets than Victoria's underwear drawer. We're trying to catalogue everything. There are no records or atlases, and it's nearly an impossible task because this place grows and changes constantly. Don't worry." His grin broadened. "The last thing I am here is bored."

I backed further into the well, and the water soaked me to my belly button. "Are you telling me the truth or just what you think I want to hear?"

He shook his head, one quick twist. "Nope. I'm being *dead* honest."

"Ba-dum-ching," I said, playing a rimshot and rolling my eyes. But my heartstrings twanged. No one could make me laugh like my brother.

He chuckled. "Go and be happy, Solina. Live your life. Try things and succeed. Try things and fail. Fall in love while you're at it. I'll be here for you when the time is right."

"I didn't get to say goodbye to you before. It sucked really, really bad."

"And now you'll get that chance. We're luckier than a lot of people."

I raised my hands from the water, and my fingers dripped as I waved a soggy goodbye. Tears burned in my eyes again, but I blinked them away. "I love you."

"And I love *you*." Mani waved, and despite his grin, he looked like a sad puppy, all big eyed and droopy eared.

I squared my shoulders and backed away, even as the seams in my heart tugged and wrenched, straining as though they might rip apart. But scar tissue is thick and hard to tear, and my heart held together. After inhaling a deep breath, I threw my arms out at my sides—a little dramatic flair—and fell back.

In the moment before the water took me under, Mani's final words reached me. "Tell Skyla I love her, too."

Heavy panting of a restless beast, like rhythmic rasps of sandpaper smoothing a rough surface. Sharp squeals of claws raking iron or steel, as shrill as fingernails on slate.

Plip, plip, plip, *drips echo in a cavernous interior.*

A howl, sung in one long note—cold and trembling it resonates— vibrates the hollows of a tormented heart.

A wolf hunkers, ears tight against his skull, tail tucked. Whimpers underscore each breath.

Val, son of Loki, kneels before a cage, and the beast inside stares back, eyes empty, sides heaving, tongue and teeth bared. Val's smile stretches his face into a ghastly rictus. On a ledge high above the cage coils a snake, not a living serpent, but an effigy of that fanged adversary, rendered in stone. The steady drips rebounding off the walls are not water but venom. Draining from the snake's sculpted mouth, poison rains like liquid fire, and the wolf burns...

...Waves break like clashing cymbals and recede in gritty whispers. Winds scream, raising strings of melodious curses as angry as sirens damning sailors to death. Footfalls from a concrete army boom, giving a pulse to the bass line of a fiendish march.

Salt and sand scourge and erode an arching metal building, industrial, utilitarian with corrugated ribs of rusting steel. Blackened veins of ice crisscross a pockmarked surface, churning asphalt rubble into scales and scabs that stretch the length of a narrow, cold, and hoary island.

A faded greeting on a corroding sign emblazoned with a grinning bear: Welcome to Amchitka...

...A windswept vista, high above a foggy gray ocean.

A rock-strewn beach.

A spear through the heart of a man's body awash in sea foam and blood.

CHAPTER 14

DARKNESS SPUN IN A SILENT tornado that gathered me up and dumped me out like Dorothy. But I hadn't touched down in Oz. Instead, I had returned to the tiny living room of Gróa's Winnebago, which was nearly as surreal as Munchkin Land. Gróa came into focus first, drawing my attention with her flouncy white hair and hot-pink T-shirt.

"Are you a good witch or a bad witch?" I said the first thing that came to mind.

Gróa and Skyla looked at each other, wearing matching expressions of bafflement. As reality solidified around me, I noticed two things: Thorin was missing from my little vision quest party, and I was drenched to the core.

"Where's Thorin?" I asked.

At the same moment Skyla asked, "Why are you wet?"

I pointed at Skyla. "You first."

Her nose crinkled. "Gróa made him go outside."

"Why?"

Gróa's gaze dropped to the floor, and her cheeks turned pink. "He was misbehaving."

I rolled my lips together and bit, swallowing a maniacal giggle. I might have returned to the present, but things inside me still felt a little... unbalanced. "You put him in time-out?"

"He would have jeopardized the process." The old seer looked up and met my eyes. "You appeared to be having a seizure at one point near the end. Admittedly, it looked pretty bad, but waking you would have been worse. You had to complete the path and overcome whatever obstacles came before you. He wanted to wake you up. There were some sharp words. If not for your Valkyrie friend here, I'm afraid the Aesir would have succeeded, but she has a way of getting through to him."

"I may have punched him." Skyla shrugged.

I slid my fur hat from my head and passed it to Gróa, who held it between pinched fingers like a soggy dishrag. "I can't wait to hear what happened," the seer said.

"What did you see?" Skyla asked.

I blinked at her, deciding whether to tell her everything or not. But what good would it have done to withhold information? She needed to know as much as I did. "Mani."

She dropped my hand and stumbled against the kitchen counter. She pressed her hand over her mouth and stared at me, unblinking. "You saw him?"

"I did. And it was wonderful and terrible—wonderful to see him and terrible to have to walk away."

"Is he okay?"

I nodded. "He is, actually. He told me to tell you he loved you."

Skyla's chin trembled. Her eyes sparkled. Her composure broke, and she turned away, shoulders shaking, wracked with sobs. I rose from my stool and shrugged off my dripping robe. I went to Skyla and slid my arms around her shoulders. She turned and buried her face in my neck, and I held her while she cried. The Winnebago's door creaked open, and Thorin's blond head poked in. Still holding Skyla, I motioned for him to come in.

"Mani's okay." I glanced over her head and caught Thorin's gaze. He returned my stare as I talked. "He's comfortable, not in pain, and in a place that keeps him contented." I rehashed the story of my walk through the woods, my descent through the cave, my confrontation with Mani, and my acceptance of having to leave him again. "At least I got to say goodbye this time."

Skyla raised her head and sniffed. She wiped her eyes and nose on her sleeve and pulled away from me. She masked her face, hiding away her distress. "You still haven't explained why you're dripping wet."

"Blame that on the Norns' well," I said, and everyone shouted questions at me at once. I waved for silence, and my three companions fell silent. Then I explained my experience of walking beneath the roots of Yggdrasil and of plunging below the waters of fate and time. "Before I tell you what I saw, though, I want to know what it looked like from your end."

Gróa looked at Skyla before shifting her attention to Thorin, who apparently had been made to leave before the final moments of my ritual. Gróa cleared her throat. "Well, the light kind of fractured the way it does beneath a pool or fountain at night. You sort of, uh, went all light and limp as if you were floating underwater. Then your eyes rolled back, and you went rigid and—"

"That's when we had to kick Thorin out," Skyla interjected.

Thorin's nostrils flared. He rolled his eyes up and glared at the ceiling as he gritted his teeth.

"After a bit, things calmed down again," Gróa said. "There was a splash, and then you were there"—she motioned to my former seat—"soaking wet and wide awake, sitting on the stool asking about good and bad witches."

"That was more literal than I expected," I said.

Skyla gave me a you-can-say-that-again look. "After all that, please tell me you saw something worth all this trouble."

I swallowed and nodded. "I'll tell you, but do you think I could have some more tea first? And some dry clothes or something? It's a little chilly in here."

"Of course." Gróa jumped up. "Come with me. I'll get you something to change into."

A few minutes later, I returned to the living area wearing pink sweatpants and a T-shirt bearing the image of an extremely unhappy Siamese cat. Skyla didn't laugh, although I could tell she was struggling not to. Thorin's face remained an impassive mask, but something powerful seemed to brew beneath his exterior. He resembled a mountain, an ancient volcano building pressure.

I sat at the little table while Gróa set about refilling her teapot. "Maybe we should start with the strong stuff." I glanced at the seer's liquor cabinet. "No one's going to like what I have to say."

Thorin's cool façade cracked, a hairline fracture. He shifted on his feet and balled his fists at his sides. I pointed at him. "Give him the first shot," I said as Gróa opened her scotch bottle. "He looks like he's going to need it."

The seer dispensed her whisky. We tossed back our drinks, and I coughed and pounded my chest as the liquor burned its way down to my stomach. When I found my breath again, I looked up at Thorin and patted the seat beside me. His shoulders slumped like knots untying, and he slid in beside me. Skyla sat across from me, and Gróa puttered in the kitchen.

"I'll start with the good news," I said. "I think I found the golems. They're somewhere called Amchitka."

"Am-what-ka?" Skyla asked. Thorin tugged his phone from his pocket and thumbed the screen.

"Amchitka," I said again. "Wherever it is, it looks windy and cold and deeply unpleasant."

"It's an old US Air Force base in the Aleutian Islands." Thorin set his phone on the table where Skyla and I could see the map he'd brought up. "After World War Two, the American government used it for nuclear testing. Now it's mostly abandoned and only accessible by aircraft or boat."

"Great place for a modern Vigrid," Skyla said.

"Nuclear testing site?" I asked. "Sounds like the backstory of a comic book character."

"If you're right about this," Skyla said, ignoring my comic book comment, "we need to call the Valkyries. Now."

"Do it," Thorin said. "Charter a flight. Cost is no concern, and we need to act quickly. Now that we know where Helen's keeping her army, it won't be long before the ravens know."

"And then Val will know that we know," I said.

Gróa broke in and passed out tea mugs. I took mine and wrapped my hands around the warm ceramic.

Thorin ignored his cup. "Val said he wasn't a part of Helen's schemes, but we can't take his word for it. We need to act before he decides to give her a warning."

Skyla stood, took her own phone from her pocket, and dialed. With the phone to her ear, she moved to the RV's door and pushed it open. "Embla?" she said as she stepped outside. "I've got the golems."

I shifted, turning in my seat and drawing up a knee to rest my chin on as I faced Thorin. "Now for the bad news."

One blond eyebrow rose. "You don't want to wait to tell Skyla?"

"What I have to say isn't for her. It's for you. You aren't going to like it." I set my hand over his on the table. His eyes darkened, and maybe he sensed my dread, but before I could say anything, he dropped his walls, and his thoughts flooded in.

From Thorin's perspective, I saw myself, crowned in my fur cap and robed in blue. Through his eyes, I looked less ridiculous than I had felt. A candlelight glow radiated from my skin. My eyes burned as fiery orbs. I sat on the stool, still and silent as a statue.

I screamed.

My body locked into a rigid pose, joints stiff, teeth bared, and all of Thorin's emotions burned, hot and stinging like touching a live wire. His heart jackhammered against his ribs. He yelled my name and grabbed for me, but Gróa threw herself in his path. They argued. Skyla tried to reason with him. Thorin shoved Gróa, and Skyla punched him, her fist slamming into his jaw. Her hit rattled him and cleared the panic from his head.

"*Get out!*" Gróa had demanded and pointed at the door.

Thorin had glanced at me. By then, I had fallen silent but seemed insensible. He growled, gritted his teeth, and stomped outside. Overhead, the clouds had gathered into an impenetrable black wall. Shards of lighting rent the sky. Rain fell like shrapnel.

The vision dissolved. I exhaled, slumping against Thorin, and rubbed my eyes until the RV's interior came into focus. Gróa had disappeared, leaving us alone. He folded his arms around me and drew me close. His breath fell in warm puffs over my temple. My bones felt raw and brittle, like spun sugar stretched into thin, fragile strands.

"Maybe I shouldn't have done that," he said, his voice low and soft. "But I needed you to know. Whatever you have to tell me, whatever happens next, I wanted you to know."

"You were afraid for me. You felt helpless. You hate feeling that way."

He grimaced. "It's more than that."

"I know. I felt it. *All* of it."

At the least, Hugh had understated. At the most, the raven had outright lied. What Thorin felt for me was a hell of a lot more than *want*. What I felt for Thorin was a lot more, too. Maybe the time had come to stop denying it. Maybe it was time to go after the things I'd realized I wanted when I left Mani at the well, the things that made living worth the pain.

Thorin pushed a tendril of damp hair from my forehead. His eyes glinted darkly, and I returned his stare without hesitancy, resistance, or fear. Before I could talk myself out of it, before I could change my mind or give in to doubt, or acknowledge all the reasons why I shouldn't, I leaned in and closed the distance between us. My lips pressed against his, and I might as well have touched a match to gunpowder.

Reality popped like the cork on a champagne bottle. Whatever I had expected, whatever I thought might happen...

Yeah... no. None of that happened.

Words failed. So did my thoughts. The world dissolved into sensation and perception. My nerve endings ignited with starlight.

There was velvet and silk and sandpaper and heat.

Lips, teeth, tongues.

Fire and rain.

Sunshine and lightning.

"You're glowing," Thorin said later, his voice low and gruff. He had pulled me across his lap, and his forehead rested against mine. One hand was knotted in my hair at the nape of my neck. His other stroked the skin at the base of my spine. My hands were similarly occupied, and his hair felt like strands of sunlight in my fists.

I swallowed, cleared my throat, and doubted I could form coherent words. My lips had gone mostly numb. At least I wasn't drooling. "Don't let it go to your head. A good cup of coffee can make me glow like this, too."

He chuckled. "Is that so?"

"And chocolate. That really good, very rich, dark chocolate."

He darted forward, capturing my lips. He kissed me until my brain melted and dribbled from my ears.

"Chocolate who?" I mumbled when he let me come up for air. Not that I cared about breathing ever again. "Coffee what?"

Thorin laughed, and it vibrated through me. And, oh, how I didn't want to tell him what I had seen in the well. *Let me have more of his joy, more of his happiness and none of his pain.*

"What is it?" His expression turned grim. "Why so serious?"

"It's your brother." I spat out the words like bitter seeds. *Do it quickly. Get through the worst part fast.* "Val has turned him into a wolf somehow, and he's keeping him in a cage. He's reenacting parts of Loki's punishment. Val's using something like venom, acid or something. He's burning Grim."

Thorin stiffened. His mask fell in place, and the light in his dark eyes dimmed. The door to the RV swung open, and Skyla and Gróa's faces popped into view. Skyla studied me perched in Thorin's lap, my face inches from his, him sitting rigid, fist bunched in the hem of my T-shirt. Her mouth fell open.

Gróa elbowed Skyla aside and climbed the steps into the Honeywagon. Her eyes twinkled. "I gather you told him that bad news you had. Softened the blow a little first, though, didn't you? Smart girl."

I wrinkled my nose at her and slid into my seat beside Thorin. He let me go but held fiercely tight to my hand. Skyla climbed into the RV and folded herself into the seat across from us, moving carefully as if taking a seat before a growling tiger. "What is it, Boss Man? What's the damage?"

He scrubbed a hand over his face. "It doesn't matter," he said, his voice rough and hoarse. "Until Skoll is dead, nothing else matters."

"You know there's no love lost between your brother and me," I said. "But what Grim did to me wasn't personal. There was logic at the foundation of his actions. And he had a point. My death would have resolved things quickly and neatly."

Thorin's eyes flashed, and his voice rumbled. "What are you saying?"

"I can't completely understand what you must be feeling right now, but I know if I were in your shoes, and if Val had my brother and was hurting him like that, I'd have to go. I'd have to try to save him. I don't like Grim, and maybe I hate him, but he's your brother, the only one you have left, and that's something I *do* understand."

"Grim's not my priority." His voice wavered.

"No. He's not *my* priority," I said. "But I'll be damned if you think I'm going to stand in your way if you need to find him. And I do think you need to find him and very soon. If there's anything of your brother that was ever worth saving, what Val is doing to him will quickly destroy it. I won't be the reason you couldn't save Grim."

Whatever Thorin and I had just created was tentative and fragile. A million other things could go wrong that would tear us apart, but Grim was a problem I could foresee and act on—something I could prevent. If Val broke Grim, the guilt of not saving him would break Thorin, and that, in return, would break us. I wouldn't let that happen if I could help it.

The muscle in his jaw worked. He released my hand, fisted his own together, and bunched his shoulders. "I promised you."

I rubbed his big, strong back and leaned into him. "I can't hold you to it. It wouldn't be fair."

"And if I left you for Grim, and something happened to you while I was gone—"

"I know. That's always the fear, isn't it? I *could* let you put me in a cage."

He shook his head. "You'd never do that, Sunshine."

"I can't go with you. I could, but it's a risk. And I shouldn't go with the Valkyries, either. They can finish off the golems with or without me. That leaves me with the task of going home to get my parents and convince them to go to New Breidablick the way I had planned. Baldur can watch my back. I think he'll help me if I ask nicely."

"I'll go with you," Skyla said.

"No." I shook my head. "You've got to go with the Valkyries. You've got to make sure those golems are destroyed. Something funny is going on with those women, Embla especially." Skyla's face reddened, and she opened her mouth, presumably to form an objection. I raised a hand and continued. "You can't tell me you didn't smell something fishy with that truck driver in Winnemucca."

She shrugged. "What are you getting at?"

"He was a setup—a red herring." I explained what the truck driver, Kowalski, had said about being told to leave the convoy and lie in wait for us. I laid out my concerns about Embla's lack of investigation and her ready acceptance of Kowalski's lame story. "Something isn't adding up, but I'd love to be proven wrong. I'd love to think we could trust the

Valkyries implicitly. That's what I'm asking you to do. Prove them loyal. Just promise me you won't blindly follow Embla."

Skyla scowled, and a vein in her forehead throbbed. "Fine," she said between gritted teeth. She shook her head as if a fly had pestered her. "Fine. I'll make you a tasty plate of crow to eat when this is all over."

"I hope you're right." I reached across the table for her hand. She let me take it, despite her rancor. I twined my fingers between hers, and she didn't resist, although her frown remained in place. "I *want* you to prove me wrong. *Please*, prove me wrong. I need those Valkyries on my side. You're the only one I trust to put them there."

Skyla ground her teeth and nodded. She squeezed my hand once and let go before rising to her feet. "Boss Man, can you get me to the hotel in a hurry? The Valkyries are waiting on me. We've got a golem army to demolish."

Thorin exhaled in a rush of breath and nodded. He stood and pulled me to my feet. "Let me take Solina to Baldur first, and then I'll come back for you."

I dropped his hand and threw my arms around Skyla for a brief hug. She returned it, patting my back. "Thank you," I said. "I owe you."

"No, you don't. This is what I was made to do. It's my purpose."

I stepped back from her and nodded at Gróa. "After everything you've done to help me, I feel I owe you more than just my thanks. But I don't have more than that to offer right now. And I'm sorry for leaving in such a hurry."

The seer shrugged. "I'm like the Valkyrie. I don't need your thanks. I'm just doing my job. We're all in this together, mostly. If you can keep the goddess of the underworld from turning this into Hell on Earth, I'll kindly take that as payment for my services."

"I hope I see you again," I said.

Her green eyes twinkled as she winked. "If you need me, you'll find me."

Thorin pulled me into his arms. "Thank you," he said to Gróa. "Your assistance today won't be forgotten. The Aesir owe you a favor, now."

She waved him off. "Maybe you'll pay to get the Honeywagon out of impound for me sometime."

"I'll do much more than that," he said in the moment before my ears popped. "I swear it."

When Thorin spoke the necessary rune, *raidho*, we dissolved into the whirl of cross-dimensional travel. But somewhere in the spinning darkness, the winds and dizziness faded. Everything went still and silent. He wrapped himself tighter around me.

"What's going on?" I asked. He had suspended us in a place without light or outside sounds. Only his touch and warmth assured me of his presence. "Where are we?"

"Between," he said simply.

"Between what?"

"Between here and there. Don't worry about it. I'll take you to Baldur soon enough, but this was the only way I could get a minute alone with you. No witches or Valkyries or Allfathers."

My heartbeat quickened into an unsteady gallop. "Why? What's the matter?"

He brushed his lips over my temple. "You're asking me to leave you, and I'm actually considering going through with it. I can't help feeling I'm going to regret it."

"You'll regret losing Grim even more."

"More than losing you? I don't think so."

"I'm going to New Breidablick. There's hardly a safer place for me, is there?"

"I still think this is a bad idea."

"All our options are bad."

"I agree. So at least let me have a decent goodbye."

"What do you mea—" He kissed me before I finished my question, demonstrating exactly what he meant.

Dizzying winds returned, emboldened and amplified. Thunder, lightning, and rain crashed, and I met and matched Thorin's elements with my own—fire, light, and heat.

I pulled away, laughing, rejoicing in our combined strength. My light set his eyes ablaze. "I believe in you." I smiled, brimming with confidence. "Never forget that."

"I won't." His tone was grim despite the smile playing on his lips. "I just hope it's enough to get us through whatever comes next."

Thorin settled me on my feet in the living room of the River's Edge Hotel suite and held me until I regained my balance. Baldur sat on the couch nearby, leg thrown casually over his knee, arms extended across the sofa's back—kingly, regal. His blue eyes narrowed, and he looked hard at me then at Thorin and back at me. A knowing grin broke out over his face. "Ah, I see. It's about time."

I ignored Baldur's comment, stepped away from Thorin, and inhaled, urging my emotions to settle, steeling myself against the desire to tell him not to go. "Allfather, I have a request."

Baldur arched an eyebrow. "I had a feeling you would. It's why I'm here, waiting for you."

I settled into a chair across from him and sucked in another big breath. "It's a long story. I hope you're not in a hurry."

Thorin cleared his throat. "I'm going to get Skyla. Then I'm heading out. If I come back here, I think…" His face fell flat, and his eyes went dull. He avoided my gaze. "I think it's best if I don't come back here until I'm done with Grim and Val."

I bit my lip and swallowed the protest rising in my throat. *I've had to separate from too many people I've cared about today. It's not getting any easier.* "Go. Be fast. Be safe."

"I'll see you at New Breidablick?" he asked.

"You'd better."

He nodded and disappeared without another word.

I turned my attention to Baldur. Both of his eyebrows rose as he stared at the empty space Thorin had previously occupied. "I have a feeling I'm not going to like whatever you have to tell me. Whatever happened to make him leave you…"

"It's not good," I said. "It was hard enough the first time. Explaining it again won't be any easier."

He leaned forward and braced his forearms on his knees. "Try your best."

"We've found the golems," I said. "And we've found Thorin's brother." I repeated my visionary experience again, editing to give Baldur only the most necessary details.

The Allfather leaned back in his chair, rubbed both hands over his face, and stared up at the ceiling. "Now you've put your life in my hands."

"It's not the first time, and you've always protected me."

"Despite your stubbornness."

I cracked a smile. "Despite that, yes."

"So, I'll take you to your parents, we'll convince them to come to New Breidablick, and you'll stay there with them—and me—until Thorin returns."

"Until Thorin returns, or Skyla completes her mission, or both. I won't take any unnecessary risks."

Baldur smirked. "Unnecessary is subjective. You seem to find ways of making that work in your favor."

"I am who I am." I threw my open hands out at my sides and shrugged as if to say, *too late to change me now.* "Before we leave, it might be a good idea to figure out how we're going to get my parents from North Carolina to New Breidablick. I don't think you want to piggyback all three of us in one day."

Crossing the country back and forth three times, carrying passengers on each trip, would certainly burn through his batteries. Baldur knew how to fight—I had seen him spar with Thorin and hold his own—but rune-making was his strongest asset, as long as he maintained his energy stores. I could do a lot with my fire, but protecting two humans and one guileless god would challenge me on my best days. Today was not one of my best days. The journey to the Norn's well had drained me, and my fuel gauge pointed toward empty.

"Magni's jet is available, I believe."

"It is?"

Baldur nodded. "He cleared the reservation list and rescinded all outstanding contracts."

"When did he do that?"

He shrugged. "He mentioned it when we were last at New Breidablick. He said if we were going to meddle in human affairs, we might need a reliable way to transport them."

"Won't the Valkyries need it?"

135

Baldur shook his head again. "The Valkyries were never his primary concern."

"Tell me about it," I muttered. If the Aesir had made the Valkyries more of a priority long ago, some of our recent problems might have been avoided. But hindsight was twenty-twenty, right? "Well, send the jet to Charlotte, I guess. It's the closest airport to my house."

Baldur took out his phone, called a number in his contact list, and made arrangements for Thorin's jet to meet us. When he ended the call, he said, "It was in Atlanta, fortunately. Should be in Charlotte in an hour or so." He leaned forward, stood, and held out his hand to me. "To North Carolina?"

I took my own deep breath as my stomach swirled. *Another cross-country journey via interdimensional means. Hooray.* The thought of facing my parents again after so much time, after they certainly believed I was dead, might have played some part in my discomfort as well. The prospect of a family reunion should have made me happy, but first, we had to get through the hard stuff, and I had already been through an obstacle course of hard stuff that nearly defeated me. Nothing appealed to me more than sitting down and catching my breath, but my moment of weakness might lead to someone else's suffering. I could rest when we all returned to New Breidablick. *Yeah, rest and worry about Thorin and Skyla.*

I eased my hand into Baldur's. He folded me into a gentle hug and spoke a single magical word.

Once again, we flew.

CHAPTER 15

"DO IT QUICK LIKE RIPPING off a Band-Aid" had become the new motto for my life. It applied to numerous situations: telling Thorin the bad news about his brother and announcing my *not-dead* status to my parents by appearing like Captain Kirk beamed down from the *Enterprise* in the middle of their kitchen just before closing time.

The bakery smelled of cinnamon, cloves, mint and all things Christmas-y. Homesickness washed over me, sudden and fierce. I covered my sob with an excessively cheery, "Surprise!"

Somewhat *un*surprisingly, my mother turned from her work table, gasped, and fainted, dropping to the floor still clutching a pastry bag of violet icing. Dad reacted better, managing to keep his feet, although he did temporarily lose his ability to form a coherent sentence.

"Uh," he said. "Wha...?" He repeated that theme with several variations before finally putting his thoughts together. "Solina? What are you doing here?"

A lunatic giggle rose in my chest, a subconscious reaction to the absurdity. I choked it down. "Hey, Daddy. Long time no see."

From her place on the floor, my mother muttered something indeterminate. Dad and I rushed to her side and helped her sit up. She blinked at me like an owl. Then she patted my face as if to assure herself of my reality. She shook her head, and her eyes rolled, but she recovered and maintained consciousness.

"I've got a lot to tell you guys," I said, still kneeling before my stunned parents. "Some of it's going to be very hard for you to believe."

"Harder to believe than you showing up out of the middle of nowhere?" Dad asked. "We thought you were dead."

"I know. And for a time, that was the best for all of us. But things have changed."

My father arched an eyebrow. "Understatement of the century, Solina."

I rose and backed away until I stood at Baldur's side again. He hadn't moved, hadn't said a word. He simply waited for the world to adjust to his presence. How many times had he made himself known to humans in all of his existence? What thoughts were running through his otherworldly head at that moment?

"What I have to tell you won't be easy for either of us," I said. "Not for me to explain or for you to accept."

Mom said something incoherent, and Dad helped her stand. She leaned on her worktable beside the wedding cake she had been covering in purple roses before my sudden appearance sidelined her efforts. Several bedraggled strands of salt-and-pepper hair straggled from her chef's toque. She breathed in and out deeply, and color returned to her cheeks in a flood. She went from ghostly pale to irate red in the passing of a few heartbeats.

"How dare you," she said, her voice low and rough. She straightened and stomped her foot. "How *dare* you."

"Mom, I—"

"Showing up out of the blue like this, like nothing happened, like you haven't been presumed dead for weeks." She stepped around the edge of her worktable, her hazel eyes never leaving mine, her voice cold and bitter. "How dare you put your family through that kind of pain, after what happened to your brother. Never in my life has anyone been so cruel, so thoughtless, so inconsiderate. My own daughter. My own flesh and bloo—"

"Mom!" I shouted, cutting through her rant. Not that she wasn't right. Not that she lacked justification for the cold glint in her eyes. Not that the tears in my throat didn't burn or the shame on my shoulders sit as heavily as a full-grown elephant. All of these things were real, but none of them mattered at that moment. I raised my hand, snapped my fingers, and a flame lit at my fingertips. I raised my other hand, and a fireball filled my palm.

My mother froze mid-step, and her mouth fell open. A rusted-hinge noise squeaked from my father's throat, and he gaped at me.

"The fairytales are real," I said. "So are the nightmares. You can hate me all you want, but you have to listen to me first. Your lives depend on it."

Dad's mouth snapped shut. He swallowed. "This isn't happening. It can't be."

I raised my chin and peered down my nose at them, equally indignant for having to justify myself and ashamed for misleading them all this time. "Can you honestly tell me you never once thought there was something *different* about Mani and me?"

"Different *how?*" my mother asked. "Did we know you could... could..." She flailed her hands toward my blazing fingers.

"Before he left for Alaska, Mani sensed something was going on. Tell me you never saw shadows dance when he walked by. You didn't notice how a space he had recently occupied felt colder than the rest of the room."

My mom blinked and shook her head. "I-I..."

"You never gave credit to my dreams, the ones where I sometimes saw things before they happened."

"We thought it was coincidence."

"It was easier that way." I released my flames, and they withdrew. "I don't blame you. I dismissed it all, too, at first. But then Mani died, and I refused to ignore it anymore. I refused to explain it all away as coincidence."

"What are you saying?" my father asked. His short hair, more gray than blond these days, stood on end as he dragged his fingers across his scalp. "There's such a thing as... *magic?*"

"Call it what you will. There's more to this world than we've been led to believe. It's a long and complicated story, and I'll tell you everything, but this is not a safe place or a safe time for storytelling. I need you to come with Baldur and me now. I'm going to take you somewhere safe, and then you can ask all the questions you want."

My parents' attention turned behind me, settling, presumably, on the giant man standing still and silent, waiting for me to make my move. "Baldur?" my father asked.

I shrugged. "Or you can call him Allfather, if you like."

My mother wobbled again, but Dad tightened his arm around her

139

and held her up. Perhaps they held each other up. They both looked more than a little peaked and unsteady.

"How much do you know about Norse mythology?" I asked. My father's gaze slid to me, and his eyes narrowed. "It's not a joke, Dad. We are standing in the presence of Baldur Odinson, Allfather of the Aesir and heir of Odin's throne. He is here to take you to his home in the Sierra Nevadas. He calls it New Breidablick, but really, it's just a super-nice house near Lake Tahoe. You'll like it. The best part is the bad guys can't get you there. And I have to tell you, there are *a lot* of bad guys."

"Solina." My mom crammed so much into that single word: disbelief, outrage, fear, worry. "How can we believe you?"

"What, the fire wasn't enough? Do you want me to show you again?" I raised my hand, but my father waved me off.

"No. Just... just give us a minute to catch our breath."

"We don't have a minute, Dad."

"She's right," Baldur said. He stepped forward, and my parents flinched. He cranked up his godly mojo until an ethereal aura glowed from him, and they stared at him, wide eyed. "There are other things, other... *considerations* that must be dealt with. Solina has many responsibilities and liabilities to contemplate beyond the two of you. My home is the safest place for you, and I must insist you pack your things and come with me now."

Neither of my parents blinked, but my dad slowly bobbed his head.

"Baldur," I hissed. "What are you *doing*?"

"Being influential."

"Well, stop it. It's freaking them out."

Baldur's glow faded, and the awe on my mom and dad's faces diminished. Mom recovered first. "We can't just shut the bakery down in the middle of the holiday rush. We have outstanding orders."

"Are you for real?" I shoved a hand on my hip and gaped at her. "I just showed you I can light myself on fire. You just got a good taste of the authority and power of one of the oldest beings in existence, and you're still protesting?" I stepped closer and leaned in until she could see the veins in my eyes and feel the heat in my breath. "A mythological wolf devoured your son." My mom's face tightened, and she grimaced, but I kept going, jabbing words at her like a weapon. "And another wolf is coming after *me*. A horrible, powerful being controls those monsters, and it's very likely she'll hurt you to get to me. She wants to kill me, Mother.

"So if Mary Beth Nesslestoff has to go to Wal-Mart for her wedding cake, it won't be the end of the world, but if Helen Locke's wolf kills me, it most certainly *will* be the end of the world. And I'm not being hyperbolic."

"Well," she said, breathless and blinking. "Well..."

"Rachel." My dad leaned in until his shoulder pressed into hers. "I think we'd better listen to the girl and her, ah, friend."

She twisted to face him. "But it's so ridiculous."

He nodded. "It is. If they're lying to us for some reason, we'll work it out, but if they're telling the truth, I don't want to find out the hard way."

I glanced back and forth between my parents, waiting for someone to make a definitive decision. *Come on, come on, quit being so stubborn, Mother. Listen to me this once.*

My mother's head bobbed in the subtlest of nods, but she had given her assent, and I wouldn't let her take it back. I stepped to Baldur's side. "Get the van, Dad. We'll meet you at the house."

Baldur and I blipped away, and I hoped the dramatic nature of our departure left an impression on my parents—the kind that got them motivated to shut down the bakery and drive home as soon as possible. Baldur transported us to my front yard. I led him to the side entrance, located the hide-away key, and let us in.

We stood in awkward silence in the middle of the living room, listening to the mantel clock tick. "So..." I broke the tension. "How's Nina?"

Baldur blinked as if my question had surprised him. "Better, I think."

"Yeah?"

He nodded. "She's more relaxed. A little less twitchy." He smiled. "She teased me this morning."

"She did?"

"Called me by an old nickname. She probably thought she'd just come up with it, but it's something she's called me for centuries."

"What nickname?"

A blush rose in his fair cheeks. "Not going to tell you."

I could have poked him, teased him, but their relationship was so tenuous, it deserved my deference. "She talk about Helen much?"

"Never."

"Are you worried about their connection?"

He stiffened. "I'm not."

"How can you be so trusting?"

"Throughout the eras and epochs, Nina and I have always found each other. Helen's not going to undo that by manipulating Nina for a few dozen years. Every time, Solina... Every single time we've been apart, Nina has *always* come back to me. I've never lost her before, and I'm not going to lose her now."

I folded my arms over my chest. "You always find Nina, but what about your children? What about Embla and Skyla?" His love for Nina consumed him, and it was like some kind of biblical blood curse—wreaking havoc on his descendants. Generations of daughters and sons never knowing the truth and suffering the fallout of parents doomed to an endless destiny of reincarnation. "You could have had them with you all along. They could have helped you find her again."

A flush rose in his cheeks again—not embarrassment this time, but anger, pain, and maybe a little frustration, judging by the way he ground his teeth together. "I told you before that I realized the mistakes I've made."

"Then stop making them. Tell Skyla the truth. Reach out to Embla before it's too late."

"Who are you to advise me on such things? A little girl who's afraid of her own feelings and who's never had a child of her own."

"You're right. It's not my place to judge. But I love Skyla, and I don't want to see her hurt. And I'm afraid of Embla and the damage that's been done to her. It's going to bite you in the ass, Baldur. Sooner or later, it's going to bite us *all* in the ass."

He said nothing but instead folded his arms over his chest and gazed, unfocused, into the shadows across the room. Silence fell between us again. We stood, listening to the clock's annoying *tick-tock* until I couldn't stand it any longer. "I'm going to run upstairs and grab a few things. Make yourself at home." I pointed over his shoulder. "Kitchen's that way if you need something to drink or whatever."

My nomadic lifestyle meant I shed necessities—clothes, toiletries, personal items—faster than birds shed feathers. Baldur would let me have anything I wanted shipped to New Breidablick, but sometimes, a girl craved her old favorites, and I still had a couple of pairs of worn jeans squirreled away in my room upstairs. By the time I finished packing my few provisions, Mom and Dad had returned home. I clamored down the stairs and greeted them as they came through the door.

Mom stopped short and squeaked.

"What?" I asked.

"I'm just not used to seeing you here. And after the way you disappeared..." Mom waggled her fingers in the air like a magician showing she had nothing hidden in her hands. Her shoulders slumped, and her gaze fell to the floor. "Maybe I thought I had hallucinated the whole thing."

I approached her the way I might approach a skittish dog. She stood in place and let me wrap my arms around her. For several heartbeats, she didn't respond, but then she sighed and hugged me back. "I'm here, Mom. I'm alive, and this is very real. And I want to take you where you'll be safe for a little while. I can't apologize for misleading you or for staying away so long. The things I did were necessary and important. But I do apologize for causing you hurt. I would have prevented it if I could have, but I couldn't think of any other way."

Dad squeezed my shoulder. "We'll get through this, Solina. We're just so glad—" He paused and cleared his throat. "We're just so glad to have you back."

The three of us embraced, and Mom tried her best to swallow her sobs. My parents smelled like cake batter, spices, and comfort. After weeks of hardening myself against homesickness and longing, the relief of standing in my parents' presence again thawed my heart into a warm, gooey puddle.

"Y'all go get packed up." I cleared my throat and swabbed the damp streaks on my face. I broke from the hug and motioned to the stairs leading up to their room. "None of us should rest easy until we get to New Breidablick."

My mom's brow wrinkled, and she glanced over at Baldur. "And exactly how are we going to get there? You said it's near Lake Tahoe?"

I grinned like a used car salesman trying to sell a lemon car, not that I was trying to mislead my parents. Well, not completely, but I needed them to trust me. "There's a jet on its way to get us right now."

My mom didn't buy it. She scowled. "I don't like it, Solina."

"You don't have to like it. You just have to do it."

"C'mon, Rachel." Dad tugged her elbow. "Let's not argue with the girl. Something strange is going on, and I'd like to get to the bottom of it."

Mom let Dad lead her away. They trudged up the stairs, and Baldur and I stood in uncomfortable silence until my parents returned, toting their luggage.

"I only packed for a few days," Mom said. "Unless you convince me otherwise, we can't be away from the bakery for long. Not during the holidays."

Maybe this whole thing would end soon. We'd find the wolf and kill him, and Mom and Dad could go home and pick up with their old routine without missing a beat. And maybe the NASA rover would find little green men on Mars. "Sure, Mom. I'm sure everything will work out."

After a little more cajoling from me, Mom and Dad closed up the house and packed their luggage into their minivan. Dad climbed behind the wheel, and Mom slid into the passenger seat. Baldur eyed the van. He turned and arched an eyebrow at me. "My men will follow and see that they get there safely. You and I should go ahead to the airport and make sure everything is secure on that end."

I narrowed my eyes at him. "You just don't want to ride in the back of that minivan, do you?"

Baldur grinned. "I have my pride, Solina."

"Of course you do. You're Aesir."

I ducked into the van to explain our plans to my parents. Then I scooted out, slammed the door, and stood at Baldur's side. "See in you in a bit."

Dad's face looked pinched and pale, but he waved as he backed from the driveway. As he pulled away, two black SUVs fell in behind him. Baldur's men, I presumed. "They've been fine all this time," I said. "Why am I so nervous about letting them go now?"

"It's because you've seen them again, touched and held them. They're more real to you than they have been in a long time. You've had to put them out of your mind for the last few months, but now, they are present and tangible, and that is very hard to let go. I speak from experience."

"I've already had to let too many people go today. I'm afraid I'll never see them again. Any of them." I turned around to face Baldur. "Skyla, Thorin, my parents... Mani. I'm more alone now than I've been in a long time."

"Hey." Baldur frowned. "You still have me."

I slid my arms around his ribs and squeezed. "And you don't know how grateful I am."

Baldur chuckled and returned my hug, both for comfort and for the practical demands of teleportation. "Hold tight, Solina. Hopefully, this is the last of these kinds of trips you'll have to make today. I know you don't care for it."

"I don't know." My ears crackled, and my vision blurred. "Maybe Thorin was right. Do it enough times, and I might get used to it."

#

Baldur and I fell out of the æther near the entrance to the Wilson Private Air Center terminal, one of the small airstrips adjacent to the larger commercial airport serving Charlotte. I had once told Val I was a simple girl, and I hadn't lied, but my one experience flying coach from North Carolina to Alaska had been enough to make me appreciate the ease and comfort of a personal jet.

Although Baldur moved through space and time in an instant, Thorin's jet had to abide by the laws of earthly physics, which meant we still had most of an hour to wait before the plane arrived.

"Everything out here seems fine," I said. "No golems. No wolves. No denizens of the underworld." But it smelled plenty evil: jet fuel, asphalt, hot rubber. *Blech.*

Baldur screwed his lips sideways and snorted.

"I'm going to go in and ask if they have an ETA for the jet." I set down my bag and turned on my heel, heading for the main entrance. Before I reached the doors, however, a pair of shadows fluttered from the sky and landed at my feet in the shape of two familiar black ravens.

I stopped, shoved a hand on my hip, and rolled my eyes. "Not you two again."

One bird shivered, shaking off feathers and gaining mass, weight, and height. I glanced around the parking lot as Hugh completed his transformation, but Baldur and I had the airstrip to ourselves except for a few mechanics in coveralls who hadn't looked our way since we arrived.

"It's a little chilly for running around in your birthday suit, isn't it?" I asked.

Hugh shrugged. "What I have to say won't take long."

"That makes me think it must be bad news."

"Is there any other kind when it comes to you?" Hugh asked. Munin pecked at something near Hugh's feet, and Hugh brushed his brother aside with a gentle, bare-toed nudge. Baldur noticed our visitors' arrival and crossed the distance between us in a blink. He loomed beside me, silent and imposing.

"Allfather." Hugh sank into a deferential bow. Then he rose and stepped back several paces, presumably out of Baldur's reach, and crossed his hands in front, covering his most vulnerable body parts.

Baldur arched an eyebrow and bobbed a subtle nod of acknowledgment.

"Why don't I get straight to the point?" Hugh said. "Thorin's in trouble."

"Already?" I huffed. "That didn't take long."

His black brows drew together, forming a nearly uniform line. "I'm not joking."

"No," I said, my tone as flat as his. "Apparently not."

He flapped his hands but remembered his modesty and covered himself again. "Technically, he's not in trouble *yet*. There is still time, but you have to act now. The vision you had, the one where you saw the wolf being burned with acid, that was not Grim."

My mouth went dry. "Wh-Who was it, then?"

"It was Thorin. Or it *will be* Thorin if Val's plan works."

"Bullshit." I clenched my jaw. "As if Val could ever defeat Thorin. And if it was possible, how could Val turn Thorin into a wolf?"

A cold breeze blew past us, and Hugh's purpling skin broke out in goose bumps, or raven bumps, more accurately. Either way, he looked like a plucked chicken.

"It's already begun," he said. "It was set into motion the day Val and Thorin fought in that field outside Portland. That fight was mostly a ruse, a chance for Val to brand Thorin with the necessary runes for the transformation. He didn't complete them, though. That's what the attack at the hotel was about. Val's man, the one with the knife, he finished the inscription."

"Then why isn't Thorin already a wolf?" I asked. "Why didn't he change while we were at the Bellestrella?"

"Because," Baldur said, having reached the conclusion much faster than I, but he was the master of rune-craft, after all. "The rune must be spoken with the rune maker's intent."

Oh... he was right. Every time a rune had been used, for invisibility, for transportation, for truth seeking, the user had spoken the rune's name. When Embla had ordered Amala to carve *Ansuz* into Nate's chest, she hadn't only spoken a simple word. Her intent had permeated her directive. I'd felt the power of her will, even if I hadn't understood it in the moment.

"As soon as Val speaks the words in Thorin's presence," Hugh said, "and applies his will to those words, the transformation will be complete. Val will turn Thorin into a wolf and set him to attack his brother. Val will use Grim's sinews and guts to bind Thorin, as the Aesir once did to Narfi. *That* is what you missed in your incomplete vision."

Why are the missing puzzle pieces always the most crucial? My heart sank to my feet. My insides turned to ash. "What can I possibly do to stop him?"

"You can get to Val first. You can kill him."

I wheezed as if Hugh had slapped me. "Ah." I breathed hard. "Now I get it. You've known this all along, haven't you? You tell me this, now, when things are the most desperate. I kill Val, and you get your freedom. What if I refuse?"

Hugh's eyelids lowered, and he shook his head. "Then Val wins. Grim may not die from his wounds, and Thorin may not die from the venom. I told you before it takes a lot to kill a god. Grim and Thorin will suffer for eternity or until Helen succeeds in bringing about a second Ragnarok. You're really the only one with the means and motivation to stop Val."

I snarled and shoved my fingers through my hair. I turned on my heel and paced as Hugh's words banged around in my brain. A young couple, a pair of men close to my age, exited the terminal and glanced in our direction. Blood drained from their faces, and their mouths fell open in comical synchronization. How must we have looked: Hugh standing naked in the cold and me bleeding light and heat as I stomped back and forth like a crazy woman? I swallowed my rage and retracted my firelight.

Baldur turned and addressed the couple. "Nothing to see here, guys." He waved in a dismissive gesture. "Move along. Move along." The two young men obeyed and scurried toward the parking lot.

"Did you just Jedi mind-trick them?" I asked.

Baldur turned to me and frowned. "Jedi?"

"Never mind." I waved away my comment and met Hugh's black, birdlike stare. "Thorin has a big head start on me. Even if I agreed to do what you asked, there's no way I can get to Val before Thorin does. I can't blip through space or fly." I flapped my arms like an idiot.

Hugh's eyes cut to Baldur. "I'm sure the Allfather could get you there in a hurry. If you leave now, I'll lead you directly to Val while Thorin wastes time wandering the labyrinth of Val's cave. Thorin will find Val eventually, though. Val *wants* Thorin to find him, but he enjoys the game. Besides, Thorin doesn't have as much of a lead as you think. He played diplomat with your *völva* when he went back to pick up Skyla. He left the old seer with enough cash to pay off the loan on her RV."

Surprise froze me in place. "He did?"

Hugh nodded. "God of Thunder is a big old softie. And after he carried Skyla to the Valkyries, he took time to arrange transportation for them out to Amchitka. Got them money to restock on supplies and weapons, too."

"He did?" I said again. "Was I right about that? Are Helen and her golems there, at Amchitka?"

"If I tell you everything you want to know, what incentive do you have to help me?"

"I'm not helping *you*. I'm helping Thorin."

He shrugged. "Either way, I'm not going to let you be distracted by the Valkyries and Helen. Not at this moment. Thorin left Portland minutes ago—the four of us can still beat him to Val. Then the Allfather can return here and escort your parents to New Breidablick."

Baldur kicked a pebble and shoved his hands in his jeans pockets. "I'll follow your lead, Solina, but I don't feel good about any of this." He scowled at Hugh. "How can she trust you? How can she know you aren't setting her up in another of Val's traps?"

Hugh raised his chin, baring the pale flesh of his throat and chest. "Mark me, Allfather. I'll tell you everything again, and you'll know it for truth. But make a decision fast. Any lead we might have is quickly shrinking."

I turned to Baldur, and his big blue eyes burned into mine. What was he thinking? If I asked for his advice, what would he say? It didn't matter, though. The decision to go after Val and Thorin was one I had to make myself. "I believe him, Baldur. He said ravens are opportunists. This is what they've been waiting thousands of years for. They want their freedom, and they'll take the necessary risks to get it."

"Val could just as easily kill you," he said. "The risks Hugh takes are with *your* life."

"Val could kill me. But then, at least, the wolf wouldn't get me, and Helen's plan will fail. Hugh is also taking a risk that I'll keep him instead of setting him free when this is all said and done. And if I die at Val's hands, the ravens won't be freed. Val will know Hugh's betrayal and make him pay for it. It's in Hugh's best interests to make sure I succeed."

"Smart girl," Hugh said.

I scowled at him.

"Is saving Magni a cause worth dying for?" Baldur asked. "He wouldn't want you to do this, and if you died, he would hate me for eternity for not doing more to stop you."

"What wouldn't you do for Nina?" I asked.

He flinched. "Do you truly love him that much?"

"I don't know, but if Val's plan works, I might never have a chance to find out."

Baldur bit his lip and narrowed his eyes. Hugh exhaled a sigh that sounded like exasperation, but he held his tongue.

Finally, Baldur nodded. "Fine. I'll take you and follow the birds."

I bobbed my head and fought the urge to curtsy. "Thank you, Allfather."

"I'd say it's my pleasure, but it's not. I'm certain this is a huge mistake, but I also understand your motivations, possibly better than anyone else. If anyone can save Magni, it's you." Baldur rolled his shoulders and stretched his neck until it popped in a very human way. He opened his arms wide, and I stepped into his embrace.

"Can the birds blip through space the way you do?" I asked.

Baldur exhaled. "They don't need to. They can fly faster than anything you've ever seen."

"Where do you think they'll take us?"

"Back to Alaska. It's where Odin and the others found Loki when he went into hiding."

I groaned, thinking of the long, dizzying journey. I threw my arms around Baldur's neck and closed my eyes. "Let's go before I change my mind."

CHAPTER 16

How did soldiers do it? How did they stand on the battlefield, crawl through the jungle, or crouch in the desert, guns locked and loaded, enemy waiting over the next rise, behind the next tree, on the rooftop? How did they face the inevitability of battle, bloodshed, killing, and death? How did they do that and keep their humanity and sanity?

Sometimes, they don't. What do you think PTSD is? Saving Thorin might mean sacrificing a part of yourself. Are you sure he's worth it?

My ears popped, and Baldur and I dropped hard on cold, rocky ground. I grunted and sank to my knees, driven by the force of our landing.

"Sorry about that." He helped me stand again.

My jaw ached. I had ground my teeth for the entirety of the journey. I sucked a deep breath and forced my teeth to unclench.

Baldur scrubbed his hands over his face. "We've done a lot of this today, and it's wearing on me."

Both in their bird forms again, Hugin and Munin alighted before us and faced the mouth of a cavern nearly identical to the one in my dreams. A massive waterfall fell in a curtain behind us, shielding the cave's entrance from outside viewers. It left us a few feet of a cold rocky beach on which to stand without getting drenched. Hugin flapped his wings and squawked as if to say, *This is the way. Let's go.*

"You have enough juice left to get to the airport and meet my parents?" I asked.

Baldur brushed an unruly forelock from his brow. "Yes. And some to spare, but I won't deny I'm looking forward to travelling by conventional means for a while."

"I can't thank you enough—"

Baldur waved aside my gratitude. "There are no favors between us. We're working together to ensure each other's survival and success. Guarding your parents means you're free to focus on what's to come. And I'm afraid what's to come will be mostly terrible for you. If you survive or if you don't, either way, you won't be the same woman you were before you went into this cave."

I swallowed and nodded. "I'm afraid, too. I'm afraid of what I will have to do, what I'll have to become."

Baldur's eyes shone as bright as the blue Alaskan sky beyond the waterfall curtain. The time changes from east coast to west had bought me several more hours of daylight, although the position of the sun mattered little in the belly of a cave. "You can still change your mind," he said. "I'll take you to New Breidablick."

"To do what? Hide behind your runes and wards while Thorin goes crazy from suffering? Hide until I grow old and die?" I bit my lip and shook my head. My throat burned from unshed tears. "No." I cleared my throat. "I can't do that, either." I turned and faced the cave. Hugin hopped forward into the shadows and cawed again. It sounded urgent and impatient. "Get my mom and dad. Keep them safe. Tell them I love them. Tell them I never meant for any of this to happen. Tell them—"

"I'll tell them everything, Solina. Everything. They'll know the truth. They'll know your bravery and honor and loyalty." He raised his voice over the roar of the waterfall. "Hear me now, ravens. If you betray Solina, if you break her trust in any way, I will hunt you down. I will stuff you and make you the newest additions to my trophy room."

Hugin and Munin squawked in unison and hopped further into the cave.

I said nothing and kept my back to Baldur. Leaving him hurt much less than leaving my brother at the well, but it wasn't easy. I took a tentative step forward. The frozen ground—rocks and scraggly little weeds mostly—crackled beneath my feet.

"Bring Magni home," Baldur said. My ears popped, and he was gone.

I raised a hand and lit it with enough fire to light the way, and I hurried after the ravens, moving as fast as possible over the uneven floor. "Can anyone say *déjà vu*?" My voice echoed off the cavern walls: "*vu, vu, vu...*" Further down the way, a raven cawed.

Unlike the cavern in my vision quest, this one neither wound in corkscrews nor sloped at a noticeable angle. It did, however, exude the same dank mineral odor and impenetrable blackness. It extended into the same never-ending, repetitious terrain. "I guess once you've seen one stalagmite, you've seen 'em all."

One of the birds squawked again, presumably urging me to shut up and move faster. I obliged. Not that I was anxious to reunite with Val again—or fight him if it came down to it. *But I will, if I have to. I will...* Maybe if I told myself that enough times, I would believe it.

Every so often, Hugin or Munin slowed enough to allow me a glimpse of a wing or tail feather, reflecting my firelight. They led me on a twisting and turning path along which I would never find my way back without help. If they abandoned me here, I'd be lost. I fingered the golden chain around my neck: Mjölnir's lanyard. Thorin could find me if he used the hammer to track the lanyard, but I had a feeling he'd lose the will necessary to maintain possession of the hammer the moment he changed into a wolf. The hammer might still find me, as it had before at Mount Rainier, but without Thorin to wield Mjölnir, what use did any of us have for it?

I rounded another corner and ran smack into Hugh's bare back. I choked on a squeal, but even my garbled gasp echoed in the darkness.

"Shhh," he said. "An elephant makes less noise than you."

"Sorry," I whispered. "We can't all grow feathers on a whim. Why did we stop?"

"Thorin's here." His head twitched like a curious bird's. "Has *been* here. He's moving faster than I would have guessed, almost as if he knows where he's going, but he doesn't. Not consciously anyway. Either he's lucky, or it's instinctual. Something to do with brotherly bonds, maybe?"

"Will we make it in time?"

"If we fly."

"Then being quiet and sneaky doesn't matter, much, does it? If you don't get me there in time to save Thorin, our deal is moot. If I kill Val..." Bitterness pooled on my tongue, but I swallowed my disgust. "If

I have to kill Val to save myself, I will. But if Thorin is turned, I won't let you go. I'll keep you to myself."

He bared his teeth at me. "The vastness of our knowledge could destroy your mind."

"Don't underestimate me, *bird*." I poked his skinny chest. "And you'd better get us there before it's too late."

Hugh mumbled something under his breath but raised his voice so I could hear the next part. "I'm going to fly fast. Do your best to keep up."

He shivered, throwing off his human form like so much dust. He flapped once and shot off in a glossy black streak, joining his brother, who swooped from the shadows overhead. I sprinted after them and tried my best to keep my feet beneath me, despite the uneven floor.

We ran long enough for my heart to throb and my lungs to burn from the effort. The ravens never stopped for a break, and I never asked for one. Whatever awaited me, whatever came next, I sprinted toward it without hesitation, without questioning. It was the same way I'd learned to ski. Mani and I had cut our teeth on the little slopes in the North Carolina mountains. If I stood too long at the start of a steep slope, I would psych myself out and lose my courage, so I had learned to never hesitate. I jumped off from the lift, headed for the run, and shoved myself over the edge without stopping. No uncertainty, no planning my attack, just go and try not to die.

I ran toward Val the same way: no uncertainty, no planning my attack, just go. And try not to die.

Don't think...

Just act.

Just survive.

Get in, do what you must, and get out alive.

The ravens and I rounded another corner into a long, narrow passage. A dim light shone from the other end. I threw on a burst of speed, lowered my head, and charged forward, a silent war cry burning in my chest. The hallway curved and spilled into a small room, one with a ceiling not much higher than my head and walls slightly wider than double the span of my arms. A simple kerosene camping lantern sat on a rock ledge, and it illuminated a metal cage squatting in one corner, a prison the size of several large dog crates stacked together.

A man's nude and limp body lay curled upon itself on the cage's small floor. His hair mostly covered his face, but red welts and dark bruises stood out on the pale skin over his ribs and spine. Despite my animosity for Grim, my heart sank at the sight of him. Maybe I should have reveled in karma's justice, but nothing about his sorry, broken body inspired my glee.

A shadow shifted in the room's opposite corner, and I shrank from it. "Rolf," I said. He wore the features of the dark-haired man to whom I had served drinks in a bar in San Diego not long ago. He was the man I'd battled in an alley behind that same bar. He was also the man who had once been my brother's best friend—a man who had betrayed us all for an ancient vendetta.

"Or do you prefer Val?" I asked. "You *are* Vali Lokison, right?" My voice came out calm and controlled despite the blizzard freezing my bones and the desert burning in my throat. My vision narrowed until it encompassed only him, and my blood thrummed against my ears until I thought my head might explode. *Keep it together, girl. Keep it together.*

A flicker of surprise crossed his face before he forced his features into a cool, neutral expression. His violet eyes glanced behind me, and a nasty grin split his lips. "You little birdbrain twits. I knew this day would come, but the two of you putting all your faith in her..." He gestured in my direction. "That's something I would have never guessed."

The ravens, perched on a rock ledge behind me, kept their silence as well as their feathers—the better to make a hasty escape if things went bad.

He raised his eyes to mine, and his cold smile thawed a little. "There's a small part of me that regrets this, Solina. I don't guess that matters to you, but it's true. I really did care for your brother. Might have loved him, in another place and time where I was still capable of such a thing." He shrugged as if to say, *Not that it matters, now.*

I gagged but recovered after a brief coughing fit. "How can you say you cared about Mani when you knew Helen was going to kill him, and you did nothing to stop it?"

He pressed his palm against his chest and bared his teeth. "I loved *my* brother, and I did nothing to stop *his* death." He pulled his fingers through his long black hair. "I killed Narfi myself. What does the death of anyone else mean in comparison?"

The little bit of compassion I still harbored for Val surged through me. My whole body slumped, and nothing appealed to me more than melting to the floor in a puddle of despair. My heart ached for all the lost brothers and the broken siblings left behind to mourn them, but I had cried enough for all of them. I stiffened my shoulders and straightened my spine. I raised my chin and peered down my nose. "I'm not going to let you do this."

He sniffed and thinned his lips into a sardonic grin. One black eyebrow flickered. "I can see how much you believe that. You think you'll do what you must to stop me, but belief is only the potential for action. Potential and reality aren't the same thing."

"I've killed before."

"Hati was a stranger to you and a beast." He rubbed his face as if washing it—washing the Rolf away. When he lowered his hands, a familiar face smiled back at me. Blue eyes instead of violet. Auburn hair instead of black. "You'll have to give yourself over to Sol to do it—to kill me. You'll have to let yourself go and lose control again. Can you do that? And can you kill someone you were in love with only a few weeks ago?"

"I never loved you. Not like that."

Val snorted. "You cared for me."

"As much as you cared for my brother, I suppose." Not complete honesty—I had more than cared for Val, but analyzing the truth of the feelings I once harbored for him would have cost me too much in a time when I needed to avoid vulnerabilities.

His thin smile fell. "Touché."

"Please." I stepped toward him, hand outstretched. Val had once said people believed lies because they were easy, and I had told him I refused to accept anything but truth. It would have been easier to believe Val was once the man he pretended to be, but none of that had been real. *Don't forget that.* "Please don't do this. Don't make *me* do this. It's not too late. There's still redemption for you if you want it."

His face crumpled into a mask of agony and rage. "Who's going to give it to me? You? You just accused me of letting your brother die. You weren't wrong about that. 'The only thing necessary for the triumph of evil is for good men to do nothing.' The only trouble is, I'm not a good man. There's nothing to redeem."

His expression softened as his anger drifted away. Val's mood was like a summer storm, quick to thunder and rage but equally quick to dissipate. "If there's anyone who can empathize with me, it's you, Solina." He crossed to the cage, crouched, and pushed a finger between the slim bars, poking at the figure inside. Grim moaned and pulled away. "Put yourself in my shoes. Would you surrender your quest? Would you forgive?"

"Or destroy myself for vengeance like you?" I asked. "Mortality puts a limit on my suffering. I have to let it go at some point if I'm going to get any happiness out of the short time I'm given to live. But if I was immortal, if the hurt could go on forever..." *Well, then I could see where it would be hard to let it go.* "You never found a reason to live? To move on?"

Val huffed and gave a sad smile. "Maybe if Mani and you had come along a few millennia ago... But, no, it's endless. It's eternal suffering. It's *hell.*"

"Will revenge on Thorin and Grim end that for you?"

"That answer requires rational thinking. I've been beyond rationality for a long time."

"If this has been your lifelong motivation, what will you do with yourself when it's done?"

Val chuckled. "Damned if I know. Maybe I'll ask Hela to kill me. Feed me to her snake or something."

I inhaled, preparing to ask about the truth of that possibility, but the crunch of rocks beneath a heavy footstep silenced me. The smell of storms and lightning filled the room, and a weighty groan exhaled behind me. Electricity, one searing pulse, shot through every nerve in my body.

"Sunshine." Thorin said my nickname as though it were a curse. "Why am I not surprised?"

I kept my attention focused on Val. If he opened his mouth to speak, to put his will into the runes infecting Thorin, I would have to act fast.

"My vision was wrong. Well, not wrong, just incomplete. Your brother isn't the wolf."

"Huh. I can see that." Thorin moved behind me, close enough for his body heat to warm me, for his breath to tickle my cheek and ear—close enough for me to see, in the periphery of my vision, Mjölnir raised and ready in his fist. "But if it wasn't Grim you saw, I have to presume it was someone else. I'm guessing it was me. *I* am the wolf. This was the endgame all along."

"He simply has to speak the runes." I focused my darkest stare on Val. "But I won't give him that chance."

Val licked his lips and opened his mouth. I cut him off before he could speak. "No!" I raised a handful of fire overhead. "You don't get to say another word. I told you I wouldn't let you do this. Open your mouth again, and I'll show you where you can stuff your *potential.*"

He snapped his mouth shut and narrowed his eyes at me. His nostrils flared. A muscle worked in his jaw. Not for a second did I think we had reached an impasse. This was a duel, a showdown between three gunslingers at high noon with their hands poised over pistol grips. Who was the fastest in town? Me and my fire? Thorin and his hammer? Val and his mouth?

"Last chance, Val," I said. "It's two against one. You could give this up. I promise to let you go if you turn right now and walk away."

Val sneered but held his tongue.

"No," Thorin said. "He doesn't get to walk away. This ends now."

He drew back the hammer, but before he released it, Val's voice ripped from his throat like a lion's roar. "*Hagalaz!*"

Thorin grunted and stumbled, and the concussion of Mjölnir hitting the floor shook the cavern. In response to his distress, my fire exploded from within me, coating me in heat and flame. He fell to his knees and clawed at his chest as if trying to free something trapped beneath his sternum, but he maintained his human shape.

It must be more than one rune. Val's not finished yet.

"Please!" I begged. "What do you want? I'll give you anything. *Anything.*"

"Give me my brother back."

I'd demanded the same thing from Nate, knowing it was impossible.

I had nothing Val wanted. We both knew it, but panic made me ask like a magician saying the magic words to reveal something that hadn't been there before. But real magic didn't work that way, and no matter how badly I wished otherwise, Val's brother was no rabbit in a hat.

"Take away my guilt." Bitterness ravaged his voice.

I stepped toward him, hand outstretched as if reaching for a man who had fallen overboard and was drowning. If Val hadn't found his own forgiveness by now, he certainly wasn't going to accept my lame absolutions. But still I tried. "I don't blame you. No one blames you. It wasn't your fault."

"No. It was *his*," Val hissed through clenched teeth, pointing at Thorin. "*Inguz!*"

Thorin bowed over, panting and grunting as his shoulders shook. Val turned and met my stare, daring me. He inhaled, preparing to speak another word—the final rune, judging by the satisfied sneer on his face. I closed my eyes and something inside me—Innocence? Hope? Virtue?—withered and died. As the first syllable escaped Val's lips, I threw myself on him and sent my walls crashing down.

The goddess inside me leapt free, and she rejoiced.

"Do it," Val snarled as we fell to the cave floor together. "Do it fast."

"What about all your plans? What about your revenge?"

"If you can make it stop, then do it. End my pain, Solina. You may be the only one who can."

"Get out, Thorin!" I yelled. "Get Grim and get out *now*."

My fire flared, rising hundreds of degrees in an instant. Instead of recoiling, Val cried out and pulled me closer. We both screamed, him begging for it to end, me signaling a fiery release.

Star light,
Star bright,
Supernova,
Goodnight.

CHAPTER 17

I BOLTED UPRIGHT, TURNED MY FACE into the crook of my elbow, and sneezed hard, twice. I blinked and rubbed my eyes until my vision cleared, not that there was much to see in the gloom. Hazy starlight and a moon half concealed by clouds shone through a pair of glass doors across from me, and the perspective suggested I sat somewhere high up. *The Aerie?*

I sniffed, rubbed my nose on my T-shirt sleeve, and balled my hands in my lap—a lap filled with... fur? I stroked the heavy covers drawn over my bare legs. The softness beneath my fingertips was, in fact, some sort of animal pelt—something warm, velvety, and dead. "Ugh." I sneezed again. I kicked off the covers, and chilly air skimmed my legs.

I heard the soft rustle of someone moving nearby. "Sunshine?" Thorin asked, his voice low, quiet, and uncertain. He rose from a chair beside the bed and settled on the mattress beside me. Soft light from a fireplace flickered on his face.

I sat up straighter. "Where are we?"

"I call it Lopteldr. It's my home."

My heart stilled. So did my breathing. Bruce Wayne might as well have told me he had brought me to his Bat Cave. "You-Your *home*?"

"That a problem?"

I cleared my throat. "No. I'm surprised you didn't take us to New Breidablick." I was surprised to be anywhere at all, actually. I'd let Sol free and given the fire complete rein. Last time I did that, I'd spent four weeks in some alternate state in which I wasn't aware of myself.

He found my hand in my lap and twined his fingers between mine. "We can go to New Breidablick if you prefer, but I thought you might

160

like to have a little less company. Fewer people asking questions and demanding answers from you."

Sharp memories pressed against the thin fabric of my mind, threatening to make me remember, but I pushed against them. *I'm not ready to remember. Not yet.* "How did we get here? I was sure..." I stopped and swallowed. "I was sure I'd be a star by now."

Thorin's silhouette ducked its head. "The geologists will probably say there was an earthquake—something volcanic, maybe. Anyway, there's a river in Alaska flowing on a different path now. It used to run above the cavern, but there was a cave-in and the river, um, sank, I guess you could say. There's no more waterfall either, which is a shame. It was a lovely waterfall."

"Earthquake?" I gasped. "Is that a euphemism for the God of Thunder and his hammer?"

"Someone had to put you out, Sunshine."

"So you doused me? With a river?"

He ducked his head. "There was a moment when I wasn't sure it would be enough."

"You're not a wolf."

He looked up and arched an eyebrow, questioning my non sequitur.

"Val didn't have time to speak the last word, but who's to say someone else couldn't finish what he started?"

Thorin scowled. "Someone would have to have his same, specific intent, which is highly unlikely. You, me, and the ravens are the only ones who know what Val was planning." His lips spread into a suggestive grin. "There are ways you could turn me into your personal, slavering beast, Solina, but you wouldn't have to use magic runes to do it."

Fire erupted in my cheeks. I glanced away, unable to meet his eyes. Despite my aversion to the furs, I tugged the bedcovers over my legs and relished the instant warmth. "You don't believe in heating and air conditioning? This place is an ice box." I rubbed my arms for emphasis.

Thorin chuckled and stood. "I haven't been here in weeks. It'll take some time for the house to come back to life." He crossed the room, crouched before the fireplace, and tossed in another log.

Mindlessly, I stroked the fur coverings and took in the details of the room, the stone fireplace, the oak paneling, the plain, heavy furniture. "Is this *your* room?"

Still crouched before the fireplace, feeding more wood to the flames, Thorin glanced back at me and nodded. "It is."

I patted the mattress. "Why the big fancy bed for a guy who rarely sleeps?"

He cleared his throat. "Beds can be useful for other things."

A blush erupted on my cheeks, and I quickly changed the subject. "How long have we been here?"

"Half a day. It's almost dawn, but it's Alaska, and it's winter, so the nights are long."

It made sense. He probably lived somewhere close to Siqiniq and his sporting goods store. "Where's Grim?"

"New Breidablick."

"Oh? I had gotten the impression he preferred to avoid Baldur. And that maybe the feeling was mutual."

"Grim didn't have much say in the matter. He wasn't in a state to argue, and one thing about Baldur is he'll never turn away anyone in need. His grace is infinite. Always has been."

"I'm starting to appreciate that fact. Grim won't be a threat to my parents' safety, will he?"

Thorin shook his head. "As soon as he's well enough, he'll leave. He promised me."

"And you believe him?"

"My brother might be a bastard, but his word is good." The fire popped, crackled, and threw dancing shadows over the room. He used a poker to readjust several logs before tossing another piece of wood on the stack. The silence thickened, and it seemed as though he had something to say but was hesitant, which was unlike him. Finally, he cleared his throat and turned to face me. "It's bad enough you keep running headlong toward death, Solina. But you keep convincing Baldur to give you a ride so you can get there faster."

I blanched, and my stomach rolled over. "Don't go there. Not yet. I don't want to fight with you." *And I don't want to think about what happened in the cave any more than I have to right now. Or ever, maybe.*

Thorin rose and moved to my side. He crouched beside me and took one of my hands in his. "We both know I want to lock you up in a box, but I've come to accept you'll never be that kind of woman. I think I wouldn't respect you if you were." He grinned and rolled his eyes. "I might relax and breathe a little easier if you were. My life would be a hell of a lot easier if you were..."

I squeezed his hand. "But it wouldn't be nearly as much fun, right?"

"Fun? Is that what you call this?"

"I call it living. And for a lot of years, I wasn't doing that. I was just getting by. This is the most alive I've ever been."

"This is the closest to death you've ever been, too."

"Funny how those seem to go hand in hand."

"Yeah. Funny," he deadpanned.

I shrugged and changed the subject again. "Skyla and the Valkyries? Have you heard anything?"

His lips thinned. "Socked in. Too much fog and a bad storm in the area. They're camped out in a little town called King Salmon, waiting for it to clear up enough for them to catch a flight out."

My heart and my head cared more about Skyla's fate than my stomach did. It let loose an angry, empty rumble. Thorin chuckled and rose up to his full height. "I stocked the refrigerator for you."

"More gourmet staples?" I threw off the covers again. The roaring fire had chased away the chill and brought a coziness to the room. Still, I preferred not to parade around Thorin's house in nothing but an oversized T-shirt. I turned, set my feet on the floor, and leaned forward, preparing to stand. "I've lost count of the number of times—" A bolt of white-hot pain sheared through my head, stealing my vision in a blinding burst of light. Then came a litany of scrambled images, like an old-fashioned newsreel on fast forward.

What is this? My visions don't usually work this way.

Thorin caught me as I groaned and sank to my knees. "What is it?"

"A-A headache." Another wave of heat and light washed over me. My stomach revolted. "I think I'm going to be sick."

"Hold on." He scooped me up. I clamped my eyes shut and breathed through the pain as he carried me from the warm bedroom into a cold, echoing space. "Is this okay? The bathroom's the first place I could think of."

My stomach turned over again, and I gagged. "Put me down, and leave me alone for a second, okay?"

"Sunshine," he said, nagging.

"Let me save my dignity as much as possible."

"I don't care—"

"Well, I do."

He hesitated, but he set me down on a cold tile floor. I pried open one eye, spotted a sparkling white commode, and said a little prayer of thanks as I knelt before it and prepared myself for the worst. He opened a small closet in the corner and pulled out a plush white towel that must have been woven by angels from fibers made of clouds. He shook it out and handed it to me. "The floor has got to be freezing."

I arranged the towel under my knees as another cramp twisted my stomach. "Go, please. I'll be okay."

"I'll be outside if you need me."

For a reply, I leaned over the toilet and retched as another torrent of fire burned through my skull. More images flashed before my eyes, random and lasting only an instant before fading away. I heaved and heaved and must have coughed up a lung and most of my intestines in the process, but, eventually, the cramps subsided, leaving me weak and shaky.

The headache eased, not disappearing, but diminishing to a bearable throb. I rolled off my knees, leaned against the cabinet beneath the sink, and panted. When my muscles stopped trembling, I worked my way onto my feet, leaned over the sink, and turned the cold water on full blast. I splashed my face, washed out my mouth, and drank until the acid burn in my throat faded.

"What the hell was that about?" I asked the woman staring at me in the mirror over the sink. Straggly haired and sallow skinned, my reflection shrugged limply and said, "Could be something to do with your fire. Could be something to do with the ravens..." I shoved that thought aside to deal with later. For now, I needed normalcy. And food.

A huge robe made from the same heavenly material as Thorin's towels hung from a hook on the bathroom door. I slid it on and cinched the belt around my hips. The hem dragged on the floor like the train of the ugliest wedding gown ever, but it blocked the cold air and trapped in my body heat, so... *Winner, winner, chicken dinner.*

When I opened the door, Thorin waited for me on the other side, holding a giant mug of coffee. A host of seraphim sang a song of heavenly praise in his name. "Please say that's for me," I said.

"Of course."

I grabbed the mug and gulped.

He gave me an unconvincing smile. "You gonna die on me, Sunshine?"

"Not today. Although my head is trying its best to roll off my shoulders."

"Food should help you feel better. C'mon, I'll make you some eggs."

I scoffed and followed him out of the bedroom. "The God of Thunder can cook?"

"I didn't say it would be a five-course meal."

"Eggs are harder than most people think. Mess 'em up, and they taste like rubber."

"Lots of butter and milk," he said. "That's the key."

Barefooted and bundled in a bathrobe ten sizes too big for me, I sat at Thorin's kitchen counter gobbling a plate full of surprisingly good scrambled eggs and toast coated in butter and honey. A month ago, if he had brought me to his house, I might have demanded to leave right away, balking at the intimacy and familiarity it would have insinuated. But being here, now, felt less like invading his inner sanctum and more like finding solace and comfort, as if I belonged here. Plush, but not ridiculously opulent, his house was the home of a *real* man, not a detached and distant god—a man who connected with the world on a human level, a man who connected with *me* on a human level.

I stirred my fork through the remaining dregs of eggs and toast crumbs. "How can you be an ancient deity and be so real at the same time?"

Thorin ran his finger around the rim of his coffee cup and frowned. "What do you mean?"

"This is a real house." I gestured to the ordinary kitchen and living room. "It's lovely and elegant, but it's not a palace, a lair, or an ice castle in the sky."

He huffed a quiet laugh. "Ice castle?"

"I just mean there are no pretenses here. No affectations. No magical anomalies, either."

He arched an eyebrow. "You expected something different?"

I set down my fork and shoved my plate aside. "I had no expectations, honestly. It never crossed my mind that I might ever be in your house. You might as well have said I would stand at the top of Mount Everest. Not because it's unattainable, just... highly unlikely."

He snorted. "I won't deny my existence is complicated in this realm. I am a simple man at heart, though. I want simple things. They are not always granted to me."

"I know how to complicate your peaceful existence, don't I?"

His eyes blazed as he took my hand and laced my fingers between his. "Solitude brought me peace, but you have brought me fire and passion—things I hadn't felt in a very long time. I'll never let you apologize for that. I wouldn't give it back, even if I could."

"I'm afraid I'll only bring you disappointment, Thorin."

"I've taken whatever you've given me, and you've never given me disappointment. I only ask for what you're willing to give."

"And that's enough for you?"

"Your being here, alive and well in my home? It's enough."

"For now," I muttered.

He heard me, though, and said, "Yes. *For now.*"

After a whole conversation that wasn't really a conversation about our future together, Thorin took me on a tour, proving just how real and mundane he liked his accommodations. Lots of hardwood, lots of stone, thick rugs and leather sofas—his house reminded me of New Breidablick but on a smaller scale. He showed me his weight room in the basement and a game room with pool and poker tables. Then he took me upstairs to what he said was his favorite place in the house.

He ushered me into an area with walls constructed entirely of bookshelves, all packed to the brim. "There's not many *New York Times* bestsellers in here, but you might find something to amuse you."

I ran a finger over a binding, not as old as some, but not new either. *Ulysses*, James Joyce. I sniffed.

"What?" he asked.

I slid the book out from its shelf and showed him the cover. "As if."

"You think in the past five hundred years, I haven't come across a little free time every now and then?"

"But *Ulysses*?"

"You ever read it?"

"I have nothing to prove. Give me Dickens or Hemingway if I have to read a classic. Shakespeare, even." I slid the book into place on its shelf and moved to another row. "Makes a good paperweight, though."

"But have you ever tried it?"

"Unlike you, I don't have thousands of years to kill. I read things for enjoyment and possibly for education, but never to prove my eruditeness."

"You think I'm erudite?"

I turned and found him pulling a face, eyes crossed, tongue out. It was so unlike him, and it utterly undid me. Despite my best effort not to, I laughed. His face softened. He stepped closer and cupped my jaw. "I wondered how long it would be before I heard that sound again."

I shrugged him off and leaned closer to read a faded title bound in leather. "*Apology*?"

"Plato."

"Jeez, and I thought Joyce was a heavy hitter."

"I was there the day Socrates gave that speech."

I arched an eyebrow. "The heck you say?"

"Look at the Greek pantheon, and see how very closely their gods resemble the Norse ones."

"So, you mean... " The possibilities made my head hurt.

"I only mean there's nothing new under the sun."

I tried to make him elaborate, but he evaded my interrogation with noncommittal grunts and shrugs. I let it go and moved to a shelf supporting a collection of books that appeared to have come from the decades closer to my short lifespan. "*The Lord of the Rings*?" I considered it for a moment. "Did you ever meet Tolkien?"

"Maybe."

"Give him some suggestions?"

"He researched his own sources."

"Like what?"

Thorin tilted his head. He tapped a finger to his jaw. A light sparked in his eyes, and he went to a shelf where he drew out several books. "Here, look at these."

I accepted his offerings and flipped through the covers, all textbook types, but contemporary enough. At least they were written in twentieth-century English and not Norse, Latin, or Middle English. Thorin pointed to one in particular. "Start with that one. Learn a little something, maybe."

After I showered and dressed from a bag of clothes that had clearly made the transfer from New Breidablick, I curled up on the sofa with my borrowed collection of books, and Thorin left me to read in peace. As I flipped through the pages, I practiced forming fireballs in my palm. The effort helped hone my control and eased my headache. A palm full of fire was the most I had managed, but my strength was returning.

Manipulating my fire put me in a paradoxical situation, though. Anger lurked like a living thing under my skin, squirming, wriggling, trying to get out. It lived close to my fire, wrapped itself around it, entwined with it. Each handful of flames brought out my fury. Memories seeped in, ones I had tried all day to ignore: Val screaming in my ear, the charred smell of his burning flesh, the surrender in his voice when he had asked me to make his pain stop.

Damn him for using me that way. And damn me for letting him.

My blood pressure soared. My temples throbbed. In a sudden fit of pique, I growled and slung a textbook at the nearest wall. The book hit with a satisfying *thunk* and clattered to the floor. I picked up another book and threw it. I stood and spun around, looking for something else to throw, and found Thorin standing on the threshold. Confusion drew his face into sharp angles. I nearly missed slinging a book against his head. Good thing he had quick reflexes.

"Solina? What's going on?"

"What do you think?" I palmed another fireball and touched it to another book. *Hope it isn't priceless.* I flung the burning missile at him, expecting him to take the hint and leave me to let my anger consume me alone.

It didn't work. He narrowed his eyes, shook his head, and flashed across the room. He plowed into me, tackling me onto the sofa. I laughed like an insane idiot, but deep down I was glad he stopped me. I couldn't have done it myself. The laughter turned to sobs. Thorin held me and let me cry.

—◆—

Later, when my tears had run dry, Thorin rolled over and pulled me to him, fitting me to his side so his shoulder pillowed my head. "I didn't know I was arming you when I gave you those books."

I couldn't say anything, couldn't even crack a joke. *I am such a fool.*

"Do you want to talk about it?"

I snorted.

"Do you want to listen to me talk instead?"

I gnawed my lip for a moment. "'Bout what?"

"About the days after Ragnarok."

"Okay. But why?"

"I'm not without empathy, Solina. I might understand a little about the way you're feeling right now." His deep voice reverberated as if a giant purring cat had sidled up next to me. He stroked my back, and I melted against him. As he talked about the devastation he had suffered, he let down his walls and let me see it in his memories.

Standing before the hearth fire of a rustic kitchen, a woman in a long woolen dress lugs a small child onto her hip. Eir... and Joren. Strands of pale hair have loosened from the knot at the nape of her neck, and a purple smudge near her neckline matches the violet smears around the little boy's grinning mouth—evidence of his recent bilberry feast. Joren clutches at beads strung across the yoke of Eir's dress. Circles of exhaustion darken the skin beneath her eyes, but her smile is bright and genuine. At the sight of her holding his boy, Thorin's heart swells. His chest aches with the strain of containing the immensity of his love.

A blackened house frame, smoldering timbers, charred rubble—nothing remains of his home or its occupants. Something glints in the cinders, and Thorin crouches to examine it. He finds a brooch among the soot and ashes. Although the fire has melted and deformed the piece, he remembers it clearly: a pair of bronze deer, a stag and a doe forming an endless circle. Heads butted together, the deer had stared into each other's eyes. He had given the piece to Eir on their wedding day as a symbol of his vows. The melted brooch is the only thing of hers that remains, and he clings to it as though it might lead him to her again. His heart, once so swollen full of pride and love, hangs empty in his chest, crushed, dried, and useless.

"I didn't know." I forced the words past the lump rising in my throat.

"No. It's not in the legends or history books." Thorin assured me only on the rarest instances, like now, could he bear talking about them. He spoke of his anger and how it drove a wedge between him and his brother—how it had crippled him for years.

"How'd you get past it? How did you ever recover?"

"I didn't." He shook his head. "You don't recover, but you learn to cope. Or else you give up. You've talked about me being a relic, and you're right. Sometimes, it's easier to retreat from the world than to engage with it and risk the pain that's bound to come. But you also miss the joy. After all these years, you'd think I would know more about living, but it never gets easier. You have to decide, every day, if it's worth it or not."

I wound a finger in a loose tendril of his hair. "You've had a lot of days of deciding it's worth it."

His shoulder shrugged beneath me. "After a while, it becomes habit. You realize there are things you can accept and endure"—his arm tightened around me—"and things you can never let go of at any cost. It wasn't supposed to be like this for you, Sunshine. You are a creature of light and were never meant to know darkness like you've suffered. It's going to leave a bad scar, but you'll heal if you let yourself. You'll heal faster if you'll accept the grace of those who care about you."

I took a deep breath and exhaled. "I haven't survived all these horrible things so I could waste the rest of my life being scared of my own shadow. But that doesn't mean I'm ready to have group therapy time."

"No." He chuckled. "But we should probably find a more productive way for you to vent."

I ducked my face against his side. He stroked my hair, heedless of my embarrassment. "I would let you tear this house down, piece by piece, if it made you feel better."

"It doesn't make me feel better. I just don't know what else to do with these feelings."

"You can use my workout room. I have one of those fighting dummies you seemed to like so much at the Aerie. You can take it out on him."

"I killed him," I said, not talking about the fighting dummy. "How do I live with that?"

"You brought him peace. You saved my brother and me."

"I don't know if that's enough."

Thorin held his breath, and I sensed him searching for the words that would fix this, fix me. Those words didn't exist, though, and he must have realized it, because he exhaled without saying anything. Instead he just held me, and I let him.

CHAPTER 18

THORIN DID HIS BEST TO keep me distracted for the rest of the day. He loaned me a knit hat and a wool peacoat that fit me like a dress, and we hiked the circumference of the private island on which he'd built his home. He explained *Lopteldr* meant "lightning" in his ancient tongue, and sitting high up on a summit in the middle of the little island, his house certainly looked like something that attracted the attention of storms and squalls.

When the wind and cold had me calling for mercy, he led me inside and kept me company while I warmed up on hot chocolate and a grilled cheese sandwich. Then he took me out for a cruise of Resurrection Bay on his fishing skiff. The beauty and majesty of the snowy peaks surrounding the bay made my heart stutter with awe. A peaceful reverence bathed my wounded spirit. I blessed him for understanding my need to absorb it all in silence. A person could heal in such a place. Maybe that's why he'd brought me here.

"You should probably call and check in with your parents," Thorin said. "Let them know you're okay. I'm not so sure they took my word for it."

I closed my eyes and leaned into the frigid breeze blowing off the water, letting it numb me, starting with my nose and cheeks and moving inward. "Is it wrong of me for not wanting to face them yet? I've done what I can for now to make them safe. But how do I look them in the eye? How do I pretend I'm still the daughter they think they know and love?"

"You don't have to face them yet. But you should probably give them some reassurance. They deserve that much at least. Don't you think?"

"You're probably right." I didn't sound very convincing.

Thorin drew back on the boat's throttle and shifted into neutral, leaving the engines to idle as he drew me into his embrace. I sank into his warmth. "I would have chosen differently for you. I would have chosen the suffering if it saved you from this. You asked for my protection, and I failed you."

I looked into his eyes, losing myself in his warm brown gaze. "'The blame is his who chooses. God is blameless.'"

"You read my Plato book?"

I smiled. "It's not God's fault, and it isn't your fault either. Don't choose the blame, Thorin."

"I could say the same thing to you, couldn't I?"

I bobbed my head once. "I know, and I'm working on it. We're both still alive. I think we've both kept our promises."

After we returned to the dock, I hurried up the hill to his house and left Thorin to secure the boat. In the kitchen, I poured a glass of water and gulped it down. Using a phone I borrowed from Thorin, I dialed the number to my dad's cell. As it rang, I concentrated on steadying my breathing and slowing my pulse. Why did I feel as though I was facing a jury about to hand down my conviction?

"Hello?" Dad said after the second ring.

"Hey, Dad, it's me… Solina." *Duh, who else?*

His breath whooshed over the airwaves like a sigh of relief. "Oh, thank goodness. Baldur has been telling us you're all right, but we weren't sure we could believe him. We're not sure *what* to believe anymore."

"I know how you feel. The world has lost its mind, hasn't it?"

Dad gave an uncomfortable chuckle. "You can say that again."

"Is Baldur treating you well? You and Mom have everything you need?"

"He's been an excellent host, but we'd feel a whole lot better if you were here with us."

"I know, Dad, but it's not a good idea. There are people, *monsters*, after me. They'd hurt you to get to me if they could. For now, the farther we stay apart, the better. There's nowhere safer for you than New Breidablick, but I plan to finish this soon. Then things can go back to normal… or as normal as possible, considering everything that's happened."

"What do you mean, finish?"

I scratched my fingernails over my scalp, loosening tangles the windy boat ride had worked into my hair. The kitchen door opened and banged shut, bringing in Thorin and a burst of cold air. I turned around to face him, and he winked at me. "I mean put an end to it. Don't ask for details because I'm not sure I can give them to you. But I have the God of Thunder and a horde of Valkyries for allies. How awesome is that?"

"I hear the words you're saying, Solina, but they're not making any sense. Valkyries? God of Thunder? Do you mean..." My dad lowered his voice to a whisper. "Thor?"

I snickered. "Don't be silly. Thor's been dead a long time. I'm talking about his son, Magni." *That'll make Dad's head spin for a while.* "Look, I have some things I need to do." I had nothing I needed to do, but I'd make up any excuse to get off the phone and end this familial awkwardness. "Tell Mom I called and I love her."

"Wait, Solina..."

"Dad, please. I don't know what else to say. You're going to have to trust me. I'll call soon, I promise. Love you, okay?"

My dad sighed again. "Love you, too."

I flicked my thumb over the END icon and passed the phone to Thorin. "Glad that's over."

"You and your parents not getting along?"

I shrugged. "We used to be nearly inseparable."

He stepped closer. "A lot of things have changed, though. Right?"

I nodded.

"Would you go home? Back to the bakery?"

"How could I go back to the way things used to be, knowing what I know now? But what else do I do?"

"Stay in Alaska." He had said it so calmly, so matter-of-factly, I thought I might have misunderstood. He leaned in, and his next words came out on a ghost of breath, but it was unmistakable. "Stay with me."

My voice was raspy and broken when I said, "Could there be two less compatible people in the world than you and me?"

His brow furrowed, and his eyes darkened. "We have more in common than you want to admit. All of this trouble with Helen has rocked a boat that has been shored up for a very long time. Ancient magic is stirring and awakening. If there is a way for us, Solina, I will find it."

His conviction nearly convinced me, but my own self-doubt was no easy thing to defeat. "I'm just saying we shouldn't be naïve, is all."

He snorted. "My naiveté has shriveled up and fallen off."

"I don't see how it's possible for us. You don't age, Thorin. Each day is forever for you."

His fingers curled around my upper arm and squeezed—his go-to way of dealing with me and his ire at the same time. "Why do you insist on picking fights with me?"

"Why do you insist on ignoring the truth?" I wanted forever with this man. It might have been impossible, but, by God, I wanted it. But want and belief weren't the same things.

"I make my own truths," he said, his voice low, tone ominous. "Never doubt that."

A doorbell rang and shattered the moment. Someone pounded on the front door. We froze in place. "It's Hugh," I said. "I-I don't know how I know, but it's him. I'm sure."

Thorin cocked his head like a dog hearing a curious noise. The doorbell rang again. "I'm surprised they waited this long. I honestly expected them to be here from the moment you woke up." He released me and marched away, heading, I assumed, to let in our feathery friends. "This conversation isn't over yet," he threw over his shoulder. "This isn't an argument you're going to win."

The ravens' presence stirred mixed feelings in me. Hugh's face brought back instant, harrowing memories, but I was too grateful for his participation in Thorin's quasi-rescue to deny his right to talk to me, face to face. Joe Muniz, Munin in human form, stood beside his brother in the middle of Thorin's living room. The pair twitched and blinked and shifted from foot to foot. Their nervousness probably had a lot to do with the ominous presence of the God of Thunder, who glared at them the same way a Secret Service agent stares at an unwelcome visitor at the White House.

"I've got this. Why don't you..." I waved in a vague way to suggest he find something else to do—something preferably in another room or outside. Thorin folded his arms over his chest, set his jaw, and stood as rigid as a monolith.

"You look like you're waiting for an excuse to pluck them and throw them in the stew pot," I said. "I don't think they're going to relax until you give them some space." Thorin's nostrils flared, and he pressed his lips together until little white lines appeared at the corners of his mouth. I put a hand to his arm and pleaded. "Just a few minutes. You don't have to go far. Just.... far enough for them to relax. Please?"

He held my stare as he deliberated. Then he exhaled and nodded. "I'll go check the crab pots I threw out this morning." He turned and jabbed a finger at Hugh. "I'll be back in an instant if anything happens to her, though. Don't try me, *pigeon*." He turned on his heel and stomped off, heading for the front door.

"I don't know how to break your bonds." I turned to Hugh. "Except for a nasty headache and some flickering images from time to time, I can't tell anything is different."

Hugh's shoulders slumped. Thorin's exit had obviously relieved some of his tension. "It's there. You just don't know how to sense it yet. Once you do, you'll find you have access to everything we know and remember. And we know and remember *everything*."

"Sounds like a terrible burden."

He shrugged. "We've learned to live with it."

"How do I sense it?"

"You have to open your mind."

"And that's the dangerous part." Joe's voice startled me. He so rarely spoke. "Dangerous for you because some minds can't handle it. Dangerous for us because you might decide you like it and refuse to cut our bonds."

"I swore to you—"

Hugh waved me off. "It's a difficult promise to keep when you can't fully appreciate it."

"I don't know how to reassure you. The only thing we can do is move forward." I gave Hugh a pointed look and shifted my attention to Joe. "I have to trust you to give me the information about the wolf you promised me. I could break this connection between us and never hear from you again. So I guess we'll just have to trust each other."

I set my hands on my hips and furrowed my brow. "Now, how does this 'opening my mind' thing work? I don't have to spin in circles or inhale paint vapors, do I?"

Joe gave a hesitant smile. I smiled back.

Hugh crossed the space between us and gestured for me to sit on the floor. As I sank into a cross-legged position, he knelt beside me. "Close your eyes. Clear your thoughts. Have you ever tried meditating before? It would be helpful if you knew how."

"I managed to do an imaginary spirit walk with Gróa, so I think I can do what you're asking."

"This requires no chanting or vision quests. I want you to try to quiet your mind. That's going to be hard after everything you've been through, but—"

"But I made a promise," I said. "Now, let's do this thing."

Meditation was supposed to be relaxing, but letting go of my tension was harder than I'd expected. Hugh tried lowering the lights and playing soft music on his phone. The effects made me sleepy, but that turned out to be a good thing. As I nodded off, something strange stood out in my mind, like a rough spot that needed filing, a mental hangnail. I gasped.

"What is it?" Hugh asked.

"Shhh." I pushed deeper into my mind and gave the rough spot a mental poke.

Hugh gasped. "That's it, Solina. You've got it. I can feel you. Keep going."

"Is this going to fry my brain?"

"*Shhh*. Just do it."

I tugged on the connection again. The dam broke, and the whole world flooded in.

I swam back to the surface with Thorin shaking my shoulders. "Solina, dammit. Don't do this. Not again."

"Chill out." I pushed myself up to a sitting position as the room spun around me. "I'm okay."

"See, we told you she'd be okay," Hugh said. Thorin growled and lunged for him. Hugh jumped back, barely evading Thorin's swipe.

"Stop it." I waved at Thorin. "They warned me it might be a jolt." Actually, they had said my mind might not handle it at all. They weren't kidding.

He shot another black glare at the ravens. "It was too soon for you to do this."

"I thought you were out checking crab pots," I said.

"They were empty, so I came back." He brushed a few stray hairs off my face and peered into my eyes. "I walked in to find you lying on the floor, still as a stone."

"I found the connection." I smiled, trying to reassure him. "It was a little bit overwhelming."

His lips thinned. "You're going to kill me slowly, aren't you? You're going to literally scare me to death, a little bit at a time."

I reached up and patted his cheek. "Not on purpose."

He pulled me in and squeezed me hard to his chest. "I thought I was a strong man, Sunshine. I never knew a little thing like you would be the death of me."

I furrowed my brow and pushed at him until he let up. "I'm not so little when it comes down to it. Now, help me up, and let's get this over with. I don't like having the whole world in my head."

He met my eyes with a solemn look. "Are you positive?"

"Absolutely."

Thorin helped me settle in a chair and leaned on the armrest beside me. Hugh and Joe moved to the sofa and perched on the edge, a couple of nervous birds again.

"Okay. Let's find that connection one more time," Hugh said. "I've tried pulling back on my end, putting an insulator on our link. It will only slow the flow of information, not stop it, so you may have to slog through some stuff to reach the connection and cut it off."

I nodded and took a deep breath. "Okay."

I closed my eyes, prepared to go back inside myself, but Hugh stopped me. "Solina, wait."

My eyes popped open. "What?"

"It won't be easy. The things you're getting right now are the most recent Thoughts and Memories. You might have to wade through some really bad stuff, if you know what I mean."

Thorin put his hands to my shoulders and squeezed. "You sure you want to do this?"

Hugh scowled. "She has to, Boss Man. If she doesn't do it now, it will only get worse. If she had crazy dreams before, she's going to be completely out of her mind when the visions and nightmares stalk her in her sleep. It takes time to learn how to control it, and she could probably do it, but she'll suffer for it. Better to get it over with all at once."

"I'll be all right." I put steel in my voice. I looked up at Thorin with my best tough-girl face. No pity, I was telling him. No indulging my weaknesses. "I want to get this over with."

He sucked in a breath, obviously working to control his protective instincts. He let the breath out with a whoosh and a deliberate blink. He nodded.

I closed my eyes, slowed my breathing, cleared my senses, and stepped deeper into my mind. Hugh was right. It was all there, swirling about me like an ocean of sounds and sights. The visions switched to rewind mode and showed me everything I had missed after exploding into a superstar. Maybe I could have skipped over it, but I wanted to see, wanted to know.

I should have realized I was pulling the pin on an emotional grenade.

I saw Thorin bringing me to his home, shifting with me from out of the darkness of a flooded cave...

Rewind.

Thorin leaving Grim with Baldur, but not before Grim drew Thorin into a feeble but brotherly embrace...

Rewind.

Thorin scooping up his brother from Val's cave in the moments before I shattered into starlight. The wails of Val's anguish reverberating against the cave's walls. My voice rising up to join his...

I screamed and charged through the flood of Thoughts and Memories, a mad woman tearing through a twisted kingdom of pain and horror until I reached the source, the connection. It rose above a swirling landscape like a pillar. A thick, ropy cable extruding sticky webs wound around the strange, glowing shape. Although I would have sworn I'd never seen it before, the figure made me think of my fire, and I supposed that... *thing* was the source of all my otherworldly abilities: Sol's eternal rune. In the past, I'd sensed it as a corporeal object hidden deep inside me, and now I had finally found it. I battered and tugged at the sticky strands, fighting a desperate attack until, finally, the ravens' connection severed and fell away.

Hugin and Munin retreated from my mind, taking everything I never wanted to know or remember about the world with them. Relief flooded me, and I puddled into a boneless heap, but the release of my connection did not remove my anger, my guilt, or the devastation of my actions.

I returned to the present in a disconcerting blink. Thorin leaned in and put an arm around my shoulders. He murmured soothing things into my ear. My stomach tugged, twisted, and turned over. I shoved him away and ran for the bathroom, barely making it to the toilet in time to vomit, over and over, until my body shook, my stomach muscles ached, and a cold sweat soaked through my clothes. *How many times can a person throw up in one day and survive?*

I sank to the cold tile floor, stared up at the white ceiling, and waited for tears that never came. Instead, the familiar numbness returned. The more trauma I experienced, the more I realized I coped by turning everything off. It shut down the pain. It shut down *everything*.

Thorin eased into the bathroom and dropped down beside me. He tried gathering me up in his arms, but I pushed him away.

"Sunshine—"

"Go away." I cut him off. Unable to face him, I turned my back.

He tried touching me again. Big mistake. My short recovery hadn't allowed for the full recuperation of my fire, but I gave him every bit of the pittance I had managed to restore. It was enough. He cursed, pulled away, and retreated from the room.

I stretched out on the cold floor and lay there until my toes turned blue and my teeth chattered. Then I pushed myself onto my knees, stripped, and turned on the shower to the hottest setting. Thorin must have installed a tankless water heater, because I stood under the spray, waiting for the hot water to run out, but it never did.

What was I trying to wash away? My shame? My guilt? The memory of the look on Val's face in the moments before he surrendered to me? But of course, the shower could never cleanse me in the way I so desperately wanted. Maybe nothing ever would.

If anyone could prove me wrong, though, it would be Thorin.

After thoroughly waterlogging myself, I shut off the shower, wrapped up in towels, and paced the length of the bathroom. I might have happily lived the rest of my life in that room, if no one interfered, but I could always trust Thorin to do precisely that. I didn't argue or fight when he pushed open the bathroom door, grabbed my arm, and dragged me out. But I did play opossum, refusing to respond to his questions or pleas.

He didn't fall for my "play dead" routine, and he spared me no pity, either. He set me on my feet before the blazing fireplace in his bedroom. When I tried to sink onto the floor, he jerked me up. "Hold still. You're going to freeze to death if you don't get some clothes on. Your skin feels like ice."

We both knew it would take a lot more than a cold bathroom to freeze me to death, but I refrained from stating such a needless observation. He wanted to take care of me. I sort of wanted to let him.

He pulled the towel from my hair and rubbed the damp strands. I accepted it all in numb silence. He dug into my luggage and found underwear, a long-sleeved T-shirt, and a loose pair of yoga pants. He shoved them toward me. "Put these on."

I took the clothes and waited for him to turn his back before I dropped my towel, not that it mattered. He had seen my bare flesh more than once. At this point in my life, who hadn't?

Thorin turned around, sensing I had finished dressing, and pulled my hand, leading me to the bed. I sat, and he made a brush appear from nowhere—but probably his back pocket—and worked on the tangles and snarls in my hair. His nimble fingers felt like magic. "You needed time for physical recovery, and I had hoped you keep you here, safe, until your fire was fully renewed. But it leaves you alone with too much time to think, too much time to wallow, when what you need is an occupation, something to keep your mind and body busy."

I started to speak, but my voice cracked. I cleared my throat and tried again. "I guess you speak from experience."

"You *know* I do."

I sucked in a deep breath and let it out. The gesture served as a physical metaphor, symbolizing the release of my most bitter emotions. I suspected it was only a temporary remedy. I needed time to heal, and as Thorin suggested, I needed a distraction to keep me occupied until then. "I happen to agree."

His eyebrows rose. "Oh? Do you have something in mind already?"

"The ravens kept their end of the bargain."

He blinked, obviously confounded, but then his expression cleared, and his eyes narrowed. "Skoll. You know where the wolf is."

I bobbed my head. My brief connections to the ravens had shown me many things—maybe too many things—but I focused on the most useful facts. "I'll give you one guess."

He furrowed his brow and scratched his jaw. Finally, he said, "Amchitka."

"Give the gentlemen his prize," I said, imitating a carnival barker.

"Helen wouldn't go far from her golems, not since she lost Nate. Someone has to control them, and not many people are gifted with her necromantic abilities."

"Good." I stood and brushed the wrinkles from my shirt. "We're agreed."

"Say the word, Sunshine. We'll go whenever you're ready."

"You don't want me to stay here? Or go back to New Breidablick where I'd be safe and sound?"

He gave me a sardonic look. "Would you?"

I snorted. "You know me better. Those golems might not be my fight, but that wolf certainly is."

"I could get to Amchitka and finish him off before you could say, 'boo.'"

"You could." I nodded. "But you won't. You respect me more than that."

He pulled a theatrical grimace. "You'll make me regret saying that, won't you?"

I stepped forward and slipped my arms around his neck. "No. I'll make you worship me."

His chuckle reverberated through his chest as he circled his arms around me. "I already do."

A blush lit my cheeks, but I played it off. "Take me to New Breidablick, Jeeves. I've got to get my parka and winter boots. From the look of it in my visions, Amchitka is *cold*."

"Jeeves?"

"It's my chauffeur name for you. Better than, 'Ya mule!' right?"

Thorin's only reply was a snort.

My ears popped, and we were gone again.

CHAPTER 19

Returning to New Breidablick meant facing my parents again, which I had meant to avoid as long as possible. A couple of days was not long enough to come to terms with the person I had become, not long enough to sort out the things I had done and how I felt about them. I wanted nothing more than to blip in, grab my winter clothes, and blip out, taking the Aesir Airways to Amchitka as fast as possible. Instead, Thorin and I touched down in Baldur's living room directly in front of my parents, blocking their view of the football game blaring on the flat screen.

No avoiding them now.

My mom gasped and pressed her hand over her heart. My dad rose to his feet, wobbled, and sat down again, spilling popcorn from the bowl he clutched to his chest like a shield. "We're never going to get used to this," he said breathlessly. "I'm too old to believe in magic."

"Hey, Dad." I waved at him lamely. "Mom." I nodded in her direction. "What's up?"

"What's up?" She flapped a hand at me. "That's all you can say?"

"Um... how's it going?"

"Solina," she said in a nagging tone. How many times had I heard her say my name that way? Too many to remember.

"I don't think y'all have ever formally met." I gestured between Thorin and my parents. *Am I really about to introduce the God of Thunder to my parents like we're on a first date or something?* "Magni Alexander Thorin, this is my mom and dad, Rachael and Tim Mundy."

Thorin stood in his most formal stance and bowed from the neck. "It's an honor to meet you both."

"Mom and Dad, meet the God of Thunder."

My mom's face flushed, and my dad gawked at us as he rose and tugged my mom to her feet. "You're not being serious, are you?"

I nudged my elbow into Thorin's ribs. "Show him your hammer. Dad, you're going to flip when you see his hammer." My glib performance was an act, a shield to keep Mom and Dad from seeing the real me. Outside, I smiled. Inside, I burned coldly.

Thorin bit back a grin as he fished through his pocket. He presented his fist, twisted his wrist, and Mjölnir in all its majesty appeared as if he had pulled the most astounding rabbit from the most miraculous hat. Thunder clapped outside Baldur's living room window, and a streak of lightning rent the early-evening sky.

"Good Lord," my dad said. Mom squeaked and dropped into her seat.

"I know you still have questions," I said, "and I promise I'll answer them, but not right now. I came by to pick up some things. Thorin and I have some... *hunting* to do. If we're successful, all of this craziness will be over very soon."

"And if you're not successful?" Dad asked.

"Then we keep hunting." *Or the wolf gets me instead, I'm dead, and the world ends.* But my dad didn't need to hear that.

I threw my arms out at my sides. "Hugs before I go? Get them while they're hot." Stunned and uncertain, my parents let me approach and gather them into an embrace. "I'll be back before you know it. I swear." I chucked my thumb over my shoulder in Thorin's direction. "I mean, look at this guy. You think he's going to let anything happen to me?"

He spun Mjölnir's handle through his fingers like a baton. At the end of the last rotation, the hammer shrank, and he stuffed it in his pocket. I smirked at him. *Show-off.*

"It's not like we can tell you no anymore," my mom said. "You've obviously got things under control here."

"I wouldn't say that..." I absolutely would *not* say that. "But you shouldn't worry, okay? Promise me you won't worry. You won't even have time to miss me."

Dad cocked his head, and his brow furrowed. "We'll always miss you."

"And we'll always worry," Mom said. "We're your parents. Nothing can take that away." She glanced at Thorin and narrowed her eyes.

"Not even mythological gods." She pressed a hand to her forehead and grimaced. "Did I really just say that?"

I laughed. "You're taking it better than I thought you would." Maybe I hadn't given my parents enough credit. Either they had more strength than I had expected, or they had learned something from the ordeal of Mani's death. Perhaps I had been wrong to assume the experience hadn't changed them. It had certainly transformed *me*, turned my world upside down, and shaken loose my courage and intrepidness. It had shaken loose my darkness as well.

A hot wave crashed over me like a fever, and I shuddered. Seeing my mom and dad again had reinforced our growing differences. They may have crawled out of their cocoon and formed a more realistic outlook about the world, but a divide existed between us, a rift none of us could cross.

"All of this has obviously changed things," my mother said as if reading my mind. "This new path for your life isn't something we're really equipped to handle."

"There's no going back to the way things were," I said. That possibility died with Val. It had probably died long before, but the events in that cave were my event horizon, my point of no return. The sooner we all accepted that, the sooner we could leave it behind. "I'm not the girl I was before."

My mother took my hands between hers and stroked my knuckles. "I've mourned you, Solina. I thought I had lost you, same as I lost your brother, and I grieved that loss." I inhaled, forming a reply—perhaps an apology—but my mother shook her head and gave me a look that silenced me before she continued. "I'm glad I was able to do that, because you're right. The girl you were before is gone, and because I've already mourned her, maybe I can let her go and accept that you've become someone else." She pulled me into another embrace, and her shoulders trembled. "Promise me that when this is over, you won't shut us out. Promise that, somehow, we'll still be family."

A lump had risen in my throat, so I said nothing. Instead, I squeezed her as hard as I could. Catching my father's gaze, I nodded at him and mouthed the words I couldn't say: *I promise*. His shoulders slumped, and he nodded back, smiling.

I let go.

Thorin slid an arm around my shoulder, tugged me against his side, and said something vaguely polite about the pleasure of meeting my parents. Then he led me out of Baldur's living room. From the closet of my New Breidablick bedroom, I grabbed a couple extra changes of clothes and my winter gear. After I zipped and buttoned my parka until only my eyes showed above the high collar, Thorin nodded, and I read it as a gesture of his approval.

I clicked my heels three times. "There's no place like Amchitka... There's no place like Amchitka..."

He snorted, rolled his eyes, and wrapped his arms around me. Then away we went.

"This does not look like my visions of Amchitka," I said. Instead of a barren wasteland covered in snow, Thorin and I stood before a log-and-river-rock cabin framed in the glow of a floodlight, illuminating a quaint rustic scene that surely adorned an Alaska travel brochure somewhere. A gravel pathway in front of the house led to a larger lodge next door before winding down to a waterfront dock hosting a collection of seaplanes and fishing boats. Cold wind tore at my parka, and darts of icy rain pattered on my hood, but at least no snow had fallen recently.

The cabin's front door opened, and Skyla and Embla stepped under the glow of the porch light. The two women hesitated, their posture going stiff and alert. Then they recognized us and relaxed. Skyla stepped forward, leaned against the railing, and waved. I grinned and waved back.

"You're brave," Thorin muttered in my ear, "and I'm strong, but I'd still rather not face Helen's hordes with just the two of us. We'd be foolish to waste the Valkyries as a resource."

"If we can trust them."

"Yes. *If.*"

"What did you say this place was? Salmon something?"

"King Salmon." He nodded. "I've led more than a few fishing trips around here."

"Adventure for the weekend warrior who doesn't want to get too far from his comfort zone."

"My clients never complained."

"Why would they?" I motioned to the deluxe accommodations as I started toward Skyla. "I'll bet this place has a spa. And a bar."

"There's a spa," Skyla confirmed. "Hot tubs, massages, pretty good food in the lounge, too."

"You sure know how to get stranded in style." I jogged the steps up to the porch. "Hello, Embla."

The older woman nodded in greeting.

Skyla embraced me, and I hugged her hard enough to squeeze a grunt from her. "Be careful, or it'll make you soft."

She cuffed my shoulder. "You take that back."

I sniffed the air near her hair. "Lavender and... rosemary?"

She scowled. "I tried, but it won't wash off."

"You smell like a girl."

"You trying to pick a fight, Mundy? What are you doing here, anyway? I thought the deal was you were going to get your parents and hang out at New Breidablick while Boss Man snagged his brother from Val."

Heat flooded my cheeks, and I looked away. "Yeah, well, plans changed."

She stood still and silent for several heartbeats. "What happened?"

Thorin cleared his throat and stepped up beside me. He glanced at Embla before he turned and stared off at nothing. "Val's dead. That's all that matters for now."

Skyla flinched and stifled whatever she was about to say. "Okay. Well, that's one less thing to worry about."

When I said nothing, she hugged me again.

I let her rub my back until Thorin shuffled his feet in an obvious gesture of impatience. "Let's get out of the cold. I'm sure Solina could use something to eat."

"Hmm, now that you mention it..." I pulled away from Skyla and patted my stomach. The morning's helping of eggs and toast had disappeared, and my recent bouts of sickness had left me empty and hollow.

"Take her in and feed her," Embla said. "I'll do a check around the perimeter."

Skyla turned on her heel and led Thorin and me inside toward the kitchen. "There's sandwich stuff in the fridge. I think there's probably a leftover pizza in there too."

She rambled off a list of snacking options as I shrugged off my heavy parka. Several other Valkyries lounged in the living room, watching TV, eating, flipping through the contents of their phones. Siobhan looked up and waved as we passed by. The other two women mostly ignored us.

"I'm going to head outside." Thorin paused in the kitchen doorway. "Get a look around. I'll be back in a few minutes."

"We've kept a round-the-clock patrol, Boss Man." Skyla narrowed her eyes at him. "We haven't let our guard down."

"I'm not saying you have. I want to get a look for myself."

She waved him off. "Knock yourself out."

Thorin disappeared. I tossed my coat over a kitchen chair and opened the refrigerator. A very welcome pizza box sat on a middle shelf. I pulled it out, popped open the lid, and studied the contents: pepperoni, sausage, mushroom. Then I rifled through the cabinets until I found a big skillet. After setting it on the stove and turning a flame on low beneath it, I slid in two pizza slices to warm.

"Stovetop?" Skyla said, glancing at my pizza. "Who does it like that? Just nuke it."

"Microwaving makes the crust chewy. Warm it in the skillet, and the crust stays crisp without overcooking the toppings."

She shrugged. "Guess you would know."

"It *is* my job. Or it was..."

"Why are you here?" she asked, apropos of nothing. I gasped and inhaled a bit of phlegm. Skyla pounded my back until I cleared my airway. "Didn't mean to upset you. I just didn't expect you to show up on the front porch, out of the blue."

I focused on pizza and shoved one slice into a different position. Then I shoved it back. "Skoll's on Amchitka," I said, almost a whisper.

"And how do you know this?"

"The ravens told me."

"And why did they tell you—Oh. Val."

I shifted my pizza around the pan again, mostly to keep from looking at Skyla. "Yes, Val."

"So, you..."

"Yeah. I did."

"Aw, *shit*," Skyla muttered and said nothing more, but her questions, her request for the rest of the story, hung in the air between us.

"It was a trap for Thorin. I had to save him. It was the only way."

"You don't have to justify it to me. You know how I felt about Val. But I know how you felt about him, too. I know it wasn't what you wanted."

"I didn't have much choice." I recounted the story in a dry and quick summary—the facts and nothing more.

Skyla followed me to the kitchen table after I plucked my pizza from the pan and dropped the slices on a paper plate she had handed me. "Do you think Val's plan would have worked? Do you think Thorin would have turned?"

"Seemed like it was working." I remembered the way Thorin clawed at his chest, how he had dropped Mjölnir, the agony on his face. "It's not like I wanted to call Val's bluff."

"Knowing Val, he wasn't bluffing."

"No." I bit into the pizza, and hot cheese stuck to the roof of my mouth. It brought up an instant blister. I barely noticed. "He wasn't."

"Killing the wolf will be worth it in the end."

"That's what I keep telling myself."

"You don't believe it yet, do you?"

I shook my head.

Skyla reached across the kitchen table and covered my hand. "I didn't make it out of the Marines without knowing what it felt like to take another person's life. I'm still not proud of it, but I've learned to live with it. It had to be done."

"How long did it take you? How long before every breath stopped hurting?" I gestured to the half-eaten pizza. "How long before you could eat without feeling guilty?"

"It's different for everyone. It wasn't so hard for me, being around others who had stood in my shoes, done the same things I had done, made the same choices. It helped knowing I wasn't alone." She patted my hand and pulled away. "You aren't alone, either."

"I know." I poked at a crumble of sausage that had rolled to the edge of my plate. "And I'm grateful for it. I am. It just might be a while before I can show it."

Her lips curled into a half smile, and she jerked her chin toward the doorway. "C'mon. We moved things around on the back porch. There's room for sparring. You know what you need right now? A way to let off some steam. Let's get in some fight practice and get you warmed up for Skoll." She pointed at my discarded dinner. "Might help you get your appetite back."

I pushed my plate aside and rose to my feet. "Guess it couldn't hurt."

I followed Skyla down a hallway to a door leading to a glassed-in porch shrouded by darkness. She flicked on a light and strode to the middle of the room. A wicker couch stood on its side in one corner, and a couple of chairs balanced on top of a coffee table in another, leaving an area just wide enough for two women to practice hand-to-hand techniques.

"No fire." Skyla rolled her head on her neck. She tugged off her sweater and threw it into a corner, leaving her in a T-shirt.

I followed her lead and stripped down to my tank top. She prowled, making a wide circle. I spun, keeping her before me, and lowered my center of gravity. "I won't use my fire. It's still a little on the fritz after... *well*, you know."

She paused, and her brow furrowed. "You're going to face the wolf without the full use of your powers?"

"I'm not completely bankrupt. And given the way the weather's behaving, I might get a few more days of recuperation before I have to face him."

"You're taking a big risk, girlfriend."

"Then you'd better make sure I'm ready." I leapt and struck.

Skyla barked a sharp sound of surprise and countered, blocking my attack. Without losing momentum, she brought her fist up, aiming for my chin. I turned, and her knuckles kissed my cheek. She chuckled. "Good move, Mundy, but you're going to have to be faster than that."

I widened my stance and turned my body, giving her my shoulder. She bounced on her toes and grinned. Her eyes flashed, so did her fist. I leaned back, avoiding her strike. Skyla reset, drawing herself in like a tightly coiled spring. "You gotta be more offensive."

"I'm just warming up," I said, already breathing hard, adrenaline spiking my heart rate. "I'm a little rusty."

"Rusty? You move like a broken-down old Cadillac."

I returned her toothy grin. "Oh yeah?"

"Like a grandma in need of a hip replacement."

I laughed and darted right. When she moved to follow me, I twisted through my hips and hurled a right cross into her ribs. She turned and stepped back, and my fist grazed her T-shirt. "Ooh," she said and rolled her shoulders. "Do I feel a breeze?"

Jab, jab, left cross, I went on the attack, not because Skyla had baited me, but because I enjoyed it, because the harder I punched, the faster I swung, the more my conscious thoughts slid away. My body and instincts took over, and emotions disappeared. Sweat pooled between my breasts and rolled along the valley of my spine. Strands of hair escaped my ponytail and stuck to my forehead and neck. Blood roared in my ears. Breath whooshed in my chest.

It was glorious.

Sometimes, I landed a blow. Sometimes Skyla did. We held back, pulled our punches, but the shock of each hit still sent shivers of pain and delight rolling over me. I embraced punishment, both the giving and the receiving. We fought until my breath came in pants and wheezes. I might have driven myself to hyperventilation if Embla hadn't arrived and called a time-out.

"Save some for the wolf, Solina." She pointed at Skyla. "You too, Ramirez."

I pouted and huffed. "Party pooper."

Embla chuckled and threw a towel at me. I snatched it and dabbed my sweat. My tank top clung like a second skin, and my jeans felt uncomfortably hot and clammy. "I'm going to take a shower."

"Great idea," Skyla said. "Glad I didn't have to suggest it."

<hr />

Skyla invited me to share her room, and after a long, hot shower and after gobbling up the rest of my half-eaten pizza, I retreated to bed, but not to sleep. Nope, no sleep for me. I dreaded my dreams too much. Logically, a night of solid rest would hasten my recuperation, but Val's ghost haunted the quiet moments, and I feared facing his memory more than facing the wolf.

I paced the cold wooden floor between the nightstand and bedroom door and chanted song lyrics, Bible verses, movie quotes, fragments of a Shakespeare play I learned in school, famous political speeches. *Four score and seven years ago...* My strategy? Keep my mind occupied and *not* thinking until I exhausted myself and passed out. Gently falling asleep was not aggressive enough. I needed instant oblivion.

Skyla walked in on me in the middle of my rendition of the famous scene from *Flash Dance*. "I'm trying to wear myself out," I said, still jogging in place. "Don't judge me."

She skipped around me and plopped onto the bed, snorting with laughter. "Girl, you seriously need some sleep. You have lost your mind."

I sobered and went still. "No, I haven't. But that's what I'm afraid of."

"C'mon." She patted the empty space beside her on the bed. "Relax a little. You might not get that chance again for a while."

I sank onto the mattress. "Being cooped up like this is making me nuts. Running from one demon while trying to track down another. It's going to make me crazy. Damn the storms and fog. I want to go to Amchitka *now*."

She exhaled and fell against her pillow. "I know how you feel. It's been a long time since I've had that mix of fear and battle lust running through my veins. It's dread and anticipation. Eagerness and hesitancy. Sometimes you feel like you're tearing in two."

"It's more than two for me. One piece for Val, one for the wolf, one for Thorin, one for Mani."

"Will killing the wolf make you feel whole again?"

I shrugged and picked at a loose thread on the knee of my pajama pants. "It'll be a start."

"And Thorin? You feel as though he's pulling you apart, too?"

"The whole immortal-versus-human thing still has me messed up. I don't know how we're going to make it work."

"Seize the day, girlfriend. It doesn't have to be forever."

I pivoted, drawing my knees up under my chin, and met her deep brown gaze. "With him? I think it's *only* about forever."

"Look, I'm not saying you should go running down the aisle or anything, but I think Thorin needs your company as much as you're trying to pretend you don't need his. Hanging out with him would be a hell of a lot better way to keep your mind off things than listening to me snore, don't you think?"

"You're not going to stay up all night with me?"

Skyla rolled over, propped her chin in her hand, and grinned at me. "Nope."

I groaned and shifted off the bed, rising to my feet. "You know where he is?"

"Front porch, last time I checked. He said he'd pull night watch."

"Sunshine," Thorin said when I stepped onto the porch, reinstalled in my heavy winter parka. "Why aren't you in bed?"

A heavy wall of cold, misty clouds enveloped our cabin. Water lapped and babbled at the distant riverbank, a ghostly noise echoing in the fog. Thorin stood at the railing, his shadow as dark as a wraith.

"Don't want to sleep," I said. "Don't tell me I should because I know. But knowing is easier than doing."

"You're afraid of your dreams," he said, not asking a question.

I sighed, and my shoulders slumped. "I'm a wuss."

He chuckled. The porch floorboards creaked beneath him as he shifted his weight. "I've said before you're one of the bravest people I know. Real monsters are sometimes easier to face than the imaginary ones, right? Real monsters can be defeated. The ones in your dreams..."

"Not so much," I finished. He reached out, his big hands enveloping one of mine, and he drew me closer to his side as I talked. "I've been trying to keep myself distracted. I'm running out of ideas, though, and I'm afraid of the quiet."

"So you want me to keep you amused?"

"You're the only one who doesn't sleep." I hoped he heard the teasing in my tone. "Skyla kicked me out. I was keeping her awake."

"What can I do to help?"

"Talk to me." I leaned against the porch rail. "Tell me a story. Something about you that isn't in the legends. Tell me what it was like before the fire and the war. What was it like growing up in Asgard?"

Thorin stepped close again and wrapped his arms around me. He lowered his head until our foreheads touched. His warm breath misted over my cheek, and his voice's deep timbre reverberated through me as he spoke. "I could tell you. Or I could show you—let you see for yourself."

I pulled in a deep breath. Then I let it go in a rush. "Okay, show me. I'm ready."

A stream glints golden sparks of light and burbles along a meadow's edge. Tall green grass and melancholy willows line a crumbling bankside. A tawny-headed boy, no more than nine or ten years old, crouches in the shadows of those graceful branches. He holds a fishing net, small, unevenly constructed, but sufficient for his purposes. Ghostly bodies flicker beneath the stream's surface, darting, scattering, eluding the net. Warmth floods Thorin's chest as he watches his brother troll the waters. Grim is beloved, his brother and dearest friend.

Grim has woven a second net, and Thorin collects it from the bank. He takes a position opposite his brother. The boys work in concert like a pair of herd dogs wrangling a flock of wayward sheep. They broaden the reach of their nets and close in on the clever trout, trapping fish in a small pool enclosed by rock walls the boys had arranged earlier. Grim catches Thorin's eye. He nods, and the brothers pounce. After a flurry of splashes, yells, and laughter, the pair come away from the creek, both sodden but each clutching a shimmering, squirming prize.

"We filled two baskets that day," Thorin said, drawing me out of the memory. "Fed the whole family and then some."

My heart had swollen until it strained against my sternum, threatening to burst. It thudded a slow, contented rhythm as if the joy Thorin felt that day had transferred into me. "You and Grim must have been nearly identical as children. You still look a lot alike, but he seems so much colder."

"Ragnarok was as hard on him as it was on me. Harder, maybe. He had more to lose."

I untangled myself from Thorin and edged toward the porch steps. His nearness still overwhelmed me sometimes. Would I ever get used to him, take his intimacy for granted? I couldn't imagine that day.

"It's still very fresh, isn't it—the memory of those you lost?"

"Sometimes." He shifted, and the floorboards squeaked again. He edged around me, descended the steps, and turned on a flashlight. Its beam failed to penetrate the gloom, but the light reflected off the fog and illuminated his pale hair. He held out a hand toward me and motioned for me to join him. I left the porch and twined my fingers in his. We turned and started on a path around the cabin—perimeter patrol.

"Sometimes, it feels like it happened yesterday," he said. "Sometimes, it feels like a dream, one that fades after waking."

"Immortality is as much of a curse as it is a blessing, I think." I turned my face up to his, searching for his eyes, but deep shadows masked his face. "It's why I'm reluctant to want it."

He nodded. "I get that."

"When I saw Mani, he was in some other place, some other plane of existence, like Asgard, but not. He had a name for it, but I don't remember—"

"Helgafjell?" Thorin asked. "It means 'holy mountain.' It's a sacred place for families to commune in the afterlife. They live out their days much as they did in life. He's in a good place, Solina."

"That's what he said, too, and I believe him. I know my brother is not the be-all and end-all. My existence isn't as consumed with Mani as it sometimes seems. I want my own life with my own hopes and dreams, but I'd like to think, after a life well lived, I could be with my loved ones again. Immortality would deny me that."

We turned a corner, and he shined his flashlight around, but the fog had reduced visibility and camouflaged any discernible landscape. If Helen Locke's entire stone army had surrounded the house, we'd never know until it was too late. I cleared my throat and blinked against the sudden burning in my eyes. "Would an eternity with you be enough to make up for the things I'd have to sacrifice to get it?"

He clicked off the flashlight. Darkness enveloped us. His voice was flat when he said, "I can't answer that. It's something you have to decide for yourself."

I took the flashlight from him, turned it on, and started forward in short, careful steps. The beam of light struggled against the fog to map the uneven, muddy terrain. "Sometimes, I feel I barely know you. How can I want eternity with someone I barely know? But other times, I feel I've known you forever, and in those moments, I can't imagine ever being without you."

"As Sol, you *have* known me forever," Thorin said from behind me. "You can't separate yourself from her, and the more you use your fire, the more indistinguishable you and Sol become."

"Did the two of you ever... before?"

"I haven't seen a physical manifestation of her in thousands of years. In Asgard, she and I had our own families. She had a husband. I had a wife."

We turned another corner and sidled along the rear of the house, stepping out to make our way around the glassed-in porch where I had sparred with Skyla earlier. The house was dark, the porch's glass now opaque. No Valkyries, no golems, no wolves. "I feel stupid asking these questions."

"Why do you say that?" he asked.

"You know more about me than I know about myself."

His heavy hand fell on my shoulder, and he spun me around to face him. "I know your past but nothing of your future. I fully intend to remedy that." He tucked me to his side, throwing his arm around my shoulders, and we finished patrolling the outside of the cabin.

Back on the porch, still in his embrace, something inside me unclenched, and exhaustion rolled over me. I sagged on my feet. "I could sleep now. I could go to bed and be okay, I think."

He chuckled. "Does my company bore you that much?"

I feigned passing out and fell against him, limp as a wet noodle. He caught me as I inhaled a loud and elaborate snore. He laughed and scooped me off my feet. I yelped, but he ignored my feeble protests. "When this is all over, I'm taking you to *my* bed, and I don't plan on letting you go for a while."

My face burned, and my heart leapt into my throat. Even if I could have formed a coherent sentence, what could I have said?

Thorin set me on my feet and stepped away. "But I guess you'll have to make do with another night of Skyla. She does snore, makes enough racket to scare away the bears on backpacking trips."

"She's never kept me awake," I said as he lowered me to my feet.

"Huh." He rubbed his jaw. "Maybe she does it just to annoy me."

I crossed the porch, opened the front door, and stepped over the threshold. Siobhan had passed out on the living room couch, and blue television light flickered over her face. "Good night, Thorin."

"Sweet dreams, Sunshine."

I pushed the door behind me, almost closing it, but stopped and spun on my heel. As if reading my mind, he closed the distance between us. He pulled me in and met my lips with his own.

My former uncertainty faded. The whole world drained away. Tomorrow, my doubts would return, but for one night, the memory of Thorin's touch would keep the nightmares at bay.

CHAPTER 20

I SAT AT THE KITCHEN TABLE, smearing cream cheese on a bagel while Skyla poured coffee at the counter. "How can you eat like that so early in the morning?" She wore a scowl as she studied my breakfast. Beside the bagel lay a banana and a hardboiled egg: wolf-fighting fuel.

I shoved the bagel in my mouth and bit off a huge quarter. Through bulging cheeks, I said, "Breakfast is the most important meal of the day. Everyone knows that."

Skyla set a mug of coffee on the table before turning away to pour another for herself. "I could see a granola bar, sure, but what you have there is a personal breakfast buffet, and it's barely"—she glanced at the time on the microwave—"six o'clock in the morning."

"Are you saying that you, a former Marine, don't know the importance of starting a day of hard work on a full stomach?"

"I know if I eat too much and go out for a ten-mile hump in full gear, I'll more than likely throw up halfway through."

"I don't plan on doing a ten-mile hump in full gear anytime soon."

Her eyebrow angled up. "How do you know what to expect about today? Have another vision?"

"Nope." I popped in another hunk of bagel and chewed. "I slept blissfully dream free for a change."

"Told you thunder was the best medicine."

I choked. Skyla pounded my back until my airway cleared. "We just talked," I croaked.

"You smelled like him when you came to bed."

"How do you know? You were sound asleep."

She shrugged. "I woke up." Her gaze flickered up and focused somewhere behind me. Her lip curled into a knowing smile. "'Morning, Boss Man."

My chest muscles clenched, and my breath froze. I inhaled and forced myself to relax. Last night, after my fire had flared and nearly seared him, I had left Thorin standing sentry on the front porch alone. My physiology equated passion with fire, and my flames had blazed out of control. With concentration and effort, I could maintain normalcy, but Thorin's touches had left me the opposite of focused and controlled.

Maybe I just need more practice.

I scrubbed my sleeve cuff across my mouth, turned to face Thorin, and lost my breath again. The overhead light crowned him in gold, and his dark-chocolate sweater matched his eyes. He wore his hair in a braid, something I had only seen him do when he anticipated a fight. *Does he know something I don't?*

He grinned at me, and despite my being seated, my knees quivered. *Quit being such a sop*, I told myself.

"The coffee's good." I motioned to the fresh pot as I stood to search the cabinets for another mug. "Want some?"

He nodded and stepped further into the kitchen, closer to me. He smelled like soap and shaving cream. I poured and passed him the mug. He covered my hands with his own and gave me a deep, dark stare before accepting the cup. "Sleep well?"

"Like a log."

"Then why are you up so early?"

"My subconscious came online at some point and insisted today was important, and I needed to get up and get ready."

"*I* woke up when all the boats and planes started up." Skyla motioned toward the river. "They've been quiet the last few mornings."

"The storm's cleared." Thorin sipped his coffee and peered out the cabin's front window. "It's time to make our next move."

I crossed the room and stood at his side, evaluating the early-morning sky. Remnants of last night's stars sparkled on a flawless field of deep violet. "Not a trace of clouds. You have something to do with that?"

"Why waste any more time?" He settled a severe stare on me. "How's your fire?"

I turned away under the pretense of going to pour another cup of coffee, but in truth, I was hiding the furious blush burning in my cheeks. His question sent my thoughts back to last night, when I had nearly consumed him in flames. "Um. Fine, I guess. I haven't really tested myself. I've been trying to, uh, conserve energy."

Skyla snorted, coughed, and cleared her throat. "Is that right?"

I shot her a dirty look, but it only made her laugh.

"Show me," Thorin said. "I know I can't stop you or lock you up or any of those things I'd love to do that might keep you safe, but do me a favor. Please. Before we go to that island and confront the wolf, Helen, and her army, show me you can defend yourself."

I set my coffee on the counter and glanced around the kitchen. *Yeah, way too flammable and cramped.* "Outside?" I met Thorin's gaze.

He jerked his chin, a quick nod motioning me to lead the way. I left off my parka and shrugged out of my long sweater. In T-shirt and jeans, I stepped out into a cold, dry, and clear Alaska morning.

"How long until sunrise?" I asked.

Thorin stopped behind me, close enough to share his body heat. "Two hours, at least."

"How do the locals stand it? All this darkness?"

"Tanning beds."

I spun around and gaped at him. "Seriously?"

"For the UV rays. A little bit every now and then to keep away the winter blues."

I cracked a sardonic grin. "Do *you* ever use a tanning bed?"

"Why would I?" He stroked my arm. "I have my own personal sunshine."

I rolled my eyes, although his comment warmed me as much as his proximity. After flexing my neck a few times and swinging my arms to encourage blood circulation, I stretched my fingers and held my palms open at my sides, elbows bent. Fire pooled into my palms. "How much is enough to convince you? I can't afford to sacrifice my wardrobe to satisfy your concerns."

"Just make it as big as you can."

I concentrated until the fire in my palms rose into flaming pillars. A blaze wreathed my head and neck. The rune inside me, the source of my power, glowed hot and sure. "Are you satisfied?"

Thorin had backed several paces away, and the look on his face was... awe? My fire reflected in his dark eyes and lit the high spots on his face, the regal nose, the broad forehead, the prominent cheekbones. "Is it enough?"

"To kill a wolf? I think so."

He arched an eyebrow. "You *think*?"

"You don't trust my judgment? Think I'm so eager to get the wolf, I might be willing to take risks?"

He exhaled, and his shoulders slumped. "Gods, I hope not."

"I don't *want* to die, Thorin. Isn't that reassurance enough?"

He jammed his hands in his pockets and kicked a loose pebble at his feet. A muscle worked in his jaw. "Hardly."

I laid a hand on his forearm, and he stilled. "We'll get through it. Together. The Valkyries have the golems. You and I can take the wolf."

His dark eyes flickered up to meet mine. His jaw clenched, but he nodded. "Let's get going."

Aboard a Cessna with floats instead of wheels, Thorin, Skyla, Embla, four other Valkyries, and I soared over the glaucous waters of Kvichak Bay and then the deeper Prussian blue of Bristol Bay. The rest of the Valkyries followed behind in a seaplane similar to ours. The horizon shone clear and unobstructed from this vantage point, and while the sky remained locked in darkness, a thin band of yellow burned along the line separating sky from sea.

Above hung the moon, and below it, the sun, both entities sharing the same sky. I took it as a fortuitous symbol of a brother and sister briefly united. I had a feeling I would be leaning heavily on my brother. I needed his courage, bravery, and impetuousness in order to survive whatever happened next. Timidity and fear never defeated a mythological wolf or saved the world.

Skyla, sitting beside me, clenched my hand. I raised an eyebrow. "Don't tell me you're scared of flying."

Her jaw muscle worked, and she shot me a dirty look.

I bit back a grin. "And here, all this time, I thought your greatest fear was being forced to go shopping."

"I'm not afraid of it," she said through gritted teeth. "I just don't care for it, especially when we're flying over the ocean in something not much bigger than a sardine can."

As if responding to her insult, the plane shimmied and bobbed. Skyla squeaked. When the plane recovered its smooth course, I chuckled under my breath. "This is nothing compared to interdimensional travel. Ask Baldur to take you for a spin sometime. Then you'll really know about scary rides."

Skyla and I fell silent, and the drone of the airplane engine rumbled in my ears. Thorin, in the copilot's seat, glanced back at me. I gave him a thumbs up and smiled. He accepted my reassurance and turned frontward again, but the stiff set of his shoulders and his fist, clenching and unclenching on the armrest, spoke volumes about his state of mind.

On his own, he might welcome the fight, look forward to it, even. But he wasn't on his own—he had me and fifteen Valkyries to consider. The Valkyries probably concerned him least of all. We had seen them fight, knew what they could do. He had seen me fight, too, but I understood that wasn't enough.

He was the God of Thunder, armed with an infallible weapon and superior might. His superiority hadn't stopped me from invading his fight with Rolf and the golems in the field outside Portland. It hadn't stopped me from flying with the ravens to intervene on his behalf with Val in the cave. It hadn't stopped me worrying, wondering if this was the one conflict that might finally do him in. He was immortal, and I believed in him, and yet I feared for him.

I could only assume he felt the same about me. Probably worse. And yet here I was, at his side, not locked in a cage as he might have preferred. He could have chained me up and accepted my hatred as a consequence. It's what most anyone else would have done, if they didn't just kill me outright. I would have understood if Thorin had taken that approach with me. I would have hated him, but I would have understood. Thorin wanted something other than my hate, and he was willing to risk a lot to get it.

My ears popped, and I woke from my reverie. The plane had started its descent. A chain of islands rose before us, dark specks afloat on sparkling waters. The plane banked and lowered again, and we lined up perpendicular to a long, slim island, dusted in snow.

As we approached, the snow gave way, revealing the outline of an empty landing strip. Streaks, tire tracks, and skid marks marred the white surface, indicating recent visitors. A few rattletrap buildings hunched against the wind and snow, one with what looked like an air traffic control tower appended to its roof. On another low structure, a sharp, slim erection jutted from a gable. *A steeple?*

Our plane shimmied again, and the engines revved. Skyla squeezed my knuckles again, and I gritted my teeth as the plane's tail end sank, plunging us toward the ocean uncomfortably fast. We touched down minutes later, bobbing off the water like a skipping stone before settling down for good. The pilot motored to the dock and idled the engines as Thorin leapt out and secured the plane long enough for Skyla, the remaining Valkyries, and me to disembark. The other seaplane touched down as we exited, and a mixture of worried and excited faces stared from the passenger windows.

Seven of us hunkered together while Thorin leaned into the plane's doorway. After a brief conversation, the pilot nodded. Thorin waved and untied the mooring line. The seaplane pivoted, the engines revved, and he shot off across the blue, rising into the sky as gracefully as the Arctic terns that had scattered upon our arrival, crying in high, buzzing chirps and clacks.

After the other plane docked and disgorged its contents—a grim bunch of green-around-the-gills warrior women—Thorin repeated whatever message he had given to our pilot, and the second plane took off, leaving us stranded. I understood why he had done it though: no jeopardizing the mundane humans. No exposing our world to them either. It was safer for everyone that way.

Our group gathered, Thorin and Embla in the lead, Skyla and I at their heels, over a dozen Valkyries behind us. Thorin raised his voice over the birdcalls and wind. "Where do we start, Sunshine?"

I shrugged and tossed my hands out at my sides. "At the airfield, I guess. I only got an image of them marching on whatever's left of the landing strip. By the looks of it, someone has been here, but it seems awfully quiet."

"There are several buildings situated around the perimeter of the airstrip." Embla pointed at the structure that appeared to have an air control tower affixed to the roof. "We'll start there."

No one disagreed, so we all started forward, footsteps muffled in a thin layer of snow. "She'll have heard the planes," I said to Skyla. "She has to know we're coming."

"Does it matter?" Skyla shrugged. "We came for a fight. Let her bring it to us."

A disappointing silence enveloped us as we neared the center of the old Amchitka encampment. Had Helen hidden her army among the few standing structures remaining in this abandoned place? Several metal buildings stooped in the snow like weathered old men. To my left, a distinctive, arched-roof structure squatted in silent dereliction. The fine hairs on my neck rose to attention. I started toward it, but Skyla grabbed my arm and yanked. "Where are you going?" she asked.

I nodded at my destination. "I saw it in my dream—that building."

"You can't go in there by yourself. You shouldn't leave the group."

I shook off her grip. "I'm not here for the golems."

"You're here for that damned wolf."

"Yes, so why are you trying to stop me?"

"I'm not stopping you. I'm simply asking you not to go alone."

Canting my head, I arched an eyebrow. "You coming with me?"

Skyla glanced at the Valkyries and at Embla marching forward, leading her group across what was left of the old tarmac. Thorin had noticed us. He stepped around the group and approached us. "Of course I am," she said. "We kill the wolf, and all this ends, right?"

I nodded. "That's the idea."

"What's wrong?" Against the backdrop of snow and a band of women in heavy-duty winter attire, Thorin looked absurd in nothing but jeans and a sweater. The wind whipped strands of his hair about his head and brought out pink highlights in his cheeks, but he never shivered or huddled against the cold. He stood straight and alert, eyes scanning the island while he awaited my answer.

I flicked a hand at the arched building. "Something about that place sticks out to me. I saw it in the ravens' memories associated with the wolf."

"You think Skoll's in there?" he asked.

"I'm not sure about anything anymore. Nothing about this place adds up. But I'm still going to take a look."

He nodded. "Grant me one favor, Sunshine."

"What's that?"

"Let me go first?"

I snorted and motioned for him to lead the way. The three of us turned for the little corrugated building as Embla and her crew carried on, presumably heading for the old air traffic tower. None of them looked back or questioned our stopping. Those golems wouldn't stand a chance... *if* the Valkyries could find them.

We've been played, said the little devil on my shoulder. *Admit it. The golems are gone.*

Possibly, I replied, *but by whom? Ravens, Valkyries, or someone else we don't even suspect?* The prospect of a double cross or betrayal had occurred to me, but that didn't stop me from seeking proof. If Helen had left anything behind, any kind of clue, we needed to find it.

Thorin's boot steps left vague impressions in the smattering of snow. I glanced around the path he made, searching for other imprints: wolf paws, flat golem feet, a woman's snow boot, perhaps. If she had even come to Amchitka in the first place, surely Helen had worn something other than her Jimmy Choos.

By the time we reached the outbuilding's entrance, I spotted no signs of company or habitation. Still, as Thorin reached for the handle, my heart rose in my throat like mercury in a hot thermometer.

"Locked," he said when the handle refused to turn. He winked at me, grasped the handle close to where it connected to the door, and shoved his shoulder into the doorjamb. The handle fell free and clanked at his feet, and the door blew open, screaming on rusted hinges.

If anyone inside had overlooked our approach, he or she certainly hadn't missed our entrance, but nothing jumped out from the gloom to attack. Only silence and dust motes greeted us. Grimy windows obscured the dull winter sunlight, so I paused and centered myself, concentrating on bringing out my light, separated from my heat. The long building stretched out like a tunnel to our left and right. A thick layer of dust coated the floor, and for the first time since we had arrived,

I spotted evidence of the existence of a visitor other than the ones I'd brought with me.

My knees creaked as I squatted and drew my finger through the dust, circling a collection of paw prints nearly as large as my hand. "Wolf?" I peered up at my companions.

Thorin crouched beside me. "I'd say so."

"Skoll?"

"That would be my guess."

"Where is he now?" I asked, expecting no answer. "Did the ravens change their Thoughts and Memories to lie to me somehow?"

"It's a possibility," he said, "but there's probably another answer."

A distant cry cut through our conversation. A raised voice shouted something unintelligible. Then came more voices. Yelling. Gunshots.

"They've found something." Skyla turned for the exit.

Thorin and I raced out behind her into the late-morning light. Across the frozen expanse of the tarmac, a roiling, boiling fracas spilled from the hangar bays attached to the air control tower. The Valkyries and a gray heap of twisting, grinding, fighting stone swirled onto the tarmac like a storm cloud full of bluster and rage.

My heart slammed against my sternum and set up a steady pounding beat. Despite its ineffectiveness against the stone men, my fire rose and licked at my skin, begging for release.

"They're here," Skyla said breathlessly. "Holy shit, they're here."

Without waiting for a word from us, she charged forward, obviously eager to join her sisters. Thorin and I hung back and studied the scene.

"Will you fight?" He glanced at me from the corner of his eye before returning his attention to the battle spreading before us. After a quick count, I estimated the Valkyries had uncovered an army of several dozen stone men. *Seems like there should be more...*

"I don't know. If the wolf's here, I don't want to risk being distracted. But I think that shouldn't stop *you* from joining in. You'd make rubble out of them in no time."

"This can't be her whole army," he said.

"I was thinking the same thing. Can't you throw a couple of thunderbolts at them?"

He shook his head. "Not without risking the others."

"So... hand-to-hand combat?"

He allowed a quick smile. "Yes."

"Don't let me stop you. I'll stay out of the way and keep my eyes peeled for Helen and Skoll."

Thorin nodded and charged forward, Mjölnir already drawn and ready for action. Piles of stone littered the field in front of the hangars, and the Valkyries made more gravel as they went. I scanned the island again, turning in a full circle, searching for signs of the wolf. After finding nothing suspicious, I moved closer to the brawl and watched Thorin and Skyla operate in their prime environment, unhindered, full powered. They were marvelous, and a cold shard of jealousy lanced through me. Standing here, useless—it didn't sit well with me. But what help was I if I tried to fight?

The Valkyries were making headway with few injuries. Occasionally, a woman fell or a lucky swipe from a golem knocked her down, but her sisters shielded her until she recovered and rejoined the fight. Thorin demolished the stone men in great swaths, and the whole thing seemed rather anticlimactic and close to ending when another wave of golems—fifty or sixty, perhaps—poured from the backside of the hanger and renewed the fight.

A cold shiver rolled over me as a new realization dawned. The Valkyries had thrown themselves into the first round of battle, holding nothing back. They had fallen for what now seemed like an obvious ploy. The women were all well trained and fit but ultimately human, and they tired fast. Tired fighters made mistakes. They ducked slower, swung sluggishly, stabbed with less force.

Embla, one of the oldest in the group, stumbled first. A rock-hard golem fist connected with her chest and sent her flying. She uttered a horrible grating scream like skidding tires. Then she hit the ground, crumpled, and fell still and silent. Naomi disengaged and rushed to Embla's aid, but I ran in and shoved Naomi aside. "You fight. I'll take care of her," I said.

The effort of dragging Embla's lifeless weight away from the center of action strained my muscles. She was small but solidly built and full of muscle. I settled her in a bed of mostly frozen grass, checked her pulse, and found it beating light and fast beneath the thin skin at her neck. Her chest rose and fell in shallow breaths.

I made her as comfortable as possible before returning my attention to the fight. More women faltered, and the golems pressed their advantage. Thorin, however, had not wavered. He pushed on, tireless and resolute. Skyla stood at his side, firing steadily into the melee, pausing only to reload.

Embla groaned beside me and blinked. She stared unfocused into the blue sky. I leaned over, and her gaze fell on me. She blinked again.

"Did you dream of electric sheep?" I asked.

Her brow crinkled. "What? No."

"Good. I guess that means you're not an android."

She grimaced. "What happened?"

"Rockslide got you, I think."

She pressed a tentative hand to her chest and gritted her teeth. "I'll say."

She moved to sit up but grimaced and wheezed. I pushed her down. "Nope. You're not doing anything else until you get checked out by a doctor. Don't take chances with internal injuries."

"But my sisters—"

"Have it under control." I interrupted her protest. "Thorin and the others are taking them down by the dozens. The fight will be over in no time."

Embla exhaled, relaxed, and closed her eyes. "Any other casualties?"

"Probably some black eyes, bloody noses, maybe a cracked rib or two. But it's winding down again. Thorin and Skyla made pea gravel out of those things." I narrowed my eyes at her and studied her face—the one that reflected elements of both Nina and Skyla in bone structure, coloring, and shape. Could she really be their betrayer? How could anyone harbor that much hatred, enough to abandon their family? "Embla, I need to ask you something."

Before I could form my question, my ears popped, and Thorin appeared at my side. I glanced up at him, expecting to find him triumphant and exultant. Instead, he wore a grim expression, and something dark flashed in his eyes. My breath caught. "What is it?"

"Baldur. He's found the rest of Helen's army."

My words turned to ice as they crossed my tongue. "Where are they?"

He held his hand out as if asking for a hug, and I forgot all about my questions for Embla as I leapt to my feet and latched my arms around his neck, ready to go wherever he wanted to take us—New Breidablick, I presumed.

Skyla, having caught on to the change in mood and tone, jogged up and stopped at Thorin's side.

In a voice filled with imperative, he said, "Bring the Valkyries to New Breidablick as quickly as you can. Baldur is under attack as we speak."

My parents. I had thought they'd be safe in Baldur's estate. Instead, I had moved them into the hottest part of the fire.

"It'll take hours to get there." Skyla's eyes went wide and fearful. "We may be too late."

"Whatever it takes, whatever the cost..." Thorin pulled me closer. "Just do it."

"Embla needs a hospital," I said the moment before Thorin whisked me into the æther.

Skyla nodded, knelt, and reached for her aunt.

CHAPTER 21

THORIN AND I ALIGHTED ON the patio at the rear of Baldur's house. He kept me locked in his arms as he settled his heavy gaze on me. Copper flecks swirled in his dark eyes. Thunder rumbled in the distance, and dark clouds blew in on stiff winds. If I had to guess, the God of Thunder was gearing up for battle. "I don't know what's going to happen next," he said. "But if I've learned anything in all my years, it's to take nothing for granted."

"What are you worried about?" I shrugged off his sudden gravity. "You're immortal."

His fingers curled around my shoulders. "My immortality isn't the problem."

I pursed my lips. "No, it's my vulnerability, right?"

The muscles around his eyes tightened. "There was a war like this before. I underestimated the toll it would take. The destruction and loss devastated those of us who survived. The one thing I regret most was never taking the time to tell them..." He closed his eyes and cleared this throat. "I shunned the prophecies. I thought nothing was strong enough to defeat the Aesir. I walked out of my home the morning of the final battle, assuming, at the end of the day, my house would still be standing, and my family would still be there, alive. I thought I would have more time."

A hard knot rose in my throat. How much had I regretted taking Mani for granted? How much had I hated not telling him, one last time, how much I loved him? But I had gotten that second chance, there at the Norns' well. I had told Mani goodbye. It wasn't as good as having him back, but for the first time since his death, I had peace and closure.

211

For thousands of years, Thorin had lived never having those things. How had he managed?

"*You have to decide every day if it's worth it or not,*" he had said.

If anyone had ever lived up to his own words...

I cleared my throat and met his ancient, bottomless stare. "What would you have done differently?"

"I would have still gone to battle because that was my purpose, but I would have lingered. I would have taken Joren in my lap and told him all the reasons I was proud to be his papa. I would have stayed up through the night with Eir, telling her, *showing* her, how much I loved her. Instead, I patted Joren's head, kissed Eir's cheek, and I walked out the door."

I leaned in and rested my temple against Thorin's chest. His heart thumped under my ear—a muscle that had beat, impossibly, for millennia. How was it I could be standing here, like this, with a being like him? How could he think I was worthy of him?

He stroked my back. His deep voice rumbled through me. "I won't have those regrets again, Solina. I won't make the same mistakes. Whatever happens next, I won't go into it knowing that I never took a moment to tell you that I love you."

Gasping, I pulled away and gaped at him. My heart strained like a newborn moth fighting to escape its cocoon. I drew in a long, deep breath, expanding my lungs near to bursting. "No. You can't." My logical side refused to accept it, but the moth beat against my sternum, testing its wings, eager to fly.

Thorin's expression darkened. "I am the God of Thunder, strongest among all of my kind." A twisted smile played across his lips. "I can do anything I please. But you..." He took my hand and curled it into a fist, all except my pinkie. He traced a tickling, winding circle from my knuckle to the tip of my nail. "You have me wrapped around your little finger."

I shook my head. "Not possible."

He smiled again, a little brighter this time. He took my chin, tilted my head back, and pressed his lips to mine. "Did you hear what I said?" he asked after he kissed me thoroughly enough to make my head spin.

I swallowed. "I-I heard you."

"But you don't believe me?"

My voice had mostly deserted me, so I whispered. "Shouldn't."

He drew me into the circle of his arms. "Why not?"

"Dangerous."

Skimming the tip of his nose along the rim of my ear, he said, "You're right. It's more than bones and bodies we're risking. Injuries of the heart are so much more grievous."

"How can it work? We're so different." I had asked the same question before, but this time, my words lacked conviction.

"Do you trust me, Sunshine?" He had asked that before, too.

I bit my bottom lip, hard. I nodded. Of course I trusted him—trusted him to my grave. That was the problem.

"Do you believe me when I say we'll find a way?"

"Damn me, but I do. But I'm also afraid of what it might cost us."

He grinned, and a new light shone in his eyes. "When have you let the fear of the unknown stop you?"

It had stopped me for twenty-five years. Then I climbed aboard a plane and flew to Alaska. That had changed everything. "No regrets?" I said as if toeing a pool of frigid water while contemplating jumping in—knowing I was going to jump in.

Thorin's grin widened. "No regrets."

Here goes nothing. I exhaled a long hopeful breath, and at the end, while I still had the air for it, I said, "I love you, too."

"We can do this."

I dared to meet his eyes, and the look in them nearly stole my breath again. I swallowed and bobbed my head. "Yes. I think we can."

CHAPTER 22

S O, YEAH.

I had admitted, out loud, to the immortal and otherworldly God of Thunder that I loved him, but only after he'd said it first, which might have been even more... amazing? Ridiculous? Absurd? Breathtaking? I was still processing the unlikelihood of my situation when Baldur stepped onto the patio to greet us. He was scatterbrained sometimes and obsessed with Nina, but he wasn't stupid. And he was perceptive—possibly empathic to some extent. He looked at Thorin, glanced at me, and scanned the horizon, the valley, the sky.

When he had satisfied himself with his search, his attention settled on Thorin. "It's like standing in the middle of a hurricane."

"What do you mean?" Thorin asked.

"There are too many things swirling about. I can't pin them down." Baldur's brow furrowed, and he blinked. "Bitter and sweet. Terror and joy. You two have terrible timing." He turned on his heel and motioned for us to follow him around the side of the house. "New Breidablick has wards. They're holding Helen's army at a relatively safe distance, for now, but keeping the wards up against her constant attack requires my active focus and attention. It will eventually wear me down, leaving me vulnerable and exhausted. I won't be good for much if it comes to an all-out battle."

Thunder rumbled overhead. "Leave the fighting to me," Thorin said.

"The Valkyries are on their way," I said. "But they're hours out, and I don't know which of them to trust. I'll be honest. Embla makes me nervous. She was wounded at Amchitka, but if she's Helen's mole, she may have allies among the other women."

Baldur flushed, and he glanced away. He stared, unfocused,

somewhere over my shoulder toward a distant ridgeline. "You think Embla's helping Hela as revenge for my parental neglect? She's not a rebellious teenager, Solina."

"It's just one theory." I crossed my arms over my chest and furrowed my brow. "I don't know what motives the other Valkyries would have for helping Helen. Maybe there's another explanation altogether."

Baldur hesitated a moment longer. He scrubbed his chin and gazed at nothing. His expression sharpened, and his posture stiffened. "Thorin, follow me. Solina, I'd warn your parents. They're already in the basement—see that they stay there. Find Nina, and get her to the basement, too."

"Then what?" I asked. "Pop some popcorn, and put in a movie? There's got to be something more useful I can do."

He raised his chin and peered down at me. "Your time will come soon enough. Gather your strength, prepare your fire, and hope we don't need it." He stepped beside Thorin and grasped his shoulder. My ears popped, and the two men disappeared.

I growled and muttered incoherent expressions of annoyance as I stomped off to find my parents and explain to them how my plan to remove them from their home and bring them to Baldur's house had actually been a huge mistake. And then I had to find Nina. Poor broken Nina... *Wait. Nina.*

As if I expected to find her hovering in some corner like a silent ghost, I rushed into the house and scanned the living room. Nope, no Nina. I hurried to the kitchen. *Damn. Empty too.* With no better idea of how to find her, I jogged through Baldur's house, calling her name at the top of my lungs. "Nina! Hey, Nina! It's Solina. Olly olly oxen free!"

"What?" Nina said from somewhere behind me. I yelped and spun around. She stood a few feet away at the bottom of the stairs leading to the second floor. She wore a gauzy white dress and a silvery-gray scarf that brought out the cool undertones in her brown skin. Regality fit her like pride fits a lioness. She clutched a book, holding her place with her thumb. "Your shrieking could raise the dead."

"You don't know the irony of that statement," I said, mostly under my breath. "I need to ask you some more questions. About Helen. Would you be willing to talk to me about her?"

Nina glanced down at the book in her hand. She frowned. "Now?"

"You've got insight no one else has, and we need your help."

Her eyebrow arched. "We?"

I exhaled and tried not to roll my eyes. *Keep your patience. Don't patronize.* I stood my ground and waited for her reply.

She sighed. Her posture relaxed. She eyed her book again and sputtered her lips. "I was at a really good part, but I guess it can wait."

"I'll make us coffee," I offered. I was going to need all the caffeine and extra energy kick I could get. Plus the chore gave me something to focus on, although I was perfectly capable of multitasking. *Look, folks! She can make coffee* and *worry about the apocalypse at the same time!*

Nina shrugged. "Why not?"

I led the way to the kitchen, and Nina trudged behind me. She wore her tough exterior like armor, no doubt a defensive mechanism she'd learned in her years living with Helen. But she had shown me her soft side the last time I was here. She had let down her barricades before. For weeks, she had marinated in Baldur's love and care and hadn't yet run away or killed the Allfather in his sleep. That had to mean something good, right?

Or maybe she's here to be Helen's backdoor key into New Breidablick. I dusted the little devil of doubt off my shoulder, and Nina gave me a funny look. I resisted sticking my tongue out at her. *As if you don't know about having voices in* your *head.*

"Baldur has told you Helen is about to unleash her undead horde on us, right?" I went to the coffee pot.

Nina eased into a kitchen chair and nodded.

"You don't seem very concerned."

She waggled her shoulders in a half-hearted shrug. "I don't have powers like you or Thorin or Baldur. What do I gain from being worried or upset about something beyond my control?"

"She could kill us all."

She winced, but her expression eased. "Nah. Thorin and Baldur won't go down so easily."

"What about you and me and my parents? And the rest of the world?"

She stared at the backs of her hands and flexed her fingers. "Why should I fear death? I'll just come back again, won't I? And so will you, right?"

I swallowed my rising irritation and anger. Confrontation would mostly likely shut her down when I needed her cooperation more than ever. "I thought you didn't believe in reincarnation."

Nina looked up at me and blinked. She almost, *almost*, smiled. "Baldur can be very... persuasive."

"There may not be anything left for you to come back to next time, if Helen gets her way."

She sat up straighter and squinted at me. "What do you expect me to do about any of this?"

I finished pouring water into the coffee machine and pressed the start button. I leaned against the counter and crossed one leg over the other. "Two things." I raised my index finger. "First, I want you to tell me who Helen's contact inside the Aerie is. Which of the Valkyries is Helen's mole?"

Her lips twisted, and she huffed. "I already told you, she would never tell me anything like that. I was always simply a way for her to take revenge on Baldur, by giving me to him a little more warped, a little more broken, and utterly useless. "

"You never heard her mention the Valkyries? How about Embla or Naomi?" I listed more Valkyrie names, but Nina only shook her head.

"Told you I'm useless," she said.

Her melancholy pronouncement stirred a warm current of pity in my heart. "Your being here is a big help to Baldur. He's been... well, he's been better since he's had you back."

A light flared to life in her dark eyes, and her face brightened. "Really?"

I grinned, encouraging her delight. If she felt at all invested in Baldur and New Breidablick, it was on those sympathies I had to lean. "Definitely."

A full smile unfurled across her lips, and a deep shade of pink crept into her ears. Nina fidgeted with the fringe on her placemat. "Didn't you have something else you wanted to talk about? You said there were two things."

I nodded. "Helen is going to try her best to kill us all. I need you to promise you won't help her. Promise you won't let her in through the proverbial backdoor. Even if things get desperate and siding with her might seem advantageous, promise you won't do it. Promise you won't break Baldur's heart."

She stared at the table top and knitted her brows. Her throat worked. She balled her fist on the table. "I don't want Helen to win. I don't want to go back to living that way."

"That's not a promise." Why did it matter? Whether she made a vow or not, it changed nothing. Helen would still come. We would still have to fight.

Baldur had one of those restaurant-style pots that kept water hot all the time. It made coffee almost instantly, and when the brew finished dripping, I poured two mugs.

Nina took her cup without looking at me. "For what it's worth, I promise. I want what Baldur is offering."

Her promise should have been enough, but I had shed my guilelessness over the past few months. *Trust but verify, they say.* Bracing myself, I slid my hand over Nina's and reached for her mind. As I had hoped, our conversation drew her thoughts of Baldur to the surface.

Our connection revealed images of the late-night suppers he cooked for her—all her favorite foods. He knew without asking what they were. He brought her tea—oolong with a splash of cream and a hint of sugar, just the way she preferred, but she had never told him those details. She thought of the day before, when she was feeling especially despondent. He played recordings of Bessie Smith and Sidney Bechet, jazz from her favorite musical era. He never touched her without asking, and even then, he was careful his posture never intimidated or threatened her in any way. He held her when she cried and didn't ask questions, never made her explain her tears.

Her thoughts shifted to flashes of images she had once dismissed as dreams, night terrors, in which she repeatedly found herself aboard a flaming ship next to Baldur's dead body. She knew better now—not nightmares but memories of dying from a broken heart.

Her thoughts stuttered across a litany of moments with Helen— lavish gifts distributed with sharp words, cold shoulders, long absences, opulent living conditions and plenty of everything, but so much loneliness...

As casually as possible, I drew my hand away from Nina's and stood, severing the connection. I went to the refrigerator and took out a bottle of half-and-half. "Baldur wants you to go to the basement and stay with my parents until this is over."

She glanced up at me as she spooned sugar into her mug. "Nowhere is safe from Helen."

I closed the refrigerator. "I tend to agree with you. But I'd also love to have someone who knows a little about what's going on stay with my parents. I'm sure they're more than a little freaked out right now."

She huffed a nervous giggle as she poured in the cream. "They're not the only ones."

"I could also use a little moral support when I explain what's going on to them."

"Moral support isn't my strongest suit."

I took up my own coffee mug and sipped. "I'll take what I can get."

After we finished our coffee, Nina and I tromped down the basement stairs, dread making our footsteps heavy. My parents sat close together on Baldur's sofa, talking quietly to each other. Light from the TV flickered over them, but they had the volume low. Although I couldn't make out the words, the tone of their conversation sounded serious and fearful. My dad looked up at me first. The worry lines on his forehead deepened as he stood and pulled my mother up beside him. "Solina. Baldur asked us to come down here but wouldn't say why."

I raised my palm like a policeman stopping oncoming traffic. "Most won't make sense. But I'll try to explain it if you'll try your best to believe me."

Dad glanced at Mom. They held each other's gaze as if communicating telepathically. Perhaps couples who had lived and worked together as many years as my mother and father *could* read each other's minds. My dad nodded and swallowed. "Okay. Let's hear it."

I exhaled and slumped into a chair perpendicular to the sofa. I motioned for my parents to sit. Without a word, Nina glided to the opposite side of the room and took a seat at Baldur's desk. A moment later, the blue light from the computer monitor illuminated her face.

"Baldur's told you most of it, right?" I asked. My dad nodded. "Okay, I'll start with what's happened since I last saw you." I talked, and my parents listened, rarely interrupting. They absorbed everything in semistunned silence. "And now we're all here, and it's our last chance to end this thing."

My mother had lost the flush that typically adorned her cheeks. Her eyes sat deeper and darker in her face than usual. "You said we'd be safe here, Solina."

I scraped my fingers through my hair and leaned back in my chair. "I did say that, and I still think it's the safest place for you. You were too vulnerable at home. Baldur has had men watching you, but we were never confident it was enough. Helen could have gotten to you, used you as leverage."

"So what do you want us to do?"

"Stay here, stay out of the way, and try not to worry." I pointed to the beautiful woman sitting in the rear of the room. "This is Nina, Baldur's wife. She's going to stay with you."

Nina looked over the top of the monitor and cocked an eyebrow at me.

"Well...you *are* his wife," I said, "in a metaphysical sense."

Nina shrugged and returned her attention to the computer.

My dad glanced at Nina before looking back at me. "What are *you* going to do, Solina?"

I cracked my knuckles and rolled my shoulders. "I'm going to fight."

As if to underscore my words, thunder boomed loud enough to rattle the house. I rose to my feet. My dad shifted as if to stand, but I waved at him, urging him to remain in his seat. "Stay here, please. I already know the things you'd say to try to convince me not to. Please don't. I won't stay. I have to help them."

Thorin's thunder exploded again. I turned and jogged up the basement stairs before my parents could protest. Outside the first-floor windows, the sky had gone twilight purple from the thickening storm clouds. Diluted light glowed in the windows, casting dark shadows over the interior. A streak of lightning tore apart the sky. Bright, phosphorescent light flared over the landscape as brief as a heartbeat before fading away. Specks of color floated in my field of vision. I blinked them away as I hurried outside.

Thorin's voice rose above the clamor of his storm, and he spoke in his ancient tongue. I followed his voice and found him beside Baldur in the broad expanse of land spreading out before New Breidablick's front door. Baldur's estate sprawled over several thousand acres, and he had told me before that the closest neighbor, a beef rancher, lived miles and miles away on the other side of a distant ridge. A protracted battle would eventually draw attention from mortal authorities, but perhaps Helen thought our battle wouldn't last that long. Most likely, she didn't care. In her mind, this was the beginning of the end.

"Where's Helen?" I stepped to Thorin's side. He pointed to a distant mountain range, but the fading light camouflaged everything beneath a cover of shadows. "I don't see anything."

"You will soon enough," he said. "Baldur's wards act like an invisible brick wall. You throw something against them long enough, they'll eventually crumble."

"How far out are they?"

"Just over a mile." Baldur gritted his teeth. "It's the extent of my reach. If I tried to push the wards any farther, they'd be too weak to be useful." He stood firm, legs braced wide, eyes focused on some faraway point. But an unusual pallor had crept into his skin, robbing him of his ruddy complexion and leaving him pale and waxen.

"Is Baldur doing okay?" I lowered my voice out of consideration for Baldur's concentration.

"Helen has been here for over an hour." Thorin studied the Allfather with an appraising gaze. "She's been throwing her soldiers at the wards like cannonballs. We underestimated the size of her army. I'm afraid Baldur will give out before her golems do."

Hairs rose along the back of my neck. At first, I mistook it as a reaction to the static electricity surrounding Thorin or a primal response to fear, but no. My sixth sense had picked up on the presence of someone new behind me.

"Brother, Allfather... Solina."

I spun on my heel and gasped. Fire pooled in my palms. "Grim," I snarled, baring my teeth. My stomach churned, and stinging, ice-cold revulsion chilled my blood.

Grim raised his hands and stepped back. He lowered his eyes and waited for me to decide whether to attack him or not. Thorin's heavy hand settled on my shoulder. *Holding me back or lending support? Hard to tell.*

"I'm not going to burn him." I'd had more than enough of killing people with my fire. For a certain wolf, however, I'd make an exception. "But I know better than to face him empty-handed."

A deep flush stained Grim's cheeks. "You have no reason to believe me, Solina. But I swear to you—I mean you no harm. I owe you a life debt."

My fire retreated, and I stepped closer, fists balled at my sides. "What's that supposed to mean?"

"He'll do everything within his power to protect you," Thorin said. "Even if it means giving his own life to do it."

"Ha! That only happens in Hollywood, like Morgan Freeman in that Robin Hood movie."

"You don't have to believe him, Sunshine. It's our way. He's not lying."

Dumbfounded, I stared at Grim. He looked up, and our gazes locked. I grumbled an ineffable sound of disgust and backed away, putting Thorin and Baldur between Grim and me. "Give me one reason to doubt you, Grim, and I'll burn you to ash. You don't have a fire sword to protect you anymore."

Thorin's brother said nothing but bowed his neck. I snorted and turned away. *How do I keep an eye on him and fight Helen and her army at the same time?*

As if reading my thoughts, Thorin said, "I'm watching him, too, Solina. But I believe he'll do what he says."

"I believe it, too," I said, my tone thick with derision, "so long as Helen continues to be a bigger threat. What happens when he gets tired of fighting her and decides it's just easier to kill me first, the way he originally planned?"

"He won't." His eyes, dark and intent, bored into me. "I won't let him."

"Why is he still here? I thought he was going to leave when he felt better."

"I asked him to stay," Baldur said without turning his attention away from whatever distant spot he'd been staring at. "We need all the help we can get."

I harrumphed but swallowed my protests. As much as I hated it, Baldur had a point. Grim was invested in Helen's defeat as much as the rest of us. If he kept his berserker battle rage pointed in her direction, he could be useful. And I'd try not to set him on fire.

"Where are the Valkyries?" I asked between rumbles of thunder and lightning strikes. Concussions of sound and light bombarded a distant ridgeline where, I assumed, Helen's army approached.

"Still hours out." Thorin gritted his teeth.

I rolled my shoulders and popped my knuckles. "That's too bad, because this may be over long before then."

CHAPTER 23

BACK AND FORTH, THORIN SHIFTED his weight, his feet, his shoulders. He toyed with his hammer, tossing it from fist to fist. I stood beside him and stared, searching distant ridges that stood out against the bruised sky like raw, broken bones, but nothing struck me as unusual.

"How does Helen transport a battalion of stone soldiers into the middle of Lake Tahoe without drawing notice from mortal authorities?" I asked. "The National Guard should already be here with tanks and helicopters."

"Out here, in the mountains," Baldur said, "those creatures are naturally camouflaged, blending in with the landscape."

Thorin twirled Mjölnir's handle through his fingers like a baton, the same trick he'd shown my parents last time we were here. *If I touched him right now, wonder if I'd get an electric shock?* "If Helen unloaded her trucks somewhere nearby and sent the golems in small groups on foot through the mountains, it's possible they could go a long way without being noticed, especially if they move at night."

"And she's had days to get them into position," I said. "While we were wasting our time at Amchitka—why do you think I didn't see this part of her plan when I was in the Norns' well?"

"She probably didn't decide to do this until she learned that we were on our way to Amchitka," Thorin said. "I think this was a last-minute decision on her part. It's the only way to outwit your premonitions."

"It still took some advance planning."

"Someone from within the Valkyries is betraying you," Grim said. "They're rotten at the core."

"Tell me something I didn't know, Captain Obvious." I scowled at

Grim's profile, but he had the sense not to take my bait. He stood at Thorin's opposite shoulder, and the two brothers, side by side, formed a formidable force. Thor had split his might between his sons, giving Magni Alexander his strength and Modi Grimr his lust for battle. One look at them and any sensible opponent would run for the hills. Neither Helen nor her stone men had demonstrated much sensibility, however.

I scowled at Grim. "I have to believe the Valkyries aren't all—"

Baldur gasped and sank to his knee. Thorin grabbed the Allfather's shoulder and held him steady.

Baldur rubbed his temples and ground his teeth. He rose unsteadily to his feet. "The wards... I don't know what she's done, but if she keeps it up, I won't last much longer."

I stared into the distance, and a shimmer of iridescent colors quivered across the horizon. I pointed. "I see something."

Thorin followed the direction of my gesture. He grunted low in his throat. "Shit."

"What is that?"

"It's the wards," Grim said. "They become more visible as they lose their strength. Helen's hitting that spot with everything she's got."

"What can we do to help?"

Baldur winced and clutched his head in his hands. "I don't know. Maybe... Maybe if there was someone who could reinforce the wards..."

"Who could do that?" An idea struck. "What about Skyla? She's a direct descendent. Do you think she could help?"

"Couldn't hurt." Baldur grunted.

"It'll mean telling her the truth about you and her."

He turned his glittering, pain-filled eyes on me. "If it means saving everyone's lives, I'll risk it. Even if she hates me."

I looked at Thorin. "Can you get her? Bring her here?"

Worry lines crinkled around his eyes. He licked his lips. "I'll get her if you can find her. But the moment Helen breaches the wards, I'll have to stay and fight. No matter what."

I swallowed past the hard lump rising in my throat. "I understand."

Thorin slipped his cell phone from his pocket and tossed it to me. After thumbing through his recent call log, I found Skyla's name and swiped the call button. Her phone rang and went to voicemail. I tried again with no success. *Where the hell are you, Skyla?*

"Call me immediately," I said to her voicemail. "I need you here as soon as possible. Thorin will come get you, but he has to know exactly where you are. Baldur's wards are failing, and there's a way you might be able to help if we can get you here. Now."

I ended the call and met Thorin's dark stare. "Do you have any of the Valkyries' other numbers?"

He shook his head. "They mostly use disposable phones. They aren't very trusting."

Baldur's wards shimmered again, ghostly greens and blues rippling from the golems' point of impact like concentric rings in a pool of water. The undulations dispersed into the atmosphere in a twinkle of glittering sparks that resounded like fireworks. Baldur uttered a steady litany of words under his breath, most likely naming the runes that had fabricated his enchanted wall. He spoke the runes with specific intent, giving them power, converting them from inert symbols into active weapons.

A crack like the felling of a massive oak tree cut through the dissonance of thunder, lightning, and wind. A web of veins—glowing and pulsing with every hue of the rainbow—clawed through Baldur's invisible barricade.

"It's going," Baldur groaned. "I can't..."

Thorin threw back his head and roared something in his ancient tongue. A glowing network of electrical highways and byways crisscrossed the clouds like a celestial map, crackling and popping with potential energy. The lightning fell apart and rocketed toward the earth, slicing the sky into jagged shards and ribbons. Thorin folded himself around me, forming a shelter against the concussion of sound and dynamic force exploding across New Breidablick as his ammunition found its target.

I clamped my hands over my ears and clenched my eyes shut, but the blast rocked through me despite Thorin's insulation. My heart stumbled and stuttered, its rhythm disturbed by the blast. I wheezed and pounded my chest until the sensation faded. Still, my ears rang, and the world swirled in a dizzying soup. He stroked my back and kept me wrapped in his arms until my senses recovered.

"Good Lord," I rasped. "Why don't you just drop an atomic bomb next time?"

He ignored my bad joke. "You're all right?"

I shifted and peered at his face. Amber flecks swirled in his dark eyes like suns in faraway galaxies. I offered a limp smile. "I'm fine."

We straightened up and surveyed the results of his literal *Blitzkrieg*. "Her army has fallen back," he said. "They're regrouping."

"I'll have to take your word for it. I still can't see anything."

"They've taken a hit," Grim said. "I can't say how many, but there are rubble piles everywhere."

My heart swelled in my chest, filling with pride and awe that temporarily alleviated the fear. *I believe in you, Thorin. I believe... I believe...*

Baldur shook himself, clearing the dazed look from his face. "I need to narrow the perimeter of the wards. I don't have much juice left in me, but I can hold out a little longer if I bring the wards in closer. It'll give us a smaller buffer zone, but I don't have the strength for anything bigger. Maybe it'll buy us some time." He turned his blue eyes on me. "Any luck finding Skyla?"

I shook my head. "Nothing yet." Common sense listed a dozen reasons why my calls had failed to reach my best friend: her phone battery had died; her route to New Breidablick carried her through spotty reception zones; she was distracted, occupied, et cetera. But a little niggling voice of doubt suggested otherwise. *Something's gone wrong*, it said in insistent tones.

Baldur, Grim, Thorin, and I retreated to New Breidablick's wraparound front porch. Baldur inhaled several deep breaths, rolled his head around on his neck, and flexed his shoulders. Then he strained as if lifting an enormous weight. A chorus of snaps, pops, and hisses sang out, and a translucent blue curtain rose before us, rippling like the surface of a glacial bay.

From our perch, we watched the golems approach. They spread themselves wide apart, diluting Thorin's target, making it harder for him to take out many at one time. From somewhere behind us, near the vicinity of Baldur's barn, a rooster crowed. I shivered, and goose bumps broke out over my arms.

Overhead, black clouds boiled and expanded, tumbling over each other. Slim filaments of electricity crawled through the tumultuous heavens, flashing, fizzing, breaking apart, and reforming. I turned to Thorin and pointed overhead. "What are you doing up there?"

"Recharging. That last blast spent a huge amount of energy. It'll take time to build up to that level again."

"What if Helen won't give you that time?"

He grimaced. "I'll make the best of what I've got."

"Have you seen Skoll anywhere out there?"

"No. And I've been looking."

"That doesn't make sense."

He frowned. "What do you mean?"

I gestured to the battlefield. "This is supposed to come last. First Hati kills my brother. Then Skoll devours me. Then comes the battle. Helen doesn't have the fire sword, either. What's she hoping to gain from this?"

"I don't know anymore," he said. "She's desperate. Her plans are falling apart."

"Maybe," Grim said, "she just wants to take as many of us down with her as possible."

"I don't like feeling useless." I stared out at the approaching army. "I want to face her. I want to fight her."

Thorin shifted closer and curled an arm around my shoulders. "Does it help to know your being here gives me more incentive to succeed? You make the cost of losing too expensive." He lowered his voice so only I could hear. "I can't lose you. I *refuse* to lose you."

I swallowed and searched for an appropriate response, something to express how much I wanted the same thing. My words were weak and insufficient. Instead, I leaned into him and held him close.

A cry rose from the combat zone, a lone voice shouting something imperative and urgent. The golems responded. As a unit, they lurched forward at a steady march. Their pace increased as they closed the distance between us. They ran, hurtling toward us—a giant stone battering ram with a hundred different points of impact. When the first line of golems reached us, they drove headlong into Baldur's wards, and the collision blasted them into dusty smithereens. The repercussion jangled in my ears, and I winced as my eardrums shrieked.

Baldur's wards violently heaved, and the Allfather cried out, bared his teeth, and sank to his knees. Another golem tidal wave raced toward us. Thorin glanced at Baldur, at his brother, and at me. A cold mask fell over his face, and my heart lurched into my throat. His decision showed plain on his face, and before I could form a protest, he leaned forward and kissed me. Then he vaulted the porch railing and threw himself over that metaphysical boundary separating us from Helen's hordes.

"No!" I screamed, grabbing for him. *Too slow. Much too slow.* Above us, the storm raged. Thunder detonated. Winds screamed. Frantic, I turned to Grim, knotted my fingers into his shirtfront, and jerked him forward. "Why are you just standing here, you bastard?"

Blackness bled into Grim's eyes, and he snarled. "Baldur. I need a weapon. Now."

Clutching his head between his hands, Baldur groaned and rocked on his knees.

"Allfather, please." Grim pulled free from my grasp. He knelt beside Baldur and implored. "You asked me to stay and fight. I can't do it empty-handed."

I sank to the floorboards beside my erstwhile enemy and addressed the Allfather. "You know how I feel about Grim. I have less reason than anyone to trust him. But we can't afford to play it safe now." I glanced up and searched the melee, looking for a glimpse of blond hair or a flash of lightning reflecting off Mjölnir. But the only evidence of Thorin's presence in the fight was the occasional spray of exploding stone and the deafening shrieks of thunder and wind.

Given enough time, Thorin might demolish the entire army on his own, but Baldur and his wards would fall long before then. Once Helen's army breached our walls, a flood of rock and stone would drown us all.

"Find Nina." Baldur forced the words through his clenched jaw. "She knows where my weapons room is. Surtalogi... Take it."

I glanced at Grim. The darkness in his eyes cleared, and his whole countenance lightened. "Stay here with Baldur," I said. "I'll find Nina. I'll bring you the sword."

Like a pinball, I ricocheted through the house and bounded down the basement stairs. "Nina." I stopped and panted for breath. "Weapons room. Now." My parents jumped up and rushed toward me. I waved them off. "No time to explain. Stay put, please."

My mom and dad clenched each other's hands and stared at me, their eyes huge and full of worry. "It sounds like World War Three up there," Mom said. "The house is shaking like it's going to come down around our ears."

"Nah." I put on a thick layer of bravado, an act to keep my parents calm. "It's just Thorin showing off. Posturing a little."

"Then why do you need weapons?" Nina rose from her seat.

I narrowed my eyes, urging her to read my body language and play along with my nonchalant performance. "Just being prepared."

Her sour expression said she didn't believe me, but she rounded the corner of Baldur's computer desk and crossed to the basement stairs. As I followed her to the exit, I slapped a smile on my face and fought against the tension in my neck and shoulders. I steadied my breathing and unclenched my fists.

"Everything's under control," I said to my parents. "I'll be back soon to give you an update." *Lies, lies, lies.* But I'd do or say anything to keep them here—out of the way, innocent, ignorant. A few months before I had cursed them for ignoring the truth about Mani and for not trying harder to uncover the motives behind his murder. Now, I'd consider it a blessing if they'd sit and wait and not ask questions or seek answers for themselves.

I followed Nina to the first floor, leaving my parents gaping at each other. As soon as the basement door closed, Nina whirled around and faced me. She arched a single eyebrow. I read the question in her face and answered quickly, summarizing all that had happened since our kaffeeklatsch in the kitchen. As I talked, she led us down the hallway and up a flight of stairs to the second floor.

"Baldur keeps the weapons room warded like the rest of the house." She approached a bare expanse of wall stretched between two bedrooms.

"Will the inside wards fall if the outside ones do?"

She pursed her lips and pressed her palm against the wall. "How should I know? This is all still mostly a lot of hocus pocus to me. I wasn't sure I believed him, but he made me practice just in case."

Nina whispered a word, and the bare drywall faded, revealing an open doorway leading into a closet-sized space chock-full of knives, swords, and things I had only seen in fantasy role-playing games. *World of Warcraft, anyone?*

Nina took in my stunned silence and rolled her eyes. "Hocus pocus."

Baldur had mounted everything elegantly, either on a wall rack or perched on display stands like a museum. I stepped into the room, and motion-sensor lighting illuminated the displays. Surtalogi, the ancient fire sword, drew my gaze as if whispering my name. Carefully, as if it were a bomb, I lifted the weapon from its mount on the wall. I also selected a slim knife covered in rune etchings from a velvet-lined box. When the sword didn't explode or immediately drain away all my fire, I turned and started down the hallway for the stairs.

Nina trailed behind me. "Why that one?"

"It's a fire sword. Works like the craziest flamethrower you ever saw. It's for Grim." My stomach turned over, but I shoved aside my discomfort and doubts. "He needs a weapon, and he's familiar with this one."

"I don't know anything about weapons or how to use them."

I paused on the stairs and studied her. Although beautiful, she was gaunt and seemed fragile. Breakable. I had once thought of her as a porcelain doll. Her outward appearance screamed she was helpless and needed protection, but it was camouflage. She had survived Helen's manipulations and emotional abuse. She had survived a car wreck and a coma. She had survived hundreds of reincarnations. I had a feeling anyone who underestimated her strength or fell for her fragile façade would wind up regretting it.

I handed her the knife I had taken from Baldur's weapons room. It resembled the blades the Valkyries preferred, and I hoped the rune carvings meant the knife carried an extra dose of lethality, should she need it. "We'll make sure to change that as soon as possible. You need to know how to protect yourself."

Nina's face fell as she studied the weapon, an elegant blade with a hilt that perfectly fit her small hand. She looked up, and a wall rose behind her eyes, but when I started forward again, she followed me. "Sometimes, getting through a single day is like climbing Mount Everest," she said.

"You're not the only one who dreams, you know. I've seen his death." I knew she meant Baldur because I had seen her thoughts and the way her memories haunted her. "I've seen his death played out, again and again, almost every night since he brought me here."

If I put myself in Nina's position and imagined the way the world looked through her eyes, from the point of view of a woman who constantly reincarnated with no memory of her past but was haunted by the ghosts from it anyway and who had spent most of her life with Helen Locke for a role model, I could see how her world might be a terribly confusing and frightening place.

"Okay." I nodded. "So you aren't an Athena. Maybe you're a Helen of Troy instead."

"What does that mean?" she asked as we reached the door leading to the front porch.

"Helen of Troy didn't fight." If I could be an incentive for Thorin's motivation to win this battle, then Nina could do the same for Baldur. "She inspired men to go to war in her name. If anyone needs your inspiration right now, it's your husband. And if there's any indecision left in your mind, may I make a recommendation?"

Nina's eyes narrowed, but she nodded.

"Choose love and family and devotion. Choose the one who has never abandoned you, the one who never will."

We stepped onto the porch, and Nina's dark eyes fell on Baldur, who still knelt on the porch, pale, tense and trembling.

"Go to him." I gave her a little shove. "Inspire him."

Nina flashed me a hard stare. She locked her jaw and nodded.

CHAPTER 24

NINA STRODE FORWARD, DROPPED TO the porch floor beside Baldur, and set down her knife. She slipped her arms around his shoulders, pressed her lips to his temple, and whispered something only he could hear. Baldur responded instantly. His shoulders relaxed. His trembling eased. He remained on his knees, still straining as though he carried a massive boulder, but I worried about him a little less now that Nina had joined him.

"What's she doing out here?" Grim asked as I handed him the sword.

"Giving Baldur a little more get-up in his go."

His brow furrowed. "What?"

I rolled my eyes. "Never mind."

Grim dismissed my sarcasm and strode down the front porch steps into the front yard. He flexed his wrist and sent the sword swirling in an arc of bright flames. I exhaled a breath I hadn't realized I'd been holding. Did I think it wouldn't work—that Val had broken it somehow?

I opened my mouth, preparing to ask him what he planned to do next, but a flicker of movement at the edge of my vision stole my attention. A familiar black bird fluttered to the ground beside Grim. After repeating the strange performance that shed his feathers and turned him into a man, Hugh stood before me in all his natural glory.

"We've *got* to stop meeting like this." Although I joked, his arrival compounded my accumulating worry. Hugh never came bearing good news.

"Don't worry. What I have to say is short." He clenched his teeth and rubbed his arms, as if that could possibly ward off the persistent cold. "Embla has Skyla. She's holding her prisoner at the Aerie. If you don't

233

come immediately, Embla will kill her. She'll work her way through *all* the Valkyries if she has to."

The fury of Thorin's storm muted as though I had gone deaf, and the world around me froze. I blinked at Hugh and waited for his words to make sense, but like the screen at the end of an old movie when the film had run out, my mind remained blank.

"Solina." Hugh waved a hand before my face.

I gasped, and everything came screaming back at me double speed and twice as loud. I cringed and cried out. Hugh grabbed my shoulder and shook it. I shoved him off and rubbed my face. "Oh, god," I said. "I knew something was wrong."

"There's more. The wolf is with her, with Embla."

I gaped at the raven. "Skoll?"

Hugh nodded. "I would have told you sooner, but I didn't know."

I shoved him, pushing hard against his bare chest. "What?"

He steadied himself and scowled. "I. Didn't. Know."

"How can you *not* know?"

A pained look crossed Hugh's face, and his mouth drew into a sour pucker. "There was something blinding us—a hole in my Thoughts." His voice cracked, and his eyes watered. "It's the same feeling I got when I tried to look into your Thoughts here, at New Breidablick. There was a wall, and I couldn't tell who or what was behind it. Not until she *wanted* me to know. Not until she set her trap."

"Rune magic?" asked Grim, who stood beside me, leaning in as if he might strike Hugh.

The raven nodded. "It has to be."

"Is that something the Valkyries are normally capable of doing?" I asked.

Hugh's black brows angled down. "The Allfathers were the only ones we ever knew who could block us."

"Well, Embla *is* the daughter of the Allfather. Perhaps she has some of his skills?"

"What the hell?" Grim hacked a guttural roar and swung his sword. A stream of fire spewed from the blade and burnt an arc in the grass several yards away. Hugh flapped as if preparing to make his getaway, but I grabbed his arm and held onto him. *If he flies away, he'll have to take me with him.*

"One more question," I said.

Hugh grimaced. "Make it quick. My nuts are about to freeze off."

I resisted the urge to kick him. "Can we trust *any* of the Valkyries?"

"As far as I can tell." He shrugged. "They all seem genuinely interested in defeating Helen."

"Are they still coming here? Or did Embla change that plan?"

"They're still on their way," Hugh said. "They think Embla's recouping from her injuries at the Aerie and that Skyla is staying with her. They don't know she faked the whole thing."

I heaved a sigh. "Thanks, Hugh. Will you let me know if anything changes?"

He crouched, preparing for his transformative leap. "I'll keep my vows to you, Solina. Beyond that, I can only say I'll do what's in our best interest." He jumped, shifted into his bird form, and streaked toward the horizon.

When Hugh disappeared, I turned to Grim. He studied my face, read the plea in my eyes, and his mouth puckered into a sour expression. With the sword, Grim would have enough power to take me—blip me across space and time and carry me to the Aerie. "Oh, no, Solina." He shook his head "There's no way in hell."

"You made a vow, did you not?" I shoved a finger against his sternum. "You *owe* me."

"I vowed not to kill you, to do anything in my ability to keep you alive. Taking you to face Embla and Skoll would be breaking that vow in the worst possible way."

Fear burned in my heart, panic formed a sea of ice in my guts, and the opposing sensations had created a churning hurricane of desperation beneath my ribcage. "What if we could kill the wolf? Kill Embla and end this whole thing? You know we'll never get a better chance."

Grim's harsh expression wavered. "And leave my brother here to fight on his own? Abandon the Allfather? Abandon your parents?" His lips twisted into an ugly, wry leer. "You of all people would do that? A minute ago, you were ordering me to go help Magni."

He was right, damn it. I paused and considered his argument. Should

I leave Thorin to fight mostly on his own or abandon Skyla and ignore this opportunity to destroy the wolf? Had I ever been stuck between a bigger rock and a tighter hard place? "Baldur's holding it together now that Nina is helping him. Your brother, as we both know, needs no help. He'll fight Helen's army as long as it takes. There's one key to winning this war, and it's at the Aerie. You can be the one to end it."

Light flickered in Grim's eyes. Appealing to his ego had weakened his resolve, it seemed. He licked his lips, and his Adam's apple bobbed. "There's also a very good chance Skoll could kill you, and we lose everything."

I shook my head. "Never. I won't let him." I poked Grim's chest again. "*You* won't let him." He wavered again, so I went in for the kill. "You want to be the hero in this story, Grim? Well, now's your chance."

He growled and lunged for me. Had he decided to kill me right then and there—go back on his word and save everyone a mountain of trouble? I reached for my fire as he latched onto my shoulders, jerked me against his side, and swore in my ear as it popped from pressure change, a sure sign we were entering the æther.

"Damn it, Solina," he said as the whirlwind of interdimensional travel surrounded us. "You'd better hope you know what you're doing."

Grim and I dropped to the ground in the Aerie's front yard. The old mission-style home perched on the cliffside above the Pacific Ocean, and a thick cloak of mist shrouded its blue-gray waters. A cold breeze stirred the air, intensifying the smell of salt spray and seaweed, but it was a paler, weaker sister of the storm we'd left at New Breidablick. Still, after Grim and I parted, I shivered and rubbed my arms. Our brief contact had given me insight into Grim's thoughts and memories that chilled me more than any storm ever could. When Thorin said Grim had lost more than him at Ragnarok, he had downplayed the worst of it.

Images of bodies—broken and burned children, dead women, dead animals, crumbled and blackened and incinerated things—had filled my head. Breathless and close to retching, I shoved the visions away and stiffened my spine. Grim kept his back to me as he surveyed the landscape, searching for Embla or Skyla, but only the eerie cry of seagulls welcomed us.

If I was immortal, if the hurt could go on forever... It was what I had said to Val, understanding that an eternity of pain could drive one to extremes. If I could find empathy for Val, could I do the same for Grim, even though he had tried to kill me not so long ago? *Time will tell. His actions today will go a long way toward redeeming him. Or not.*

I fingered the gold chain around my neck—Mjölnir's lanyard. With it, Thorin could track me anywhere. Grim and I had left Lake Tahoe without explaining our departure. Thorin would find me if I didn't return to New Breidablick soon, and he would surely be pissed when he did. I'd take his wrath though. It was an acceptable price for saving Skyla. *I'll take Thorin's anger because he has to be alive to be pissed off at me. I'll take anything from him, so long as he's alive and well when this is over.*

"I don't like this." I observed the stillness and silence.

Grim huffed. "Neither do I."

We could separate and cover more ground, but anyone who had ever seen a thriller or a horror movie knew splitting up meant certain death. Despite my aversion for him and the horrible things inside his head, I grabbed Grim's shirt sleeve, careful not to touch his skin. "No matter what, we stick together."

He thinned his lips, and his nostrils flared. "Obviously."

I started forward, and he fell into step beside me, heading for the Aerie's front door. I jiggled the handle, and the door opened, swinging on silent hinges. No creepy horror house screech—the Valkyries kept their home well maintained. Our footsteps echoed through the foyer as we crept inside. The interior smelled musty, as if no one had opened a door or window in a while, but a lingering undercurrent of smoke perfumed the air. The ghost of the Aerie's fire would haunt the house for a long time.

"I guess you and Tori were right," I said as we tiptoed through the dim interior. A watery, late-afternoon sun provided enough light for us to make our way, and we kept our heads on a swivel as we eased into the kitchen.

"Right about what?"

"There being a traitor within the Valkyries."

"Of course I was right."

"But you didn't know it was Embla?"

He shook his head. "I thought it was all of them."

A chill swirled through my gut. "I hope you're wrong."

He stopped so suddenly I nearly face-planted into his back. Wearing a grimace, he peered down at me. "If the bird was telling the truth, we only have Embla to worry about." He turned around and started forward again toward the rear of the house. "One woman is no threat to me."

"You think I'm not a threat?" I nearly growled.

Wisely, Grim refrained from answering.

"Embla is Baldur and Nina's daughter," I said. "She's a direct descendent. Doesn't that make her as much Aesir as you or your brother?"

We wandered into the Valkyries' vacant living room and paused. "Embla has never trodden on Asgardian soil, breathed its air, ingested its nutrients, bathed in its sunlight." Grim tossed me a smug smile as he said the word *sunlight*. "She's too much of this world. She's too human."

His statement stirred an uneasy feeling in me. I had walked through Asgard, had breathed its air, had eaten Idun's apples, and, arguably, was the physical embodiment of Asgard's sun. *Still haven't figured out how that one works yet...*

What did that mean for me? Had I changed somehow—more than I already had?

"Not so human if she's working runes to keep Hugin and Munin out of her head."

Grim had no reply other than a shrug. After making quick work of searching the rest of the house and finding nothing more than shadows and dust, we eased out the back door and surveyed the rear of the Aerie. A short, stubbly lawn dropped off at the edge of a cliff descending several dozen feet into the Pacific. Clearing the main house left us few other places to search.

I pointed toward the outbuilding housing the Valkyries' School of How to Be a Badass. "Maybe they're in the training barn."

Grim shrugged and motioned for me to take the lead. As I stepped forward, a shout rose through the mists below us. A broken, strangled voice cried out. He looked at me, and our gazes locked.

"The beach," we said in unison.

Grim drew his sword and darted forward, heading for the path winding down to the rocky shore, and I raced after him. As we descended into the fog, a faint memory rattled in its storage box in the back of my mind. I grabbed his sleeve and tugged. "Wait. There's something..." I furrowed my brow and worked the lock on my memory box.

"There's no time—" he started, but I yanked his arm again and cut him off.

"Yes there is. This is *dèjá vu*..." I gasped as understanding hit me. "No. It's a premonition. I had a vision—Thorin, stabbed through the heart with Odin's spear on that beach. There was fog like this. The wolf was there. He attacked me."

Grim drew back and gave me a wary look. "Odin's spear?" He shook his head. "No way. I've been looking for it for centuries."

"My visions never lie."

"Thorin's not here, so what are you worried about?" Grim twisted free from my grip and worked his way down the precarious path until it leveled out on a stony beach enrobed in thick, oily fog.

Unsatisfied with his response, I followed close behind and explained my concerns. "I had the vision the first time we all came to the Aerie. I thought I had prevented it coming true by sending Thorin away. I thought that was the end of it, when we left the Aerie, but I saw the tail end of that dream again when I was in the Norns' well."

Grim stumbled to an abrupt halt. He looked at me over his shoulder and narrowed his eyes. "You were in the Norns' well?"

I flapped a hand, tossing aside his question. "Long story. But trust me, it happened. I saw Thorin bleeding out on the beach, and the spear was in his chest." In my mind's eye, I zoomed in on the image. A man lay prone and unmoving, awash in blood and sea foam. Blank, empty eyes stared from a familiar face that looked so much like the one glaring at me that same moment. I gasped and blinked at Grim. "You and Thorin look *a lot* alike, sometimes."

He raised his shoulder and dropped it. "So?"

Before I could express my concerns, a sharp *thwak*—half mechanical, half musical strum like a guitar string—echoed through the fog. Without thinking, without considering the danger or my own mortality, I flung myself at Grim and tackled him. My attack surprised him, and he lost his balance as well as his grip on the fire sword.

As we tumbled down, a hoarse, raw scream clawed from Grim's throat.

"*Shit.*" I grunted and rolled away from him.

He lay beside me, his face crumpled in an expression of agony. He bared his teeth and groaned. A short shaft protruded from his shoulder, and the weapon's point had buried itself deep in his deltoid. But a deltoid wound was not lethal. At least, I didn't think so.

Grim cracked an eyelid and peered at me through a dim slit.

"You believe me now?" Spitting hair and grit from my mouth, I rose to my feet only to wind up flat on my face again, inhaling more sand and salt. A hundred-plus pounds of claws, teeth, and fur strained my ribs and ripped at my spine. As I screamed, fire bloomed over me, intense and bright. I inhaled, screamed again, and called my flames higher, hotter.

My attacker hacked a wolfish complaint and leapt from my back. I rolled over, ignoring my screaming flesh and the warm blood oozing from my wounds. I would heal. My fire always renewed me. Slowly, I stood, spread wide my stance, and centered my weight on the balls of my feet.

Two or three strides away, Skoll crouched low, waiting, watching as greasy mists swirled around us like an ensemble of dancing ghosts. Twisted scar tissue disfigured his muzzle, revealing evidence of the damage I had inflicted during our fight in the desert. His ruddy fur stood in a rigid line down his back. He crouched low, tail flicking, ears lying flat against his head.

There stood my greatest adversary—not Helen Locke, not a fire sword, not Val, Grim, or Embla. From the beginning, it was the wolf, and I cursed myself again for having forgotten that so many times over the past months. Perhaps everything that happened since Mani's death could have been avoided if I had never taken my focus off finding and killing Skoll. If I had discarded my need for vengeance and taken him down that night at Oneida Lake instead of his brother, we could have all avoided so much pain, torment, and loss.

But Thorin had said the Aesir were beholden to fate, and all evidence suggested the truth of his claim. Skoll and I were here now because this was the way it was supposed to be. I had finally become the woman, the warrior, who could defeat the beast, and I vowed I wouldn't leave this beach until Skoll was dead.

I sneered at my adversary. "You've tasted my fire three times. Haven't you had enough yet?" I felt like Atreyu taunting Gmork, the wolf who was the great Nothing's agent. If Helen had her way, that never-ending story would come true. She'd take our world and leave us with destruction and chaos.

Skoll snarled, and his lips rippled over his long, horrible teeth. I laughed at him. "I'm not afraid of you anymore." I waved him forward. "Come for me. Let's end this already."

Perhaps Skoll was as fed up with Helen's plots and schemes as I was. He wasted no more time on posturing. He threw himself forward, and I charged to meet him, two steam engines hurtling forward on the same track, head-on collision imminent. Fatalities guaranteed.

As he lunged and closed the inches between us, I raised my flames to full capacity and welcomed Skoll into my embrace. I crumpled under his weight, and we crashed to the ground, rolling as his fangs sank into my shoulder. His claws raked my belly, shredding flesh. Pain flashed like lightning before my eyes.

The fire will heal, I chanted to myself—no fancy fighting moves, no Krav Maga or Valkyrie fighting techniques needed. I gritted my teeth and locked my arms around him. *Just hold on. Just hold on.*

Skoll wriggled like a monstrous eel, slipping from my grasp. My body screamed with the pain of his bites and scratches, and my arms shook from the effort of restraining him. He was muscle and might and power, and I was only a woman. But I wasn't helpless.

I reached to the depths of my powers. The farther I sank into the flames, the more the goddess took over, and the less I felt Skoll tearing me, taking me apart bit by bit. *I have to hold out longer than he does...*

Whose motivation was greatest? Skoll had hatred and revenge. I had those things too, but they were nothing more than a small, dark closet in a fortress I had built from love, hope, devotion, and second chances. Most of all, second chances. Skoll's claws and teeth would never be enough to take that away from me.

My conscious self drifted away as the goddess rose to power inside me, but a scream brought me rocketing back, crashing hard into reality. Every cut and gash and bleeding place inside me roared. Over the protests of my own body, I heard my name as a desperate cry.

"Solina!" Skyla screamed at me with a raw and distressed voice. "Don't let go. Finish him!"

Still wrapped in a massive Skoll bear hug, I centered what was left of my fire in my hands, arms, chest, belly, legs. I shut out the agony and pain and held on. Skoll's panting came hotter and faster in my ear, each breath underscored by a high-pitched whine. The acrid stink of burning fur invaded my nose and mouth, and his struggles grew anxious, frantic.

"Go on, you bastard," I snarled. "Your brother's spirit is out there somewhere waiting for you. Go find him. Leave Helen and all this bullshit behind. It's not worth it. *I* am not worth it."

Skoll uttered a long, ear-shattering howl that drowned out everything else: my heartbeat, my shuddering breath, the ocean. Then with a strangled gasp, he kicked, once, twice, and fell silent, limp, and still.

Utterly still.

My flames guttered and died, leaving me chilled to the bone and empty. *Oh, so empty.* I was spent, exhausted, and lacked the energy to do anything more than sprawl beneath the dead wolf and breathe moist, salty sea air that tasted so very good because it meant I was still here. It meant I hadn't lost myself to the starlight.

It meant I had won.

Somewhere in the depths of my mind, my body shrieked at me. The wounds Skoll inflicted had not healed. Perhaps I had run out of fire before my flesh had mended, but I was too tired, too anesthetized on adrenaline, to appreciate or acknowledge the extent of my injuries.

The clatter of shifting rocks and bitter, sharp voices drew my attention to a spot closer to the water's edge. A gust of wind blew the fog aside momentarily, revealing Grim, who was on his feet again but pale, shaky and blood soaked. He swung his fiery blade at a little redheaded sprite, Siobhan, while Skyla and Embla struck and lunged and yelled at each other.

Grim stumbled, and the sword guttered. Siobhan danced around the flames like a pixie, dodging in and out and striking when she could with her own small sword. The mists drifted, concealing the fight again, but the fog threw their voices at me and amplified their words.

"Why?" Skyla demanded. "*Why* are you doing this, Embla?"

"To recreate the world," Embla said. "You know that."

"But Helen—"

"Helen Locke was a pawn. She was desperate and angry, like all the Aesir. So easy to manipulate."

"You hunted and fought her golems with us at Amchitka," Skyla said.

"It's a nasty game we played, but necessary. A magician's trick to distract the audience."

"Helen will be dead soon if she isn't already," Grim said, but his voice was hoarse and full of pain. Gungir may not have killed him, but it had apparently inflicted a grievous wound. The fog opened and showed Siobhan rolling away from a spew of Surtalogi's fire. The petite Valkyrie fought from a stance near the waves, and she used the water to her advantage. When she gained her footing again, she hurled a blade at him, but Grim swung, and the sword's flames shielded him.

"You're right." Embla huffed for breath. She and Skyla faced each other near the water's edge. Waves lapped at their feet. Sand coated their legs like armor. Neither held a weapon other than her own cunning and fierceness. "She's another necessary sacrifice. Helen will surrender everything for a chance to reclaim Baldur"—she paused and panted—"just like she always does. It's ingrained in her. The ancients... abide in their patterns. They cannot break free. It's their... greatest weakness. Makes them predictable... so simple to control."

Skyla charged her aunt again and landed a solid punch in Embla's ribs. Embla hissed and twisted away, moving like a greased snake.

"If Helen's the pawn," Skyla said breathlessly, "does that mean you're the queen?"

"Don't be so surprised." Embla circled Skyla, slashing at her with an open-handed jab. "You figured out a lot. You know my lineage. You know... You know my father abandoned my sisters and me... all of his children the way the Aesir abandoned the Valkyries or used them as their whores." Embla bared her teeth. "He abandoned you too."

Skyla recoiled. "What are you talking about?"

"I'm talking about the Allfather. Your grandfather. Baldur."

The mists closed over them again like curtains at the end of an act. Everything fell silent except the crashing waves. My heart thumped several slow, stuttered beats, before Siobhan cursed. Then she screamed. Embla screeched, and Skyla coughed a strained grunt. When the fog lifted again, Siobhan was crumpled on the beach. A horrible scorch mark fanned across her chest. Waves lapped at her red curls, and her blood dyed the sea foam pink.

Well, that much of my vision came true, anyway.

Grim turned the sword toward Embla and took a spot at Skyla's side, but Embla was already down on one knee. Blood seeped from her nose, and she clutched her ribs. Then things went fuzzy, and not because of the fog. Something colder than the wind and water chilled my insides, turning my guts to ice.

I closed my eyes and concentrated on breathing. *Shit. Skoll must have done more damage than I thought.*

"So you were going to burn the world to ash and start over again?" Grim asked, oblivious to my flagging condition. His words sounded as though they came from a distant place, although I knew better. He stood only a few yards away, the sword sparking and spitting flames at his feet.

"The Valkyries and I…" Embla panted. "We'll build a world where we're not forsaken or taken for granted."

"How were you going to survive?" Skyla asked. "After you burned everything down?"

Embla chuckled hoarsely. "That's a secret I'll take to the grave if I must. This isn't over. Not by a long shot."

Darkness swirled, sucking me toward an infinite, bottomless void. But a shout of horror mixed with outrage yanked me away from the edge. The bellow had sounded a little like my name. It also sounded a little like a grizzly bear imitating Thorin's voice.

I pried my eyes open in time to see Skyla's attack. Distracted by Thorin's sudden appearance, Embla never defended herself. Skyla's fist slammed into her jaw, and the older woman's head rocked back. She collapsed as if her bones had turned to water, and she did not move again.

My satisfaction was bittersweet. How could it be otherwise, when I was pretty sure I was bleeding out, one heartbeat at a time? I looked away from Embla's lifeless body and found Thorin standing at the edge of the surf, Mjölnir clutched in his fist.

Skyla followed the direction of his stare until her gaze fell on me. "Solina... Oh, *shit*." She blanched and stumbled toward me, horror showing clearly in her wide eyes.

Thorin blipped out of sight and appeared at my side. He fell to his knees and gathered me in his arms. "You gonna die on me, Sunshine?" he asked, his voice hoarse and rough.

I swallowed and shook my head. The effort nearly took me out. "Trying not to."

Fury filled his eyes, and he glared at me. "Try harder." He ground the command through a clenched jaw.

I locked my eyes on his as the æther's whirlwind rose around us.

My ears popped.

The void sucked me in.

Blackness swallowed me whole.

CHAPTER 25

THORIN'S HEARTBEAT HAMMERED BENEATH MY ear. His heat enveloped me, and he smelled like the rain that falls in heavy sheets, bringing flood, destruction, and plague—an angry deluge of doom and death. Part of me wanted to linger in my semiconscious state where nebulous detachment shielded me from my own pain and his anger. But I was not the kind of woman who avoided reality.

I had never hidden from truth.

Thorin's presence sharpened along with my awareness. He held me in his lap, arms folded around me, lips pressed against my temple. He must have sensed my wakefulness because he shifted and raised his head. "Sunshine?"

Sweet and cloying, the flavor of Idun's apples coated my mouth as if I had drowned in a vat of their juices. I smacked my lips and swallowed. "Why do I feel like I have an apple cider hangover?" My voice was raw and gravelly.

He huffed. "Because you probably do."

I sat up straighter, meeting his gaze. Unrelenting darkness stained his eyes—the kind of blackness that accompanied his strongest emotions: rage, fear, ferocity, need. I raised an unsteady hand to his cheek. "Tell me. Tell me everything."

"You threw yourself over the cliff." Thorin's tone was cool, stiff, restrained.

"And took you over the edge with me?"

He grunted. "I said you would, didn't I?"

"And we landed in Asgard?" I looked around, studying the familiar surroundings, the lush green lawn, verdant orchard dripping with golden fruit, a partially reconstructed home that had belonged to the garden's former occupant. During his last visit to Asgard, Thorin had erected a lean-to from the old home's remnants. We sat on the shelter's floor, and he leaned against the only fully erect wall, cradling me in his lap.

"You're surprised?"

I glanced at his dark eyes again and resisted the urge to shiver. All was not right between us. Thorin wore a calm, composed mask that hid something volatile and potentially explosive. I was sitting on a powder keg, and his fuse burned fast and hot.

I shifted to get up, but he growled and closed his arms tighter around me.

"Okay." I settled against him. "Okay, I'm not going anywhere."

When I relaxed, so did he.

"If I am here," I said, "then where is the rest of me?"

"My house."

"How—" I stopped and swallowed. "How bad was it?"

Thorin released me only to cup my face in his hands. He leaned his forehead against mine and dropped his walls. "See for yourself."

Surrounded by stone warriors, Thorin fights, swinging Mjölnir in a blur. Rubble rises in piles around him, and storms rage in the heavens. A lightning blast demolishes a half dozen golems, and they lie in jagged, smoldering heaps. But for every dozen felled, another dozen takes their place, an endless stream of tireless warriors. Through his millennia-long connection to the Allfather, Thorin senses Baldur fading, despite Nina's reassurances and faith—a source of power Baldur had been lacking for decades. But even with Nina at his side, the Allfather struggles. Helen's onslaught is relentless.

Thorin wonders, who wants Baldur more? Nina, or Helen? The answer to that question might decide the conclusion to this battle. Thorin knows he'll outlast the golems, but how much longer will Baldur hold up? If the wards fail, how long until New Breidablick falls? Solina, her parents, Nina, Grim...

Thorin grits his teeth and leans into battle. He is a machine, locking away emotions, focusing on his duty, singularly determined. His attack develops a rhythm—step, turn, swipe, hit, kick, punch. Over and over, golems fall before him. His thoughts drift away, and he fights the way a bird flies, with instinct and eons of muscle memory. Step, turn, swipe, kick, punch...

He loses track of time and place until the moment Mjölnir swings a full arc through thin, unresisting air. He stumbles, blinks, and his narrow focus expands, taking in the battlefield as a whole.

Baldur's wards are gone, and the buzz of their energy, like high-voltage electric lines, has fallen silent. The golem army has gone still, frozen in mid-fight poses.

Thorin extends his senses, listening, feeling, searching for a cause...

There!

Across the way, Nina crouches in the midst of the petrified army. Shadows shroud her in darkness.

What has she done? And how?

Like popping a taut string, Thorin releases the bond connecting him to the storms. Heavy black clouds disperse like smoke in a breeze, and warm, late-afternoon sunlight drapes Nina's shoulders. He crosses the space between them, arriving at her side in a blink. The sun's rays illuminate a crumpled figure at Nina's feet: a woman in fine clothes drenched in blood. Nina strokes her hair with bloodied hands, staining Helen Locke's single white stripe with red. Mismatched eyes, one blue, one black, stare unblinking at the sky.

Baldur appears at Nina's side and kneels. He draws her into his arms as she collapses against him, sobbing. Still, she clutches the knife that struck Helen down, and sticky red residue clings to her fingers. "It's done," Nina moans against Baldur's chest. "For me... for us... I had to."

"But how *did you do it?" Baldur asks, mirroring Thorin's own questions. "How..."*

Nina shakes her head and drops her blade. It clatters to the ground, its rune carvings dark with blood. "Solina gave me the knife—said to protect myself with it. But the only way to protect myself was to—" She chokes on the words. Baldur holds her until she recovers and motions to the battlefield's perimeter. "Took the long way around. She never saw me coming until it was too late. Even then... She thought I was coming to help her. I told her if I made a display of my loyalty to her, it would break you, make you easier to defeat. It never crossed her mind I was betraying her instead. She took me for granted. Underestimated me. She always has."

Nina was the ultimate secret weapon—one they hadn't known they had. The only person who could get through Helen's defenses, and they'd never thought to use her. Or perhaps Baldur had thought of it but was afraid to ask Nina to choose. Thorin wonders if Solina suspected Nina's potential. Had she gotten a glimpse of Nina's thoughts in making the decision to give her that knife? Or was it simply fate at work again—the one power stronger than all the Aesir combined?

"She's really dead?" Thorin asks. "Truly?"

A muscle in Baldur's jaw works as he grinds his teeth. His blue eyes flash as he releases Nina and lowers into a crouch beside Helen's still body. He places his hands over her chest, and a faint glow envelops his fingers. "I will make certain of it."

At the sight of Baldur inspecting Helen Locke's body, Thorin's thoughts shift away from the battle and its unexpected conclusion. He reaches for the connection to Mjölnir's lanyard.

Solina...

He senses her absence, and his heart shudders. Where the hell is she? What has she done?

Responding to the tug of the hammer's connection to its leash, Thorin throws himself into the æther. He withdraws moments later at the stony beach beside the Valkyries' Aerie, and as he studies the scene, his mind forms instant connections.

Embla, prostrate and defeated at the feet of her niece,

Skyla, exultant, a warrior goddess in righteous fury,

Grim, wounded and bleeding,

Siobhan, limp and lifeless at the water's edge,

Surtalogi, the fire sword, dormant at Grim's side,

Gungir, Odin's spear, half buried in sand,

Skoll, the wolf, burned, charred, decimated... ash and bone,

Solina, glazed in blood, flesh torn to ribbons and shreds... light fading from her eyes.

Thorin roars. His conscious thoughts retreat, and he is action, fury, and fear.

He is her savior...

If he's not already too late.

I drew away and blinked until my vision returned to the present, if being a detached soul in Asgard qualified as "the present." I met Thorin's gaze again. "I told Nina to be Helen of Troy and inspire Baldur. I didn't know if she could be a Trojan Horse, too, but I had hoped."

"So when you gave her that knife...?"

I wagged one shoulder in a feeble shrug. "Tempting fate."

"Well, it worked."

"What happened next, after you found me? You took me back to your house?"

Thorin nodded. "Left your body there with Baldur. He's working healing runes as we speak."

"What about Skyla and Grim? Are they okay?"

He nodded again. "Skyla hasn't left your side. Grim's wound has been problematic, and Baldur's working on patching him up."

"Embla?"

He paused, and his nostrils flared. "Under lock and key until we can decide what's to be done with her. Baldur is keeping her at New Breidablick for the time being."

The conundrum of Embla wasn't one any of us would solve easily, and so long as she was safely locked away, I had more pressing concerns to address. "You still haven't explained why everything tastes like apples."

"You remember what you told me when I found you here when Grim had you? You said you ate the apples and felt like they were giving your strength back." Thorin shifted, rearranging me in his lap. "I came here as soon as I left your body with Baldur, and I found you in a heap out there in the yard." He jerked his chin, indicating some vague location beyond the wall at his back. "Lifeless, unresponsive, getting colder by the second."

"So you fed me apples—or the juice from them." I glanced down at my chest and stomach, concealed beneath the white gown that always covered me in Asgard. After poking and prodding my flawless skin, I opened my hands and examined my smooth palms and unblemished knuckles. Diaphanous flames flared from my fingertips, only for an instant, and disappeared. "Guess they did the trick."

He sneered. "*Did the trick.*" Thunder rumbled in his chest like a far-off storm, and I tensed, sensing the coming tempest. "Like some kind of magician pulling a rabbit from a damned hat."

I braced myself for his potential anger. Earlier, I'd said I would welcome his wrath so long as it meant we had both survived. *I'll welcome it, but I won't apologize for causing it. I did what I had to. Either he'll accept that, or he won't, but I won't say I'm sorry.*

"You're not fooling me."

"What are you talking about?" Thorin's voice sounded like a grizzly warning away a hunter.

"Don't think I don't know that I'm sitting on top of a volcano. You're so close to blowing up at me, I can feel it like an earthquake. I know…" I exhaled and paused to gather my thoughts. "I know you're mad."

Thorin made a strangled noise in his throat. "Mad? *Mad?*"

"I felt it," I said before he could launch into a tirade. "When I saw your memory, I felt what you felt. Your fear… it was *cold*." Reflexively, I shivered, remembering the iciness of his terror. "Colder than Grim's ice cave. I felt your anger, too, and it was hot. Almost as hot as my flames. You were fire and ice at the same time, and it was—" My breath hitched. My voice broke. "It was *horrible*."

Thorin coughed, and it sounded like a roar. He clasped me tighter, and his words were raw and strained. "There was a moment when I was certain you were already dead, that I had come too late. That I had lost everything. *Again*."

I balled my hands into the fabric of his shirt. "I didn't do that to you on purpose. You *know* who I am. You know the things I was willing to do. It's not my fault you fell in love with me, you stupid idiot."

His eyebrows arched high, and he blinked like a startled owl. I shoved against him, and he loosened his hold. I had to get away, clear my head, and put some space between us to allow us room to process our feelings. *Is it over? Has the nightmare finally ended? The wolf is dead. Helen is dead. Embla, the betrayer, is dead.*

After slipping free from Thorin's grasp, I strode out to my garden. The sky shone a blue so pure and sharp it stung my eyes. The sun burned hot and welcoming, and in its light, my golden apples shone like miniature stars.

Sensing Thorin's approach, I turned to face him. "I keep trying to think of the words, but they don't seem to exist. I can't say I'm sorry, Thorin. I won't. I know you told me not to fling myself over any cliffs, but that wasn't what I was doing. You have to believe me."

"I know," he said, low and gruff. At his sides, his hands flexed, forming fists. A muscle worked in his jaw. "If I hadn't been willing to accept that you had your own fate to pursue, your own will to exert, I would have put you in that cage we've always talked about. You needed freedom, and as much as it pained me, I wanted you to have it. This"—he made a sweeping motion to encompass my whole figure and insinuate the nearly mortal wounds that necessitated my current dual existence—"is the consequence. It may take me a little time to accept it and find my peace."

He stepped closer, approaching me like a fox stalking a hare. "From the first day you walked into my life, my greatest fear was finding you'd been devoured by that damned wolf. When I found you at the Aerie on that beach..." He drew a clawed hand down his neck. He raked his fingers across his chest and stomach, mimicking the wolf's attack on me and the injuries I'd suffered.

Thorin's expression darkened, and reading his thoughts required no magical touches. His pain shone clearly in his eyes, in the lines on his face, in the stiffness of his back and shoulders, and especially in the physical distance he kept between us. He stood a few feet away, but it felt like miles.

In my nightmares, night after night, I had watched Hati devour my brother. I had experienced firsthand the shock, terror, and helplessness Thorin felt when he found me bleeding out on the beach at the Aerie. I had suffered those exact same feelings for Mani. But I had survived. Thorin would too.

I allowed a thin smile. "You still want to punish me a little, though, don't you?"

He closed his eyes and exhaled, but the tension in his shoulders did not ease. "I want to shake you until your teeth clack. I want to bring down the thunder and lightning and rage at you." His eyes popped open, and they smoldered. A grin played on his lips, and his voice reverberated like a purring tiger. "But I also want to drag you down in this grass

252

and have you, possess you... *own* you. I held you, lifeless, in my hands, Solina. Now I want to feel you come alive beneath my fingertips."

No questioning what he meant. A different kind of fire flared inside me, one not necessarily under my control. Thorin closed the distance between us but kept his hands at his sides. "I respect your autonomy. You deserve that from me. Rather than my anger, I owe you my respect, my awe, and my gratitude. Your fierceness has likely saved us all."

Undone by his confession, I sagged. He caught me before I slumped to the ground, and I welcomed his touch, his comfort, his grace. "It is over, isn't it? It's really done?"

"I'm almost afraid to hope." He touched his lips to the curve of my jaw, below my ear. "But yes, I think we've won."

I turned, bringing my mouth closer to his. "These apples, do you think they could answer the question of my mortality?"

His thumb stroked my jawline, and I sank further into him. "I think it's very possible. It would explain a lot about how you've managed to survive so many things that should have killed you."

"Does the fact I've eaten them mean I'm immortal now?" A mixed blessing, immortality. I wanted forever with Thorin, but I also wanted to reunite with Mani again someday. Perhaps, as long as I retained the lessons Gróa had taught me—the ways of the *völva*—I could have my cake and eat it too. Such a thing seemed like too much to hope for, but it was a promising kind of day. We had defeated our enemy. We had won.

"I think it means your timeline is less limited than it was before." Thorin leaned lower and plucked a kiss from my lips. "More than that is hard to know. Your presence in Asgard is unprecedented." He snorted. "*Everything* about you is unprecedented."

"I'll take it as a compliment." I closed my eyes and leaned into him. He shifted, taking my weight, and eased me to the ground, laying me like a treasure upon a blanket of grass. There was possession in the way he kissed me, slowly, deeply, as if he meant to claim me. Sometimes, despite our best intentions, there is ownership in love. For once, I didn't mind being owned—not if Thorin was the one to whom I was bound.

His lips trailed down my neck, and I buried my hands in his hair. I breathed him in, and he smelled like rain, the kind that came with wind gusts and thunder, turning the heat and humidity of a Southern summer into steam and mist.

His hands explored my skin, and I pressed against him, begging for more. I burned for his touch.

Is it my fire? Or is it desire?

I didn't know.

I didn't care.

There was me; there was him and no one else in all the realm of Asgard.

Nothing else matters.

CHAPTER 26

SKYLA AND I SAT AT the table in Thorin's kitchen, stuffing our faces with scrambled eggs and buttered toast. Nestled on a mountaintop on a private island in Resurrection Bay, his isolated home discouraged interference from the outside world. I could think of no other place I wanted to be.

Before Thorin disappeared with a vague excuse about checking on something at his sporting goods store, he had cooked us breakfast and demanded we eat it all. Skyla picked at her plate while I, like a steam shovel, piled eggs and bacon in my mouth as fast as I could chew, filling a stomach that had gone several days without solid food. The apples had saved me, but butter and eggs and toast and honey would restore me. And coffee. Lots and lots of coffee.

Beneath my robe and pajamas, great swaths of pink scars curled over my stomach, ribs, chest, and neck. Baldur's rune work had prevented the need for stitches and reduced my healing time to days rather than months. A quick bath in my fire's restorative powers would likely remove all remaining evidence of the wolf's attack, but I had a way to go before my flames were up to that task. *Time heals all wounds...*

At the kitchen table, sitting across from me, Skyla poked her fork tines at a few fluffy yellow bits on her plate. She supported her chin in her palm, elbow resting on the table, and stifled a yawn. Dark smudges underscored her eyes, and her curls sprang wildly about her head.

"Go get some sleep," I said. "Bedside vigils are exhausting."

She smiled sheepishly and set down her fork. "If I take my eyes off you, how do I know you won't disappear on me?"

I reached across the table and squeezed her hand. "I have a feeling I won't be going anywhere for a *very* long time."

Her cheeks colored. "Thorin told me. Idun's apples, huh?"

I leaned closer and captured her gaze. "Nothing's changed, Skyla. Nothing between us is different. Whether I die tomorrow or live for a thousand years, I love you more than life itself, and you're my best friend. The best I've ever had. How could I have survived a minute without you?"

She looked away. "You wouldn't ask me that if you could see yourself when you go Super Sunshine. You *are* a goddess, Solina."

I chuffed. "So are you."

She leaned back in her chair and scowled.

"No, really," I said. "You're at least a demigoddess, anyway. Baldur's your grandfather. That's got to come with some interesting..." I choked down a snicker. "Side effects."

Her scowl deepened. "It's not funny. He lied to me."

"He didn't want to hurt you."

"That's everyone's excuse when they lie."

Sensing the freshness of her pain, I sobered and dropped my smile. I wasn't quite willing to call Baldur's omissions lies, but his resistance to admitting his flaws had cost us all dearly. Skyla's bitterness toward him wasn't misplaced or undeserved, but I didn't want to see her anger take her down the same path that Embla's rage had carried her.

"You're right," I said. "Absolutely. But he's family. Do you have so much that you can afford to lose him?"

The subject of our conversation had retreated to New Breidablick to tend to his affairs, and he had taken Grim with him. The wounds Odin's spear had given Grim had improved, but his injuries required more of Baldur's finesse. Grim and Baldur had also seemed to understand that the only invalid Thorin wanted to nurse was me, and the two had left not long after I awoke back inside myself, fully ensconced in the human world. I suspected Baldur had gone home to lick his own wounds. *Nothing like finding out your daughter's abandonment issues almost brought on the second Ragnarok.*

A flame burned in Skyla's eyes when she answered. "I have *you*. I have the Valkyries." She folded her arms over her chest and frowned. "What's left of them, anyway."

"You trust the ones who are left?"

"I will. I'll make them prove themselves to me."

The look on Skyla's face left no question about her future goals and intentions. She was a Valkyrie with Aesir blood, and she'd undoubtedly take the Aerie by force if she had to. But I had a feeling the remaining Valkyries would welcome Skyla and her tough-but-fair brand of leadership. Embla's betrayal had torn them apart and nearly destroyed them. Skyla's strength and verve and love would knit them together again.

"What about the rest of your family? Your father and your brother? I looked for them when you went missing after Oneida Lake. Thought one of them might have a lead that pointed back to you."

The fire in Skyla's eyes dimmed. "Haven't heard from either of them in years. Paul and I were never close. He had a substance-abuse problem. He was an addict. Before I was old enough to help him, he disappeared. I always figured he lived on the streets until he overdosed or died from something he got from a bad needle." She shrugged, and something flashed in her eyes. I had seen that same look in my own eyes in the months after Mani's death. She understood about lost brothers, and it was another shared pain that reinforced our bond.

"And your dad?" I sensed she didn't want to talk about Paul.

Skyla's expression hardened. "He died. Little over a year ago. Lung cancer."

"I traced him to Camp Pendleton when he retired. It was one of the reasons I went to San Diego in the first place."

Skyla's eyebrows arched, and she blinked at me. "Really?"

"Yeah. But there was never another word about him."

Skyla shook her head. "There wouldn't be, not in San Diego. I moved him into hospice care in Siqiniq. He only lived a few months after that. I spread his ashes in Resurrection Bay."

I took Skyla's hand and forced her to unfold her arms. Then I slid out of my chair and squatted next to her, one arm around her ribs, holding her close. "I'll be your family, Skyla. As long as you need me."

"But you think I should embrace Grandma Nina and Grandpa Baldur, too, don't you?"

"Yeah, I do. They need you at least as much as you need them. But it doesn't have to be today. Just... just try to keep an open mind."

"I won't make promises."

"I didn't ask you to."

She shifted, pulling away, and peered at me. "What about *your* family? Your mom and dad are crazy worried about you."

"Tell me something I didn't know." I rolled my eyes, stood, and collected our dirty dishes. "Thorin's taking me to see them as soon as I feel well enough to travel."

"You're going to North Carolina?"

I piled dishes in the sink and filled it with soapy hot water. "Only long enough to say goodbye."

"Then what?"

I glanced at Skyla over my shoulder. "What do you mean?"

"What do you do after that? What are your plans for the rest of your life, now that you've saved the world from annihilation?"

I scrubbed a dishrag against my sticky plate, removing a stubborn honey smear. "Then one day at a time. I've never had many choices before. Now that I do, I don't intend to rush into anything. I have the most valuable commodity of all, and I'm in no hurry to spend it."

"What commodity?"

"Time." My ears popped, announcing Thorin's arrival. I grinned as he appeared beside me and drew me into a sudsy hug. "I have lots and lots of time."

EPILOGUE

THORIN AND I PAUSED WHILE I caught my breath and rehydrated, gulping from my water bottle. I might have lived and dreamed in fire, but Alaska's cold climate gobbled my energy and snuck between the gaps in my clothes, tickling me with chilly fingers. The views though... those were what left me truly breathless. Thorin had stopped us on a pebbly beach beside a frozen ice field called the Knik Glacier. Electric-blue striations banded the jagged ice formations, giving the scene a touch of the imaginary and fantastic—as if we stood in some fairytale land.

Not so long ago, Thorin had promised to take me on one of my brother's favorite hikes, and now he was fulfilling his vow. "I can see why Mani liked this place so much. There's magic here. *His* kind of magic."

"His kind?" he asked.

I motioned to the glacier. "Cold, ice..."

"And I take it you prefer white sand beaches, sunshine, and tropical weather?"

I snorted. "I haven't been anywhere close to a beach—a *tropical* beach—since I was a kid. Mani and I went to the beaches in North Carolina as kids, some, with an aunt or uncle." I closed my eyes and sketched a memory of briny sea air and sand between my toes. Hot sun and seashells. "But the only place I *prefer* to be is wherever you are."

His breath caught, and he pulled me close, cupping my face in his hands. My eyes popped open as I sank into the warm brown depths of his stare. Would his touch ever stop affecting me, ever stop feeling like lightning and storms? "It still amazes me to hear you say it," he said. "A part of me still can't believe it's real."

I swallowed and licked my lips. "What do you mean?"

"I can't say a part of me hadn't given up, Solina. The hope of having something, some*one*, meaningful in my life again had started to die."

I inhaled a deep breath and savored his scent of wind and rain. "And now?"

"Now anything is possible."

I pressed a quick kiss to his jaw. "Now you believe in me a little bit, too, don't you?"

Thorin smiled, stunning me again with the beauty of his joy. "I believe in you very much."

"Say it again," I whispered.

He chuckled and held me tighter. "I, Magni Alexander, Son of Thor, God of Thunder, believe in you, Solina Mundy, Daughter of Sol, Goddess of the Sun. I believe in you, and I'll say it as many times as you need to hear it."

My fire responded to his faith—increasing, swirling like a rising tide, overflowing its well and spilling out, spreading through my veins and bones and muscles, reviving and renewing.

It was power.

It was faith.

It was hope.

But greatest of all, it was love.

ACKNOWLEDGEMENTS

For their assistance in helping me bring Molten Dusk to life, I'd like to thank:

Red Adept Publishing, and specifically, Lynn McNamee. Your support, passion, and integrity is inspiring. Thanks for giving me and my characters a home. Also, thanks for throwing the fiercest parties.

Mai Harrison, for reading this manuscript in its infant stage and offering expert feedback and insight.

Mary Fan and Erica Lucke Dean, who have been mentors, beta readers, hand holders, walls off which I could bounce ideas, and brilliant authors who inspire me daily.

The Red Adept Publishing editorial staff, particularly Suzanne Warr for editorial mentorship that guided this series from the start and Karen Allen for not only polishing this book, but for getting my jokes and being nice enough to laugh at them. Also, thanks to Jessica Anderegg for helping me get this book cover perfect and for working with Streetlight Graphics to develop all the outstanding covers in this series.

To the bloggers and online friends who have helped me get the word out: Nicole Kaderabek, Kelly Donavan-Roberts, Tricia Ballard, Sharon Stogner and the folks at *I Smell Sheep*, Nicole Platania, and Sarah Dale.

My family, both the ones I married into and the ones who had no choice in the matter, I love you all.

ABOUT THE AUTHOR

Karissa Laurel always dabbled in writing, but she also wanted to be a chef when she grew up. So she did. After years of working nights, weekends, and holidays, she burnt out and said, "Now what do I do?" She tried a bunch of other things, the most steady of those being a paralegal for state government, but nothing makes her as happy as writing. She has published several short stories and reads "slush" for a couple of short-story markets.

Karissa lives in North Carolina with her kid, her husband, the occasional in-law, and a very hairy husky. She loves to read and has a sweet tooth for speculative fiction. Sometimes her husband convinces her to put down the books and take the motorcycles out for a spin. When it snows, you'll find her on the slopes.

Karissa also paints and draws and harbors a grand delusion that she might finish a graphic novel someday.

www.ingramcontent.com/pod-product-compliance
Lightning Source LLC
Chambersburg PA
CBHW050722180626
46814CB00002B/559